Enchanted Flight

For the young at heart,

Donijo Ash

Enchanted Flight

Donijo Ash

Rev. date: 04/29/2013

To order additional copies of this book, contact:
Xlibris Corporation
1-888-795-4274
www.Xlibris.com
Orders@Xlibris.com
133837

Contents

BAD SMOKE!

The dragon leaned close with his tail curling back and forth like a cat playing with its prey. His eyes blazed orange and smoke curled from his nostrils.

Razzi felt the dragon's hot breath and stepped backward. "Don't look at me that way. I taste awful! Go away you oversized furnace!"

The more Razzi said, the more smoke rolled over the monster's sharp teeth. The giant lizard's tongue slithered in and out around the little fellow's head, taunting him.

Razzi's heart pounded fiercely. He was far too small to fight this beast who could easily flatten him with one foot. He knew running from this speedy creature was hopeless. His mind whirled. "Yuck! I'll cook when he swallows me! Wow, this is really bad!"

With no way to escape, Razzi took a deep breath and cowered into a tiny ball, throwing his arms over his head. Nearly fainting from fear, he waited for the dragon's fiery jaws to snap . . .

ACKNOWLEDGMENTS

About thirty years ago, I penned the original Enchanted Flight. My mom, Sharlene Solomito, sister, Rita Riggs, and our daughter, Bambi Rhoades, eagerly helped me in many ways. To my surprise, my dad, Joseph Solomito, an avid Western bookworm, loved my tale. Two boys (now grown men) read and enjoyed my novel. My lead male character was named after Krispian Ian McCullar, at his request. The other boy was Kris Rhoades, who loved the story and has kept after me to publish it. John Ash, my husband, spent endless hours over the years teaching me about computers, and giving me technical assistance. Others in the family, my brother, Tony Solomito, and our son, Randy Ash, urged me to continue.

Friends and writers over the years likePat Boatner, Dorothy Henry, Sue Ellen Hudson, and Joy Margrave guided me, but have since passed on. Toni Anderson, Donna Bond, Connie Green, Elizabeth Howard, Lou Kassem, Gay Martin, Denise May, Mary Kay Remich, Brenda Rollins, Denise Stafford, Jo Stafford, and Phyllis Tickle gave of their time and wisdom. For each of these dear ones and those I failed to mention, I'm grateful.

For many reasons my book took a backseat to my busy life. It waited patiently in my desk until 2010. When the time was right, I tackled it again with eager determination. A good friend, Faye Martin, offered to edit my work. She efficiently worked through a third of my book before our computers verbally croaked. Pam Engles read and marked typos on a preliminary copy. Other supporters were Rita Bruno, Hugo Fruehauf, Dr. Samantha Graber, and Lorrie Knoepflein. The staff at Robertsdale Library were helpful. Scott Underwood with Underwood Printing and Office Supplies was caring and supportive with technical advice, assistance, and services. For all who helped me, please accept my sincerest appreciation.

CHAPTER 1

A FATE WORSE THAN DEATH

Ian McCullar smiled early that morning in the year 1738 when he left his cabin, ax in hand, walking into the thick forest. His trade was making fine furniture and he needed a perfect oak for his work. It was strange no one warned Ian about those teeny-weeny witches living in the area. The townsfolk had long feared the witches' evil spells. As Ian stepped quietly along the animal paths, viewing each tree on his property with an artist's eye, he unfortunately selected the very oak tree the fiendish sisters called home.

Ian had no idea the dire consequences his action would have on his life that fateful day as he briskly swung his sharp ax. Instantly, lighting zinged around his head and a blustery thunderstorm forced him to run for shelter.

"His ax struck our *house*! Where is that *louse*?" Zelda screamed. The tiny witch's fiery red hair bristled wildly as she ran from knothole to knothole. She peered downward with her beady eyes, inspecting the ground and woods as the thunder clapped and the lightning flared.

"That brainless Ian *McCullar* must have hightailed it down the *holler*." She watched the rain toss this way and that in the howling wind. "I'll catch that stupid *man*! He'd better run while he *can*!"

Zelda trembled as she recalled Ian's tan arms bulging with mighty muscles, swinging his sharp ax. Her icy heart thumped wildly as she muttered. "I hate to admit it, but that Ian fellow is truly handsome . . . what rhymes with handsome? Oh hooey! I can't think of a *rhyme* at such an emotional *time*.

"If that man wasn't so human, mean, and *tall*, he would make a fine date for our witch's *ball*. Aha, maybe I could make him *small*!" Her face scrunched with instant glee. "Right now, my red curly *locks* are not as tall as Ian's boot *tops*. I could zap him with a little *spell*, and forever never *tell*. If he was short just like *me*, we could marry for all to *see*. Oh, what fun that would *be!*"

Her enthusiasm poured out louder than she intended. Zelda slapped a hand over her mouth and peeked across the room. Had her foolish fancy been overheard by her sister, Vel?

Sitting across the darkness was a small figure; her head bent over a tiny desk and her eyes scouring a mystic scroll by lantern light. She wore a sparkling black turban to restrain part of her wild red hair. A gold necklace draped over her rumpled black blouse. Vel was so absorbed in her reading that she didn't hear the cracking thunder, much less her blathering sister.

Sighing with relief, Zelda turned her eyes back toward the outside and her anger rekindled toward Ian. "That ax-wielding dingbat nearly destroyed our *tree*. He could never be a dream husband for *me*! Ian ruined my devilish *dreams*, sooner than the sun could show its *beams*. I was bounced off my bed like a rubber *ball*, across our wooden floor and into the *hall*.

"I grabbed my wand and ran to the *knothole*, to see Ian's horrid ax taking its *toll*. I began a chant to slay that crazy *sap*, when Vel crafted a storm before my wand would *zap*." Zelda shuddered as she imagined their home crashing to the *ground*, leaving only a stump to be *found*.

"That evil man nearly did us *in*. He's committed a terrible *sin*!" Zelda clinched her fists and shrieked above the storm's fury. "If Ian McCullar thinks his ax can take us *down*, he's a clown whose mind is not fully *sound*!"

Zelda marched across the room screeching toward her sister. "Vel! Did that man know our home is in this *tree*, or are we so secret he could not *see*?"

Vel slammed her fist on the desk and shouted. "Ian McCullar's dreadful deed was no mistake! That fool tried to kill us! Our life here has never been a secret!" Her fiery eyes scorched the edges of her tattered aging scroll.

Leaping upon the rickety chair beside her sister's desk, Zelda's wild hair sparked with electricity. She pointed her ugly finger accusingly at her sister's bloodshot eyes.

"If Ian tried to kill us, why did *you* create a *storm*? I could have slain that spiteful man this very *morn*! Look what you've done to my *hair*! It's really more than I can *bear*." Zelda vainly pulled the unruly locks from her eyes.

"Your silly lightning won't keep Ian *away*. He will bring his ax back and it is us he will *slay*!" Zelda barked. "With his muscles and *might*, he will ruin us if we don't *fight*. We must attack him *tonight*. You know I'm *right*! If we go to his cabin right *now*, we could destroy that fetching devil *somehow*!" She angrily stomped her foot on the teetering chair causing it to lurch. She flipped head over heels and smacked back down on the wobbly seat.

Vel rasped in anger as her evil eyes glared at her dizzy sister. "Zelda, sit on my desk before that chair kills you! My fast thinking stopped you from killing that no-good this morning. The way I see it, Ian McCullar committed a savage crime against us. Death is far too merciful for a wicked wretch like him. I want him to remember his stupidity and punishment for a long, long time!"

"I won't *wait* or even *debate*," Zelda ranted. "Ian's doom is in our *hands*, so we must hurry with our *plans*."

"Listen to me, sis. I found the perfect punishment in our ancestors' diaries. This flawless incantation lasts two hundred years! Think of it! Two hundred years of misery! And remember, I decide his fate! I am the oldest!"

"Stop saying that, Vel! The thought of you being *older*, makes me *smolder*. Our birth I *remember*, born twins in *November*. You are certainly *bolder*, but only two minutes *older*! You are bossy and can't *rhyme*, so try it my way this *time*."

"Zelda!" Vel screamed. Her words spewed out. "Stop being childish! When I tell you my plan, you'll simply adore it. It's worse than death for Ian McCullar."

"Nothing's that *bad*! You're making me *mad*! Kill him *now*! I'll show you *how*!" Zelda screamed.

"That's enough Zelda! Shut your blabbering mouth and listen to me! This spell is deliciously evil. It'll make Ian McCullar's fate worse than death itself! It's a perfect spell!" Vel's lips spread into a villainous snicker, showing her rotting green teeth.

"Oh, pooh! I will listen *reluctantly*, if you stop smirking so *exultantly*! Your conniving mug shows me, *Vel*, that I might like your flawless *spell*. You have pricked my *curiosity*, so hurry and tell *me*. TELL ME!" Zelda leaned toward her sister, listening closely to every depraved word.

They whispered so quietly that even the insects could not hear their sordid plans. Moments later screeching laughter erupted inside the giant tree and echoed through the woods.

"I'll *be*! Now I *see*!" Zelda cried. "Your perfect *plan* will destroy that *man*! Toe to *toe* and away we *go*!"

At that very moment, far, far away from the spiteful witches, a storyteller was living in a small cabin hidden among snowy cliffs high in the mountains. Inside the cozy cabin, the clever Majiventor, Theodore Bumbles, preferred being called just plain, Bumbles. He always enjoyed telling a new tale. This day, the story is all about Ian and the evil witches, and being told to his beloved nephew, Bobby.

Bumbles switched off his visual storytelling wall, yawned and stretched in his floating chair. "I love telling and showing stories to you Bobby, although, those witches are about to make tons of trouble for Ian. I think Vel and Zelda get . . ." he hesitated with a teasing grin across his face, "I think they get meaner every time I tell this story."

Bobby giggled as he spoke. "That's okay Unc. But please don't stop your story now. I want to see what those witches do. Zelda is funny and mean at the same time. But, what does Vel mean when she calls a spell 'worse than death?' What could be worse than death?"

"Good question, Bobby, and it will be answered soon. You are a wise young man and I am pleased that you are my nephew. Having you here for your school holidays is always such joy for me."

"I look forward to it every year."

The older gentleman, small in stature, lowered his floating chair and stood on the floor extending his arms into the air. "Right now, I need a rest. My legs are stiff and my throat's dry as sand." Glancing outside through an ice-covered window, he shivered. "It is cold out there. The snow is extra deep."

"I had no trouble flying here through your time tunnel! That was a blast, Unc. It was more fun than a carnival ride. You make everything fun. I wish you could make my school more amusing."

"Learning new things, Bobby, should always be fun. After our story today, will you tell me all about what is happening in your school?"

"Sure! But the subject will totally bore you."

"Never, Bobby! You are always interesting to me. By the way, I need that hot tea to warm my bones. Are you in the mood for some hot chocolate?"

"You betcha and some cookies if you have 'em."

"Give me a jiff." Twirling his golden wand, the little man lifted off the floor in his long purple robe. He swooped into his kitchen where cups of steaming liquid and cookies mysteriously danced toward his tray.

The nine year old boy chuckled as he watched. He couldn't remember a time when his uncle was not a light-hearted man. Once in a while the Majiventor truly did blunder; yet, he was still performing greater deeds than anyone living on earth. A steaming drink and cookies floated toward the boy on a fancy tray.

"Grab it before it chills, Bobby."

"Thanks, Unc! Now, watch my supernatural powers," Bobby teased. He stuffed a whole cookie in his mouth. "See! It disappeared! Ah, and it's yummy. I can't wait to be a Majiventor like you. If I study hard, do you think I can do the things you do?"

Smiling, Bumbles replied. "The way I see it, you have all the talents needed; physical aptitude, brains, wit, and most important, you are a good person. That is a total necessity for being a Majiventor!"

"Okay, what else is needed?" Bobby asked.

"Added to that, you must learn how our universe works and study to help mankind with their complex problems. The job is not always easy or fun. Alas, after nine hundred years of doing my best, my abilities are waning. We Majiventors need good recruits to take over. There is still much to do. Helping others is a full time job."

Bobby sat forward in his chair. "I want to learn everything you can teach me, so I can be just like you. I'd like for us to mess around in your lab after your story?"

"Nothing makes me happier." Bumbles replied, sitting back in his chair. "For now, we will finish our story."

"Great! I can't wait to see what those witches do."

"Before we turn on the story wall, I should explain a little about Ian McCullar's background and his special friend, Deborah Devin."

"Is this the 'mushy' part, where the guy and girl fall in love? Ugh!" Bobby wrinkled his nose.

"They do fall in love, but other things happen. When Ian McCullar was four, his mother died, so from an early age, Ian learned to help his father make furniture. Everything they made was England's best. The lad was only twenty when his dad died from the Black Plague.

"The sad young man sold all he owned and sailed from Europe across the ocean to settle near an area called Richmond, a town in the Virginia Territory. After a lengthy search on horseback Ian bought a large parcel of land.

The land was a day's ride from town with his horse-drawn wagon. He built a cabin, half as a home and half for his workshop. He followed in his father's training and enjoyed making fine furniture from his own choice trees.

"After a while though, he felt lonesome. When Ian learned about the town's social and barn dance the last Saturday of each month, he made it a habit to attend.

"He would pack his wagon with his new furniture and leave on a Friday morning to go to town. He liked traveling the bumpy path made by his own wagon wheels and his brown mare's clomping hooves.

"In town he cared for his horse at the stables and rented a room at the Inn. It was a good place to eat and rest. On Saturday, Ian sold his furniture to various shops. Folks loved his work and thought his prices were fair.

"When the wagon was empty, Ian refilled it with monthly supplies for himself. The stable keeper kept the packed wagon until Ian's departure. When his work was done, Ian bathed and dressed for the evening's festivities.

"He looked fine in his tan fringed deerskin shirt, tan cotton pants and high top boots. His shiny dark brown hair and sparking brown eyes set off his handsome smile.

"Everyone gathered in a big barn on the edge of town. They clapped their hands, played instruments, square danced or talked while enjoying refreshments. For Ian there was a deeper motivation for savoring the evening. He was always anxious to once again see and dance with the lovely Miss Deborah Devin.

"Now Bobby, don't look at me that way, Bumbles said. "I know you don't like mushy! But I must tell you this before we return to the witchy part."

"Okay, Unc. But hurry please," Bobby begged.

"I promise. The first time Ian saw the beautiful Deborah standing by the refreshment table, he hurried to meet her. In his excitement to shake her hand and get acquainted, he nervously tipped over two glasses of punch. The bright red liquid splashed over her pale yellow gown."

Bobby laughed. "I bet Deborah didn't like that!"

"You are so right. She squealed angrily and bolted away from him and did not return that night. Ian was deeply hurt and sure she hated him. He was wrong of course. At the next month's dance, she greeted him across the room from the punch table and soon they danced. He tried to pay for her gown, but she explained that cold water had washed the stains away. They soon became regular dancing partners. Because of his shyness around her, she did most of the talking.

"Ian knew he was falling deeply in love with Deborah and truly wanted to marry her. However her family was very wealthy. Her family's barns were larger than Ian's cabin. Deborah loved riding fine horses. Just seeing her courage and grace on horseback took Ian's breath away. She and the horse seemed to fly as they sailed across high fences. How could Ian compete? He feared he could not give his beloved the fine things of which she was accustomed.

"Ian felt it best to remain silent about marriage. Deborah would never enjoy living in his meager cabin.

"One night as Ian's horse clomped along the moonlit path, pulling the wagon back to the cabin, Ian felt incredibly lonely. A hoot owl called out, "Whoo-whoo?"

"Deborah! That's who, you noisy owl!" Ian shouted. "I want to marry her! I love her!" As the bird flew away, Ian knew he must find the courage to tell Deborah how he felt.

"We're back to the mushy stuff again!" Bobby mumbled, and he restlessly twisted in his chair.

"That's all for now. Watch and listen." Bumbles swung his wand to and fro. A forest magically appeared; and a long-eared rabbit popped out of a hollow tree and landed squarely on Bobby's lap. The boy giggled as the jack rabbit bounced all over the room, including the top of Bumbles' head, then back to the boy's lap.

Bobby smiled and petted the animal's soft fur. "May I keep him, Unc? He likes me."

"He prefers being wild. We will find a tamer pet for you. Off he goes." Bumbles moved his wand again, saying strange words, "Bara-fee, bara-foe, wina-ree, wina-roe."

The rabbit disappeared, and before Bobby could feel sad images on the wall appeared so real that he could feel the mist and coolness from the raging storm.

The Majiventor pointed to the screen. "See, Bobby, that is Ian. He is lifting Miss Deborah from her damaged carriage and carrying her inside his cabin, away from the rain and lightning. We can watch them as they settle by Ian's warm fireplace."

Deborah stroked her fingers over the soggy material of her long emerald dress. "My gown will shrink and never fit again. My father bought it for me as a present. Woe be-it to his wrath!"

Ian's brow raised and his muscles tensed. "Your father would never hurt thee, would he?"

A smile swept over Deborah's face. "Daddy? Never! He may bluster a bit, but he loves me far too much to hurt me." Her eyes cast sadly downward to the floor. "In fact, I wish he could be home more often. His tobacco business keeps him traveling too much. Yet, he does find time to buy me many fine dresses."

"Thy lovely smile tells me he is a good man."

"Dad is good. You have a fine smile too, especially when ye dance your jig." She saw his face turn crimson.

Ian turned away and poked at the fire, trying to keep his shyness from her searching eyes. Staring at the flames, he asked. "When did you see me dance?"

Deborah giggled softly. "One evening, we ladies watched from the upper floor as all the men shared their country's dances. We kept real quiet, but I liked your jig best of all. It was brilliant, bold, and well performed."

She said brilliant and bold! Still facing the fire, he groped for words. "I will look to the upper floor next time."

"I hope you do," she replied. "So where did you learn such a splendid dance?"

When she asked questions, it was easier for him to talk. "My father danced the jig back in England. I imitated him when I was a wee lad. He also taught me his trade. He used fine timber and I do the same. My land has hardy cherry, walnut, and oak trees."

Relaxing a bit, he turned toward her, noticing tiny bumps moving up the soft flesh of her arms. She shivered ever so slightly and stretched her dainty fingers toward the warmth of the fire.

"Your clothes are soaked and you are chilling!" Ian blurted out, as he quickly found a large gray robe and some woolen socks. "These are not fancy milady, however; they are clean. I'll fetch you some hot tea while you change into this warm robe. We can hang your dress by the fireplace to dry. For your privacy, bonnie lass, I will close the door while I work in the kitchen."

Rising up from her chair, she accepted his robe. Her sea green eyes gazed deeply into his. "Thank you, Ian," she murmured. "Thou art quite kind as always."

Ian stood still a moment enjoying her smile. They stared deeply into each other's eyes and he longed to hold her. Her fragrance reminded him of the delicate wildflowers in the woods. Seeing a drop of water fall from Deborah's velvet hair ribbon jogged him back to reality. Against his wishes, he pulled away and hurried to make tea.

By the time Deborah was dressed, the hot cups of liquid were steaming when Ian returned to her. He carried a hand carved wooden tray. His eyes widened as he saw her damp golden hair framing her beautiful face and cascading in ringlets over her shoulders. His gray robe had never looked that good.

"Biscuits, too," she said with a fetching smile.

He set the tray on a small table beside their chairs. "Are you warmer now?" He asked while sitting next to her.

"Yes, thank you." She accepted the cup he handed to her and a biscuit on a cloth napkin.

Concern filled his voice. "I keep wondering, how in blazes did you find my cabin, bonnie lass? Your carriage canopy was ripped off! It must have been dreadful!"

Her fingers fidgeted on the teacup's smooth surface. "The sun was bright one moment," she began, "then without warning, a great bolt of lightning flashed and the sky turned black." She trembled as she spoke. "A tree near me was damaged and a falling limb hit the carriage top, just missing me. My horse bolted and galloped out of control for a long way. I was sure we were lost.

"My hands were freezing and I could barely rein in my panicked horse," she told him. "Then I saw wagon tracks in the lightning flashes. I felt certain they belonged to your wagon, and finally seeing thy cabin was a prayer answered. I truly thank thee for carrying me inside as I was quite cold and exhausted."

Ian placed his hand upon her soft arm. "That was my pleasure, Deborah. I am grateful ye are safe."

"You are a good man, Ian McCullar." She told him, drinking her last drop of her tea. "Thee must wonder why I traveled this long distance to see you."

"Do I understand you correctly, bonnie lass? Ye made this long trip just to see me?"

"Yes! Of course! You told me your wagon made ruts so wide it looked like a road. I was sure I could find them."

"But, I never thought about ye making that long dangerous trip by yourself." His concern was obvious.

"Only the storm frightened me." She shrugged and continued. "The news I have for you was far too exciting to wait until the end of the month." She giggled. "Daddy discovered your work at the Barclays Mercantile and loved it. My dad wants to sell your furniture in city stores along the coast. He also wants several pieces for his office. I had to see you again and tell you my good news."

Ian nodded. "You must be the bravest lady I have ever known, and your news is excellent to my ears." She was lovely and truly captivating. He realized thinking about business in her presence would certainly take a lot of concentration. "What office pieces will thy father need?"

While the couple talked, the tiny witches boarded their dirty mops. They flew from their big oak straight to Ian's cabin. They dropped their mops and stretched upward to peek into Ian's window. They could see a woman in a gray robe talking happily to Ian.

The older sister whispered. "That's a surprise. The woodman has a wife!"

"It's better to zip-zap a *pair*, than our tree to become a *chair*." A snaggle-toothed grin crossed Zelda's face. "That rhyme was pretty *fair!*"

"You might possibly be improving, sis." Vel grunted as she sauntered toward the cabin door.

Inside the cabin, Deborah laughed happily. "It is good to be here in your cabin with you."

"If not for the lightning, I would still be outside working on that big oak tree. Now, I am glad the storm drove me home."

"Me, too. You truly are my hero, Ian."

He blushed and quickly changed the subject. "Did you say oak would be good for your father's furniture?"

"I think oak would be perfect," she purred. She leaned over and kissed him on the cheek very gently, taking his hand into hers. "You must know the furniture was only an excuse for me to see thee. I missed you and needed to be here with ye. Ian, I love you."

Her kiss and loving words sent lightning bolts from Ian's head to his toes. He was astounded she could so easily voice her feelings. For the first time, he felt her words released him to share his intense love for her.

Ian gently drew her hand to his lips and kissed the smooth skin atop her hand. While he had the nerve, he leaned toward her and kissed her lightly on her upturned ruby lips. Fireworks flashed in his head. He tried with great effort to find the words to tell her once and for all, what was in his heart as her cheek pressed against his.

By her ear, Ian whispered tenderly. "Miss Deborah, I have wanted to tell you since I met you, how I feel. I . . . ."

At that very wrong moment, the door crashed open and the two miniature sisters rushed inside, shouting and waving their hands. They looked alike, except one witch wore a sparkly black turban and gold jewelry. The other let her wild red hair spray in all directions and wore no jewelry. They both dressed in black blouses, trousers and pointed boots. Their feet never stood still.

Ian was jolted when he saw his splintered door and the strange acting, little ugly women, who broke it. "Ye could have knocked! Who are you and what do ye want?"

Deborah grabbed the woodsman's arm so tightly her fingers dug into his flesh. "Ian! Be careful. They must be the witches from the forest! I heard they are evil!"

Ian looked at Deborah quizzically "I know they destroyed my door, bonnie lass, but what do you mean by evil? Surely they could not harm us."

"Believe your woman's words this *day*! For your dirty deed you'll *pay*," Zelda screeched.

The sisters began marching in a circle around Ian and Deborah. They appeared so petite and harmless; yet, their red eyes glowed with malice.

"What dirty deed?" he asked, turning as they walked around him. "I have done nothing wrong."

"The lousy *liar* can't take the *fire!*" Zelda screamed, pointing her finger at Ian's wide eyes.

"Stop this. I tell you," Ian said. "I do not lie! What deed are you talking about? Tell me so I will know."

Vel narrowed her eyes and shook her fist at him, showing a golden bracelet on her wrist. "Don't give me your innocent act. We saw you with your ax this morning, trying to chop down our home." His blank expression angered her even more. "You dumb idiot! That giant oak is our home! You planned to cut down our home!"

"Wait! You are telling me that the oak tree on my property has your home in it?" Ian could not believe his ears. "I honestly had no idea you lived close to my cabin. If I had known, I would not have disturbed you." Feeling a bit embarrassed, Ian tried another tactic.

"My ax only chipped a few notches in 'your' home before the lightning hit. I can repair those easily," he told her sincerely. "And I could make you several fine pieces of furniture at no cost to make up for my mistake. We need not be angry. We can find a peaceful solution. My door can be fixed. I do not hold grudges. So can we return to being good neighbors and get along?"

Zelda grinned and stopped moving about. "Hummm. New furniture, I *declare*! We could use a brand-new desk *chair*." Her unkempt teeth caught light.

"Stop grinning Zelda!" Vel's voice was loud and sharp. She leaped upon the fireplace mantel, screaming. "A desk chair will not mend his terrible deed! No amount of furniture can repair our wounds. Let it be known, Mr. Woodsmen; your fate is sealed! No bargaining at this time can mend your horrible deed. You and your woman will both know a fate worse than death!"

Ian clinched his fists. "Leave Deborah out of this," he demanded protectively. "This has nothing to do with her. This is between thee and me."

Jumping back on the floor, Vel took Zelda's hand. In unison they moved faster around the room. Their angry red eyes glared at Ian. They circled the couple, chanting even louder. Ian's voice was drowned out by their strange words. "Rocka this way, rocka that. Rocka this way, rocka that."

Deborah held her hands over her ears as tears streamed down her cheeks.

"Enough!" Ian shouted. "This is foolishness. If ye cannot be friendly, I must throw ye out!" He lunged forward toward Zelda. His feet were numb and stuck to the floor. His legs were rigid as stone. "What have they done to me? I cannot move!" He attempted to catch the little creatures with his hands, but they reeled past him beyond his reach.

Vel taunted him. "Rocka this way, rocka that. Rocka this way, rocka that. Where are your big strong muscles now, Ian McCullar? Come on, mighty ax man; show me how tough you can be. Or do you understand now, we little folks are in complete control? Big strong man, my foot! Tee-he. Rocka this way, rocka that."

Then Zelda screeched in rhyme. "You will be under our evil *spell* two hundred years we hear *tell*. Rocka this way, rocka that. Rocka this way, rocka that."

"What are ye saying? Tell me!" Ian shouted. "What will be two hundred years?" Ian knew the witch's rhymes were pathetic, but their frightful spell was working. He was frozen in place as the sisters circled so rapidly that they created a whirring noise.

The loud chanting drowned Ian and Deborah's voices. Tiny arms and hands slashed through the air like miniature knives as the evil witches moved ever closer. Their fiery eyes locked on their victims, forming a glowing red wheel around the couple, as Vel and Zelda sped around and around, faster and faster.

Deborah held tightly to Ian, hiding her face against his chest. He wrapped his arms around her, trying to protect her while he watched in horror as the witches blurred into a reddish-black tornado of wind, whirring around and around, chanting again and again, and repeating their vile chant over and over.

"Rocka this way, rocka that."

The spinning and unrelenting words hammered at Ian and Deborah's ears. "Please," Ian shouted. "I am sorry! I promise never to hurt your home again!"

"The words you say are so *true*. This spell will be perfect for *you*." Zelda called out with hateful laughter. "Rocka this way, rocka that. Rocka this way, rocka that."

Suddenly a blinding bolt of lightning followed by a thunderous explosion crashed through the cabin. The relentless chanting stopped, replaced with nothing but chilling laughter. After a while, the laughter slowly faded as the two wicked witches flew away across the forest toward their home in the giant oak.

Only an eerie silence remained in the cabin.

For the most part, the cabin remained the same. The fire still burned in the fireplace, the tea cups remained on the table, and the door was still broken into pieces. A damp emerald dress still hung beside the fireplace. However, Ian and Deborah were nowhere to be seen.

In the quiet, quiet room where the couple had once stood and enjoyed a few exceptional moments, were two very large wooden horses with tall stiff legs attached to thick curved rockers. The female rocking horse was white with a golden mane and tail. A thick dark brown mane and tail adorned the male horse's golden body. Both had friendly faces with bright happy expressions, but each was chillingly silent. The icy stillness proved the spell had begun. Ian and Deborah's fate would be worse than death.

They rocked this away and that, this away and that.

CHAPTER 2

GHOSTS IN THE ATTIC

The rocking horses and the cabin faded from the story telling wall when Bumbles waved his wand. "Every time I show and tell this part of the story, Bobby, it makes me sad. Poor Ian and Deborah never had a chance against those evil witches."

"I didn't expect that," Bobby said, shaking his head. "Are Ian and Deborah going to live?"

"Do you remember Zelda saying, 'They will be under our *spell*, 200 years I hear *tell*?' If we leave this dismal time in 1738, we can move forward in time to 1938. I think we can find a few answers there." His wand pointed toward the story wall.

Bobby looked puzzled. "Can we do that?" Before his uncle could answer, new images appeared on the wall and Bobby's thoughts swiftly changed.

"It's a steam engine!" he cried out. "Look at that steam rolling and listen to that loud whistle. But, Unc, it's moving this way awfully fast! Yikes! Watch out! It's going to hit us!" Bobby fearfully ducked his head.

Bumbles reached over and patted the boy's shoulder. "No, lad, the train turned and is beside us. These new special effects are more startling than even I realized. I am truly sorry."

"That was special effects?" Bobby asked.

"Yes, Bobby. Take a look now. We are visiting 1938 exactly two hundred years after the witches turned Ian and Deborah into wooden rocking horses."

Bobby sat up and warily looked around. "Honest?"

"Honest lad. In fact, that train is carrying two children important to our story. They have traveled a long way from an orphanage in New York City to this area in the California vineyard country.

"Tony is ten years old and his sister Molly is two years younger. They are small children for their age, but size makes no difference."

Bumbles chuckled. "Look at me, only four feet tall and I have done well enough. Some folks think critically toward others, for their size, color, or anything slightly unusual. Jumping-Jupiter! If we all looked alike; how boring would that be?

"People made fun of me for years. Being small and having a name like 'Bumbles,' I was a perfect target for cruel jokes. My real friends saw past my name and flaws. They liked me for being friendly and trustworthy. For those same reasons, I can also like myself."

"But you are a Majiventor, Unc. I never imagined you would have problems like regular people."

"It is sad, but it happens to nearly everyone. It always hurts. Remember, Bobby, our hearts and minds are what sets us apart. The love and kind deeds we do for others are what count in life. Real friends are a great treasure. I cherish my friends like precious gold."

"I'll try to remember," the boy promised.

"Well I swayed from our story. We can now join Tony and Molly on that fast moving passenger train. Hold tight to your seat, Bobby!" Bumbles lifted his wand. Zoom!

"And here we are sitting behind Molly, Tony, and their escort!" Bumbles said grinning, "This will be fun. We are invisible so no one can see or hear us."

It felt so incredibly real that Bobby leaned forward in his seat to look out the window at the passing landscape. That's when a sharp sound caught his ear.

The wooden ruler had struck. "Tony! I told you not to fidget! Button your shirt! And for Pete's sake, sit still!" The escort turned in her seat and also smacked the ruler across Molly's hand. "I told you a hundred times, good girls do not wear red crayon on their lips.

"Your mother would flog you good if she were alive." The annoyed woman grabbed the red crayon and threw it into her purse that lay on the floor by her feet.

She buttoned her dark blue suit jacket and tilted her matching pillbox hat. Next she smoothed her graying hair. In a flash, her cold hand grabbed Tony's arm. She puckered her lips and her voice rasped in his face. "Sit still! Your bad habits surely come from your worthless Pa. He was a no-good, dreadful man!"

Tony's face scrunched up as he barked back at her. "Don't talk about my daddy like that!"

She peered down her long nose into Tony's angry eyes. Frostily, she spit out her words. "Your Pa left you and Molly on the snowy orphanage steps and he never came back. I repeat your Pa is totally no good."

The boy bit his lip to keep from yelling at her again. Why did she say such ugly things? I've had enough, he thought. I'll fix her wagon!

As the woman turned toward his sister, Tony unbuttoned his jacket pocket and found his newest pet, a lively green lizard. Holding it gently in his hand, he pretended to tie his shoe, but instead he secretly slipped the reptile inside the escort's purse.

Sitting upright, Tony grinned, thinking about the beastly surprise the tiny lizard might deliver to his infuriating escort!

Seeing his grin, the woman demanded. "Why are you smiling that way? What have you done now?"

A muffled hiccup directed the escort's attention back to Molly. Tears seeped from the young girl's brown eyes as she tried to sit very still. The harder she struggled to be quiet, the louder the hiccups became.

"Not again! You silly child! You are disgusting." The woman waved her bony hand for the porter. "The stupid hiccups are back. Get water immediately!"

A plump man in a small-billed hat promptly arrived and handed Molly a glass of water. "This is the fifth time that poor child started hiccupping. We just entered Kirbyville so she will be home soon. That might help her feel better." As he spoke, the train slowed to a halt.

Tony pulled his prized duffel bag out from under his assigned seat. The bag was a present from his mother before the dreadful car crash that took her to heaven. He always kept his treasured tote close to him.

"That old bag is unsightly," the escort grumbled. "Your grandparents will burn it and I say good riddance. You are so willful they will soon send you back to me!"

"Never! You ole prune face!" Tony yelled. "I hate you!" He grabbed Molly's arm and hastily yanked her past the escort. The girl's chilly water was left unattended in midair to splash over the chaperone's lap.

The two children scooted down the aisle as most people were rising from their seats. It did not take long for the little ones to run all the way outside.

The escort leaped to her feet, her hands pressing the cool water from her skirt. Her face twisted with rage.

"Stop them!" She shouted.

People stopped a moment and then went about their business of stretching and moving about.

The escort pushed passengers aside down the aisle looking for Tony and Molly. She squawked in high tones, with her hat and mouth flapping in unison. "Stop those troublemakers! Come back here, you unruly no-goods."

Charging down the steps she abruptly stopped, face to face with an elderly gentleman holding a sign. The frown on her face altered to big-eyed surprise. She quickly forced a smile and her voice mellowed.

"Oh! Mr. Apple, sir! You must be the grandfather of these precious children, Molly and Tony." The words nearly stuck in her throat. Her smile faded into a nervous twitch. "You appear exactly like the photo you sent. And I see you found . . ." she paused, "your darling grandchildren."

"Well, they found me!" he told her cheerfully as the children hid behind his floppy pants. "I printed the names TONY and MOLLY on this board and they ran right to me. It's good to know they can read. But they look mighty pale. Are they ailing?"

The escort's face stiffened. Her words were defensive and curt. "I assure you, sir, these children are perfectly healthy! I have delivered them safely to you. The porter is bringing their belongings as we speak so my work is done." She held out her hand, palm up, with no smile.

Gramps placed his money in her hand. "Just as we promised," he told her. "We're beholden to yah."

Big drops of rain abruptly fell from the sky. "Hurry kiddos! Climb inside thet blue truck parked by the lamppost, before you get drenched. Thank yah, Ma'am. I'll carry their luggage. Have a safe trip home and good day."

As the man turned away, the woman called out the door. "Just ring me if things don't work out. I'll fetch the dears myself."

She ducked back into the train car away from the rain, clinging to the money he paid her. Returning to her seat, she glared through the window as the old man rushed to his truck, carrying two tiny bags of clothing. Soon his pick-up rumbled off and was quickly out of sight.

"Good riddance you worthless troublemakers," the escort grunted. "When they send you back to me, I'll get even! No one calls me names!" Idly she lifted her purse from the floor, opening it to place her cash safely inside.

She felt a strange feeling on her skin. Something was wriggling and scratching its way up her bare arm underneath her suit jacket.

Instant piercing screams rang out, causing all the passengers to flinch with fear.

The reptile squiggled up the woman's neck to her nose and from there he leaped to her pillbox hat.

Her shrieks were surely heard for miles. The escort's hands flew in all directions swatting her neck, smacking her forehead, and everyone close to her. Yet, she failed to make contact with the slippery little devil.

From her hat, the little green streak leaped wildly toward a safer place onto the Porter's sleeve as the man tried to calm the screeching escort.

It was a circus ride for the speedy lizard as he leaped and swung from one person to the next. Like a trapeze performer he grabbed the tip of a long feather attached to another lady's hat. His weight made the feather bend and it swung back and forth in front of the startled woman's eyes.

The reptile clung on for dear life to the wild whirling feather as the terrified female howled and raced outside the train into the rain.

Seeing his chance to escape, the lizard leapt to a luggage cart. He dashed across the baggage, and sprang upon a low hanging tree branch. There he happily found a drink and his well-earned freedom.

Inside the passenger car, a grinning porter fanned the waxen face of the escort who had fashionably fainted.

The children's grandfather drove the noisy truck through the wet city streets. "Just call me Gramps. Everyone does," the man introduced himself with a pleasant voice. "I'd known yah anywhere with your brown eyes and hair. You remind me of your sweet mamma. Oh my, we do miss her. Thet accident was terrible." He swallowed hard as the busy town turned into small farms scattered about the countryside.

They drove steadily upward on a bumpy mountain road and around many steep curves. Since the children refused to talk, Gramps carried the conversation.

"Grandma Meme and I couldn't wait to see yah. It's been two years since our lawyer located yah at thet orphanage. We wondered if he would ever find yah. But thet is all behind us. We're grateful you're here now."

Instead of the rowdy sounds he expected, the children were silent, so Gramps resumed. "Meme cooked all week. If we don't tarry, we can be home by suppertime.

"She wanted to be with me at the train station when you arrived, but this old truck is far too small for all of us. Maybe we can afford a bigger one someday.

"My brother, your Uncle Joseph and his wife, Aunt Sharlene wanted to be here also, but they decided to wait until tonight to meet you. Maybe they will bring yah their surprise gift when they come over."

"Gift?" Tony broke his silence. "What kind of gift?"

"It's a surprise, so I can't tell yah."

Abruptly Gramps pressed the truck's brake pedal and they quickly stopped. He grabbed his raincoat and scooted out into the rain. "Sit real still kids until I get back." His voice was not mean, but firm. Moving to the front of the truck, he glanced back to see the children leaning on the dashboard watching him with curious eyes.

A large round boulder was blocking the narrow road. Gramps began pressing his weight against the rock. He pushed and grunted until it began crunching forward and rolled off the road's edge. It tumbled down the steep walls of the canyon, making a loud clamor.

He returned to the truck, tossed his slicker behind his seat and began driving again.

"That was strange." Tony's eyes were quizzical. "Why do people leave big rocks on the road?"

Gramps chuckled. "People don't. It seldom rains here, child, but when it does, rocks slide off these high cliffs. Now and then our road gets plum blocked."

The truck halted at an observation point, high on the mountain top. A vast view of a valley loomed before them through a veil of light rain. Gramps set the brake so the children could take a real good look.

"Thet white house way down there in the valley is your new home." He heard a soft sound of amazement slip out of Molly's mouth.

Gramps continued like he never heard. "The house is old but sturdy. We own all thet land you see over to the mountains, the fields and trees, all of it. It's been in our family for generations."

His eyes misted as he surveyed the view. "Yes sir," his voice trembled, "a long time." We've added the big barn, and several other buildings. We have cattle and chickens. There's a creek and pond over yonder, good for swimming and fishing. You'll like that.

"And do yah see those tiny green lines in the fields? They are rows of grape vines. When the grapes ripen later this year, we'll pick 'em and send 'em to the factory to dry. Like a miracle they become raisins."

"Grapes can't turn into raisins!" Tony scoffed. After a second thought, he asked, "Can they?"

"Sure as my name is Gramps. This rain will make the grapes grow and later they will be sweet and juicy. Wait and see." He moved the gear shift. "Let's go home."

Tony and Molly stared at each other in awe. What would home be like?

Meme met them on the porch with smiles and big hugs. Her gray hair was pulled into a knot on top of her head and she wore a cotton print dress. After settling in, everyone sat around the kitchen table covered with bowls of food. Gramps gave thanks and they ate well.

Later, with raisin pie still on his chin, Gramps began talking again. "Thank yah Meme for the fine vittles. By their messy faces, I think the kiddos enjoyed their meal, too." He was sorry the children had eaten in silence. "Tell us about yore trip on the train. Was it fun?"

Tony nearly dropped his milk. "Why?" he asked.

"Well, I noticed yore escort didn't seem very friendly. She looked sort of, well . . . sort of angry."

Tony became instantly furious. "That woman was always angry!" He blurted out. "She hit us with that awful ruler. It hurt! And she never smiled."

Meme's face flushed as she spoke. "That woman promised me over the phone she would treat you kindly!"

"She lied!" Tony scowled. "Ole prune face was my secret name for her. She made us sit like statues until our legs hurt. She hated Molly 'cause she wears red crayon on her lips, like Mama's lipstick."

Meme hurried around the table and pulled the children into a secure hug. "We are so sorry you poor dears went through all that." When she released them, she pulled a small doll from her apron pocket and handed it to Molly. She also gave a little metal truck to Tony.

"We'll love you so much, you'll forget those bad times and love our wonderful farm." She hesitated with an instant shiver. "Gramps, we should move to the living room and sit by the warm fire. It's always cool in this kitchen when it rains. I'll clear the table in a jiffy."

Soon, the children sat on an over-stuffed couch in the warmth of the fireplace. In the big chair next to them, Gramps rubbed his tummy and stretched out. Meme soon joined them in her rocking chair and began knitting with long needles, humming a little tune.

"Give her a moment of quiet and she hums." Gramps looked lovingly at Meme, and toward the boy. "What's in your knapsack, Tony?"

Tony's face paled and his answer was defiant. "It's nobody's business, but mine!"

Gramps flinched. "I'm sorry lad. I just wondered," he replied. "How do you like thet cute little doll, Molly?"

Wordless, Molly laid the doll down, folded her hands, and stared at her feet.

After an hour with the children not talking, Gramps asked Meme to join him in the kitchen. "This is discouraging," he whispered. "I never expected silence."

"We must be patient, dear. This is all new to them. They will warm up after a while. My goodness, it's been a long time since we had little ones in our home."

"Meme, yah just gave me a grand idea." A happy glint filled Gramp's eyes. They returned to the children, but he kept walking to the hallway and lit a lantern. "It's adventure time, kiddos!" He called out.

"What do you mean?" Meme asked.

"Don't fret. Just follow me," Gramp's spoke jovially. "Come on slow pokes."

Tony protectively took Molly's hand and they joined Gramps. Meme followed.

Gramps opened what Tony thought was a closet door; instead there were steps leading upward. Holding the lantern high, Gramps warned them. "Be careful not to fall down these steep wooden stairs." With each step he took, creaking sounds were heard.

Nervously, Meme asked, "What are you doing, Gramps? We haven't been up here for years. It's far too chilly and dusty for the children. There might even be mice and spiders up there."

Molly was wide-eyed and kept a tight hold on Tony's hand. She saw shadow creatures creeping across the walls from the lantern light. Worn hinges rasped as the old man opened the seldom-used door at the top of the stairs. A musty smell filled their nostrils.

Gramps held the light high just inside the door and pointed around. "This big area is our attic. Through the years, we stored all kinds of things up here."

He shuffled forward with the lantern's glow exposing a portion of the room. They could see a wooden floor and weathered gray ceiling rafters. A steady rain pattered on the metal roof as the children and Meme followed Gramps in the dim light.

The lantern left much of the large space around them black as a moonless night. Odd sounds, eerie moving shadows and cobwebs made the children's imaginations run wild.

Tony wanted to run away, but Molly was clutching his hand. Besides, he didn't want to be called a sissy.

Hearing the children breathe fast and occasionally gasp, Gramps acted scared also. "By the way, kiddos tell me if yah see any ghosts," he whispered.

"You're joking! Ghosts are not real!" Tony asserted. After a moment's thought, he asked. "Are they?"

Molly hiccupped.

"Sure," Gramps replied. "I've heard tell ghosts are likely to hide behind old desks or lay in wait in dark corners. They jump out and scare yah now and then."

"I've never seen a ghost," Tony whispered. "What do they look like?" His wide eyes peered all around.

"Our sons used to see 'em. But, our ghosts never hurt us. They just smell musty and have glowing eyes." Gramps was enjoying their adventure.

Molly's fingers dug deeper into Tony's hand.

"Take it easy, Molly," he whispered. "Gramps is sure the ghosts won't hurt us."

At that moment, a mouse ran up the boy's pant leg. He yelled and jumped around like popcorn. When the mouse leaped back to the floor, Tony's face felt hot with humiliation. "I'm okay," He insisted. "I had to scare that mouse so he would run away!"

Molly had leapt sideways, never letting go of Tony's hand. Her large eyes explored the floor for more mice. She saw a broken broom leaning against an old trunk. It reminded her of a pirate's chest she had seen in a storybook. She wondered if these ghosts were pirates.

The floor groaned and both children feared what might happen next? Even Meme was quiet.

Gramps muttered in a low voice as he lowered his head and shoulders. "We're close to the edge of the roof now, so don't hit yore head on these lower beams."

The family watched as Gramps bent over in the narrowing space. "This is the place I remember." He handed the lantern to Meme. Then he bent his knees and crawled back into the dark.

Tony and Molly watched their grandfather in awe. What was he doing? They wondered.

The hair on Tony's neck stiffened. "What are you looking for, sir?"

The man did not answer, but groaned as he stretched and felt deeper into the sinister darkness.

"Maybe our sons moved whatever you want to another spot," Meme suggested. "This dampness cannot be helping your rheumatism. I'll make hot cocoa if you'll just forget this and go downstairs."

"I'm okay," Gramps insisted. "Have a little patience my love. Isn't that what yah told me to do in the kitchen?"

"Uh . . . So I did," She looked sheepish. "So I did."

"I must admit," Gramps chuckled as he chatted. "This was easier when I was young." He reached out a bit further. "Here it is. I found it!"

Tony stepped back. "What is it?"

Mice squealed and scurried as the old man's taunt arms tugged at something in the dark. "It's stuck," he grumbled. He pushed and tugged some more until he and the dusty form could be seen in the dim light.

Meme sucked in her breath. "Gramps, how did my good blanket get way back there? I looked all over for it." Her voice was higher than usual. "Those mice have ruined it."

Moving the form loosed more dust into the air. It whirled around in the lantern light. "Sorry, dear," Gramps said between sneezes. To everyone's shock, he moved back into the same black space. After a suspenseful wait, another shrouded form slid into sight behind him.

Tony and Molly stood amazed.

Gramps grinned. "Look here, everyone. I've found two forgotten ghosts! Yah couldn't see 'em but they were there!" Dust swirled everywhere.

Meme hung up the lantern and pulled the children close to her. "We've had enough talk about ghosts," she spoke protectively. "All your ghost nonsense is scaring our grandchildren."

Molly liked Meme's reassuring words. It felt good to be held tenderly again.

Tony was still thinking about Gramp's words. "If those dusty things are ghosts, why are they so dirty and not moving?"

Gramps shook his head. "Now thet I think about it, I may have gotten carried away. These dusty old things are not really ghosts. In fact these critters may become yore best friends."

Bewildered, Tony asked, "What do you mean? What kind of critters?"

Molly watched dust wisp around Gramps as he wrestled with the tight rope knots. The fine particles drifted in the air, mingling with scary shadows and dangling cobwebs. She saw the ropes fall away one by one. The dirty blanket began to sag.

Tony's muscles tensed and he was all set to run.

As the first blanket fell to the floor exposing a wooden form, Tony gasped, and bravely told Molly. "See, it's not a ghost at all. It's just a big rocking horse, and look, his ears are higher than my head."

Gramps began talking as he worked. "He's a fine beauty, carved from a solid piece of wood." Soon the second dusty blanket fell to the floor.

"That's a girl horse," Tony declared. "And look at her golden hair."

Molly murmured. "Bee-u-tee-full!"

Meme pushed a strand of graying hair back from her eyes. "I forgot all about them. You and Joseph must have put these horses in the attic years ago."

Gramps smiled, "They came to my mind when Meme told me our kids had been away a long while. I wonder if Meme recalls the story behind these horses."

"I truly do," she confirmed. "However, it's cramped here. If we move all this to the middle of the attic, you can sit down and tell the children yourself."

Gramps agreed. Soon, he settled on a nail keg by the sinister pirate chest that Molly had seen earlier.

"As I recall," Gramps began. "Long time ago, my great grand-dad, John, lived in a town named Richmond, Virginia, where he went to a big auction. There, he heard a puzzling story. It was about his distant relative, a nice lady named Deborah who loved a furniture maker named Ian.

"That lady picked the wrong day to travel to Ian's backwoods cabin. A bad storm hit. Folks found her damaged carriage close to his cabin but, both of 'em had vanished and were never found.

"After a long time, the grieving girl's parents stored the missing couple's belongings in some fancy barn loft. It was a real tragedy that the girl never returned to her family. Time passed and the stuff was forgotten for generations. When it was finally found, the girl's distant family decided to sell it.

"When my great granddad, John, saw these wooden horses at the sale; it was love at first sight. He bid the highest and they became his. Later, he moved west and carried these two horses inside his covered wagon. It was a long and dangerous trip to California. Later, he bought our valley and built this very house where we are now. John was a hard worker and a good man.

"All the kids that grew up in this house rode these two fine rocking horses; yet, the horses still look new. They are yore horses now, if yah want 'em?"

"Really?" Tony asked with excitement. "They are terrific." Then his smile faded. "But, Gramps, do you think I'm too old to ride a rocking horse?"

Gramps shrugged and answered. "If these horses were tiny, I might say yes, but they are extra tall and strong. My brothers and I rode 'em until we were much older than you."

"Did you have saddles?"

"No, Tony," Gramps replied. "But there might be something in the trunk, if the goblins haven't taken 'em."

Molly listened but kept very quiet. She still clung to Tony's hand like a lifeline.

Gramps opened the old trunk, and gazed inside. In a spooky voice, he called. "Are any goblins hiding in here?"

Molly stared closely at Gramps as he leaned forward, reaching deeper into the dark cubicle.

With a quick movement, the man pulled his hand up. His clinched hand was covered with wiggling things that glowed red and yellow. They blinked eerily in the light.

"Goblins!" Molly screamed out. She broke away from Tony's hand and bolted into the blackness, shrieking as she ran. Clattering and clunks were heard, then a loud pop, followed by an alarming silence.

"Molly!" Tony cried out. "Answer me."

"Where did she go?" Gramps asked his voice trembling. He grabbed the lantern. "We gotta find her!"

Tears brimmed Meme's eyes. "Yes and hope she is not hurt," she whispered.

Tony peered into the darkness listening for his sister's voice. "Molly! Answer me. Where are you?"

Carrying the light in his outstretched hand, Gramps zigzagged through obstacles.

"There! I see a movement over there." Tony pointed to a dim corner.

Working their way to where Tony directed, they heard a hiccup. Something blue in the lantern light was swaying to and fro. Little knees and feet were hanging over a wicker basket full of brown feathers. A lamp shade topped that.

"Child, are you okay?" Gramps asked as he pulled the lamp shade off her head and handed it to Meme.

"I'm fine," she blubbered.

Please don't cry, Molly. I'm sorry I scared yah. I didn't mean to. Everything is okay, I promise." He and Tony gently helped her from the basket.

Meme heaved a sigh and a smile tugged at her lips. "Molly looks like a chicken in all those feathers!"

"Where'd the feathers come from?" Gramps asked.

Meme shook her head. "I'd guess Molly landed on one of our big feather pillows and it popped. She must have hit it really hard."

Molly suddenly grabbed the man's hand. She spoke loud and clear. "Did that awful goblin eat your hand, Gramps?" She held his hands and looked at them. "Are you bleeding? I saw him eating your fingers!"

"Look child." Gramps held his hand by the light. "My hands are fine. I was only teasing. Come see for yourself. There ain't no goblins."

They worked their way back to the trunk, with Molly still shaking and hiccupping. "See, kiddo," Gramps told her gently. "These leather harnesses have glass jewels. When I held the jewels up they glowed in the lamp light. I promise you, there ain't no goblins."

"I was sure those shiny things were eyes! You told us ghosts have glowing eyes, and I saw all those crawly legs! I ran so they wouldn't eat me!"

Gramps hung his head. "I'm sorry Molly. Long ago my brothers and I made up silly games about ghosts and goblins in our attic. We loved scaring each other. It was a fun game back then. Now, I feel ashamed that I let a foolish game scare you.

"It was only a game?" Molly asked. She suddenly hugged Gramps' neck. "I'm really glad it was only a game and your hand is okay," the young girl told him. She looked around at her brother and Meme. Little giggles burst forward. "Now I feel really stupid," she admitted. "I must look like a silly goose with all these feathers stuck to me?"

"Cluck, cluck-cluck, cluck!" Tony imitated a hen, with his arms flapping like wings. "For a quiet kid, your scream was enough to scare off any goblin."

Soon, the attic filled with light pleasurable giggles, chitchat, and happy laughter.

When the rain on the roof grew louder, Meme picked up the harnesses saying, "I'm cold. Bring the horses and we can warm ourselves downstairs."

After hot drinks, the children enjoyed cleaning their wooden horses with soft rags, while Meme warmed herself more by the fire.

Gramps busied himself, oiling the leather harnesses. As he worked, he began reminiscing again. "When I was young and first saw these harnesses hanging in the blacksmith's shop, it was love at first sight.

"They were useless for me on the farm. The blacksmith told me these fancy harnesses were made for circus horses. The leather straps fit around the animal's shoulders and chest, and buckle under their belly. The bareback riders in a circus used 'em. I couldn't do that!

"I still wanted 'em. The owner told me he'd keep 'em for me until I saved the money. Thet blacksmith died a short time later and the shop was sold. I saw two men cleaning out the shop, so I asked about the harnesses.

"After they teased me for not looking like a female bareback rider, they decided to bargain with me. We haggled and I ended up trading my saved money, a pocket knife, and my leather belt for these harnesses.

"Those men must have doubled up laughing at me when I walked away. I was tiny and thin back then. It took both my hands to hold the harnesses, and without my belt, my pants kept falling down. It was a long walk home. But, still to this day, I like these bright glass jewels."

Tony chuckled as he buckled a harness around the biggest horse. "These red and yellow jewels look good with my gold horse and his thick brown hair."

Gramps gently corrected Tony. "On a horse, thet long neck hair is called his mane, the same as a lion's mane."

"Mane? Okay, I'll call the hair, mane. I'm glad he's tall, 'cause he's perfect for me to ride. But he needs a name."

"I want to name my horse too," Molly decided out loud, while combing her white horse's golden mane.

There was a knock at the door, and Meme soon guided their uncle and aunt toward the fireplace. Sharlene had curly gray hair. The man looked like Gramps, except taller. Joseph smiled and he carried a bundle of gray fur in his arms. "So this is Molly and Tony," his voice was joyful. "I'm pleased to meet yah."

Tony wondered why all the men said 'yah' instead of 'y-o-u.' "We are glad to meet you, too." Tony replied.

Aunt Sharlene gave each child a hug and a candy bar. "We are excited that you are finally here, and we hope to become good friends."

"I love candy bars," Tony told them politely. "But what is that gray furry animal? And why is he wearing a mask?" Tony asked Uncle Joseph.

"This is our pet raccoon," the man answered. "Razzi is his name and he's real gentle. All raccoons have black around their eyes. This guy has an extra big black and gray ringed tail. We don't know what happened to his right ear. Part of it was missing when he found us.

"He showed up one night at our door nearly starved to death. After we fed him, he stayed. We don't have enough time to play with him, so we thought you might like him. He enjoys playing with kids."

Tony moved closer to touch the strange appearing animal. After a few tender strokes, the boy looked at Molly and assured her, "This little bandit is soft as a kitten. I like him. Come and feel his fur."

She watched shyly, but stood still.

Joseph bent over examining the rocking horses. "Well I'll be henpecked. Thet's our Clyde and Gerty. Our oldest brother named 'em before I was born, and we played on 'em for years."

Tony's mouth dropped open. After a moment, He frowned and protested, "Clyde is sort of a corny name for a horse. Why didn't you call him Thunder or King or something good?"

"Well, child," Joseph said softly, his face turning red. "Our brother was bigger than me so the name stuck!"

"Oh, okay." The boy replied, realizing he had embarrassed his uncle. "If you and Gramps call him Clyde, then I'm sure it's a good name."

While everyone talked, Molly edged toward the raccoon. She pointed one finger and reached out gingerly to touch his fur. After barely touching him, she quickly pulled her finger back. She repeated her actions until she let him smell her hand. He didn't bite. After that, Molly trusted him.

Tony helped Molly climb onto her rocking horse the first time. He then boarded Clyde and they rocked back and forth. Razzi quickly jumped up behind the boy, holding Tony's shoulders as they rocked.

Molly called Razzi to ride with her and he did. The three promptly became friends.

After a while, Uncle Joseph yawned and declared it was past his bedtime so they put on their raincoats.

Tony was hugged by his new relatives. "Thanks for Razzi," he told them. "We'll take good care of him."

Molly nodded yes as she was hugged too.

After their Aunt and Uncle left, the children played until bedtime. Their laughter sounded so good to Gramps and Meme, they just held hands and smiled.

After the children were bathed and tucked into their beds, Meme talked with Gramps in the kitchen. "These children are like a breath of fresh air and our farm is the perfect place for them to grow up. We must find a way keep our house and land."

"Yes darling, yore right." he answered. "We'll find a way to hold on. As yet, I just don't know how."

In the bedroom, Molly whispered to her brother. "I think Meme and Gramps are nice. They didn't yell at me or slap my hands. Gramps scared me in the attic, but then he apologized. This might be a real home for us."

Tony was in bed with his hand on Razzi's head, while the raccoon snuggled on his soft blanket in a box between the twin beds. Soon, Tony plumped his pillow and pulled the sweet-smelling covers up to his chin.

"Home," he murmured. "It's okay, but we'll wait and see what tomorrow brings."

CHAPTER 3

MIDNIGHT AWAKENING

Molly and Tony fell asleep quickly the first night in their twin beds. Razzi slept in his box. Gramps and Meme snoozed in another room. None of them were aware of the unusual events taking place in the family room. It began at midnight with the fireplace embers still glowing on the tall grandfather clock which struck twelve distinct times.

The irritating bongs disturbed Ian's deep slumber; yet, he tried to ignore them. In his half awake, half asleep state, he knew the clock was not his. He decided it was the clock at the Richmond Inn. The thought cheered him. It must be time for the monthly social, and he would soon see and dance with his beloved Deborah again.

When the clock quieted Ian returned to his dreams. Deborah was smiling and her eyes sparkled as the couple frolicked merrily around the dance floor. Each time their hands touched, his heart soared. Her smile and exquisite face was framed with soft fluttering golden hair.

She was everything Ian had ever wanted for a wife. Deborah had a lively personality, a gentle way with people and animals. Yet, she was daring when she rode her jumping horse over high fences.

Ian loved everything about Deborah, even her occasional flare of temper. Like the time he spilled punch on her yellow gown. She ran off angry, but forgave him quickly. He knew she was perfect for him.

In his fantasy dream, Deborah's soft pink lips kissed the side of his face ever so tenderly. Life was good. He wished this blissful feeling would last forever.

The moment was short lived as a sense of reality crept into his flawless dream. The kiss felt quite real. Was it? If so, had he kissed her or shared his feelings with her? The answers hid in a murky haze and were unreachable.

A flash of lightning and loud thunder turned his questions to anxiety. Still dreaming, he saw Deborah shivering in a cold wind and rain, her emerald gown soaked. Wet hair clung to her face. How could he help her? He lifted Deborah into his arms and carried her from her broken buggy into his warm cabin, by the fireplace.

He sensed reality again. Was he still dreaming or . . .

Before Ian could knit the real and unreal events together in his drowsy mind, the vision turned cruel. Two tiny witches, ugly as sin, broke down his cabin door and charged angrily into his home. Their loud chanting hurt his ears. Deborah screamed warnings. Ian tried to seize the witches, but his legs were rigid and unmoving. As the couple clung to one another, Ian felt horribly helpless.

Ian's perfect dream crumbled into utter reality. He abruptly knew the witches were real and this was his memory returning, not just a dream. But what happened?

Ian eyelids popped wide open. With a rush of wild emotions, he peered around. Where were the witches?

Before seeing much, he realized he could not turn his head or move his body. What was wrong? Was he tied up? Where was Deborah?

At once he searched the room, rotating his eyes, without moving his head. Nothing looked familiar. Nothing was his; not the fireplace, the furniture, or the clock. Next to him was a carved horse with a lovely golden mane. But where was Deborah? Fear clutched his heart.

As his mind raced with unanswered questions, he heard a faint sound? "Deborah?" He whispered. "Did I hear thee yawn?"

"Who is waking me at this time of night?" Her voice expressed sleepy annoyance. "First the clock clanged the midnight hour, and now ye intrude upon my rest?"

"This is urgent, Miss Deborah. Wake up! It is I, Ian McCullar. Can you remember my cabin and the witches?"

"Uh-huh . . ." she muttered drowsily. "They were spinning around us. Spinning and spinning . . . Oh dear, Ian! The witches! Where are they?" Her eyes opened. What have they done to us? What happened? Did I faint? I cannot get up. Can you help me, Ian?"

"I would love to help you, bonny lass, but my body feels bound, almost like stone. So far, I have not seen the witches; yet, I fear they are lurking nearby, so I will keep my voice low. I cannot see you. Are ye in any pain?"

"Thankfully, I feel no pain. Where are you, Ian? Thy voice sounds very close; yet, I cannot see you either."

"This is very strange. I am grateful to hear you and know you are not hurting. I feared for you."

"Those evil witches are to blame for this! My Gram warned me about them. I thought Gram was just teasing me with her scary tales. I never believed her until now."

"Who is Gram? What are ye saying, Deborah?"

"She's my grandmother. She told me witches lived in the woods, and they were evil, and they can place dreadful spells on us. Oh, Ian, could that be our fate?"

"Merciful heavens, I remember my legs failed when I tried to catch those red-haired pests. I still cannot feel my legs or my body! Maybe we are under a spell . . . That makes as much sense as anything. Did your Gram tell you how long spells usually last?"

"I never asked. I thought it was all make-believe at the time. I wish Gram was here to help us."

"Aye! This is a mystery," Ian spoke with a long sigh. "How can we talk; yet, not see one another? You must be close to me. What do you see around yourself?"

She rolled her eyes around. "I can see a fireplace, furniture, a desk and clock by the far wall. Beside me, where I hear your voice is a fine golden rocking horse with thick brown mane. His ears must be five feet tall."

"I see the same," Ian exclaimed, "except to my left, where I hear your voice, I see a finely carved white rocking horse. The uncanny part is that it has a golden mane the same color as your lovely hair."

"Are you suggesting . . . . ?"

"No, Deborah! Not that! There is no way we could be rocking horses! If I could turn my head I would see you, sure as I am named Ian."

"It infuriates me that we cannot see each other," Deborah declared. "Why are our voices so close to these rocking horses?" Her breath caught. "I just thought of something very fearful."

"Uh, I doubt I want to hear it, but t-tell me anyway."

"Do you remember those bizarre words the witches kept repeating when they circled us, Ian? Was it 'Rock-a this way, rock-a that?' Maybe it was something else."

He repeated the words to himself several times. "Aye, that is what they chanted. Now that I think about it, ye are absolutely right. Those are the exact words! Why?"

Deborah voice quivered. "Because rocking *this way and that* is back and forth, just like rocking horses do."

"No! Great mercy! That cannot be true! Surely, even witches cannot be that vile. I will not believe it!"

"Definitely! Please keep talking, Ian, or I shall surely faint from my fears."

"I have no answers, lass." Ian's voice was tense. "That wooden horse idea is too bitter for me to think about. I must change the subject."

"Ian, I am so terrified, you may talk about total nonsense and it is fine with me. Just please keep talking!"

"Okay, Deborah. First of all, I am surprised those two witches did not kill us. I am thankful we are still alive and not in pain. Things could be better than we think."

"I like the way ye are thinking, Ian. It is good we can talk. It occurred to me that mother knew I was visiting you. Since I have not returned home, she will surely send folks to search for us. They will indeed find us!"

"I want that, lass, although . . ." his voice trailed off.

"What did you almost say, Ian?"

"How will your parents know us, if we, well . . . if we do not look like ourselves?"

"They would know my voice," Deborah assured him. Abruptly her warm voice chilled to icy. "Ian, something bad is about to happen. I hear the witches returning!"

Ian fell silent. He also heard tippy-toe steps coming toward them. Could it be the witches? He wanted to embrace Deborah to keep her from being so alone and scared. Instead, all he could do was hold his breath.

Holding a stick in his black forepaw, a raccoon crept toward the wooden horses on his hind feet. He cocked his head side to side looking directly at them.

Ian sighed with relief. "I cannot believe my eyes. Look! It is just a curious raccoon; not some evil witch."

Deborah spoke in a low whisper. "This is not good, Ian. Raccoons do not live inside homes, and he is holding that stick like a weapon! Why is he walking upright and watching us so closely? He must be a witch in disguise."

Was Deborah right? Ian wondered. Could this innocent looking raccoon be a witch? Try as he might, he had never seen a raccoon inside a home. Ian wished he could protect Deborah if this was a witch or at least run away with her to a safe place.

The masked animal with a large ringed tail calmly laid down the stick. He sat down in front of them and opened his mouth. English words poured out.

"Don't worry your sleepy heads about me. I'm not a witch. Your voices startled me. I figured you were robbers so I grabbed this stick to protect myself. By what I heard you say, I feel you just awoke from a long sleep."

"Blimey!" Ian exclaimed. "Is that animal speaking English? Did you hear that? How can this be happening?"

Before the raccoon could answer, Deborah cautioned Ian. "He is a witch for sure! Beware!"

"No, you're wrong." The raccoon wrapped his tail around himself to pick at the fur. "When I saw you last night, you were dead silent. Now you're talking and asking questions. You must be waking-up from a witches' spell."

Deborah warned Ian again. "This is a trap! How can any animal know about witches' spells? Do not trust him!"

"Lady, I just told you I am not a witch!" His voice was assertive. "This is my first night in this home and your voices, well, I must admit, you sort of scared me. By the way, my name is Razzi."

"Ian, do not believe a word he says." Determination filled her voice. "He is pulling your leg. He is a witch!"

As the animal's eyes squinted angrily, Ian hurried to speak. "Before we say more, bonny lass, I think we should see if Razzi can answer some of our questions."

"I'm glad one of you has a brain." Razzi relaxed a bit and continued talking. "I heard the scaredy-cat call you Ian, but what is her name?"

Quickly Deborah pleaded, "Do not tell him my name, Ian. He does not need to know anything about me. I am still quite sure he is a witch, no matter what he says."

Razzi's fur bristled. "Miss Stupid is what I will call her, since her real name is so secret. Let me tell you, Ian, I wouldn't be a witch if my life depended on it. I double-hate witches! But your foolish friend doesn't believe me so I will leave her out of our conversation."

Ian heard a groan from Deborah's direction.

Razzi ignored her and continued. "Okay Ian, between us chaps; I'm guessing some mean witch put you under a spell. Am I right?"

Deborah's temper exploded and she lashed back. "Miss Stupid! How dare you call me names! I am not foolish! I will have you know, I made A's in school and my father always tells me how clever I am."

"Ian, tell her, 'Clever is as clever does.'" Razzi smirked, saying it. "I try to be friendly with her, and she yells at me. Her dad just didn't see her acting like a fool."

"Stop calling me names! And do not talk about my dad," Deborah howled. "Witches frighten me and that is what you are doing. You are surely an evil witch!"

"And your accusations and distrust are making me crazy. I'm a talking raccoon! I swear I'm not a witch! I'm trying to help you," he barked with his fists clinched.

Ian interrupted. "Will you both please stop this? Arguing helps no one. How can you help us, Razzi?"

"I'll talk to you, Ian, but not her!" Razzi turned away so his tail faced the female rocking horse.

"Bonny lass," Ian called softly. "Maybe Razzi can answer some of our questions. I plan to talk with him without using your name. Will you please agree to that?"

"I trust you, Ian. If you feel talking to him is best, then go ahead. Thank you for not saying my name. I am still extremely fearful of him."

"I respect that." Ian told her, and then he directed his words to the raccoon. "I apologize, Razzi, for my doubts in this matter. My name is Ian McCullar and my craft has always been making fine furniture. This whole mess is my fault. My friend was an innocent bystander."

Ian continued. "It all began the day I went out on my own property and tried to cut down one of my trees. That particular tree was apparently the home of two very tiny and unforgiving witches.

"The only mistake this fine lady beside me made was visiting me. While we were talking, the witches burst in my cabin. We believe they may have put a spell on us."

"Uh-huh," Razzi agreed. "I figured that. It's not every day I hear voices coming from two rocking horses."

Deborah's loud shriek filled the room. "Noooooo! Please say it is not true. Please say it!"

"Sorry lady. Truth is truth." Razzi replied.

Shock filled her voice. "Is that why our bodies will not move? Are we honestly imprisoned inside these wooden horses? Why? We did nothing wrong!" Sobs drowned out the words that followed.

"Aye . . ." Ian murmured. "All you said and more!"

Razzi's head and shoulders drooped. "I know this is a terrible shock, because I was human once myself. I kind of know how you feel. Being changed into a raccoon was terrifying in the beginning, but it is better now. Do you want to hear my story?"

"You were human, too?" Deborah spluttered. "Honest? That sheds a new light on things. I would like to hear your story; yet, I have not forgotten your rude words."

Razzi defended himself. "When you yelled at me, it brought back some really bad memories. It hurt."

Not wanting another conflict, Ian pleaded, "Please Razzi, tell us about thyself. Maybe your encounter will help us. Was it a witch that changed ye?"

"It was." Razzi confided. "I was a tiny kid, alone with no family, living on the poorest streets of London, England, back in 1526. My food came from the garbage and I slept in the alleys. Bad times got worse and I walked for hours one night looking for food. I was starving.

"Walking along a new street, an amazing smell tickled my nose. It was fresh baked cookies cooling on a window ledge. I snatched a handful, thinking how good they would taste. Before I could run five paces, a really cruel witch appeared in front of me. She was gigantic!

"She cackled and grabbed the cookies from me. I tried to run, but she grabbed my ear. See this notch. Part of my ear is missing. That rotten hag swore I'd look like a bandit forever and zapped me."

Ian's voice wavered. "But, you were hungry. That unfeeling ingrate should have fed you. What happened next, and how did you get here?"

"She scared me so bad I never wanted to meet up with her again. I left that place and wondered many years. One year I slipped into a supply ship that brought me across the sea. I barely escaped with my life, and then years later, in the excitement of the gold rush, I hitched a ride on a wagon and came to California. It was a wild. scary adventure!"

"Ian, this is all rubbish," Deborah spoke without emotion. "He simply cannot be telling the truth. If he was a child in 1526 and you subtract that from 1738, Razzi would be two hundred and twelve years old! We both know that is impossible. Even I am not that foolish!"

Razzi stood tall. "It is not rubbish! And since you are so clever, tell me why you subtracted from 1738?"

"I can answer that!" Ian said. "That date is this year. Although, I must say, Razzi, the idea of you living over two hundred years sounds doubtful, even to me. Did you intend to say you were young in another year?"

"No, I told you correctly." The raccoon cocked his head. "Ian, your friend is good with math. The problem is you are both still thinking about normal time. You will have to adjust to understanding witches' time."

"How can time be different, Razzi?" Ian' voice was perplexed. "How can you be that old and still be alive? Tell us what we do not understand?"

"I will try. Actually, I'm much older!"

"That is utterly impossible!" Deborah protested defiantly. "No one lives that long! Or are you a witch?"

"Don't say that!" Razzi exclaimed. "I guess I better tell you more facts. Can you handle more bad news?"

"What are you making up now?" Deborah asked.

Ian took a deep breath. "Just tell us what you know, Razzi, even if it hurts. I cannot stand all this confusion."

"Okay. Just don't get mad at me if the truth is not what you want to hear. It's like this . . . the year of 1738 is long gone; to be exact, 200 years departed!"

"This is stupid, Ian! Razzi is totally unbelievable!" Deborah voiced coldly. "Why are we listening to him?"

"I'm telling the truth!" Razzi said defiantly. "You evidently slept through those years. This year is *1938*. I told you I was a tiny kid in 1526 so I'm actually over *four hundred* years old! The good news is that I'm still alive!"

"This is boggling my mind," Ian stated. "If this truly is factual, Razzi, can you please show us some proof?"

"Uh . . . Let me think." Razzi scratched his head. "Yep! I know how!" He ran to the desk across the room.

Deborah whispered to Ian. "Could any of this . . . be true? Razzi seems so sure. I was twenty three when I visited you. If he has real proof, I may faint."

"Merciful heaven, bonny lass, here he comes. Try to be calm. We will get through this. Why is he smiling?"

Razzi walked back to them holding papers in his paws. He held a calendar up so both could see. "Place your sharp eyes on this! I borrowed it from the lady of the house. It is store bought and exact. Look on the top. It says 1938 in bold red letters. All the days past are marked. You don't have to believe me. This tells it all."

"Oh, my gracious word, Ian, it looks genuine," Deborah moaned. "It says May, 15th, 1938.

"I told you I do not lie!" Razzi boasted.

"My stars," Ian exclaimed. "How is it possible?"

Deborah's voice shook. "That changes everything!"

"If this is true," Ian's voice quaked. "We have lost everyone and everything . . ." His words halted when he heard Deborah's agonizing moan. Ian wanted to take back his words and say something to help her, but his pain was far too gut-wrenching to speak.

Deep heartbroken sobs filled the room. The reality was more than Deborah could handle.

Razzi lowered his head and padded into the kitchen. "I'll be back in a while." He whispered.

Ian wished he could take Deborah in his arms to console her. The witches had clearly made that impossible, replacing their closeness with endless separation.

As he listened to his beloved sob, he dug through thoughts of his own. The world as they knew it was gone. And if the spell was broken now, they would surely die.

Ian's anger grew as he surveyed the facts. He loved working in wood, making it beautiful, but not living in it. The witches had turned his craft into his final permanent prison! How could anyone, even witches, be that cruel?

I should have cut down that loathsome oak! I should have set it on fire, or cut it into kindling! Those vicious ugly hags do not deserve a nice home.

They broke down my door and purposely robbed us of our precious freedom! They purposely left us in total misery!

They cheated us out of being married. Why did they drag Deborah into this mess? She did nothing wrong! Why her? Why me? I detest this! Will we be like this forever?

I want my freedom back! He silently screamed inside until a deep moan of agony escaped his throat. Without freedom to be a man, to live my life, to hold Deborah, what am I? He filled with extreme pain and defiance. Without freedom, he would rather be dead! This horrible spell was truly *worse than death* itself!

The sounds of Deborah's heartbroken crying began to seep into Ian's personal thoughts. He realized she needed some kind of assurance. Knowing his beloved needed him, he began to gradually calm down. As he listened to her sobs, his thoughts began to clear.

He reasoned that his rage could not bring back the past or make the situation better. As he thought about Deborah's needs, he knew his temper would only make things worse for her. Like turning a leaf, he knew in his heart, he must push away from the anger and face rationally the cards that were dealt to him.

Ian's resentment turned to steadfastness to carry on and somehow help Deborah through her agony. He became personally determined that those evil witches would not win! He and Deborah would survive!

As her sobs subsided for a moment, Ian spoke calmly and quietly. "Bonny lass, can you hear me?"

Her voice bristled. "Of course I can hear thee! There is absolutely nothing wrong with my hearing!"

"That is good, lass, let thy anger out. This is such a strange and frightening mess. If you can talk it out or scream it out, please do. If ye wish to become really furious and yell at me, I honestly will understand."

"No, Ian, I could never be angry at thee. You bear no fault in this," she told him quickly. "I am sorry I snapped at you. This has shocked me, but I realize you are hurting too. I just feel angry, so very hurt, and utterly lost."

"Can you share your thoughts with me? It might possibly help." Ian chose his words carefully.

"My heart aches. It aches for thee as well as me. This is all so dreadful. My family surely felt this way when I vanished. They must have felt this ghastly misery for years, never knowing where I went or why. I feel so sad for them." She stopped a moment to steady her voice.

"When I hugged momma, I had no idea it was the last time. I already miss my parents. Oh, Ian, I am so angry and hurt. It is all so wrong!"

"Aye, it is not fair. It is a total tragedy."

"All our relatives and friends, our homes, our lives are gone. They just vanished in our sleep and will never come back." She struggled to catch her breath.

"Oh Ian," she went on. "Those witches cheated us out of our youth! There are so many things we cannot do. I need your strong arms around me and I know you would hold me if you could. Life like this is unimaginable! I am thankful we can talk, but I must admit, I want more, and I know you do, too."

"Aye," he admitted. "You are absolutely right."

Deborah's voice rose. "We did nothing wrong Ian! I feel so angry, I want to scream! I hate those grimy, utterly disgusting, evil creatures. I hate them!" She shrieked. "I hate them! I hate them! I hate them!"

Ian whispered gently. "Let the anger out, sweet lady. I am here." He soothed her with kind words, imagining he was holding her in his arms. As she cried out and sobbed, he wrestled with his own feelings.

The clock struck four as the raccoon tiptoed back to them and whispered. "Are you able to talk? If not, I'll come back another time."

"Please stay, Razzi. I need answers to a lot of questions." Ian insisted. "You told us how you traveled to California. Is that place still in the Virginia Territory?"

The raccoon nearly choked. "Double wow! We have a lot to talk about. The territories are all divided into states now. You were near the Atlantic Ocean, thousands of miles to our east, where the sun comes up first. Now you are in the west, in California, near the Pacific Ocean."

"Is California a state?"

"Yes. You have it right. We have forty eight states. Together they are called the United States of America."

Deborah took a deep breath and mumbled. "One time, my father told me there would be many states. He was a man with great foresight."

"That is amazing!" Razzi said as he walked to a lamp by the couch. He turned a knob and the room filled with light. "Did your dad tell you about electricity and the light bulb? We don't use lanterns much anymore."

"Ian, did ye see that?" Fear filled Deborah's voice again. "Razzi did not use a flint, a candle, or anything to make fire. He used magic like a wit . . ."

"Don't finish that thought, Missy. I apologize for calling you foolish. You truly are clever. I realized that when you figured out all those dates in your head. We sort of got off on the wrong foot. Can we start again? You could begin by telling me what the heck to call you?"

"Yes, that would be good. I accept your apology. My name is Deborah Devin."

"Wow! We finally said two sentences without anger. May I tell you, without you getting mad about some changes folks have made in our English language?"

"I will try," Deborah answered.

Many of our words are different today than they were years ago. Today people just say, 'you.' They don't say such words as thy, thee, thou, or ye."

"Ye say you for thy, thee, and all those words?"

"Yes, Deb. You catch on quickly," Razzi told her.

"It may take a while, "she admitted. "Deborah is my name, not Deb."

Before the steam popped another lid, Ian broke in. "Changing will be a challenge for both of us," he told them. "I will try to learn your new language and your new ways, if ye, I mean 'you' will teach us. Could y-you tell us more about that light? Is it truly magic?"

"I could tease and say yes, but I won't. New inventions are coming out every day now. Electricity is a force you can't see. It runs through these wires and gives the bulb the power of light. I can't understand how it works, but I know it does.

"I can show you all kinds of new stuff. There are vehicles with motors, and even some that fly up in the sky. We can talk on telephones, and you'll like the radio, too. If I showed you now, I would wake up the family."

"Mercy, this is more than I can grasp tonight. I want to learn everything! However, will you please explain about the family you just mentioned? Are they trustworthy? Will they hear our voices as you do?"

Razzi sat down again. "This is a good family. They can't hear me, so I doubt they can hear you."

Taking his time, Razzi explained all he could about each member of the family. He told about meeting Tony and Molly, and the stories he heard all about the attic adventure. "Actually the family found you just hours before you woke up."

"Oh dear," Deborah moaned. "What if we were in a dusty dark attic now without Razzi to help us?"

"Keep thinking that way!" The raccoon told her with a little chuckle. He cocked his head and surprised them with his next words. "Molly and Tony will need your help."

"Surely you jest, Razzi," Ian groaned. "What on earth can we do? We cannot even help ourselves."

"Just listen to their needs, Ian. If you hear them complain or they need attention, you can tell me," Razzi explained. "Being orphaned was really tough on them. Maybe together, we can find ways to help them."

"Aye," Ian agreed. "It would give me great pleasure to help them. Count me in. I love children and had planned to have a large family." His voice faltered.

"Another stolen dream!" Deborah blubbered.

"Things will look better in the daylight. I'm going back to bed," Razzi stated. "Before I leave, there is one more thing I should tell you. I doubt you like it, so should I tell you now or later?"

"Tell us now," they both ordered in unison.

"Okay. While you were sleeping over the years, many kids grew up in this house and you were their toys. Years ago, you were given special names. Ian, you were named Clyde. And Deb's name is Gerty."

"That is worse than Deb!" She cried out as if stuck with a knife. "I knew a Gerty once and she was very old."

Razzi snickered, "Have you forgotten your age?"

"But, I do not feel old," she groaned. "The name Gerty is not the right name for me."

"Sorry Miss Deb," Razzi teased as he sauntered away. "Whether you like it or not, everyone will call you Gerty. So bye-bye, and I will see you later, Gerty."

"How can he be so mean?" Deborah fumed.

"I can already tell Razzi loves to tease you. He is a rascal, but I feel he is also our friend. I am grateful for him. Just think, Deborah. We have two hundred years to learn about." A touch of optimism was in his voice. "How many people have the opportunity to live in two worlds during one lifetime? It is strangely intriguing."

"Ian, you amaze me. With all our problems and fears, you actually sound . . . well, hopeful."

"I will never forget the past, and it will take me a long while to adjust and grieve," Ian took a long breath, "yet, life will go on whether I accept it or not. I can either slowly die of hate the rest of my life, or I can push that hate away. Once I can let it go, I hope to fully enjoy all the good I might find. As for me, I prefer letting go and looking forward as soon as I possibly can."

"It will never be easy," Deborah told Ian. "Will you have patience with me, if you hear me weeping? Losing my family and freedom all at once will be a tough fence to leap. You are my only friend, my only link to my past, and also my future. You are very important to me."

"Just being close to you will always give me great pleasure, Deborah. However, I feel great anguish in my heart and extreme guilt, that you were caught in this trap meant only for me."

"That is pure nonsense, Ian. It is those selfish witches whom I blame and certainly not you."

"But bonnie lass, you might have lived a normal life with a husband and children."

"Yes, it is true. And if I had lived that life two hundred years ago, my life would now be over. We still have each other, Ian, and we are alive. Like you told me, how many people actually have a chance to see and experience a new world? I feel it is important we at least try to find some happiness."

As he heard her words, a rush of excitement ran through his being. "We do face a whole new world, and a whole new beginning. In that spirit, would you mind calling me by my new name, which I believe is Clyde?"

"But, I am so fond of your name, Ian." She fought with her feelings then forced herself to speak. "Yet, as I think about it, I would love you no matter what you were called. If you want me to call you Clyde, I will try to do as you ask. It would be something I can do."

She paused, took another deep breath and spoke again. "Losing my parents was a big shock for me. It may take a while for me to honestly enjoy anything about this new way of life. However, before the tears take over again, I want you to know this. I will try hard to learn with you everything about this new world. To show I am serious, although I still despise the name, please call me, G-Gerty. And as you so gallantly expressed yourself, this truly is a *new beginning* for us."

CHAPTER 4

THE STORM

"School's out. School's out. Teachers let the mules out!" Molly sang out as she slid down a high stack of hay.

"You're crazy, sis! Summer's nearly over and school will start soon." Tony happily called as he made his way up the back side of the hay stack to join Molly. "Jeepers, we've been here in California for three months now."

Standing on the mound, Tony's eyes scoured the big barn from floor to high loft. "Molly! Where are you?"

"Hidden away, hidden away, like a needle in the hay," a little voice called out. "Find me or here I'll stay."

Tony made up his own childish rhymes as he slid down the haystack. "Needle, needle, hid away. I'll find you quickly today. Is needle in the haystack? Is she behind the tool rack, or hiding behind the horse tack? Where are you, Molly? Am I getting close?"

She giggled.

"I heard that, sis! It won't be long now," Tony wailed. He searched the stalls and the hay wagon. "I'm getting closer," he yelled again. He saw feed barrels and looked behind them. There, in lots of hay, he spied an old trunk. Quickly he jumped on top of the flat wooden chest.

He knew she was in the chest when he heard his sister gasp. Teasing her, he yelled. "You've been found by a big mean cat, and you're trapped with a big fat rat!"

Molly let out a muffled scream and beat her hands against the upper slats. "Stop that! Get off the lid, Tony! That's not fair! Let me out of here!"

"Sure its fair," Tony teased. "The question is should I let you out? Or should I . . . ."

His mirth and wisecracks quickly stopped when a ball of gray fur hit the back side of his knees. The boy buckled, yipped, and tumbled into the thick hay.

His sister promptly pushed the lid up and swiftly leaped out. She saw the raccoon sitting on top of Tony's back. "Thanks, Razzi! It serves him right for scaring me."

"No fair, two against one!" Tony objected, then he gleefully flipped Razzi into the air and onto the straw.

As the two wrestled, Molly darted up the tall mound of hay again, challenging her playmates to chase her. "Last one to the top is a monkey's uncle."

They, of course, followed. The pranksters scurried and climbed all over the barn, through the stalls and over the wagon, chasing one another until each of them panted for breath. They eventually fell upon the straw, high in the barn loft, where a cool breeze stirred through the wide open upper window.

As Molly pulled at the straw entangled in her sun-streaked brown hair, Tony looked out across the countryside. "Did you ever see anything so wonderful as our valley and mountains? I never imagined a farm like this when we lived in that awful orphanage."

"Ugh!" She moaned. "That place was awful! I love this farm. I want to stay here forever and ever."

"Me, too," Tony replied as he gently rubbed the raccoon's tummy. "I love fishing in the pond with Gramps, trying to catch that fish they call Big Sam. Someday, I'll catch that monster. Then I'll let him loose again so he can grow even bigger and we can catch him again."

"That hook is sharp! It hurts those little worms and it will hurt Big Sam." Molly protested, wrinkling her nose.

"Fess up, sis. You're just scared of fishing worms."

"Not on your life!" She retorted. "Your silly fishing isn't as much fun as eating the cakes Meme and I make."

"Those cakes are mighty good," he conceded.

"And fishing is boring compared to reading here in the loft by my big open window. I travel all over the world in my imagination. And the view from this window is . . . . Look, Tony! Uncle Joseph and Gramps are coming up the path. They were working in the chicken house, so I betcha they don't know we're still here."

Tony's eyes filled with mischief. "Be real quiet! We'll surprise them when they get closer."

The men stopped by the barn in the shade below the hidden children. Uncle Joseph's voice carried to Tony ears. "Don't fret, Gramps, you'll ketch Big Sam next time."

Tony prepared to look out and yell when he heard Gramps say, "Not if we have to move away from this valley. I'm worried sick. If we lose this crop, we'll lose our farm to thet money-hungry banker."

Molly opened her mouth to call out, but Tony clamped his hand over her face and whispered in her ear. "Be quiet! Something's wrong. Listen!"

She heard Uncle Joseph's voice. "Lose your farm? What do yah mean? What's wrong, old man?"

Gramp's voice wavered. "You see, Joseph, we had to take a loan on the farm so we could pay the lawyer fees and the travel costs to bring Molly and Tony to us."

The children shared a startled glance as Tony took his hand away from Molly's mouth. They leaned forward to quietly listen to every word.

"Don't get me wrong Joseph, we love our kiddos. We're just in a terrible bind. Thet loan must be paid in full the first week in September."

"But, Gramps, will the crop be ready by then?"

"I don't know, Joseph, and they won't give us any extra time. The bank man drove out here and offered to buy our place for next to nothing. We'd be foolish to take his stingy offer this close to harvest."

"Yah know I'd help, if I could, but our medical bills have hurt us this year," Joseph confided. "We're feeling better, but our pockets are next to empty."

"Thank you Joseph. Yore mighty kind. But even if you were rich, this is something I must do myself. Besides, if this good weather holds, our grapes will ripen fine in a few weeks. Thet will give us time to harvest 'em and pay off our debt, then carry us through next year."

"But Gramps, thet's what we thought last year. It was a swell crop until those doggone starlings ate every solitary grape on our land. What if they come back?"

"Don't even think about it, Joseph. Last year is what got us behind. Surely the birds won't come back two years in a row. I don't want our kiddos losing this home."

"By gum," Joseph exclaimed. "We'll beat drums in the fields or make scarecrows thet look just like me! Thet ought to ruin their appetites and they'll fly away."

Gramps laughed, saying, "Yore funnybone always cheers me, brother, but we've jack-jawed enough. Time is wasting. I'll get my tools from the barn. Do yah have time to help me inspect our crop baskets in the shed?"

The children peeked through the open window and watched the men walk back down the path to the shed.

"I never thought about our escort, ole prune face, costing a lot of money," Tony declared. "And I never had any idea that those grapes were so important."

"What are starlings?" Molly asked her eyes filled with fear. "They must be horrible creatures."

"Not really." Tony answered. "Gramps showed me a couple of them the other day. They look like blackbirds; only starlings are slightly smaller. Gramps told me they can flock together and make big black clouds. When that happens, they eat every grape they see for miles."

"Maybe I can beat a drum with Uncle Joseph," Molly told him, shaking her head sadly. "This is awful. We better go swimming while we can."

"Let's take the back way," Tony suggested, "so Gramps won't see us and guess that we overheard him. Come on, Razzi. Let's go to the creek."

———

While the family gathered for supper, Razzi talked to Clyde and Gerty. He told them about the children playing in the barn and the bad news they had overheard.

"Those poor kids," Clyde whispered. "They love this place. It kills me that we cannot help them."

"Face it. We are helpless," Gerty snarled. "I knew that bank man was trouble. He smiled like a fox. If he ends up owning us, anything could happen. If he separated us, I would die of loneliness. Or what if he uses us for firewood?"

"Please Gerty, stop that kind of talk." Clyde told her. "All this 'what if' stuff is more than I can handle."

Razzi plucked straw from between his toes. "Yeah, and making matters worse, I heard Gramps say his joints were hurting so he expects rain. He told Joseph that a bad storm could easily ruin the grapes."

Gerty moaned. "Woe is me. This is depressing."

"If you two happen to hear more bad news tonight," Clyde grunted, "kindly do me a favor and keep it to yourselves."

———

After lunch the following day Gramps sat on the porch swing talking with the children.

"I'm driving Meme to town for supplies this afternoon. If we have time, we'll check on her sick friend in the hospital." He wiped perspiration from his head with his sleeve. "It sure is hot, but it don't look like rain today."

"When will you be back?" Tony asked.

"Hopefully before dark, child. Yore Aunt and Uncle will check on you around four, and stay with you if we're late. Can yah handle thet?"

"Sure," Tony answered bravely. "Me and sis will take care of Razzi and the farm."

Meme hugged the boy and corrected his last sentence. "Remember Tony, it is sis and I." She then hugged Molly and climbed into the old vehicle.

The children waved and watched until the little truck was completely out of sight. Molly's lip quivered, so Tony ran into the house to the rocking horses, with Molly and Razzi on his heels. A ride on Clyde and Gerty relaxed Molly and she began to hum. While riding Clyde, Tony tried to lasso a chair with his rope. Razzi held on to Tony's shoulders and dodged the line as it swung around.

After a time, the children ate cookies in the kitchen, and Tony decided to play outside with his toy truck under the shade tree. Molly moved to the porch swing and read to Razzi from her fairytale book. In the warmth and quiet, they fell asleep. Tony stayed busy digging dirt roads and pushing his little truck, lost in his make-believe world of travel and boy sounds. The afternoon slipped away.

Unnoticed, the blue sky turned to an ominous blackish gray. Without warning, a deafening explosion of thunder shook the earth, startling both children and Razzi.

Jumping up, Molly gripped her book and ran in the house with Razzi on her heels. Tony grabbed his toy truck and ran toward the porch. The gusty wind and sudden heavy rain drenched him before he could run inside. He dripped while closing the doors and windows.

Molly shivered with fright each time the lightning illuminated the home's interior. Tony was trembling from his wet clothing. While he went to the bedroom to change into dry clothes, his sister draped two blankets over Gerty and Clyde making a temporary tent. She quickly filled the floor space with pillows and her book then sprang inside.

While Molly petted Razzi, Tony skidded under the draped covers and plopped down by his sister. At once he saw her sad face. "I love your tent, sis. Don't worry. The lightning will soon pass and we'll ride Clyde and Gerty."

"I miss Mama holding me when it storms."

"I miss her, too." Tony felt a deep ache in his chest. Liquid quickly brimmed in his eyes, but he pretended to sneeze, rubbing away the moisture with his shirt sleeve. "Aunt Sharlene will be here soon," he reminded her.

"It's late. Why isn't she here now?"

Tony peeked out from under the makeshift tent. Molly was right! Their aunt and uncle was an hour and a half late. "I'm glad they didn't try to drive here in this bad storm," he said quickly. "Let's sing until they get here. Row, row, row your boat, gently down the stream . . . ."

Molly liked singing with Tony. They sang every song they could remember, and even giggled a time or two, as the storm raged noisily outside.

An unexpected piercing ring gave them a start.

The boy stumbled out of the little tent and ran in the kitchen to the phone. "Hello? Yes, Gramps, I'm glad to hear you. Sure, we are fine. Yes, it's storming. We closed the windows . . . What?

"Aunt Sharlene is where? Sure, we can do that. Why? It's blocked? Okay. We'll do as you say. Gramps are you there? Gramps? Jeepers! The phone went dead."

Molly ran to his side. "Are they coming home? What about Aunt Sharlene? And how does a phone die?"

"Gramps wants us to eat so let's talk in the kitchen. The storm seems quieter now. Come on, Razzi." Tony found bread, cheese, carrots, and half a cake. They ate as Tony explained the details to Molly. "Gramps found uncle Joseph at the hospital. Our aunt is having chest pains."

"Oh, no, I hope she's okay."

"I hope so, too, Molly. That isn't all you need to know. Do you remember the day we arrived and we saw that big rock blocking the road?" When she nodded, he said, "Well, this rain made lots of big rocks block the pass. Folks will try to clear it tomorrow, but our grandparents can't come home tonight."

"We'll be all alone?"

"Gramps said he and Meme are really sorry. But it's okay, Molly." Tony struggled to sound grown up. "I told Gramps not to worry. You know I have always taken good care of you before, and I always will."

"I know . . . ." Molly murmured. "But where will Gramps and Meme sleep tonight?"

"They have friends in town and that's all I heard before the phone died."

"Will the phone ever live again, Tony?" She asked with a mouthful of chocolate cake.

He tried hard not to giggle. "Yes, it'll live again. When the weather clears, someone will fix it."

"I wish it was fixed tonight," Molly confided.

In the other room, Clyde listened to the children talk. "They are so scared," he whispered. "It pains me that we are here but cannot help them. I hate being wooden!"

"Those despicable witches ruined us!" Gerty gushed. "After three months, I still hate being this way. It never gets any better. And this irritating weather makes me feel uneasy like something bad is about to happen again."

"Great mercy, Gerty, I do hope you are wrong."

The children ate the last of Meme's cake as a gust of wind hit the windows. The sky lit up with crackling electricity and loud clapping thunder. Molly and Razzi raced back under the tent, both trembling.

Tony lit dry kindling Gramps had prepared earlier in the fireplace. The thunder crashed again as the child grabbed his knapsack and ducked under the makeshift tent. The electric lights flickered off, back on then off.

"Oh, no, what will we do?" Molly whimpered.

"It's okay, sis. We ate and I have some food in my knapsack for later. The fire is started to keep us warm and look at this, Gramps left his flashlight with me."

"Oh, look! That light makes me feel safer," Molly affirmed. "Do you think that awful lightning will kill our grapes like it killed the phone?"

"I hope not," Tony told her. "We can't fix them."

What will we do if the crop dies and that banker takes our house? I can't go back to that orphanage!"

"I won't let that happen!" Tony insisted. "Besides, you know our grandparents won't let us go back. They love us too much. Just relax now and let me read to you."

Tony sprawled on his stomach, between the two wooden horses. He propped the flashlight on a pillow, so he could see the storybook and turn the pages.

As he read out loud, Molly clutched Razzi close to her, listening to every word. After a while, the children and Razzi drifted off to sleep, leaving the flashlight shining on the open book.

Gerty whispered to Clyde, trying not to awaken Razzi. "I will be relieved when this storm stops. These children are as miserable as we are. Maybe some sleep will comfort them and us, too."

"Aye," Clyde answered drowsily. He also figured sleep might help pass away more hours of boring time, so he closed his eyes.

A moment later a gruff voice sounded in Razzi's ear, arousing him. He looked about. His eyes bulged and his hair stood on end when he spotted a weird sight.

He peered closer toward a page in the open book. A curtain in the tiny window of a rustic cottage stirred and the front door tilted open. The gruff voice sounded again!

"Turn off that confounded light!" A man ordered.

Razzi backed away when he saw a tiny fellow with a pointed hat step out on the cottage porch. Something in the man's hand looked like a weapon. Razzi shivered behind Clyde's legs.

Again, the man howled. "That light is hurting my eyes! Turn it off!" The little man shook his fist.

Razzi wanted to run, but before he could blink, the man was standing inside the tent. Even with his hat on, he was not tall as Clyde's ears. His white beard fell below his waist over a purple robe. The raccoon nearly fainted.

"Ian, look! I knew something bad was going to happen. Another witch is here!" Gerty's voice quivered.

Surprised by her words, the old man spun around, looking at the white rocking horse. "Who said that?"

In shock, Clyde blurted out, "Blimey, we are in trouble now. He heard your voice, Gerty."

The man spun toward the male voice. "So there are two of you? If you had turned that confounded bright light off, I would not be intruding on you."

Surprising even himself, Razzi swiftly reached out and turned off the flashlight. "It's off, sir. You can go home now." He muttered then cowered back again.

"Now there's no light and three voices!" With a twist of his wand, a gentle glow filled the area under the blanket. The man gazed upon the scene with great curiosity. "This is very unusual indeed. A do-it-yourself tent, rocking horses, a raccoon, two children, and . . . Oh, oh, I see sadness and fear in the tear on this little girl's face. What is wrong here? Someone explain at once."

"Sir," Clyde forced himself to speak. "Neither we nor the children had any idea the flashlight disturbed you. In fact, we thought we were totally alone. Please do not be upset with these two innocent children. The light helped them read and settle their fears during this loud lightning storm. Then mercifully they fell asleep."

The little man's voice mellowed. "Thank you, for explaining that part of this mystery. Even though the light hurt my eyes, I did not intend to frighten you."

"That is good to know," Clyde declared. "It amazes me that you can hear us. Could you please tell us about yourself? How did you get here and who are you, sir?"

The older gentleman's face blushed. "Where are my manners? My name is Theodore Bumbles. The truth is I don't like my first name so please call me just plain Bumbles. I am a Majiventor, and definitely not a witch."

"And sir, what is a M-Maj . . . . ?" Clyde questioned.

"Majiventor, sir. To ease your minds, Majiventors try to help folks. If we ever create evil works, we automatically lose our powers. In all my years of traveling around many worlds, I find this situation most unusual. Wooden horses do not ordinarily talk and neither do raccoons. You must tell me all about yourselves and how this happened."

"Aye, however sir, may I ask how you found us?"

"That is easy," Bumbles said. "I have urgent business around the world early in the morning. I had several hours to spare, so I decided to visit an old school buddy and his wife at their cottage in the children's fairytale book.

"In the middle of my visit, we were trying to drink our cocoa and talk in the couple's parlor when your light . . . well you know the rest. I cannot read minds so please tell me your names and the reason you have all gathered under this uh . . . temporary shelter."

Clyde and Gerty told their stories to Bumbles. He heard about the witches' spell and what the couple learned after they slept 200 years.

Razzi overcame his fears and told his history, and he also informed Bumbles about Molly and Tony. After that, Clyde told about Meme and Gramps and ended the story with, "Gerty and I love this family and wish with all our heart we could help them."

"Yes," Gerty agreed, "yet we also need help. Living inside these wooden statues is ghastly. If the grape harvest is ruined by this terrible storm, I fear Clyde and I will be parted or even worse, turned into firewood."

Bumbles stroked his beard as he listened. "Yes, Gerty, your fears are understandable. You must be in total misery. The problem for me is this; without knowing the magic spell the witches used, I cannot break it. So I must concentrate on the children right now."

The Majiventor stared at the sleeping children, thoughtfully. He fidgeted with his wand as he talked. "My spare time is running out. I must soon be on my way. I have urgent obligations to meet."

"Sure!" Razzi quipped. "You're just like everyone else. You say you'll help, and then you're too busy."

"Please Razzi, let the Majiventor talk." Clyde urged softly. "This kind man will help us if he can."

Bumbles placed his hand on Clyde's back. "Thank you for your respect, sir. The way I see it, the most vital problem is saving this farm for all of you. My brother, Esel, is two hundred years younger than me and in his prime. Esel is said with a long E and sell. If we can find him, he could possibly help you."

"Could you bring him here?" Clyde asked quickly.

"Normally, yes, but I do not know his current locale. He may be on a secret mission. I expect him back in Dome City soon. If you were there, you could find my brother."

"I would, sir, but without legs, that is impossible."

"Well, Clyde, I am still able do certain tasks. Sending you to Dome City is not a big problem."

Gasping, Clyde asked, "Are you serious, sir?"

Bumbles said, "Watch me!" He raised his wand and shrunk to a little butterfly and flew to the wooden horse's nose. "Do you believe me now, Clyde?"

"Yes sir! You are amazing! If your brother, Esel, can help us, we want to find him. Will you help us?"

Back to his normal size, Bumbles explained, "You must realize Dome City is not across the state, but far beyond the moon. It is an amazing city, beautiful to see with fine warm-hearted folks. However, there are evil places and great dangers outside the city. You might save the farm, but I must tell you, your lives could be at risk."

"What life?" Clyde asked. "I have no life since those witches took it away. Hearing Gerty's voice and talking to Razzi are my only true pleasures in life. We barely survive. I wish to go to Dome City."

"I will prepare you for your journey," Bumbles said.

"Wait!" Gerty exclaimed. "If Clyde goes, I go."

"Gerty," Clyde pleaded. "Bumbles said this trip could be dangerous! I hoped to keep you safe from harm."

"Does dying of heartbreak or being turned into firewood sound safe? I will go crazy here without you."

"I am sorry, Gerty. In my excitement I rushed to a conclusion. Of course you should go."

"She will go." Bumbles assured them.

"Have you lost your minds?" Razzi blurted out. "You just met this guy. How can you trust him with your lives?"

"Razzi, try to understand. Gerty and I want to help you and the children keep this farm. Mr. Bumbles offered us a real possibility. If Esel can help us, we must try."

Razzi's voice rose higher. "I want to help these swell kids too, but I'm staying here. If this crazy idea fails, don't say I didn't warn you!" He slunk backwards again.

"If it fails, we at least know we tried." Clyde told Razzi. "Now, I must ask the Majiventor for details. If we go to that city and look for your brother, can folks hear us talk and how can we move around once we get there?"

"No worries there. The kind people of Dome City know your language and perhaps they will give you air rugs or vehicles to help you travel."

"Air rugs?" Clyde repeated fully astonished.

Bumbles pulled his time piece from his pocket. "It is time," he said, "if you are ready, I will send you to Dome City. You will ask for my brother, Esel. Are you ready?"

"Yes," Gerty confirmed. "I want to help Molly and Tony. Most of all, I want to be with Clyde, wherever he is. Besides just being out of this house will be an adventure."

Razzi barked in disgust. "This is total lunacy! How can you trust him when he said his powers are failing?"

Bumbles shrugged. "Razzi is right. I cannot promise anything. I use the skills I have and do the best I can."

"We hope it works," Clyde exclaimed. "You have given us possibilities to help this family that we never knew existed. That alone gives us a great hope."

Perplexed, Razzi muttered, "I honestly hope you can save this farm, but I want you back here alive. Bumbles! You CAN bring them back alive, can't you sir?"

"When they are ready to come home, I will help them." The Majiventor affirmed as he stood on his toes trying to look as tall as possible. "The talking is done. Dome City is your destination and Esel is the Majiventor you need to find. Are you ready?"

"I wish I could hold your hand, Clyde."

With a pang of hurt, he ventured, "I feel the same."

Silently they watched the Majiventor swing his wand in circles, saying strange words.

Purple smoke filled the blanket tent. A spinning sensation was felt by Clyde and Gerty. Happy music filled their ears and all at once, they were rising upward. They saw trees, flying birds, mountains, clouds, and oceans below them. It was beautiful, joyful, and totally exciting.

Faster and faster they sped with the sights blurring into glowing light. Soon a great silent dark space wrapped a blanket of glittering stars around them. The moon grew bigger for a while, then smaller again as they flew onward.

They drifted for a time in total awe and silence. Rainbows began to appear, lighting the way, taking their glittery view away. A bright white light hurt their eyes, and vapor touched their faces. The bright white turned to dark gray. Their noses filled with smells of smoke and putrid odors. A treacherous evil laugh throbbed loudly in their ears. What was happening? Everything turned black.

Crash. Thud. Thud. Crash. Thud.

CHAPTER 5

ATTACKED

When Clyde's eyes opened, his high hopes of seeing a beautiful city and finding Bumble's brother, Esel, were instantly shattered. Gnarled trees with long beards of drab gray moss draped eerily from each crooked limb. The ground was spotted with puddles of slimy green water and the thick humid air smelled foul. Scores of threatening yellow eyes peered through brown scrubby swamp bushes. Dread and panic filled Clyde's heart.

This is definitely not Dome City like the Majiventor promised. Why did we trust that strange little fellow? What have we done and where is my beloved Gerty?

"Gerty! Can you hear me?" Clyde bellowed. His abrupt outcry sent huge birds into flight with a chaotic rush of squawks and flapping wings. They quickly departed.

"Yes, Clyde, I hear you. Those huge birds petrified me." Gerty moaned. "This horrid place is not the lovely city Bumbles explained? Look skyward and you will see me. I am stuck in these high tree limbs. What shall I do?"

Clyde gasped as he rolled his eyes upward. She was hanging upside down. "Are you in pain, bonnie lass?"

"Not my body, but my pride is seriously bruised."

"Aye! When I could not see you, I feared the worst. Hearing your voice is indeed music to my ears. I will help you someway," he vowed. Yet, in truth, he did not have the foggiest clue how. He was helpless.

Clyde thought and thought. As the moments ticked away and no remedy came to mind his despair grew. The place was hot and forbidding and Gerty was in great peril. He had no arms or legs to climb to her side. How could a powerless wooden horse help her? He wanted to cry out in frustration. The minutes felt like long tormented hours.

As Clyde prepared himself to tell Gerty the bleak news, a loud unexpected voice jarred his senses.

"If this is Dome City, I'm a gorilla! This place is nightmarish and it stinks! Where are we, Clyde?"

"Razzi! You surprised me! You must have changed your mind and let Bumbles send you with us?"

The irritated raccoon padded to the front of Clyde. "That bumbling fool sent me without my consent. Good grief, Clyde! Your back leg is busted. How painful is that?"

"Busted? Oh, you mean broken? It does not hurt! It is Gerty that has me troubled."

"You mean that bumbling old geezer sent me instead of her? I told you he was an idiot!"

"No, Razzi, look upward. Gerty is way up there."

"Wow, Clyde, that crazy Majiventor really goofed. Hey Gerty, how do you like the view from up there?"

"It's not a picnic and you know it! I hate this. Are you going to help me or just stare at me and grin?"

"Yes, your highness." Razzi bowed. "I'll rescue you!"

"Be careful Razzi. That high limb will not hold much weight." Clyde said as the raccoon began climbing.

Gerty could have said please, Razzi thought while crawling up the tree. His memory went back to the night they met. She had insisted he was a witch and wouldn't tell her name. I think this is payback time!

Clyde peered upward and called out. "Be brave, Gerty. Our friend Razzi is coming to help you."

The raccoon crawled out to her on the shaky limb.

"Finally, I can get down from here," Gerty greeted him. "I am so angry at that horrible Bumbles, I could wring his neck! But where is your rope, Razzi? You have to let me down easy. You really need a nice long rope!"

"Do you think ropes grow on trees?" he asked curtly, nearly slipping off the slender limb. "A small push will work. Since you are wooden the fall won't hurt."

"You must be jesting! The fall will surely kill me!"

"If you can find a rope, Gerty, I will use it."

Peering downward, Gerty let out a squeal. "I think Tony has a rope in his knapsack. He will loan it to you."

"Now, who's jesting? Tony's not here!"

"But he is! Look for yourself!" Gerty spouted.

"Well, I'll be a monkey's uncle. Hey Clyde, Bumbles sent you another surprise! Tony is right behind you."

"No!" Clyde cried out. "This is no place for a boy!"

"Jeepers, this can't be happening. I heard Razzi and Clyde talking about me. This must be a dream!"

Excitement filled Clyde's heart. "You're not asleep, Tony! We were speaking so you honestly heard us."

"I'm not asleep?" Tony asked. "This can't be . . . ."

Another voice called out. "Can you hear me?"

Tony saw her. "Gerty! How did you get up there?"

Before she could answer, Razzi shouted, pointing his paw. "Tony! A big snake is going to eat Molly! This is not a dream! Run fast and get her out of there!"

Tony shrieked all the way to Molly, who was lying quietly under several low hanging tree limbs.

Hearing her brother's screams, Molly opened her eyes. Suspended above her was a huge scaly snake's head swaying back and forth with malicious green eyes, an open mouth showing fangs, and a slithering tongue. Under him were branches that were cracking from his weight.

Molly froze in fear.

Not able to reach his sister's hands, Tony grabbed Molly's pigtails. The boy slid her away from the tree just as the limbs gave way and the heavy snake plopped down on the ground where she had been, branches and all.

Tony pulled Molly to her feet and they quickly ran back to Clyde and the others.

"Ouch!" Molly yelped, rubbing her tender scalp.

"Sorry, sis. Your hair was all I could reach."

"I'm alright, but where are we? Was that big snake a dream? I never saw one so close or so big!"

"No dream, sis." He peered over his shoulder. "I'm glad he didn't eat you. I don't think the snake followed us."

"Aye, finally something is good happened."

Molly backed away, her eyes about to pop out. "Tony? Did Clyde just talk? Where are we? What is . . . ?"

Shrieks high in the tree grabbed their attention.

"No, Razzi! If you push me, the fall will kill me!"

"We must try, Gerty. Tony's rope is way too short! This is the only way. Here goes. Enjoy the ride."

Screaming and tumbling, she bounced from one bough to another, hitting headfirst in mud close to Clyde.

In a quick and firm voice, Clyde instructed the children. "You must help Gerty immediately. Pull her head from the mud or she will suffocate. Please hurry!"

With one child on each side, they tugged on Gerty, until her head snapped free from the black sucking mud.

"Clean the mud and slime from her nose so she can breathe." Clyde directed as he watched helplessly.

Tony did as he was told. He used his shirt to clean Gerty's nose and eyes. Molly watched with loud hiccups.

Gerty gasped for air. "My word, you saved my life! That heathen Razzi pushed me! He nearly killed me!"

"You're safe now," Razzi cried out, "so live with it! I had no choice. I just wish I'd done it sooner."

Molly looked at her brother with questioning eyes. "Tony, what is happening? When did our horses and pet raccoon start talking? I don't understand any of this."

"Me neither, sis. Like you, I woke up and heard them talking. Maybe Clyde can give us some answers."

"I am truly sorry we shocked you, Molly. And you too, Tony," Clyde apologized. "This place looks mighty dangerous. We must explain fast then move on. Gerty's and my story began with two evil witches . . . ."

When the stories about witches and Majiventors were told, Molly had one question. "Do you think the Majiventor can turn you back to humans again?"

"That would be great," Clyde answered. "However, our real goal is getting help from Esel to save your home."

Tony looked around. "This is a weird place to find anyone for help. But I love our farm so what can I do?

"I want to help," Molly volunteered.

A burst of noise filled their ears as birds once again rushed into the air. A great ugly beast plodded into a nearby clearing, thrashing his sturdy tusks against everything in his way. His grimy snout lifted, sniffed the air, and his keen eyes immediately spotted them.

"Quick! Climb this tree," Clyde ordered. "Scramble up there fast and hold on for dear life!"

Tony helped Molly to the first limb then he pulled up behind her. Razzi hastily passed them, climbing further upward. The wild beast dashed recklessly toward them, running at full speed. The creature collided with their tree causing a terrible impact. The tree jolted from side to side.

Molly's footing slipped. Still holding on for dear life, she cried out as her body dangled dangerously in midair.

Tony grabbed Molly with his free arm. As she was pulled back to safety the beast hit the tree again. "Go away you crazy hog!" Tony ordered. "Leave us alone!"

"Listen to me, children," Clyde instructed. "Keep still, stay calm, and I promise he will leave you alone."

"What can I do, Clyde?" Gerty whispered.

"Relax if you can and remain stone quiet."

The beast cocked his head toward the voices. He trotted to the wooden horses and sniffed each one. He pushed his hairy head and nauseating wet snout into Gerty's muddy face. His hot repulsive breath made her gasp. Hearing her, the animal responded, digging his split hooves into the ground ready to attack.

"Forget her!" Clyde yelled. "Come on you lily-livered over-grown boar. Only show-off cowards attack ladies. Come on, big guy, show me how mean you can be."

Molly looked at Tony with fear in her eyes. She could see the brute's pointed tusks and hear his menacing sounds. Poor Clyde, she thought, he will be killed.

The angry beast rushed forward and slashed his razor-sharp tusks against Clyde, spinning him around, only to hear more heckling. The wild beast's eyes burned orange and spittle drooled over his dagger-like teeth.

The demon grew angrier with the invisiblevoice, and bored his sharp teeth into Clyde's back leg. The gush of salty hot blood that the animal expected was not there! Only hardwood splinters filled his mouth.

The beast rolled his tongue and jerked his head to and fro. Maddened by the splinters in his lips, the monster became more enraged as he crunched his teeth into the wood again. He repeated the deed several times.

Clyde laughed out loud. "Having fun big guy?"

The beast backed away appearing confused. His mouth was full of his own blood and his tongue full of splinters. He shook his head in pain. Turning away, he grunted brashly. With his hind feet he kicked sod all over Clyde and Gerty. Then like lightning, he ran off through the swamp, squealing like a startled piglet.

When the swamp grew quiet again, Clyde called out. "Come down from the tree folks. The bully is gone."

Gerty gave a long sigh. "That stinky boar was horrible, but Clyde, you were absolutely wonderful!"

Feeling elated from his first achievement in what felt like a lifetime, Clyde chuckled and declared. "I am happy to be of assistance fair maiden."

Once Molly's feet touched the ground, she couldn't stop talking. "I slipped and Tony caught me. Even Razzi nearly fell. There's mud on our horses. You were so brave Clyde. Are you in pain?" She stopped for breath.

"For once, child, it is great to be wooden. I am fine and in no pain. In fact I truly feel chipper for a change."

Molly hugged Clyde, saying, "You saved our lives!"

Gerty followed with flowing admiration. "You knew exactly what to do, Clyde. I was so scared I nearly fainted."

"You were really smart and brave, Clyde!" Tony's voice was heartfelt. "Thanks a lot!"

"For a wooden horse, I am amazed," Razzi added. "Who would believe it? You even surprised me!"

"It was my pleasure folks. I almost felt human, at least for a moment," he reflected. "And it did feel good."

"Gramps told us in the attic that you might be our best friend, but I never expected a rocking horse to save my life." Molly brushed dirt off the horses as she talked.

"Nor did I," Clyde replied. "Now, we must decide what to do next, before another beast comes our way. The children will need shelter before dark. Did you happen to see Dome City while you were in that tall tree, Razzi?"

"Just lots of swamp and a few grassy hills . . . ."

"Hills might be good. Which direction?"

"That way, Clyde," Razzi pointed his paw as he spoke. "But how do we get you there? You can't walk."

Tony pulled his cowboy rope from his knapsack. "This might help," he suggested.

"I told you, Razzi! Tony has a rope!" Gerty snapped.

"And look at it! I told you it was too short to help." Razzi declared. "You are safe so stop nagging me."

Razzi, you are a self-centered non caring heathen!"

"And you are a name-calling, ungrateful person!"

"Whoa you two, we need to save our energy for finding shelter." Clyde warned. "We must move on."

Tony was quick to cut the rope into two pieces with his pocketknife. He attached them to the horses' front legs, and was tying knots along the rope to help their grip. "I think I can pull Clyde, if Molly and Razzi can pull Gerty."

"No sir, not on your life. I'm not pulling Gerty!" Razzi grunted. "I'm sick of her attitude. Besides, I'm starving."

"My attitude! You nearly killed me!" Gerty retorted.

"I saved your selfish hide!" Razzi yelled. "You didn't even thank me for that! I'm not helping you anymore!"

"We cannot stay here," Clyde asserted. "We must find safety for the children. This is not a safe place."

Molly tried to pull Gerty by herself and failed.

"Please Razzi," Clyde pleaded. "We need you."

"Just leave Gerty here," Razzi fumed.

"No!" Molly exclaimed. "We can't leave her!"

"Yes, we can," Razzi contended. "She's trouble!"

Gerty's voice was trembling. "Being left here alone scares me senseless. I would walk if I had legs! I apologize for my unkind words. Please Razzi, I beg you to help me."

"Too late!" he grumped. "I'm leaving you here."

"If Gerty stays here, I will too," Clyde maintained.

Tony pulled a carrot from his tote and dangled it in front of Razzi's face. "If you will help us, I'll give you the two carrots I stuck in my knapsack during the storm."

"You have carrots?" Razzi's voice brightened.

"I learned in the orphanage to hide extra food in case of bad times. You can have one now, Razzi, and one later today, if you will help Molly pull Gerty to safety."

"You made a deal. Give me the carrot, Tony. I'll hate pulling her, but that carrot looks as good as a trout."

Razzi ate his carrot and soon the wooden horses were being lugged over the wet smelly land. It was hot and miserable work for the strange little group to move amid puddles, trees, and underbrush.

Gerty watched Molly and Razzi's feet sliding in the mud as they struggled to pull her. She kept quiet to keep peace. She also watched for lurking dangers.

Clyde did the same. He hated that Tony had to work so hard in this loathsome land to pull him, a rocking horse, through a swamp. It was mortifying; yet, a necessity.

The imprisoned man, once independent and strong rambled in his thoughts as they moved along at a snail's pace. How had he been so wrong believing in Bumbles? Or had Bumbles just messed up? Would Dome City still be out there in the hills? If not, how would it be possible to keep the children safe in a place like this? I must think positive. Everyone seems to be depending on me.

The children panted in the heat but never stopped. Razzi complained the whole way, talking about that idiot Bumbles and his hairbrained ideas.

Bit by bit, the trees began to thin, as the group found the low hills covered with brown grass. The first knoll they climbed rose about twelve feet higher than the swamp. Even that height seemed impossible for the worn-out trio, but their high hopes helped as they topped the hill and settled in the middle of a wide grassy field.

"Stand on my back, Tony," Clyde said. "You might see Dome City or a place we can find help?"

Tony did so, peering around. "I don't see anything. What does Dome City look like?" the boy asked.

"Bumbles told us it was beautiful," Clyde recalled. "Any kind of civilization would be fine with me."

"All I see are more hills," said Tony. "There are no signs of people, animals, or even birds."

Clyde reflected back. "When the woods became quiet with no birds in sight, it always meant trouble."

"I hope not." Tony groaned as he crawled to the ground and fell in a tired heap. "The worst part," Tony added, "was I never saw any food unless we eat grass. I'm really hungry and my knapsack is empty."

Molly sat by the boys, whimpering. "I wanna go home now, Tony. Can Clyde call Bumbles to take us back? My stomach is growling, and I sure don't like this place."

"I would call him if I only I could," Clyde told her.

"All that work pulling you guys for nothing." Razzi grumbled. "I told you not to trust that old geezer called Bumbles. He's a menace. But no one ever listens to me!"

"I am truly sorry, Razzi," Clyde's voice broke with emotion "Being cautious never even entered my mind. I just wanted to help save the farm. Besides, the plan was only for Gerty and me to travel here. But, nothing is happening like the Majiventor told us. There is no beautiful city, no food and no help in sight. Why did I believe him?"

"Because you have a kind heart and wanted to help everyone," Gerty replied gently. "When you heard there would be dangers, you wanted to go alone. I chose to be with you. We had no idea Bumbles would send all of us. It is not your fault . . . ." Gerty stopped mid-sentence. "Oh dear," she whispered. "I see something on the next hill."

Sitting up, Tony blurted out. "Jeepers, that's a Brontosaur! It's an honest-to-goodness prehistoric beast, and it's alive and walking! They died out on earth years ago. Just look! That guy is very much alive!"

"There's not just one!" Razzi warned, leaping behind Tony. "I see three of them! They are walking this way."

"How dangerous are those creatures?" Clyde asked. "Should you be hiding?"

"I don't think so," the boy affirmed. "Our school books showed pictures of dinosaurs with long necks and small heads, eating only plants and insects. We're okay."

"If that book is wrong, we'll be their supper tonight." Razzi watched the creatures munching grass then stretch their heads upward, smelling the air. When their heads were high, they were taller than a barn.

Molly tugged on Tony's arm. "Let's go!"

"She has a great idea," Gerty quickly agreed.

Peering around, Clyde spotted boat-sized birds circling overhead. "Look! Even the birds look mean here."

"Those are Pteranodon reptiles, part of the Pterosaur family that flies like birds. Doggone, I'm glad I studied about prehistoric beasts last year. Those guys don't have feathers, just scales and sharp beaks and claws." Tony sounded too excited to be scared. "Their wings must be at least thirty feet wide. We can't hide from them. Let's just watch and see what they do."

"Great mercy! Another beast just topped the other hill. Look at that creature's big head, small front legs and he is walking like a human on his back feet!"

"Yeah, Clyde," Razzi's voice shook. "And his giant head has giant teeth! Oh no, there's another monster just like him. Let's get out of here!"

"Great idea!" Tony agreed. "Those are the meanest of all! The Tyrannosaurus Rex eats meat!"

The fear stricken travelers tried to back away as the terrifying sights and sounds moved closer to them. The earth trembled. All the hefty monsters moved at once in the direction of the newcomers. A giant long-necked beast approached the earthlings first with his head and neck showing before they could see his lower half.

The children and Razzi pulled Clyde and Gerty backward to the edge of the hill, but their eyes never left the scary sights drawing nearer.

As the tall dinosaur observed the little group, his thick eyelids blinked over enormous yellow eyes. His long neck arched so his head was close over them. Peering down at the earthlings the curious Brontosaur placed his nose close, sniffing with his wide nostrils.

"His head's big as a truck," Tony mumbled.

The beast's eyes began to glow as his head drew upward and his body quickly jerked around to face his attacker, a giant Rex. Their boisterous screams and hisses toward each other were deafening. For long moments, they faced each other, waiting for one to make their move.

"Leave us here and run for your lives!" Clyde ordered. "Find some place to hide! Don't look back!"

Another T. Rex dashed toward the stand off. He gave a challenging roar arousing more dinosaurs to join in the coming fight. The ground shook.

As Razzi darted away, he yelled, "They're arguing over who eats us first. Run fast!"

The closest long-necked dinosaur broke his stare to glance upward at the circling giants in the sky. The irate T. Rex seized the moment and struck. His sharp teeth grabbed a mouthful of the Brontosaur's long throat. Warm sticky blood splattered through the air and over the onlookers. The battle had begun.

Huge swinging tails whipped the air in long swoops.

Large clumps of dirt sprayed from their heavy feet, and green metallic scales thudded on the ground around the helpless rocking horses. The rebellious howls, bellows, and groans filled the earthling's ears.

Hiding behind a tree, Molly cried. "We can't leave our friends to be smashed! We must do something!"

The uproar was so savage and powerful, the great fowls in the sky went unnoticed. They formed a single line then each bird plunged into a fast dive, one behind the other. Their strong wings stretched open and their sharp claws reached forward.

Gerty screamed frantically as the first bird lifted her from the ground with his claws forming a cage around her.

"Let me go!" Gerty shrieked. "Help me, Clyde!"

"Bring her back!" he yelled. The pain he felt as he watched her being carried away cut into his heart like knives of fire. He could only watch. This was not like the boar. Clyde could not trick his foes this time to save her.

Witnessing Gerty being taken, the children and Razzi rushed to save her, all too late as she was out of reach. One by one they were caught up in the talons of other Goliath fowls. As Tony was carried upward, he saw Clyde seized last and whisked above the dueling dinosaurs.

Together the great birds flew upward in a V formation. Their huge wings carried them higher and higher until the battling beasts grew small in the distance and disappeared from view. The flock continued steadily upward into thick smelly clouds.

In the darkness, Clyde tried to figure out where the birds might take them. Some birds take their prey to their nests. Will they feed the children and Razzi to their baby chicks? This is a horrible nightmare! It is strange that the birds would take Gerty and me. Surely they know we are wooden. What possessed me to listen to Bumbles?

Clyde's thoughts were broken when the birds lifted above the dark clouds into a dazzling brilliance. The fresh air was an instant relief as a new world opened up before him. He could see a large sun setting over the edge of the thick clouds at a far distance. The cloud layer below was no longer brown, but glistened like new fallen snow with tinges of orange from the sun.

If these are our last moments to live, it is entirely pleasing, Clyde thought. He breathed in the clean air and for a moment just soaked in the splendor all around him, which was more striking than he thought was possible.

Wait a minute . . . What do I see off in the distance? It looks like a golden pearl floating on a sea of glistening foam. Is it an island?

As the birds carried him closer to the immense transparent pearl, it was possible to see inside the dome. There was an island inside the see-through material.

Clyde felt an abrupt surge of pleasure, energizing his extremely exhausted soul. "Hallelujah!" he cried loudly to the others. "Look, everyone. Can you hear me? It truly is Dome City!"

CHAPTER 6

DOME CITY

Carrying the earthlings safely in their claw cages, the prehistoric birds glided down to the sea of clouds near the floating massive transparent dome. One by one the beasts hovered over a slightly raised cloud, where the captives were released on a solid surface still hidden by clouds. At that time the birds instantly vanished.

A jubilant Molly hugged her friends. "We're alive! They didn't eat us!" Tears ran down her smiling face.

"Sis, hold my hand!" Tony warned. "We're moving! Jeepers, look up there! I see a . . . a flying turtle!"

A tiny gray turtle with whirring wings and wearing a white vest was above them. His high-pitch voice quivered as he shouted. "Move faster, I say! We must hurry."

The earthlings were carried slightly above the cloud layer. Faster and faster they sped directly toward the round topped dome on a collision course. The dome towered above them like a great daunting mountain.

Razzi screamed and ducked down just as an entrance opened in the dome, letting the flying vehicle pass safely through. The gap immediately closed behind them, and the cloud vanished around their transportation vehicle. It was long and sleek with seats and handrails.

Razzi stood up and peeked around in amazement.

Out of breath, the winged turtle settled on a handrail beside the travelers. He put on eye glasses and observed the earthlings much closer. "Dreadful days of Sinbad, you look ghastly! All that mud and dinosaur blood stinks to high heaven!"

Molly backed up and a frightened hiccup escaped.

"Forgive my rudeness, Molly. I did not intend to alarm you! Sometimes I speak before I think. I am Professor Jay-T Tuttle, the overseer of this domed

Septar, which is a floating island. We have many kinds of Septars with cities and such that float around Bumble's world.

"I will accompany you to Dome City which is sixty miles away, although our limojet will travel quickly."

"Blimey, we may live to see Dome City after all!" Clyde declared. "This is a dream come true. By the way, Mr. Tuttle, sir, how do you know Molly's name?"

"Please call me Jay-T. Instead of fussy titles, we prefer keeping things relaxed and totally friendly. Earlier Bumbles sent us word, informing us about your arrival; however, he sent you with more speed than we expected. In our world, it is referred to 'a small miscalculation.'

"We saw you pass over our Septar's dome this morning and we could not safely stop you. Our Rangers began looking for you immediately. When they lifted you above the clouds, they informed us that they had barely rescued you from several attacking dinosaurs."

"Your Rangers saved us just in time," Clyde affirmed. "How can we thank those brave chaps for rescuing us?"

Jay-T smiled. "You just did. My transmitter is still on and they thank you for your kind words. Our invisible Rangers reside outside the dome to guard us. They are always ready to help folks in need, like they did today."

"Being invisible is amazing," Clyde declared. "Great mercy, this is a marvelous place. Everything is a surprise! I never saw a turtle with wings before."

"Prepare yourselves for more amazement. Dome City has as many wonders as Old World has dangers."

Razzi groaned. "Is Old World where we were? If so I never-ever want to go to that horrid place again."

"Yes, Old World is below our cloud layer," Jay-T told him. "Since we have some time before reaching the city, I will tell you a little about Old World's past. It was once a paradise like your planet earth. We had forests, clean air, and there were many peaceful nations."

"What happened?" Clyde questioned.

"A small part of our population turned greedy and desired greater power. They quarreled over who was most powerful which led to wars. Finally it ended with nuclear explosions and the air was filled with horrible pollution."

Jay-T shrugged sadly and went on. "The all-wise Bumbles anticipated the horror and created many floating islands beforehand. He was young when the toxic clouds formed around Old World. Our wise Majiventors floated the islands on the outer cloud layer. As I said before, many Septars now exist around Bumble's World."

The turtle frowned. "The clouds still give us problems. The chemicals distort our communications to and from Old World. Our Rangers cannot commune with us below the clouds. It was a suspenseful wait for us."

"It was no piece of cake for us!" Razzi growled.

"I know it was traumatic," said Jay-T. "It was a bad introduction to our world. I can tell you the pollution levels have declined down there so you were not harmed. Long ago, the toxins changed all the creatures left down there. That is why dinosaurs flourish on Old World."

"That's old news, Jay-T!" Razzi asserted. "We already met six of 'em and nearly became their supper!"

"It was scary," Gerty affirmed.

"You can relax now in the safety of our Septar's dome," Jay-T assured them. "For that, we thank Bumbles for his great abilities. He is our greatest hero."

"Are you talking about the same Bumbles who nearly killed us?" Razzi asked, his fists clenching.

Gerty whispered. "Control your temper, Razzi."

"Stop henpecking me, Gerty! You're not my mum!"

"And glad of it!" She retorted indignantly.

"Look!" Tony pointed upward. "There's a man up there in the sky! He has a red cart and winged horses!"

Everyone stared above the dome. A string of black flying horses flew in a long line. Leading was a mighty black stallion, pulling a chariot with a giant man riding inside, cracking a loud whip.

"Halt, Black Fire!" They heard him yell. He yanked hard on the reins, hovering in plain view of the earthlings.

The huge man stood up, placing his foot on the carriage rail. He wore black except for his cape's red lining that framed his powerful body. The scowling man pointed his finger toward the group and his harsh voice bellowed.

"Earthlings, listen well! I'm the great Zor Zanger, soon to rule this world. Your quest is hopeless! If you enjoy living, go home immediately. You've been warned by the great Zor!" His offensive laughter filled their ears.

Zor dropped onto the chariot seat, snapped his whip, and away the horses went. Even out of sight, the smoke trail still eerily snaked across the evening sky.

"I heard that same dreadful laughter before we landed in Old World's swamp," Clyde conveyed to Gerty.

"Yes, a very evil laugh," she remembered.

"That man must be the devil himself!" Tony declared. "I saw fire sparking from the horses' hooves!"

"Zor is evil as any devil." Jay-T warned, still peering upward. "He is the reason I hurried you inside our dome today. This is the only safe place away from Zor."

"How does he know us and our mission, Jay-T?"

"Good query, Clyde. A while back, when one of our Majiventors was away from his castle, his laboratory was robbed. Zor Zanger is most likely the culprit, and he is using Esel's gadgets to listen in on our communications."

"Is 'Esel' Bumble's brother?"

"You are correct, Clyde. And like Bumbles, Esel is wise and kind. His castle is on another Septar. He used to visit us often until recently. His sisters, the Wise Ones, live in Dome City and they are a bit worried about Esel."

"Bumbles told us to find Esel. The storm back on earth was bad and we need help right away to save Molly and Tony's home. We wasted far too much time in that awful swamp. Will you help us find Esel immediately?"

"We will try, Clyde," Jay-T said. "It is possible the Wise Ones can help. Before meeting anyone, you have needs, such as food, a bath, and rest. Truly, I must say your swamp perfume is ghastly!" He held his nose.

Gerty chuckled. "We must smell revolting."

Jay-T glanced around. "Darkness is setting in. I will try extra hard to find Esel while you refresh and recharge. Maybe by then, he will hear about you and want to help."

"That is kind of you, sir," replied Clyde. "If Esel can save the grape harvest in time, we can go home."

"And back to a ho-hum life," Gerty muttered. "I so admire your wings, Jay-T. Can all turtles in this world fly?"

"We are given the choice. I happen to enjoy flying."

"Having freedom of choice must be splendid! I wish Clyde and I had that option. When I was young and named Deborah a long time ago, I rode jumping horses. When my horses leapt high in the air over tall fences, I pretended I was flying. That was a marvelous feeling!"

Tony joined in. "I wanna fly airplanes when I grow up." Holding his arms out shoulder high, he turned in circles. Lights caught his eye. "Hey, look at that!"

Glowing beams crisscrossed the dark sky over a modern city full of glitzy buildings. The lights reflected on a lake which made the metropolis look twice its size.

"Welcome to Dome City," Jay-T announced as they soon floated over all kinds of shops and homes.

"I don't see any people," Molly commented.

Jay-T's brow wrinkled. "It happens every time Zor Zanger appears. Folks prefer to stay indoors."

"I thought you told us we are safe under this dome," Razzi snapped brashly. "Are we safe or not?"

"Safer than anywhere I know," Jay-T assured him. "You will feel better after you eat and that will be soon." The limojet halted by an unattractive plain building.

"This is the Renovation Center which Bumbles built years ago for relaxing after his frequent long journeys. He kept it ordinary to keep attention away from it. He has expanded the facilities to help others, like you, tonight."

Jay-T flashed a tiny beam toward the wall and it opened. The opening was barely big enough for the limojet to float inside. The outer door hastily closed.

The dim lighted room was full of gentle rushing air. "The breeze you feel is decontaminating you," Jay-T explained. "The air kills the germs that make you sick."

Razzi shivered. "Big words like you are using are scaring Molly! Stop it!"

"I'm not scared." Molly sang out. "It feels good."

Jay-T noticed the raccoon trembling. "This air will keep you fit, Razzi. In this case, big words are good news."

"I never heard of germs before, Jay-T, but I know about being hungry. I don't like it. How long does all this air-stirring take?" Razzi asked impatiently.

Secretly smiling, Jay-T turned away, pulled a lever, and an inner wall slid aside. "Okay, the stirring is over."

Clyde sucked in his breath. "I have never seen such artistry and workmanship! Great China winds, this is incredible. The room is like a cathedral. And look at the tall floor-to-ceiling wooden arches decorated with jewels!"

"Yes." Jay-T confided. "The gopher wood arches are adorned with genuine rubies, diamonds, and emeralds."

"The shimmering aqua reflections and surroundings make everything look like it is under water," Gerty said.

"What do the arches do?" Tony asked.

"Each arch has a unique task," Jay-T told them. "The first will inform us about your health. The second will seek your family history. We call the third arch Miss Mabra. She analyzes your mental state. She also studies and evaluates all the details from arches one and two."

Jay-T faced Clyde and Gerty. "The information is used to help individual needs. It is all coded now and private, except for the Wise Ones and myself. By the way, they want to meet with you tomorrow. You will like them."

Continuing, the turtle pointed to the fourth arch. "The last arch lessens all your worries, anxieties, and . . . ."

"That's enough of this mumbo-jumbo, Jay-T!" Razzi howled. "I don't need a silly arch to tell me I need food!"

"Stop being rude, Razzi!" Gerty snapped.

"Leave me alone, you bossy name-caller. Jay-T promised me food, not a speech!"

"Yes, I did, Razzi," Jay-T answered. "No more delays! We will go to the kitchen double fast."

The limojet jerked forward swiftly under the arches and sped directly toward the wall at the back of the room.

"Not this fast!" Razzi howled. "Don't hit the wall!"

The children and Razzi hid their faces, expecting a loud crash. Coolness enveloped them and they opened their eyes in another room. The limojet landed quickly on the floor, and like the rescue birds, the vehicle vanished.

"Shut my big mouth!" Razzi muttered. "I thought Jay-T was going to kill me!"

"Not just you!" Molly's face was red as she pointed her finger at Razzi. "You behave yourself! You nearly got all of us killed! That really scared me!"

"How did we get through that wall?" Tony asked.

"Air and light rays serve us well for some of our walls." Jay-T shrugged. "Razzi told me to hurry, so I did. I am sorry for scaring you. Now, before you eat, wash your hands in the rooms through the blue doors."

Soon the trio returned with clean hands, and Jay-T opened another wall. Razzi stood speechless for once.

Molly filled the silence with pure excitement. "It's Gramps and Meme's front room and kitchen! I can smell bread baking. Are we really home?"

"No, child, this is an imitation of your home, taken from your memories," Jay-T enlightened her. "Our Miss Mabra arch created these rooms so you will feel at home tonight. Your food awaits you in the kitchen. It is real food and will taste just like your Meme's cooking."

Razzi shook his head. "This is unreal. Let's eat!" He bolted to the kitchen table with the children close to his heels. They whooped and giggled seeing all their favorite foods. As they settled around the table, Tony quieted the group for a serious moment and said, "Gramps can't give thanks, so I will." They bowed their heads."

"Gramps would be proud of Tony," Clyde affirmed. "And hearing them laugh is music to my ears. There were times in these past hours I thought our lives were over."

"Me, too!" Gerty confirmed. "This place is unreal. How can a house and food be here so fast?"

Jay-T stared at his hand-held screen with code on it. "Creating material things are rather easy," he said. "Other things are not so easy. I am receiving some early findings from our arches. The children and Razzi are basically happy other than their farm problems."

Jay-T shook his head. "You two are a different story. Already, the findings are showing great sadness in your hearts. Your misery levels are off the chart. You are my greatest concern and helping you will be more difficult."

"We try to keep that part of us hidden," Gerty replied with a deep sigh. "Yet, our hearts do hurt. If we could just do simple things like walk, touch, and eat, life could be more fun and meaningful."

"Aye, Gerty speaks the truth." Clyde agreed. "We make the best of our circumstances; yet, it is sad to think we can never touch each other again."

"It must be dreadful," Jay-T spoke caringly. "We can mend your wooden bodies, even Clyde's damaged legs. The rest is more complicated. While you are being refreshed, we will examine your special situation. If we knew the incantation the witches used, it would easier."

Clyde gasped. "You know about that? Bumbles must have told you. Dare I ask if the spell can be broken?"

"Why ask that, Clyde?" Gerty grumped. "We are far older than humans can live. If they break the spell, we will die! Nothing they can do now can help us."

Jay-T slumped. "She may be right. I spoke too fast again. You are going through enough without me raising false hopes. Some spells can never be broken. We will talk more after Miss Mabra and I sort out all the facts."

The joyful children and Razzi returned from eating. They talked and giggled like they had at the farm.

Razzi smacked his lips. "The fried fish was good!"

"The chocolate cake was better," Tony added.

"No!" Molly giggled. "The strawberries were best!"

Jay-T beamed. "I think they liked the food," he said smiling. "Now it is time to enjoy your unique rooms."

He placed a weightless chain and pendant around each of their necks. "Please leave these on. They will instruct all your robot helpers about your likes and needs."

He pushed a button on his hand-held monitor and five carpets sailed through the wall. "These are your happy-mat robots." Two slid under the rocking horses and the others waited for the children and Razzi to board them.

"Okay children, take hold of the handles provided and hang on. Each mat will take you to your special areas. Molly and Tony are next door to each other. In the morning, when you are ready to eat, board your happy-mats and they will find me. Have fun and sleep well."

The happy-mats swooped away carrying the children and Razzi one way and the wooden horses another. Molly and Tony called out and waved goodbye.

When the mats carrying the wooden rocking horses stopped in front of their separate doorways, Gerty whispered softly. "Since we awoke after the witches' spell, we have always been close and able to talk. This is our first real separation. I love you, Clyde, and I'll miss you."

"Aye, Gerty, I will miss you, too." His mat began moving into his assigned room. "Good night, bonny lass!" he cried out as she disappeared from view. He instantly felt lost without her. His love for her was still as heartfelt as ever. Why couldn't he say the simple words, I love you, out loud to her?

CHAPTER 7

ESEL'S INVENTION

Clyde liked his personal robot, an exact and comforting image of his beloved dad. During Ian's teenage years, he and his elder were real buddies. Just hearing the robot talk with a familiar accent and reassuring voice was truly uplifting. Ian, now Clyde, had missed his dad, teacher, and friend. Many fond memories rushed back.

When the chatting slowed down, the robot hummed while he worked on Clyde. The easy sounds relaxed Clyde's worries and doubts, and all the while, his outer shell was being repaired, polished, and painted like new. Even the work area was cozy with a flickering fireplace, giving the room the smoky fragrance he loved. Clyde soon fell asleep feeling assured all was well.

Gerty also liked her robot helper; a replica of her Gram, whose caring voice soothed Gerty's frayed nerves and her exhaustion soon melted into restful sleep. She slept deeply while her wooden body was being renewed.

In another chamber, Razzi chased glow fish in a heart-shaped concrete pool. He played with a pair of frisky raccoons, exact copies of himself. They cheered each other as they raced through the aqua water, dived from a high board, and splashed each other. "Double wow, this is fun! Who needs sleep? I'll just play," he yipped.

In a pastel pink and white fairytale room, Molly washed her hair and scrubbed in a tub teeming with soap suds. She happily blew bubbles into the air. Her robot helper, Molly-2 was like an amusing twin. After feeling fresh and clean, Molly donned a velvety pink gown and her robot dried and curled her hair. Both giggled and babbled while playing with powder, rouge, and lipstick. They twirled and laughed in front of a mirror, fully admiring their reflections. Being mortal, Molly yawned and fell into her canopy bed. The robot kneeled beside her and read stories aloud until the real child fell into a contented sleep.

Tony's robot was the spitting image of the boy's favorite imaginary Indian friend, who always appeared during lonesome times. The kind Indian brave wore soft buckskins with colored beads and fringes, a feathered headband, and beaded moccasins.

The room was a place Tony always dreamed about; a campsite by a brook in the middle of the forest. Overjoyed, Tony and his friend put on loincloths, jumped into a bubbling creek, lathered up with suds, and rinsed under a sparkling waterfall. They splashed, yipped, and chased big green frogs and fireflies.

Tiring of swimming, they put on tan cotton pajamas with intricate Indian symbols printed on the material. They toasted marshmallows over a small fire and sang under the stars until Tony relaxed into a pleasant sleep.

Clyde was fast asleep when a happy-mat jiggled him awake. He felt dazed until he spotted Gerty being carried down a hallway in the same direction as him. They were placed beside each other on a big table.

Between yawns, Clyde spoke to Gerty. "You look brand new!" He wished they were human so he could hug her. "Have you any idea why we are here?"

"It must be important," she whispered. "Maybe they actually found a way to break our spell."

Her suggestion jarred him wide-awake.

Jay-T rushed through the wall, panting, and carrying his little hand-held screen. "I have worked nonstop," he blurted out. "Facts have come to light that the Wise Ones and I thought you might want to consider."

"We are listening," Gerty responded promptly.

"First, I must tell you our background findings. We traced back to Vel and Zelda, the twin witches who cast this appalling spell on you."

"Great mercy, you actually know the witch's names?" Clyde exclaimed. "What else did you find?"

"Their last recorded evil deed involved a farmer, who raised bees. The tiny witches hated bees, according to hearsay. Vel and Zelda decided to kill the insects. They used their customary trick and made a fierce storm."

"Gerty and I recall one storm quite well!" Clyde declared. "It happened the last day we were human!"

"This storm was perhaps their downfall," Jay-T said. "A tornado dropped from one witch-made cloud, picked up the evil duo, and we can find no record of them after that."

"Well I for one will not miss them," Gerty scowled.

"Their own brutal pranks probably killed them," Jay-T asserted. "What we know for sure is their home in the giant oak was searched. The ancient scrolls we wanted so desperately were not found. I am sorry to tell you without those incantations, we cannot return you to your former human bodies again."

"Y-You woke us from our deep sleep to tell us bad news?" Gerty's expectations were crushed and her temper flared. "Those crazy witches were our last hope! Now even that is gone! Why did you tell us? Our lives are ruined forever now! We have no hope left! I hate those witches!"

"She is right!" Clyde grumbled. "Those evil witches bragged about our fate being 'worse than death' before their spell put us to sleep."

"It is true! I would rather be dead than living in this wooden prison," Gerty whimpered. "How could you do this to us, Jay-T? I was sure you were our friend."

"I am!" Jay-T cried out. "You failed to let me finish. We have a new option for you, but we must discuss it."

"What kind of option?" Clyde quickly inquired.

"It is called transference." Jay-T said. "Esel is always advancing our medical techniques. Two years ago, he invented a fine way to help critical accident victims. We feel your condition is mentally severe."

Jay-T resumed. "Please know, this work is still experimental, although our results with animals are brilliant so far. The machine transfers feelings and logical matter from one body to another. Because we feel your mental state is at risk, I have permission for you to try it."

"I am confused, Jay-T," Clyde said. "It sounds like Greek to me. Please say it again slow and simple."

"Yes, I talk too fast when I am excited," Jay-T admitted. "This invention will take everything you feel and know, and transfer it to a new non-aging animal body. I am sorry to say, human forms do not exist yet."

"We are in animal forms and I hate it!" Gerty said.

"Yes, but if the transfer works, you could walk . . . ."

"Walk!" Clyde blurted out. "We could honestly walk? I understood that word! How? What kind of animal bodies? Hurry Jay-T. I need to know more!"

"See! You are excited, too. We have all kinds of animal forms. You might enjoy being a turtle like me, or a cat, dog, horse, or a wild animal. It is your choice."

Gerty's voice quivered. "Are you saying I could be a real live horse? I could run, jump, and eat real food; yet, I could still talk and think as I do now?"

"Exactly correct, Gerty!" Jay-T affirmed. "I am sorry we cannot make you exactly as you once were; however, this would give you many of the freedoms you desire."

"It sounds too good to be true!"

"Not this time, Gerty," Jay-T insisted. "Here are some details. The changeover is painless. Failures are rare. If it fails, you will remain the same. And you must know, this is a one-time procedure. Consider well as we cannot transfer you a second time."

"Existing like this is agony," Gerty moaned. "I love horses. If I were a real horse, I could walk and run. This is a chance I must try. I want to be a real horse."

"Horses are fine animals," Clyde mumbled while thinking it through. "Horses are strong, graceful, and full of spirit, just like Gerty. And I want to be with her. Aye, a horse must be my choice also."

"This is the most excited I have felt since falling in love with Ian," Gerty admitted. "I cannot wait to be free of this horrible wooden torture chamber."

"Aye, how quickly can we begin?" Clyde asked.

Jay-T smiled. "We will set up at once, my friends."

"Please, Jay-T, forgive my temper."

"No problem, Gerty," the flying turtle told her with a smile. "Off to the laboratory!" The happy-mats heard and obeyed. It was a fast trip to a very large room.

Clyde studied the enormous gray transference box, with twinkling lights on its side. He recalled when a candle was his only source of light. What a difference now. In this world, he would trust strangers to give Gerty and himself a chance to walk again. Could it really be true?

The happy-mat moved Gerty toward the gray box. "No matter what, Clyde," she called out. "I love you."

"Yes, no matter what." He answered, wanting to say more, but she disappeared into the square structure. He was quickly taken to another compartment inside the same box. Clyde was in a lonely black-walled room and his fears surfaced. What if he remained wooden and Gerty became a real horse, or visa-versa? What if . . . . ?

Jay-T's gentle voice interrupted his doubts. "You will be pleased with your choices, Gerty and Clyde. Take a deep breath and relax. Listen to the soothing music. You will feel small vibrations, warmth, and become sleepy."

Soft music filled his ears and a tingling sensation flowed through Clyde's body. He wondered about Gerty and remembered her words. She still loves me! His eyes closed and his mind drifted back to dancing with the girl of his dreams, his beloved Deborah.

———

Early the next day, Razzi left his barely used bed and splashed noisily into his pool. He yipped with joy.

Tony stretched, dressed, and left his forest room to watch Razzi. He met Molly outside his door, dressed in a clean shirt and jeans. They both hurried to watch Razzi.

Hearing noises, Clyde's head jerked upward. He smelled fresh hay. His eyes popped open and his mind awakened. The transfer! "Great mercy, I can feel my legs!"

Like a new born colt, he thrashed about until he was able to barely stand. He wavered on wobbly legs, turning his head this way and that, and twitching his nose. "I love this! Yet, having four legs may be a challenge."

Stumbling forward in an awkward manner, Clyde's legs fought for self-rule. He hoped no one was watching. His heart beat with excitement. Being able to move his legs no matter how poorly was a true miracle.

To Clyde's delight, he discovered his image in a large mirror. His body was golden, and his shiny thick mane and tail were chocolate brown. Clyde wiggled his graceful ears and blinked his big brown eyes. He swished his long tail. He had never seen a more handsome stallion.

At the same time, unknown to Clyde, the children were watching Razzi chase glow fish in his pool.

"Tony," Molly tilted her head in the sunlight pretending to be a mature lady, "how do you like my lipstick color and my new curly hairdo?"

Heheld her hand high as she twirled around and around. Using a low voice he once heard on the radio, Tony said, "My dear, you look like a fairytale princess!"

"Is she famous and pretty?" Molly asked.

"Uh . . . she sure is. Her name is Princess, uh, Mary. She's a beautiful lady with curly hair and a big smile."

Razzi jumped from the pool. Curtly, he shouted, "Molly's no princess! She's just Molly with lipstick. Your foolish jibber-jabber is driving me crazy! I'm starved. Let's go eat." He shook a spray of water from his fur all over the children and jumped on his happy-mat.

"Razzi! You ruined my curls!" Molly yelped.

"Personally, I like your pigtails best," Razzi quipped circling them on his mat. "You have plenty of time to grow up and be a woman! Now is the time to enjoy being a kid!"

Seeing Molly's joy fade, Tony leapt back into character. "Is that really you, Molly? All this time, I was sure you were a real princess," helping her smile again. As their happy-mats arrived, Tony took Molly's hand. "Come, my lady. We must eat with that grumpy ole raccoon this morning, but maybe Jay-T will cheer us."

Molly grinned. "Razzi's always grumpy! Okay happy-mats, take us to the cheerful Jay-T," she ordered.

At that same moment, Clyde stepped outside the barn. His legs were stronger. He saw fields, trees and ponds. "This place is truly lovely. Where could Gerty be?"

Clyde was impressed with how fast his moving parts improved. After walking fast, he trotted, exploring the park as he practiced. He moved up to a canter. His newfound powers excited him. Finally he tried a fast run, galloping with the wind in his face and mane. The ground slipped beneath him faster than he had ever imagined.

It was amazing; yet, where was Gerty? He stopped to peer around. Pawing the ground, he snorted then he chuckled. This is fun. I want to share it with Gerty.

As if summoned, a pure white horse leapt gracefully over the bushes and stopped abruptly by his side. Her golden mane and tail sparkled in the sunshine and her large green eyes were very familiar.

Clyde shook his head in delight as he recognized the dazzling mare. "Gerty! You look splendid! And you jumped those shrubs like you had years of experience."

"I love it," she cooed gleefully. "And you, my dear, have become a handsome stallion while we slept." She reached her nose over and gently touched his nose. "I can feel your face! This kind of freedom is beyond words."

"Your touch is amazing! My heart has ached to touch you again. We may not be human beings, but this is great! Did you have trouble learning to walk?"

"It's good you didn't see me." She giggled.

"Me, too," he said joyfully. Seeing her beauty, Clyde felt his knees shake as they had years ago. He hastily bolted away, only to have Gerty speed along beside him. They galloped wildly together across the meadow, their manes sailing in the wind. They were alive again!

While they savored their new-found freedom, Jay-T greeted the children and Razzi for breakfast. He made a point of telling them about their table on top of a slight hill. "You can see most of the park while you are eating. Did you enjoy your rooms and helpers?"

Everyone had stories to tell. They chattered all at once, eating between talking. When Tony finished his food, he asked. "Jay-T, were you able to fix Clyde's leg?"

Molly cut in. "Look at those *bee-u-tee-full* horses running in the park. Their colors are like Clyde and Gerty."

"Jeepers, they are fine! I wish Clyde and Gerty could run like that. But, that's an impossible wish."

"Sometimes, Tony, our wishes can come true," Jay-T told him with a slight grin.

"Sure!" Razzi ridiculed. "Now, who's kidding? Wishes are a waste of time Jay-T and you know it! I once wished I was rich and you can see where that got me."

"You have good friends and that is a fine source of wealth if you think about it," Jay-T suggested.

"I like my friends, but I asked for real money. That was as hopeless as Tony's wishing Gerty and Clyde could run. It'll never happen!" Razzi scoffed indignantly.

Molly pushed a limp curl from her eyes. "Those horses can run fast. What are their names, Jay-T?"

"You call them Clyde and Gerty," he said gently.

Razzi sat up straight. "Is that a brainy-man's joke?"

Molly jumped up with a wide grin on her face. "It's not a joke! It's real, you silly waterlogged raccoon! I knew it before Jay-T told me. But how is it possible?"

"You are quite observant for your age, Molly. Last night we tried an experiment. It worked! Go meet them."

"Sis, you're a genius!" Tony exclaimed. Grabbing her hand they began running down the slight hill.

"Wait for me!" Razzi yelled and hurried to catch up.

Clyde heard the children's voices carry across the field and turned to see. "Look who's coming to see us."

Gerty kissed his nose again, watching his surprise. "I can get there faster than you!" The race was on.

———————

At that same moment, in another part of the city, the Wise Ones had gathered together for a special meeting to discuss the earthlings. Jay-T had already given the three sisters all the new facts from the arches. The information lit up a big screen on a wall in their meeting room. They also carried hand monitors like the flying turtle.

Earlier that morning from the park's cameras, the Wise Ones watched the children and raccoon frolic around the pool. The ladies especially enjoyed Clyde and Gerty learning to walk, their first steps and new found freedoms.

As the sisters began their meeting, the youngest sister, Rose, complained. "Zor shouted so loud yesterday that he wilted many of my fragile flowers."

"He's a menace!" Birdie agreed. "All that noise made my hens stop laying eggs. Zor is endless trouble."

"True," Queen Pearl, the eldest sister agreed. "Zor is away today so we will concentrate on the visiting earthlings. Our arches confirm they are kind and friendly souls, who seek help from Esel to save their grandparent's farm. That home is the only place of comfort for the children since their beloved mother died."

"That is so very sad," Birdie noted.

Pearl went on. "After their mother died, the children were taken to an orphanage. It was unpleasant because of the woman Tony refers to as *'ole prune face.'* She never smiles or gives love to anyone. The thought of returning to that orphanage panics Molly and Tony. We must query the children more about their problems and needs."

"As you know," the queen went on, "Our older brother, Theodore, sent the earthlings to Esel for help. Each day I am more concerned over Esel's safety since he usually contacts us daily."

"Something is wrong!" Birdie said anxiously. "But Bumbles knew about Esel's absence when he sent the earthlings to us! *Why did he do that?* He knows we have *powers* too! Is this a *'guy thing?'* Does our brother feel Esel is smarter than we sisters?"

"No." Queen Pearl assured her. "Our brothers are not like that! Theodore is aging; yet, his reasoning is quite sound. I think we should honor his wishes . . . there is more to Theodore's thinking than we can see! Between Zor Zanger's powers growing and Theodore's obligations on earth, I believe our eldest brother hoped these earthlings could somehow help us locate Esel."

"I cannot understand his thinking, but today while tending our flowers," Rose recalled, "I was wondering how Zor messes with our various means of communication. Could it be possible, Esel is simply unable to reach us? If these earthlings could find him, it would certainly ease all our minds about our eldest brother's safety."

"But Rose," Birdie squawked. "May I remind you, that these naive earth folk have no idea of Zor's evil powers? They have no weapons and we cannot by our own law give them any. If they leave here, their lives would be in terrible danger. I for one do not want to be responsible!"

"Me, neither," Queen Pearl admitted. "So this is my suggestion. We will warn the earthlings of the many dangers. If they wish to continue their search for Esel, we will provide them with as much knowledge and equipment as our law allows. If they choose not to find Esel, we can help them return home. They can decide their own destiny. Does anyone have more to add? Or do you disagree?"

No one added or subtracted. The queen's suggestion was respected and approved.

CHAPTER 8

HIGH EXPECTATIONS

Clyde and Gerty galloped across the field eager to greet Tony and Molly, who squealed and waved their hands all the way down the gradual slope.

When the gap narrowed between them, Razzi slid to a halt, exclaiming. "Double wow! You're huge! You look like those fine Arabian horses I once saw in a parade."

The children stopped and gasped with excitement as they gazed upon their fully-grown, very alive horses.

Cautiously Tony asked. "Is that really you, Clyde?"

"Aye! I'm taller with the dark mane. Gerty's snow white with lovely golden mane the color of Deborah's hair.

"*Bee-u-tee-full!*" Molly purred.

"I really like your golden coat, too," Tony said.

"Yes! He looks splendid!" Gerty gushed. "And being free from those wooden rocking horses is a miracle."

"Aye, Jay-T couldn't make us human again so this was the next-best option," Clyde added. "We can run like the wind! All this new freedom is nearly overwhelming."

Gerty pranced about. "We feel young again! We're both so excited we feel giddy."

Molly stared in disbelief. "If you had wings, you would look exactly like the horses in my dreams."

"That's right!" Tony affirmed. "Molly always told me her dreams, and you look like the horses she described."

"It's just chance, if you ask me," Razzi shrugged and pointed to Clyde's hind leg. "That looks strong now."

"We're both strong," Clyde answered. "Never again will you have to pull us! From now on, we'll carry you."

"You even talk more like us now," Tony noted. "How did this incredible miracle happen?"

"Climb on!" Clyde invited his friends gleefully. "We'll talk and show you this magnificent park all at once.

Molly pulled on Tony's hand. "I want to ride, but Gerty's too tall. How can I get up there?"

"I'll help, dear." The mare bent her foreleg and bowed down. "Use my bent leg like a step and grab my mane. You can pull yourself up."

The girl struggled at first, so Tony helped. Molly's face turned red. "I'll get up here by myself next time!"

Clyde also stooped low and Tony climbed aboard. "Come on Razzi. Take my hand," the boy called.

The raccoon popped upon Clyde's knee, caught the boy's hand and swung up behind Tony. When Clyde stood up, Razzi yelped out and grabbed Tony tightly. "Wow, climbing trees is easy, but they don't jolt around!"

The children held tightly to their horse's manes. Joy filled their hearts and everyone wanted to tell their stories about robots, pools, decisions, and even curly hair.

After they caught up with their recent events, the children wanted to go faster. Giggles filled the air and all their jitters vanished. Even Razzi relaxed.

The happy earthlings trotted along a wooded path, cantered across the valley, and loped beside a field of purple violets. They splashed in a bubbling brook with cool water spraying over them.

They passed white swans on the lake, wild ducks beside a pond, and great long-necked birds perched in trees. Butterflies flitted in the air as they passed colorful flowers, and blue birds sang in the weeping willows.

The morning was a whirlwind of fun, speed, thrills, and energy. Laughter filled the air as the earthlings investigated every corner of the park. No one fell off and it was a perfect morning for all.

Far too soon, Jay-T called them to lunch. While eating, the professor made an announcement. "The Wise Ones wish to meet with you this afternoon at two."

"What kind of people calls themselves Wise Ones? They sound uppity to me." Razzi smarted off.

"The ladies were named long ago by our Dome City citizens, who adore them. The sisters rule over our Septar," Jay-T stated proudly. "They are diligent, wise and kind. It was their idea to give Clyde and Gerty this chance at a new life. And hopefully, they can help you find Esel."

Razzi knew he had miscued. He hid his pink nose inside a cup of milk and quietly grunted incoherently.

"Great mercy, in all our excitement, I forgot our mission. We must find Esel at once!" Clyde exclaimed.

"Do not feel bad," Jay-T replied. "Our expert arches knew your high stress levels and dulled your logic so you could rest. It is standard procedure. Once you leave here, you will feel fine; yet, reality will be clearer. Come now, we have a thrilling afternoon planned," offered Jay-T.

"This is already the best day I've known for two hundred years! I cannot imagine more thrills in one day."

"Nor I, Clyde," Gerty giggled as she talked. "We are delighted down to our toes, uh . . . I mean hooves."

The happy group chuckled as they departed the Renovation Center through a single green arch where their medallions vanished. A heavily locked door opened and they left with a sense of hope instead of despair.

A puff limo, not the limojet, waited outside the exit, near a bustling sidewalk. The limo's invisible puff filling formed around each passenger, seated or standing, keeping them secure. Razzi was safe even moving about.

While floating between the shiny buildings and over grassy avenues, everything was festive. Venders sold vegetables, fruits, and flowers to a variety of living souls.

The residents had all colors of skin, even purples and greens. The city hummed with contented chatter and jovial laughter. Their clothing, accessories, hairdos, and hats were all diverse from wild to quietly simple. Some animals talked and others walked on their hind feet.

Floating silently between long rows of tall buildings were all sizes of bright vehicles. When on the ground waiting on their owners, the vehicles shrunk to shoe box size and waited, or followed the owners like pets.

Razzi stood at the very front of the limo where he could see both sides of the avenue. Tiny children pointed to his natural mask and giggled shyly. When he waved to them, they smiled and waved back. "This is great! I love this place. Maybe I won't go back to earth after all."

Jay-T smiled then said, "You and the children will enjoy our first stop at the city museum." The vehicle halted in front of a wide building. When the group left the limo, it reduced in size and waited by the entry.

Inside the building, they were encircled with the past. War weapons, machines, space vehicles of all sizes, and odd looking inventions filled the ceilings, shelves, and walls. The earthlings were amazed. History of Old World and Dome City were all over the immense building.

Jay-T led them. "One exhibit is especially for you."

Standing proudly in an impressive showcase with a light blue background were two wooden rocking horses. They were mended and appeared brand new. The children were overjoyed; however, Gerty and Clyde backed away.

"They give me cold chills," she hissed."

"Aye," Clyde agreed. "Those prisons are fine in this museum as long as you and I are free."

"Where are their harnesses, Jay-T?"

"They are fine, Tony. The Wise Ones have them."

"Good! Those harnesses mean a lot to Gramps."

Tears formed in Molly's eyes. "I really miss Meme and Gramps. They must be sad without us. Do you think we are too late to help them, Tony?"

"I don't know, sis. I just hope Esel will show up and help us. Maybe he will be with the Wise One's today."

"Do you think so?" Molly's mood brightened. "Let's go see! I want to find him soon as possible."

"Good idea," agreed Jay-T feeling relieved that Molly was not crying. "We will leave immediately."

While walking away, Molly blew a kiss to the wooden horses, saying, "I'll never forget you."

Soon their limo whisked from the city to large pastures with lush trees, bushes, and green grass. The limo landed in a well-tended courtyard where a grand fairytale castle met their eyes. Lovely trees and flowers filled the yard. A cobblestone walkway lead to the porch where two women in long dresses waved.

"Rose wears pink, and Birdie wears yellow. They are kind and will guide you," Jay-T promised. "My work in the city needs me. I will join you later today. Go, now."

As the limo departed, the earthlings walked along the cobblestone walkway toward the ladies.

Molly whispered in Tony's ear. "Look! Their hair is the same color as their dresses and shoes!"

"I see . . . ." Tony answered quietly.

"Welcome," the lady in pink said. "I am Rose."

"And I am Birdie," the other sister said. "Come inside and we will find refreshments and chat."

Gerty stalled. "Thank you but I can't. I'll wait outside. Your home is far too fine for horses to enter."

Rose turned toward the mare and spoke gently. "Gerty, my dear, you and Clyde are our honored quests. Kind and honest hearts are always welcome in our home. Our sister, the queen, awaits your arrival. Please come."

"Oh . . . ." Gerty replied. "Thank you." She followed, knowing it was against all her childhood training. She heard Clyde behind her and knew he felt the same. We have much to learn in this new world, she thought.

They walked through a flower-filled glass room into a long hallway. Soon, they entered a good-sized room with no windows. A blending of yellows, pinks, and purples made the room cheery. A scenic mural covered one wall.

A tall woman walked toward them, her clothes, shoes, and hair were violet. "Welcome to our home. I am Queen Pearl and quite happy to meet you. I had the girls greet you while I gathered more reports for our meeting. Please make yourselves comfortable."

Feeling unsure, the horses stood behind the children and Razzi's chairs. Each Wise One had a rocking chair the same color as their clothing.

Queen Pearl wore fine pearls. Even her violet cane had a glistening pearl handle. She appeared regal, but pleasant. She stood by her purple rocker.

When the group settled, the queen raised her cane to begin the meeting. "This is the first time our brother, Bumbles, has sent us visitors from another world, so we have much to discuss. We always honor Bumble's wise decisions and wishes. And we are happy that our earthling friends uh . . . dropped in to visit us."

"We not only dropped in, we crashed, and nearly got killed a dozen ways!" Razzi whispered behind his paw.

Hearing him, but pretending not to, the queen said, "The first business today is finding how Clyde and Gerty feel inside their new bodies."

"We feel great!" Clyde replied. "We are indebted to you kind ladies and forever grateful."

Gerty nodded. "Yes, you saved us from a horrible existence. The freedom we feel is heavenly. Thank you!"

"Good," the queen and her sisters smiled. "It pleases us that Esel's invention worked well and we also made the right decision. We hope all our choices today are just as successful. With so many scraps of odd information we made a movie of sorts. As we watch the pictures on our info-screen, maybe some of our questions will be answered. Feel free to eat the popcorn or fruit from our side tables."

"Whoopee!" Razzi yipped with glee. "I love popcorn. Is the movie a western, Miss Queenie?"

Hearing Gerty groan, the queen continued. "There will be no western today, Razzi. These little clips are personal to you folks." She touched her cane to the wall mural and it transformed into a familiar farm scene.

Tony leaped upward. "It's our farm," he cried out. "Where's Gramps and Meme? Are they looking for us?"

The queen tried to answer, but a buzzing noise roared over her voice. The screen zigzagged and new images abruptly appeared on the wall-sized screen.

Tears flowed down Meme's cheeks and Gramps called out, "Bring our kiddoes back!" They stared in horror from their porch as a tall thin woman in a pillbox hat yanked Molly and Tony from the yard into a strange car.

"No!" Molly screamed. "I don't want to go!" Peering around, the girl's face turned pink. "What is happening? We're here with you wise ladies, not back on earth!"

"Does this mean we're too late?" Tony asked.

"No, children, I apologize. Please try to relax as I explain," the queen's voice trembled. "For some reason our info-screen just went haywire. You were not supposed to see this scene until later. I intended to prepare you first and explain that these are scenes taken from your own worries, recorded when you passed under our arches. This was honestly an unplanned and untimely foul-up."

The flustered queen turned to her sister. "Birdie, check all our warning lights in the sensor room in case it was Zor Zanger. My screen has never jumbled my data before! It is very upsetting." Pearl turned to the children, smiled, and made a suggestion. "May we start over?"

"Don't you dare scare Molly again," Razzi warned.

"It's okay Razzi," Molly said. "I'm sorry I screamed. I know the queen didn't purposely frighten us."

"You are very caring, Molly. We appreciate your kind attitude. I will begin again. Theodore Bumbles told us your train ride from the orphanage was miserable. We also heard Gramps and Meme have given you kindness and love, and you love them. Is all this correct?"

"That's so correct!" Molly said. Tony agreed.

The queen continued. "Why do we see images of rocks on a road. Can you explain that, Tony?"

"Yes, ma'am. Us kids didn't go to town over the big mountain with Gramps and Meme 'cause the truck is too small. A sudden storm caused the rocks to slide and block the mountain pass. Gramps phoned us from town to tell us they couldn't get home. Then the phone cut off."

"They left you unattended?" Pearl asked.

"Not on purpose. Our uncle was supposed to join us that evening. But his wife got chest pains, so our uncle took her to town before the storm came."

"Hence, you were left all alone. Can you explain why the grapes are so important, Tony?" Pearl asked.

"Well, last year the birds ate all the grapes. Gramps had to borrow money to bring Molly and me to the farm. If the grape harvest is good this year and is sold, Gramps can pay back the money. If not, he loses the farm to the bank then we won't have our home anymore."

Tony hung his head. "Molly and I feel responsible for the problem. We really want to ask Esel for help."

"That is admirable," Pearl told them. "However, I am sure your grandparents do not blame you."

Molly piped up. "Did you know, Queen Pearl that ripe grapes turn into sweet delicious raisins?"

The smiling queen answered. "It's like a miracle!"

Popcorn clung from Razzi's chin. "I didn't want to come here, but that idiot Bumbles sent me anyway. The farm is my home, too, so I intend to talk to Esel, also."

"That is big of you, Razzi," the queen said. "Esel enjoys helping others. The problem is . . . Esel is missing."

"Missing? How is that possible? I thought he was the wisest Majiventor around!" Razzi cried out.

"Our brother simply cannot be found. He has not contacted us and we are uneasy about his well-being." The queen nodded to her sisters. "We discussed your situation and feel obligated to advise you about your options.

"If you wish, you may wait here until Esel's return. Or if you prefer to go home, we will help you. And if you choose to search for Esel, we can make that possible."

"They need to know more details before they can makeup there minds correctly," Rose insisted.

"Yes, Rose. First, we will show you Esel's castle on another Septar." Pearl tapped the wall but it remained blank. After three failed tries, she called to Birdie. "Is our system totally broken?"

"No, sis, we have outside intrusion." Birdie shouted back from an adjoining room. "I cannot find the source."

Troubled, the queen continued. "Our guests can see Esel's castle later. Right now we will discuss the risks."

"We know some of the dangers first hand," Clyde affirmed. "If we search for Esel, how could we travel?"

"We will make a way, Clyde," Pearl promised.

"Would we travel above the cloud layer like the rangers?" asked Gerty.

"Yes, exactly. The upper clouds change daily, but they are safe and the air is good. Zor Zanger is the problem. He can show up anywhere at any time. Rose can tell you more about this subject while I help Birdie."

The lady in pink stood up. "Travel outside our dome is not easy. Only a few miles from our Septar, you are totally on your own without safety nets, military, or Rangers to rescue you. Zor knows that. If you get into trouble, Old World waits below the clouds."

Razzi cut in. "Why can't the Rangers help us?"

"The Rangers only work close to our dome. You landed close enough to get help. To save you, they had to become visible, a true act of bravery. If Zor sees them, the evil man kills the birds to show off his powers."

"Because of us, they might have been killed?" Tony blurted out. "We had no idea! Don't you have airplanes to rescue folks? We have them back on earth."

"It would be hard to land airplanes here with our dome. It was created to keep Zor Zanger away. At one time, he wanted to make our Septar a military airbase. Bumbles wisely designed our dome. He is our hero and definitely not the idiot you called him, Razzi."

"Well, he didn't show his smarts when he sent us to Old World!" The raccoon retorted.

Clyde stared at Razzi without his usual kind eyes.

Razzi glared back. "So now that you are big, it's you and Gerty both against me." The raccoon barked. "Stop gawking at me! I'm too old to boss around."

Clyde spoke firmly, but quietly. "These fine ladies are helping us, Razzi. Bumbles may have made a mistake, but we were rescued. We were given help and respect. Please give our hostesses the honor they are due."

"I will. But I won't change my mind about Bumbles. I'm not going to lie for you or anybody!"

"Fibbing is always wrong, Razzi." Rose agreed. "We understand your experience in Old World was horrendous. Please let us make up for that. We are honestly trying."

Rose's kindness deflated Razzi. "Uh, okay. What were you saying about airplanes?"

"Thank you, Razzi," Rose replied. "After the bombs ruined Old World, survivors came here. Back then, we had no dome, and that is when we first met Zor Zanger."

The color in Rose's cheeks brightened. "Zor was not a big man, but he was full of anger. He kept folks stirred up, hoping to rule us. The man planned to use armed planes to become king of our Septar. We talked with him to no avail. Finally, we had to banish him from our Septar.

"When Zor left, he vowed to come back and take over. At that time, Bumbles made our protective dome for safety. Still today, it shields us against Zor's vile deeds."

Rose shrugged. "A few folks still use small flying vehicles on occasion. Most of our citizens actually have their own wings. Our need for large planes ended, so we simply banned them. Our limos are quite handy."

Continuing, Rose said, "Zor still dreams of ruling us and also the complete universe! He has no heart or love. His drive is greed, power, and always playing mad games."

As Rose talked, the blank screen flashed on with images of Esel's castle. It was easy to see there was no dome around the quiet gray castle.

Birdie rushed toward them. The queen followed. Birdie was speaking quickly. "My up-to-date report is not good. We have no word from Esel. Our smoke sensors are flashing wildly so Zor is close. And the Kingobe volcano is getting brighter."

The screen suddenly filled with Zor Zanger's huge face. "You're right, Birdie! I'm close! Your sensors need updating. Don't worry your wise heads about the volcano; it'll cause no harm." His deep mocking voice was cold as the north wind and forbidding as a lion's roar.

Zor's weather-beaten, smoke-smudged face looked sunburned. His penetrating red eyes glared at them under bushy black eyebrows. A thick black mustache covered his upper lip and a long knotted goatee hung below his chin. His head was bald with two bumps like tiny horns.

Razzi leapt recklessly behind his chair.

Zor's voice boomed. "Hide behind your chair, Razzi, but I'll find you. I can't stand cowards, and you're the worst!" His laugh was so loud it rattled the lady's tea cups.

"Your beloved brother, Esel, is not missing. He's helping me reach my goals. As my partner, he's far too busy for these childish outsiders and their petty requests. Esel wants these brats to go home immediately."

The giant winked and whispered. "Next time, ladies, we'll sip tea together." He vanished as fast as he came.

Clyde collected himself and asked. "How did Zor do that? And how did he know Razzi was behind his chair?"

Rose trembled. "I wish we knew," she muttered. "He must be using all of Esel's newest equipment."

Queen Pearl sat down, her brows pinched tightly. "One thing is certain," she declared angrily. "Our brother would never work with a man like Zor Zanger! In fact, Esel would die first!" Birdie and Rose nodded in agreement.

"Zor's words chilled my heart." Pearl shuttered. "Something is very wrong. Zor is either playing mind games with us, or he has captured Esel. But, how? That is nearly impossible! It has never happened before."

"He is playing mind games, Pearl," Birdie stated. "Esel is too wise to be captured, but where is he?"

Razzi crept from behind his chair. "Zor hates me! Forget about me finding Esel. I'm going home!"

"Yes," Clyde told Razzi. "Going home sounds best, but without Esel's help, we have no home. Maybe you can live at Joseph's home again. However, where would Meme, Gramps, Tony and Molly live? What about Gerty and me? Our only hope to save the farm is to find Esel. I won't give up unless Esel personally refuses me."

"That is totally impossible!" The queen interjected. "Refusing you is not in Esel's nature. Majiventors cannot refuse good deeds. Zor is a liar! The truth is not in him!"

Clyde raised his head. "Queen Pearl, could I try to find Esel by myself?" he asked. "Zor might not expect me to go alone. Besides, I don't want my friends in danger. I could investigate Esel's castle for clues. Someone might know where Esel went. Is my request possible?"

Molly hurried to Clyde and hugged his leg. "I know you want to help us, but I would rather go back to the orphanage than see you hurt."

Clyde nearly choked hearing her words. "Thank you Molly, your personal sacrifice is amazing. The problem is, if I went home now, and you were sent to the orphanage, I could never live with myself. Please know I must find Esel."

"I'm going, too," Gerty told Molly. "Esel holds all the answers. We're no longer helpless thanks to our new friends. I intend to travel with Clyde."

"No!" Molly cried out. "Please stay with us, Gerty."

Clyde chuckled. "You can beg, Molly, but I have lost that battle before. If Gerty's mind is set, she is braver than most men!" He turned to the Wise Ones. "Is it possible for the two of us to look for Esel, Queen Pearl? If so, we need a safe place for the other three to stay, while we travel."

"Last night's accommodations will be open as long as any of you need them," the queen answered.

"Oh, boy!" Razzi yipped. "I can swim again!"

Tony's eyes were determined as he faced Clyde. "I helped you in the swamp, sir. Remember? I will help you now. Molly and Razzi can stay here. I'm going with you!"

Molly looked at her brother with her hands on her hips and spoke firmly. "Tony, you can't go without me! We both helped in the swamp. If you go, I go, too!"

Razzi covered his eyes and groaned. "I knew this would happen. Everyone has to be a hero! Oh heck, count me in! I can't let you guys go without my help."

Queen Pearl gazed upon the five earthlings. "We feel appreciation for each of you. We accept your offer to search for Esel, and your needs will be prepared."

Birdie quickly invited everyone to the veranda.

Clyde felt stunned by the ladies' quick decision to allow the children to go on such a risky trip? Perplexed, he followed the group to a large shady back porch, with many chairs. The yard was huge, green, and flat. They gathered around a table full of colorfully wrapped boxes.

"Here Molly," Birdie handed her a present. "Open your gift first. We think this will make your day brighter."

Molly pulled out a small pink purse. It fit perfectly in her hand or hung from a shoulder strap. Little squeals slipped out then she peeked inside the purse. Two silver lipstick tubes, a silver powder box with an attached mirror, and a pretty comb and hair brush set were seen.

"Look Tony!" She cried. "I have lipstick and powder for my very own! These are *bee-u-tee-full*!"

"The powder and lipstick will never go empty, child. Just rub the tube or case and wish for your favorite color," Birdie guided her. "They will last your entire life."

Molly grinned brightly. "Thank you! This is perfect." The child could not wait to peek into her new mirror.

Rose handed Tony his box and he unwrapped it.

"It's my knapsack," he cried out. "It looks brand new! I love it! Look at the extra straps." He stared inside and grinned with delight at the long nylon rope, a case with a compass, a canteen, wrapped chocolate bars, and a see-through box with carrots and celery.

"Your pack will never be heavy and these straps will allow you to carry it snugly on your back. Your hands can be free." Rose told him. "The knapsack was especially treated to be waterproof and to look new. We knew your love for keeping extra food for bad times, so all the food items will replace themselves immediately as you use them. And your canteen will always have fresh water."

Before Tony could speak, Razzi yipped loudly. "Double wow-wow! Look at this! My own red bow tie and a matching red cane! Wow! Thanks everyone. How did you know? I never told anyone my secret wish."

"That is why they call us the Wise Ones," Birdie joked with a smile. "Your cane holds a surprise. It opens into a telescope so you can see things far away."

When the excitement settled, Queen Pearl stood in front of Clyde and Gerty. "Before you receive your gifts, will you please grant us an unusual request?"

"Anything," Clyde answered. "But what could we possibly do for you, Queen Pearl?"

"Years ago," the queen explained. "As humans you were named Ian and Deborah. Those names belong to the engraved tombstones where you lived years ago."

The horses both drew in deep breaths. "I should have guessed that," Gerty whispered.

The queen went on. "We learned those facts while researching for the twin witches. And as you know, the wooden horses, named Clyde and Gerty are presently in our museum. Their names rightly belong to them! Your divine spirits now have new bodies; yet, you currently have no personal names to identify yourselves. With your personalities in mind, we have chosen unique names for each of you. First, we need your permission."

"Yes! The name 'Gerty' was never right for me."

"Aye, permission granted!" He told them quickly.

"Thank you both." Pearl placed her hands on each of their heads and looked at Clyde as she spoke.

"For this handsome stallion, strong in physical power, who is also a human male with a caring spirit full of intelligence, courage, zeal, loyalty, and love, we christen you with the name, *Gallopade*."

The queen turned to Gerty and said. "For this lovely mare, strong in physical power, who is a human woman with a caring spirit full of intelligence, courage, zeal, loyalty, and love, we christen you with the name, *Heija*.

"The names Gallopade and Heija also reflect caring, honesty, and swiftness on the wind.

The horses gazed at one another, slowly repeating their new names. After a few moments, Heija said, "I'm thrilled with my new name! And I love the name Gallopade; it fits him well. This is a grand surprise."

Excitement filled Gallopade's voice. "I'm happy with our new names. We'll try hard to live up to them."

The children and Razzi ran out to hug Heija and Gallopade, and kept repeating the new names.

"And now," the queen raised her cane. "We have more to do. Please open this box, children. The harnesses Tony inquired about are here."

Tony and Molly quickly tore open the wrapping, and the queen said, "We added real jewels, new tassels, and a bit of Bumbles mystique. What do you think?"

"I love them and Gramps will, too!" declared Tony.

Birdie poured red liquid into a long golden bowl on a stand close to the horses. "This sweet elixir is made from rare flowers, honey and herbs, especially for our fine Heija and Gallopade. Please drink. We wish you good health, wise decision making, and a long happy life."

Fully trusting, the couple both drank the fine elixir.

"It is well," the queen agreed and commanded the harnesses, "Go to your new owners!" The jeweled leather straps floated to Gallopade and Heija, wrapped around them perfectly, and snapped closed without help.

"Double wow-wow," Razzi muttered in awe.

The queen raised her cane again and her voice was strong. "Stand back, children. The Wise Ones now give Heija and Gallopade a truly special gift. Your imprisonment was unfair, so prepare yourselves for high expectations and new freedom. Each of you, kindly press your nose against the middle emerald of your harness."

Gallopade looked toward Heija quizzically.

Heija did not see his gaze. She just obeyed. At once, she sensed a strange buoyant feeling.

"Great thunder, you have huge white feathered wings!" His voice quivered. Quickly, he touched his nose to his emerald and felt instantly lighter on his feet.

Heija gasped full of wonder. "Your golden wings are amazing, Gallopade. The queen said '*high expectations*.' Could that mean we are supposed to fly?"

Molly's eyes grew large. "Tony, my dreams are coming true! Our horses have *bee-u-tee-full* wings!"

Gallopade felt excited but an unexpected fear clutched his heart. "Blimey, horses are not supposed to fly!" His eyes begged Heija and the Wise Ones to say no.

"Why would we have wings, if not to fly?" Heija asked. "We must give it a try."

The queen smiled at Gallopade. She and her sisters waved their arms and called out. "Push your wings down, fly up. Push down, fly up."

Heija watched the ladies and dropped her wings. She zipped upward. It happened so fast, it startled her. She lifted her wings slightly, and she floated easily back to the ground. "My word, that was wild! I went up in the air light as a feather. Give it a try, Gallopade, please."

With Heija's encouragement, he fortified his nerve. He held his breath and quickly pushed his wings firmly downward, shooting upward like a bullet. The ground fell beneath him so fast his stomach turned.

"Blimey! I'm in the air!" He leveled his wings and hovered with his heart hammering. It was fun; yet, scary. He dared not look down at his friends on the ground.

Heija joined him, face to face, thirty feet in the air. "This is more fun than I ever had before. It is so easy. We can fly to the stars now." Her eyes were twinkling.

The whites of his eyes showed. "This is quite high enough, Heija. I think I should go back down, but how? This is not easy for me."

"But, Clyde . . . oops, I mean Gallopade, we are free! The witches have lost their hold on us. We have wings to fly anywhere now." Heija's eyes sparkled. She bobbed around, giggling like a child. "We can fly like birds!"

Watching her enjoyment gave Gallopade pleasure. He wanted her to remain happy. "I'll try," he ventured.

Gallopade followed Heija, doing as she did. They flew up, glided, hovered and soared in circles. Their flying skills were soon like second nature. As the flying grew easier for him, he still dared not look down.

Heija was a natural. Her joy was almost more than she could stand. "Flying with you makes this the most amazing and fun day of my entire life," she told him.

On the ground below, Razzi rolled on the ground in laughter. When he caught his breath, he said, "I've never seen birds with four legs before. This is hilarious!"

"I don't see anything funny about it. They are the most *bee-u-tee-full* horses I ever saw."

"And they are flying even higher," Tony remarked. "Wouldn't it be great if we could fly that high with them?"

"You're crazy!" Razzi barked. "What if you fall off?"

"We didn't fall off in the park," Molly reminded him.

"Yeah, but . . . that was a not such a tall fall," Razzi huffed. "Look at them now. They're really, really high!"

"I'm not scared," Molly chirped. "I always wanted to fly like that, just like in my dreams all these years."

"I can't wait," Tony chimed in. "It'll be great!"

Razzi sat back wrapping his tail around himself and frowned. His big eyes gave away his fright, but no one was watching. They looked upward as the horses flew around.

After an exhilarating flight, the horses glided back to the ground. "I can't believe this," Gallopade kept saying. "It's easy and fun! I can even look down now."

"Can we ride?" Tony pleaded. "Can we?"

"Is it possible?" Gallopade asked.

"Just do it!" Rose answered with a shrug. The ladies rocked back and forth, watching with great pleasure.

The children prepared to ride. Razzi backed away.

"Get on Razzi," Tony called out. "Don't be a sissy!

"I'm not a sissy!" Razzi howled, looking around at the Wise Ones. "Help me up Tony. I'll show you!"

"Fly high!" Tony told Gallopade. "Hey, Razzi, stop choking me!"

"Molly and I want to go slow and low," Razzi tried to sound concerned for the little girl.

"I'm ready to go high like Tony," Molly said with a wide grin. "Heija will keep me safe. We'll fly like in my dreams, with the wind in our hair."

"Hold tight," Gallopade called out. "We're off!"

As the horse's feet left the ground, Razzi let out a wild terror-stricken howl. Tony yelled with glee. "We're flying!" And Molly giggled with pure joy.

The Wise Ones chuckled as they watched.

"I gave up hoping for freedom," Gallopade admitted. "I was dead inside. Now I feel alive and free!"

"Alive and free, and I love it!" Heija repeated merrily. They raised high in the air and made wide circles. Even Razzi relaxed and soon stopped strangling Tony. They flew for a long time, enjoying their marvelous enchanted flight.

After a time, while zooming across the sky, Tony yelled loudly. "We'll find you, Esel. Watch out, Zor Zanger. Here we come."

CHAPTER 9

SASHA

"Farewell friends! I hope you find Esel, but beware of Zor Zanger!" Jay-T called out before he closed one of the dome's secret exits. He watched as the earthlings flew out of sight toward Esel's castle. "Poor helpless babes," he muttered. "If they survive this quest, it will astonish me."

Gallopade and Heija soared with ease through the sunny morning's crisp air, even with the weight of the children and Razzi on their backs. Below them were soft fluffy clouds stretched as far as they could see.

"Is this truly happening, Gallopade? Or am I having a great fantasy that will vanish like a dream?"

"We'll hope it lasts a long time, Heija. Flying like this together is too grand for words. Our time in Dome City transformed us from helpless prisoners to vital beings on a mission. My life as a furniture maker is forever gone, but I can live with that. You always wore lovely clothes and went to lady's meetings. Will you miss all that?"

"I was devastated when I woke up in a stiff wooden prison. As time passed, I realized freedom was my greatest desire. I had taken my liberty for granted. Now, our freedom is worth more than all the dresses and money in the world. I'm happy! Do you miss seeing me in gowns?"

"I thought you were beautiful back then. Yet, as I look at you flying beside me, you are even more exquisite than ever. I feel grateful to have you by my side." When the words left his mouth, he suffered a sudden shyness attack and quickly turned his eyes away from her.

"Thank you, Gallopade. I'm pleased you're beside me, too." Before Heija said more, she noticed the raccoon clinging to Tony's knapsack. "You can open your eyes now, Razzi. The scenery is breath-taking."

"Leave me alone, Heija!" He snarled. "Yesterday was not so bad, but if I fall off today, I'll go clear down to Old World." His eyes remained tightly shut.

"But, you are missing a perfect day."

"Just nevermind, Gallopade, I've seen nice days before!" He squeezed his eyes so tight his face wrinkled.

Tony stretched both arms out enjoying the breeze. "Back on the farm, I pretended to be an airplane. In this world I don't have to make-believe. Riding a flying horse is better than any pretend game."

"It's exactly like I dreamed," Molly bubbled, "except I flew over land, not clouds. This is beautiful and fun!"

"Aye, Molly, this is fun." The stallion agreed. "Just remind me to stay on course. It would be easy to get lost. Tony, are you watching your compass? Are we okay?"

"It's a cinch, Gallopade. I have a map, and my compass is working well. We are going due east and there are Septars along the way where we can rest."

"Tony always wanted a compass," Molly recalled as she pulled her powder box from her purse. "The Wise Ones really are smart. I adore my new mirror and . . . . Oh! What's going on? Meme's in my mirror! Can you see her, Tony?"

"I'm too far away. What is she doing?"

"She's holding my doll and your little truck, and she looks really sad."

"Talk to her!" Razzi urged. "Meme might hear you."

"Meme, can you hear me?" Molly called out. "Oh no, she's fading away. I can't see her now."

"Doggone it!" snarled Tony. "I wanted to tell her what is happening and that we miss her and Gramps."

Molly's only answer was a loud hiccup.

"I wish Gramps and Meme knew we were trying to help them," Heija said caringly. "We'll hope Molly can talk to her next time. Say, Razzi, what do you see?"

"I hoped to see Meme in my telescope, but I don't. Meme is like a mum to me." An unusual sadness filled his words. "I guess I'll watch for that mean ole Double Z."

"That's a good name for Zor," Gallopade observed. "Thanks, Razzi. Your help will help ease our minds."

The day passed without further events. By evening, Razzi searched for the island where they hoped to spend the night. "Double wow! I see it, but I don't believe it! The city looks like stacks of blue ice cubes coated with snow, but it's not even cold! This world is sure weird."

"That's Cubical City on my map," Tony verified.

"I hope they have a place to rest," Heija voiced. "Flying a long distance is more tiring than I guessed. I wonder how safe this Septar will be without a dome."

"Well if you ask me, I think Zor's warnings were a bunch of hot air." Razzi noted flippantly. "This traveling stuff is a piece of cake. We haven't seen anything scary all day. I think that giant ugly guy was just bluffing."

Heija flinched. "Shush, Razzi! Zor might hear you."

"Heck," Razzi frowned. "You are always such a worrywart. Can't you relax once in a while?"

"I want to stay alive, Razzi," Heija answered. "We were warned for good reason. Zor might be anywhere and he is terribly dangerous. You saw him! He's mean!"

"I'm looking everywhere and I don't see smoke." Razzi barked curtly. "Zor is not here. So stop being such a fussbudget. You don't know everything! Besides it's not possible for Double Z to be everywhere at once."

"I know that," Heija stressed. "Yet, we should be vigilant. Zor knew we were with the Wise Ones and he even knew your name. The Wise Ones told us he is tricky like a fox, so I'm just asking you to be cautious."

"Thanks for your la-di-dah concern," mocked Razzi, "but don't be such a scaredy-cat. Remember the time you thought I was a witch! You nearly nagged me to death."

"Stop being so mean and calling me names!" she snapped. "I'm not helpless like the time you pushed me out of that tree. Now, I can bite your ears off!"

"If you bite me, I'll . . . ." Razzi's words were lost when his seat swiftly dropped a foot lower.

"Whoa!" Gallopade commanded, catching their full attention. "The Wise Ones warned us about this risky trip. Staying safe and finding Esel is our priority! To have a strong team, we must help each other. Call a truce now!"

"You're right, dear," Heija stated. "I'm sorry."

The stallion resumed his normal flight pattern beside Heija, close but not in the way of her wings. "Jay-T suggested an inn named The View," Gallopade told them. "I was told they have good food. Do you see it Razzi?"

"Not yet." Razzi answered still glaring at Heija. "I can bite, too!" He snapped, getting in the last word.

Heija bit her lip and said nothing. She continued to search for the restaurant and finding it a short time later.

'The View' was a restaurant on the top floor of a high building with huge upper windows, giving its patrons a grand place to view the city. The horses landed easily on the upper deck, pulled their harness tassels to hide their wings then lowered down so their riders could slide off.

An ostrich with a long neck, wearing a black bow tie greeted them in an open door. "Please come in and rest after your long trip. The Wise Ones said to expect you. Our décor looks icy outside, but inside we are warm and friendly. Few travel these days so we value your business. Your table is ready and the sky show will soon begin."

Tony looked puzzled. "What is a sky show?" As they followed their host, they passed odd shaped tables where all sizes of people and animals were eating. Their table was by a large window. Even the ceiling was clear glass.

The friendly host said. "After dark, you will see a meteor shower like fireworks. It happens most every night. Also, the Kingobe volcano is glowing again in Old World, making the clouds shimmer like an ocean of fire."

"Is the volcano dangerous, sir?" Gallopade asked.

"Not at this distance. I hope you enjoy your meal and the show. Your servers will help you now."

The cushions were designed like the puff limo. The softness fit snuggly around them, giving them security with freedom of movement. Even the horses sat so their heads were over the table. The servers adjusted the adaptable table and eating containers for their personal needs.

Razzi boasted. "My red tie is perfect for dinner. I always wanted to eat out. People on earth take us out to the porch but not out to restaurants."

"You do look fine," Heija complimented him, trying to keep peace. "I hope you enjoy your first restaurant."

Trays of food were delivered. Animal guests were pampered the same as humans. After the long flight, the horses enjoyed the comfort and fun of sitting.

"I must say," Heija admitted, "I actually feel relaxed indoors. I thought a horse inside a restaurant was totally forbidden. Back on earth, people would not understand."

"Aye, this is a surprising world." Gallopade talked between crunches on his fresh carrots. "I fully expected Zor to attack us today. Instead, we are eating in a luxury hotel with a sky show about to happen. The Wise Ones even paid all our expenses. They are extra kind ladies."

"This is unreal but totally grand," Heija purred, "I want to forget our problems tonight and just enjoy these special moments as fully as possible."

"Great idea Heija," Gallopade affirmed. "This will be our night to celebrate all our newfound freedoms."

After gobbling his food, Razzi rolled backward with his feet waving in the air. "This meal was worth the trip! But I ate too much," he groaned. While up-side-down, his eyes were drawn to a pair of large sparkling eyes, peeking up from a stairwell. Her long eyelashes fluttered flirtatiously and then she timidly backed away.

Razzi sat up and rubbed his eyes. He stared toward the stairs. Had he really seen a female raccoon? Those flirty eyes filled him with excitement. Who was she?

Just then, Tony spotted the first meteorite passing across the darkness. He pointed excitedly and talked a mile a minute. "Look! A purple one just zoomed across the sky. There's a silver one and there goes a green one!"

Razzi could not look up for watching the stairwell.

Again, long lashes fluttered over diamond eyes. She gave a charming smile, and motioned her paw for him to follow her. She winked and disappeared again.

The wink made Razzi's heart flip-flop. "Ho hum . . . ." He yawned. "Meteors bore me. I'm going downstairs."

Tony's eyes were riveted to the sky. "Sure, pal. I'd go with you, but this is too exciting. There's a red one!"

The other earthlings were enjoying the show also.

Razzi zipped down the stairs to a lower floor. He searched the hallways and all the unlocked rooms. Not finding her, he scrambled downward to other floors. He darted here and there, as fast as his legs would carry him.

He clumsily knocked over flower pots, lamps, and left a trail everywhere he ventured. On the lowest floor, he became frustrated and angrily searched pantries and under work tables in the kitchen. When jars of milk, sugar, flour, and oil were spilt, the furious cooks threw pans at him.

Razzi could not find those flirty eyes. He scurried around gift shops, a barber shop, and exotic food shops. He blundered through a Bistro, a sandwich eatery and a Tea House, knocking over a stand of tea cups. As folks yelled at him, he fled under the cover of a lush flower garden, part of an indoor oriental park.

"Where could she be? Why can't I find her?" He moaned. His tail dragged as he walked beside a fish pond. Even the fish did not distract him. "I searched everywhere. She must have left the hotel. Double dang! She was cute. I guess I need to go back and watch the sky show."

The gloomy little fellow padded slowly up one side of a steeply arched red oriental bridge and was abruptly face to face with those gorgeous fluttering eyelashes!

Jerking backward in dismay, he reacted. "Who are you? I followed like you asked. Were you hiding from me?"

Turning her head shyly, her lashes lowered. With a tiny giggle, she spoke softly. "My name is Sasha. What do your friends call you?" The words rolled from her tongue with an accent slightly foreign.

His heart thumped like an Indian war drum and his frustration melted. "I'm Razzi. Sasha is a pretty name. Are you and your family staying here at the Inn?"

"No, uh, I'm alone. I only came here to see the, yes, to see the sky show. Let us walk. It is a lovely night, Razzi. Yes?" They walked outside on a walkway.

Not as lovely as you, Razzi thought. "Yes, Sasha, it's a perfect night." His paws wrung nervously behind his back as they walked by a hat shop. "Where do you live?"

"Not far. It's called Plentiful Valley. We have big dewberries, a pond with glow fish, and fresh corn.

"Dewberries! Wow, I love 'em. It's been years since I tasted any." He kept staring at her charming eyes.

"We have lots of berries ripe for eating, but I suppose you already have plans or maybe even a wife?"

"Not me! Are you married?" Razzi asked.

"No," She giggled. "We could go to my place and eat berries together. It might be fun."

"How far away do you live? I should tell my friends."

"Yes, you should. Although, your friends are watching the sky show and it is quite long. We could take my Bubble Craft and be back before the show is over."

"You have a flying vehicle? Double wow!"

"Yes. It moves very fast."

"I've never ridden in one of those," he admitted.

"You can ride in mine!" She affirmed with a giggle.

"What about Zor Zanger? It might be dangerous!"

"No, Razzi, my vehicle is faster than his horses."

Razzi hesitated. "I should still tell my friends where I'm going and when I'll be back. They worry about me."

"Sure, Razzi, I always tell my family where I'm going. You go tell them," she offered. "And tell them I'm sorry we are disturbing their show. Just hurry back and don't keep me waiting too long." She winked again.

The wink melted his good intentions. "I can't make you wait." Razzi told her. "Besides, I'm not a kid. Let's go! What they don't know won't hurt them!"

They giggled as they walked toward her vehicle parked by the edge of the Septar. After she boarded, Razzi jumped into a plush seat beside her. "Now this is the way to travel," he declared as a glass dome closed over the vehicle and they slipped into the thick dark cloud.

"Wait! Are we are going down toward Old World?"

She smiled and gazed at him innocently. "But of course, sweetie. That is where I live."

"Plentiful Valley is in Old World? Oh no! As much as I hate to say this, please take me back to the hotel."

"If that is what you want." Her paw touched his cheek and her velvet voice calmed him in the dim light. "But dear one, did your friends not tell you the good side of Old World? Shame on them! You'll be missing out. I live there and as you can see, I'm fine."

She lowered her chin sadly and began turning the vehicle. "I'm sorry. I so hoped I could share this evening with you. You're so interesting and irresistibly cute."

Her words made his head spin. "Really? I am? I honestly want to be with you, but . . . ." he hesitated.

"Then come with me! You'll love it!" Her charming eyes begged. "If you don't like my home, I promise I'll bring you back to the hotel right away."

"Well, okay. I'll go with you." Her promises defeated his better judgment. How could he resist her coaxing eyes?

Soon they broke below the dark clouds and landed in a clearing between a corn field and rows of dewberry bushes. The place was lit with a round floating illumination that Sasha called her make-believe moon. They jumped from the vehicle and began eating extra-large juicy berries.

"These are even better than you told me. Wow, what a nifty place! I can't wait to tell my friends." He smacked his lips loving the taste. "I was sure there was nothing good in Old World. This is totally amazing."

"You haven't seen the best part," Sasha boasted. "Follow me." She pranced down a little path to the edge of a shiny pond. They sat on a grassy knoll in the moonlight and watched big glow fish play and swim in the water.

The moon beams on her beautiful face made Razzi have feelings he had never felt. She was fun. His heart raced far too fast, so he challenged her. "Let's go after those glowing critters." He pulled off his bow tie to keep it dry and dived into the pond.

Sasha giggled. "You are so cute." She splashed in with him. They bobbed up and down, chasing the fish and each other. The two of them laughed and played until they at last tired. After shaking the water from their fur, they dried in the moonlight.

Razzi put on his red tie. He thanked her for a grand time and kissed her paw. "I'd like to do this again, but now I should return to my friends. They will worry."

Her voice filled with sadness. "But I enjoy your company so much, sweetie. Surely you can stay a while longer?" She fluttered her lashes and begged. Please?"

Razzi tried to act casual, but being called 'sweetie' filled his heart with new feelings, making it hard to talk. "I guess . . . if that is what you really want . . . ."

Her nose touched his. "You know that's what I want, sugar. You are such fun and I love you being here."

Swallowing hard, he replied. "My friends can wait! I enjoy being with you, too, so I'll stay a while longer."

"I like that!" she purred. "Let's walk a while."

They ambled down the path bumping gently together. She gave him a kiss on his ear then darted away giggling. She dashed into the tasseled cornfield and for a moment disappeared. A second later, she leaped out in front of him with a teasing smile, and the pursuit was on. They played hide-and-seek in the light of the moon.

"How did I get so lucky? Maybe wishes can come true like Jay-T said. Sasha is better than all my dreams." They ate sweet corn together then raced up and down the corn rows. Sasha slid to a stop in a clearing directly in front of him. The moonbeams glowed on her fur. Razzi gazed at her pretty face and sparkling black diamond eyes.

"You're terrific!" Razzi murmured, wanting to kiss her lovely lips. "You make me hear music and my heart dance. Is this love?" He watched her head tilt toward his, her pink lips coming toward him. He closed his eyes and leaned forward, his lips puckered as he waited for her touch. His mind whirled with her absolute perfection.

As he waited, a noise caught his attention. His eyes popped open. "What was that? Sasha? Where are you?"

A haunting laugh filled the night air, a laugh he had heard before. His hair stood on end. "Zor has taken Sasha! I must save her!" Razzi scrambled toward the laughter then skidded to a quick stop.

His lovely Sasha was in her vehicle as it hovered in front of him. Before Razzi's eyes, the beautiful Sasha began changing. Her adoring eyes filled with hatred and her shiny fur turned to rough smudged skin. She vanished as Zor Zanger materialized! His laughter thundered, mocking the shocked raccoon.

"How terrific am I now, sweetie? Fools like you are a dime a dozen. Enjoy Old World! I hope your berries and corn were good, because they were your last meal! I told you to go home. You're too late now! Bye-bye, fool!" The bubble arose and veered toward the volcano's glow.

"No!" Razzi cried out. "This can't be. It's all a horrid dream! I have to wake up!" He turned and ran until his chest heaved. When he finally stopped to rest, panting for breath, the bright moon was gone. He was in a dark rank-smelling place without the lovely Sasha or his friends.

"I can't get Zor's laughter out of my head!" he sniveled. "How did this happen? How could my beautiful Sasha be dirty ole Double Z? How was I so blind? Sasha stole my heart! Dang it! How will I ever forget her?" His anger erupted in such a fury he swung his fists wildly at the dark smelly air until his rage finally calmed a bit.

"That dirty rotten bum! How could Zor do this to me? He played his game until my heart opened to love so he could add to my pain. And his stupid tricks worked! What did I do to deserve this? Worse than that, my friends don't know I'm here." Razzi fell to his knees, folded into a knot on the ground and let out a spine-tingling howl.

———————

In Cubical City, the sky show continued for all to enjoy. Molly watched until she became drowsy and dropped her purse. "Is my mirror broken?" She exclaimed.

The friends gathered to see, when images of Razzi darting wildly between corn rows with terror etched in his face appeared in the mirror. He was screaming for help.

"He looks so real," Tony held the mirror in disbelief. "But how can he be in a cornfield? He went downstairs."

"I don't know, but Razzi needs us! We must find him!" Gallopade said leading the way downstairs. They found a messy trail with annoyed personnel along the way, but no real answers.

Molly checked her mirror again and screamed. "It's Zor Zanger!" The girl held up her mirror for all to see!

Zor's deep voice thundered forth. "Go home, earthlings! Esel will not help you. Your friend, Razzi, is gone forever! Be wiser than him and heed my words. Go home now!" Smoke filled the mirror and Zor was gone.

"Oh, Razzi, what happened to you?" Tears filled Molly's eyes. "What has Zor Zanger done to you?"

CHAPTER 10

OLD WORLD AGAIN!

The earthlings followed Razzi's cluttered trail from the highest to the lowest floor, searching for him. Along the way, employees picked up spilt flower pots and waste baskets, complaining about a wild bandit. The kitchen floor was covered with spilt oil, flour, sugar and milk.

The cook fumed as he talked to the horses and children. "Look at this sticky mess! Your friend is crazy! His pranks cost me time and money! What was he thinking? If you must find him, follow his sticky footprints."

The prints led to the Tea House, where dishes littered the woven-grass covered floor. "Our hotel guard knew a raccoon arrived with you, so he notified the Wise Ones in Dome City. The sisters will reimburse us for our damages," the annoyed owner said. "The guard told me the hat maker was the last person to see that pest before he left this Septar. Just go two doors down the sidewalk."

After apologies and thanking the man, Gallopade and his friends hurried to the hat shop. Large windows overlooked the island's edge. The walls were filled with bizarre hats of every color and shape. A plump lady with long orange hair and a green neon hat greeted them.

"We were told you saw our friend, Razzi, a raccoon, leave this Septar . . . ." Gallopade began nervously.

"Yes." The woman said with a welcoming smile. "Actually, I saw and heard two raccoons by my window. The male called the female, Sasha, who batted her eyelashes a lot. Sasha invited him to ride in her flying machine and eat dewberries in Plentiful Valley. I wanted to stop them, because traveling at night is very dangerous; however, I had customers waiting for me.

"I quickly buzzed for our hotel guard, but he only witnessed them sink into the clouds toward Old World."

"Razzi went to Old World?" Gallopade blurted out. "He hates that place! None of this makes sense."

"Nothing ever makes sense when Zor Zanger is involved and I believe he was," the lady admitted.

"What do you mean?" Heija asked.

"I have heard incredible stories about that evil man. A short time ago, my friend shared her story with me. Let me tell you her account, and you can judge for yourselves.

"Last week, a rich man landed his flying machine by my friend's business. The man demanded six dozen blue-shelled eggs, each with three yokes. She filled his order and he stood there and broke a whole dozen eggs, one at a time onto her clean floor. Then he screamed that one egg only had two yokes. He refused to pay her!

"My friend told him to pay her or return the remaining eggs and leave. His ruthless anger scared her, so she ran to another room, locked the door and peeked out her window. What she saw was startling. The man went to his vehicle and in front of her eyes turned into a 'hen' like her layers, and he flew into her hen house.

"She called for help and when my friend returned to the window, her chickens, the man, and the vehicle were gone. A message was tacked on her door, printed in blood. It read, 'Never refuse me again! I'll be back! Zor Zanger.'"

The earthlings stared at each other. "How is that possible?" Heija asked. "I never heard of such a thing!"

Thoughtfully, Gallopade said, "Well . . . If Zor can become a hen, I suppose he could just as easily become a female raccoon! A charming lady raccoon could easily entice Razzi without him knowing he was in real trouble."

"Oh dear! This is bad!" Heija reacted.

"In my mirror, he was running in a cornfield," Molly remembered. "Could he still be there?"

"Not on our Septar," said the hat lady. "But I have heard that Zor bragged about raising corn on Old World. Of course, he brags about everything."

"Jeepers," Tony reacted. "When we saw Razzi running, we didn't see a bubble vehicle or Sasha. He was terrified and all alone!"

"He's alone with monsters chasing him!" Molly concluded. "He needs help! We have to fly down there right now and get him back! I know how scared I was when I thought those dinosaurs were about to eat us."

The girl's words moved the group to action. When Gallopade proposed he go alone, his words landed on deaf ears. After quick preparations, they returned to the hat shop to leave the Septar. The children waved to the hat lady as their steeds sunk into the dark cloud layer.

The children hung on tightly as the horses over-lapped their closest wings, and glided in a wide spiral downward through the blackness. Eventually they broke through the dense clouds into an eerie red haze coming from the distant volcano. The smells were rancid.

They were greatly disappointed when no cornfields were in sight. Precious time would be lost searching for Razzi's location. Hopefully he could survive until then.

At that moment, lost in the vast corn fields, Razzi stood as if frozen, listening intently to the sounds around him. Unusual footsteps padded ever closer. They were too quiet for dinosaurs. He could hear a light step here, there, and in-between. He quickly ran again, zigzagging from corn row to corn row, hiding below the stalk's long leaves.

What beast walked that quietly? Maybe they were stepping lightly to listen for him? As the soft steps came dangerously close, the raccoon laid quietly in a tiny ball on the ground, not even breathing. He rejoiced inside when the sounds passed by him and faded in the distance. He wanted to remain curled up and sleep a while.

A foul-smelling rat crawled from his hole next to Razzi. The rat abruptly howled like a coyote, "Trespasser! Over here! Trespasser, I say!"

Razzi's hair stood on end. "Shut up, you traitor!" Hearing footsteps approaching, Razzi darted into the darkness. Glancing back, he glimpsed great glowing eyes bobbing above the corn stalks close behind him. What could be that gigantic, he wondered? His fears mounted.

He scurried along faster, dashing by mistake into a small clearing where he slid to an instant stop. In the red haze, a spider taller than the corn stalks leered back at him with a half dozen bright glowing eyes. He was a black hairy spider with eight long legs that pushed into the soil as he charged toward the raccoon.

Razzi shrieked and skidded back into the corn stalks on a zigzag course, just missing the spider that had already chased him. I can't believe they are spiders! I hate spiders! They'll wrap me up and suck the life outta of me! What can I do? Even the rats are against me! I gotta hide!

After running at breakneck speed as long as he could, he stopped to listen. Tears welled up in his eyes.

Why didn't I tell someone where I was going? Why did I trust Sasha, a total stranger? Was it her beauty or her flirty ways? Maybe it was because she treated me so special, and she shared her bubble vehicle to go get tasty treats. She tempted me with things I wanted. Why didn't I see that? The truth is I know I should have told my friends.

What if I never see them again? They are my first real buddies, and they'll never know how much I care for them. Why didn't I tell them? A tear trickled down his nose, as soft padding sounds advanced closer. Razzi pushed himself to move on, hoping to find a place to hide.

————

Gallopade and Heija found Zor's cornfields near morning and landed to rest in a small clearing. Tony shared his food and water, and they rested until the dark red haze turned into a lighter gray.

After a nap, Molly whimpered. "Poor little Razzi."

"He's a scrapper," Heija said. "He'll be okay."

"We must find him soon," Gallopade warned. "This morning light will make him a moving target."

They lifted up and soared over the fields. At length, through Razzi's telescope, Tony noticed a dust cloud above the corn stalks. "I see dust in the air," he told them.

Immediately, they winged toward the dust swirls.

"Oh, no! It's giant black spiders running around." Tony's voice shook. "They're chasing something!"

Molly hiccupped and Heija gasped.

As the winged horses neared the commotion they could see huge hairy spider backs above the corn stalks.

"I see Razzi!" Tony wailed. "He's staggering from side to side, but the spiders are about to catch him!"

"Are you sure it's Razzi?" Heija queried.

"I'm sure. I see his red bow tie. Oh, no! He fell!" Tony cried out. "They're circling him!"

"Great Mercy," Gallopade moaned. "He must be terrified. I see him! Those brutes are making a trap!"

"How can we help him?" Heija squealed. "If we try to grab him now, the spiders will catch us!"

Screams pierced the air. Razzi shrieked as he tried to get away from the shrinking circle.

"They'll kill him!" Molly howled. "We gotta grab him now! He needs us. Do something, Gallopade!"

"I want to, Molly, but Heija is right," he answered. "Those excited spiders will trap us if we go down in that circle. I wonder if Razzi could catch a rope."

"My rope is good and strong," Tony offered.

"Let's try, Tony," the stallion urged. "Tie one end to my harness and make a hand loop on the other end."

"Yes, sir, I will," Tony replied working feverishly.

"When you are ready, we'll fly over and see what happens. I hope they are not jumping spiders. They look strong and I doubt they scare easily," the stallion stated.

"They look fearless!" Heija responded.

Gallopade remained calm. "If the spiders fail to jump, our rope might work. But those monsters will still fight like devils to keep Razzi. Heija and Molly can help by distracting the beasts at a safe distance."

"We're ready!" Molly quickly agreed.

"Yes, we'll help," Heija promised. She moved her body so her head was closer to Gallopade. "It's important that you guys stay safe. There's no need to fret over us."

"You know I do," Gallopade answered sincerely.

"Yes, I know," she murmured. "I love you, too."

The stallion cherished her words. It gave him an unseen strength to return safely to her. Before he could reply, Razzi's pathetic yelps filled their ears.

Breaking his gaze with Heija, Gallopade sprang into action. "They have caught him! He's dangling between two spider webs! We must get him soon. Are you ready, Tony?"

"Yes, sir, let's get him! I'll hold tight."

Gallopade and the boy swooped over the circle.

The hairy spiders watched with sticky white silks dripping from their bodies and claws. Razzi was already dangling off the ground in the center of three long webs.

Watching the horrible scene, Molly screamed out. "Let him go, you bullies! He's my friend. Let him go!"

Gallopade flew over the circle and Tony shouted down to the raccoon. "Razzi, we're here! Look up!"

Barely hearing the boy's voice, the raccoon opened his tightly closed eyes. "Help me!" He pleaded.

As they passed over a second time, Tony screamed out. "Hold your paws up." The third time, Gallopade hovered over the circle expecting trouble any moment, while Tony dropped the rope's end loop toward Razzi.

The spiders raised their ugly legs reaching for the rope when it fell from Tony's hands. As the spiders leaned forward trying to grab the rope, the center of their web holding the raccoon dropped lower to the ground. Each time Razzi stretched to catch the dangling lifeline with his front paws, the center of the web dropped too low.

"I can't reach it!" Razzi's cry was filled with terror. "I can't reach it! Drop it lower!"

"Gosh, Gallopade, those spiders reach really high."

"I know, Tony. Lower means trouble for us and staying higher means trouble for Razzi. Call it Tony."

Seeing the crisis, Heija and Molly swooped down over one edge of the circle to distract the spiders from their prey. They screamed and hissed while over the circle.

One excited spider broke away from the circle and raced after them. He was quicker than Heija expected. One of his long hairy legs lifted up, reaching for Molly.

The child shrieked when she felt him catch her hair. She ducked down and held tightly to Heija's harness, feeling her pigtail grow taut.

Heija pressed upward away from the monster, screaming. "Molly, are you all right, child?"

"That doggone bully stole my hair ribbon!"

"I was afraid I had lost you, Molly," Heija cried out.

Molly stared at the action below her. "Gallopade and Tony are too close! We have to help 'em, Heija!"

Heija could not believe her ears. Was all this courage truly coming from their shy little friend? "But Molly, it's terribly dangerous for you. I almost lost you!"

"I'm fine. I'll hold on. Hurry! They need us!"

The girl's anxious pleading filled Heija with renewed determination. "Hold on, dear!" They flew across the circle much faster, fully knowing the dangers.

The boy jerked the rope away from a spider again, after the raccoon barely missed it. "We don't have a choice," Tony yelled. "We gotta go lower or Razzi will die."

"If they grab us, Tony, it's over for us, too."

"We can't leave him this way, Gallopade," Tony protested. "We have to try again. Just drop down a little. Razzi almost reached the rope last time."

Gallopade flapped his wings for a moment to scare the spiders back then he lowered closer to the irate mob. "Quickly Tony, drop the rope!"

Heija flew by him. "Gallopade, you're too low!" She warned. "They'll pull you down!"

Razzi struggled to reach the rope, touching it, but not able to grab on. "Dang, double dang," he groaned. His eyes stung as he watched the rope go by. "I never wanted anything so bad in my life! Please guys, come a little closer. I promise I'll catch it!"

Tony screamed from excitement. "Razzi nearly caught it! Just go a little lower."

Gallopade knew they were in huge danger. "Great Mercy, Tony, any lower and we'll be sitting in their laps!"

"But Razzi will catch it next time!" Tony persisted. "He's trying really hard to catch it."

Gallopade felt his strength dwindling. He was breathing in dust and trying to stay in one spot far too long. "Okay Tony. Make it fast!" The horse pulled his legs near his body, and lowered closer to the clutching claws.

The more Razzi wallowed about in the adhesive webs, the more entangled he became. "Throw the rope," he called out with a pitiful voice. "You're my last chance!"

Spider webs whizzed through the air, now falling across the stallion's aching body. White goo was dripping from each beast's busy front legs, some pulling, some throwing, and some reaching upward.

The webs grew heavier with each added strand. Just as the hovering steed knew he must pull up, Tony's joyful voice rang through the air. "Razzi caught the loop! Raise up, Gallopade! Hurry! Get us out of here!" The boy's voice was jubilant and strengthening to his friends.

The exhausted raccoon held the rope with one paw. "Pull me out of here! These suckers have terrible breath, and you should see the cooties in their hair."

"That's the Razzi we know and love." The stallion declared as he pushed hard to rise upward.

"What's wrong? We're not moving!" Tony asked.

"My back leg," Gallopade groaned. "They're holding my back leg. I can't lift all this weight and fight too." Dread filled his voice. "I hope Razzi can hold on. Great mercy, this is bad! What can I do?"

Heija gulped when she saw the spider grasping Gallopade's hoof. "Our guys are in trouble. Hold tight, Molly. This may be a rough ride but we must help them."

"Hurry, Heija, we can do this! I'll make lots of noise." As they flew downward, Molly ducked her head close to Heija's neck, holding on for dear life. The girl shrieked loudly hoping to frighten the spiders. Dust filled her mouth, flying spider webs were everywhere, and below them was a sea of angry glowing eyes peering upward.

The mare hovered behind Gallopade, trying to kick at the strong spider leg holding the stallion's leg. Her sharp hooves made contact and even brought blood, but the spider would not let go. The spiders under the girls become more excited and grabbed higher toward them. Fearful, Heija pulled up, not succeeding in her mission.

Heija raced upward taking webs with her and giving Gallopade a moment with less weight to endure.

Molly tossed webs off as they swung around.

With fire in her eyes, Heija shouted. "Molly, we must do more. Lay low on my back and hold on even tighter." They dove again as fast as Heija could fly, hitting the webs full force, pulling many off the stallion and Tony.

The sudden motion of pulling and snapping silk webs made a few spiders momentarily draw back.

Gallopade rose up slightly, but his leg was still in the firm grip of one muscular spider.

Heija repeated her actions two more times and Gallopade managed to pull up again, but only inches.

During the hassle of up and down movements, Razzi managed to grab the rope loop with his other paw. He tried to climb up the rope, but the sticky web around his waist and feet held him tightly in place. "Don't drop me, guys. I want outta here! Pull up!" He begged.

Heija continued breaking the web ropes only to find the faster she worked, the faster the spiders worked. They were determined to pull the stallion down. Even with Tony pushing webs away, the spiders kept making more.

"We are losing them!" Heija's voice was filled with panic. She flew downward toward the spider's leg holding Gallopade. She crunched her teeth into the creature's leg. Nothing happened. She tore at the beast's flesh over and over, taking hair and flesh off; yet, it held tight.

"Bite him Heija!" Razzi called out in a feeble voice. "Bite the tar out of him! Make him let go!"

"Heija, get out of here!" Gallopade's voice rang out. "The spiders will pull you down. Save yourselves!"

"If you go down, we will too!" She managed to spit out while still chomping at the spider's bloody leg. "These spiders must be made of steel!" She groaned with disgust. "What else can I do?" She bit again and again.

Molly screamed out as a spider claw brushed her side and nearly caught her purse. "Get away and leave us alone! Don't touch my purse!" Her flustered voice was angry as she pulled her purse close to her. Then an idea flashed through her head. Molly grabbed her powder case from the purse, rubbed it, and begged. "Please little box give me lots of powder." With that, she began shaking powder on the sea of glowing spider eyes.

The spiders blinked. Some rubbed their many eyes with their numerous legs. Others even pulled back when they were temporarily blinded.

Molly continued spilling the powder everywhere, including Heija's back. "Close your eyes, Razzi!" The girl called out. The sticky webs absorbed the powder and began falling off Heija's back.

The monster holding the stallion's ankle swayed blindly, lost his balance, gave a final jerk, and lost his grip.

"You're free, Gallopade!" Heija screamed as she strained upward, trying to carry more webs off the stallion and boy. The mare was also tiring quickly.

Razzi was still stuck in the main web, which weighed too much for Gallopade to carry upward. The remaining spiders grouped together to pull on the webs still across Gallopade's back.

"Great job, Molly, keep up the good work!" Heija told the girl. "I'll try to break more of their webs." She zipped back and forth, striking the webs with her wings, while Molly sprinkled more powder.

Gallopade rose higher, thankful for each inch.

The powder that had fallen on Razzi's sticky bonds abruptly let him break free from the main web. He recklessly swung to and fro, wailing as he passed each annoyed monster and their wild grabbing claws.

Gallopade's strength was spent; however when Razzi broke loose the excitement boosted his energy. He strained upward with all his strength against the remaining webs that still confined him.

Heija was working in an exhausted state but her love and determination for her friends kept her fighting on. She spread her wings wide and swooped across the circle at full speed again and again, continuing to break the final webs. In her hurry the last dive, she failed to see the rope holding Razzi which swung directly in front of her.

Then it happened. The lifeline that Razzi still clung to, collided with Heija's fast-moving wing. The rapid jolt spun the little raccoon straight upward as if shot from a cannon. He sailed past Gallopade and Tony toward the smoky cloud layer, screaming all the way upward.

Razzi was traveling far too fast for Tony to reach out and grab him. Heija had not yet seen Razzi's dilemma. She was turning to prepare for another dive.

"Heija, catch Razzi!" Gallopade and Tony screamed at once. They felt the request was impossible; yet, they wanted so badly to help the little fellow.

"Poor Razzi," Tony whimpered. "He's flying like an airplane! We have lost him this time for sure."

Molly heard Gallopade and Tony call out, then she heard and saw Razzi spiraling skyward. "Heija, look up! Razzi is way up there!" She yelled.

Puzzled, but hearing the urgency in Molly's voice, Heija peered upward, seeing the raccoon still slowly rising.

"How did that happen?" Heija asked as the reality sunk into her tired mind. Her adrenalin surged and she reacted, pushing on her wings, darting quickly upward.

Razzi's upward momentum slowed and he hung in the air a moment. Glancing around, he felt himself begin to fall and moaned. "I've had it now!"

Heija's fast rise put her close to Razzi as he began his fall. The mare knew Razzi's weight could easily knock Molly off, or do dreadful damage to whatever he hit. What should she do? She was close as she dared.

Molly stretched her hand out. Her fingers momentarily clutched his outstretched front paw only to have it pull away with great force. Like a blur, Razzi's body rolled over prompting his back leg to slap smack-dab into Molly's grasping hand. She held as firmly as she could.

Can you hold me? Razzi wanted to ask her, but there was no time or strength for words.

Molly held on tightly, but felt his paw slipping away. He was too heavy for her. Just before his paw escaped the girl's grip, Razzi twisted and grabbed Molly's foot with his front legs. He could not hold on but swung under Heija's wing. The tiny pause gave him time to grab Heija's hind leg as he fell downward.

A miracle just happened! Heija thought. She wanted to yell out in glee, but it was not over. She had to find a safe landing area for Razzi, away from the spiders. Heija could see the monsters below watching, waiting and dancing with excitement, hoping Razzi would fall into their webs. She stayed high in the air but flew toward the place they had rested earlier in the day. Flying with Razzi's extra weight was hard work for the weary mare.

Panic again filled Heija's heart as she felt Razzi's little paws slipping down from her midleg to her ankle. He was barely holding on. His strength was gone.

Molly nearly fell off, trying to reach Razzi. He was too far away to help. She watched and cried in horror as his tired paws slipped low on Heija's ankle. His little body swayed in the wind like an autumn leaf ready to tumble.

Hardly audible, Razzi pathetically muttered. "I'm sorry, Molly, I can't hold on!" A second later, he was once again plunging downward, toward the spiders and Old World. The wind whistled in his ears. He closed his eyes, giving up on his fight for life. He had lost. His friends gave their all, but this was the end and he knew it.

A sudden warmth and gentleness surrounded him like a soft warm blanket. Was he in heaven? He timidly opened his eyes to see Tony's twinkling brown eyeballs staring gleefully at him.

"How did you do that?" Razzi whispered.

"You did it, Razzi! You hung on long enough for Gallopade to fly under you and I caught you when you started to fall again," Tony told him.

"I thought I was a goner. Double wow-wow," Razzi uttered with tears swamping his face. In moments, he relaxed and fell asleep in Tony's safe arms.

Gallopade and Heija landed outside the cornfields.

Molly was able to reach into Tony's knapsack and give out food and water while the boy cradled Razzi in his arms. It gave Heija and Gallopade the needed energy boost they would require to fly up through the thick cloud layer and back to Cubical City.

As the spider's glowing eyes approached, the group began their journey upward. The horses shared the ends of the rope between their teeth to stay close in the darkness.

They broke through the cloud layer near the Septar. It was morning and folks were busy on the little island. The hat lady waved at them as they flew to their hotel. The city was awake, but they were ready to sleep.

"Will we look for Esel tomorrow or turn back?" Heija asked. "Zor Zanger is no joke. He meant to kill Razzi."

Exhausted, Gallopade whispered. "We'll all decide after we get some needed rest. The only thing I know without a doubt is what you said. Zor's brainless games are truly deadly! Finding Esel may be an impossible task for us, whether we like it or not."

CHAPTER 11

RAINBOW SURPRISES

After rescuing Razzi from Old World, the exhausted earthlings slept all day. Later, during the meteor show, they gathered and ate in the View's upper room. After the meal, Razzi wanted to apologize to the hotel's personnel so the children tagged along for support. Heija and Gallopade waited outside on the highest balcony.

"The meteors are so beautiful," Heija murmured. "It's good to be alive! I know finding Esel is very important; yet, I wonder if it is wise for us to travel tonight."

"We have lost precious time, bonnie lass. I worry about Gramp's losing the farm if we don't find Esel soon. Zor might not expect me to fly to Esel's castle tonight. This time I must travel alone! It's too risky for all of us."

Quietly Heija asked, "Could you have saved Razzi from the spiders all by yourself?"

He stared at his hooves. "Must I tell the truth?"

"The truth is, you told us what to do and together we helped each other. I cannot stay here and worry myself to death about you. I'll go with you and that is that."

"We do work well as a team. However, if those spiders had hurt you, it would have destroyed me! Were your words true and you still love me?"

Heija kissed his nose. "How can you not know? I loved you the first night we met over two hundred years ago. And I love you today even more. Being beside you is all I want, now and always, even in the face of danger."

Gallopade's hooves pranced and a happy snort told his story better than his words. He wondered why sharing his love was more fearful than facing Zor. He finally said, "You faced a lot of danger for me last night. When we were human, I . . . uh, never dreamed you could love a furniture maker who would never be rich like your father."

"You truly felt that way? In my eyes, you were always rich in kindness, talent, loyalty, and bravery. You are still exactly who I love and will always need."

"Mercy, I never felt worthy!" He managed to respond. "You're so dear to me. I-I have intended to tell you my . . . uh f-feelings for a long time now. I t-truly . . . ."

The patio door swung open, filling the upper deck with happy chatter. Gallopade groaned and shyly pulled from Heija's gaze as the children and Razzi ran to them.

"The store owners were nice, but the cook wanted Razzi to wash dishes," Molly giggled as she talked.

"I promised I would when we return. That sudsy water didn't look bad. After two baths I still feel creepy. I despise spiders and their sticky webs!" Razzi shivered.

Gallopade shook his head, saying, "Aye, little buddy, we're thankful you are alive and with us tonight."

"I am too! No one ever cared for me as a boy. Now I'm a silly raccoon and you risked your lives for me. Why?"

Molly's' voice rang out. "That's simple. You're our friend and we love you!" She embraced him.

Razzi's eyes stung. "In all my y-years, no one ever told me t-that," he stammered.

Tony gave the raccoon a hug, too. "You're our pal."

Heija popped a kiss atop his head. "All is forgiven friend. I'm truly happy you are safe and back with us."

"Wow! I didn't expect that! From now on, I promise to be a better f-friend." His nose turned pink. "Thanks everyone. I owe you!" He quickly wiped away a tear. "Enough of this! W-What are our p-plans now?"

Gallopade took over. "I thought it was best if I traveled alone. Heija disagreed. I hope the three of you will be smart and stay here until we return from Esel's castle."

Razzi's fur bristled. "I'm going, sir. I thought Sasha was real! Ole Double Z stabbed me in the heart. No matter where I hide, that viper will find me. I feel safer with you."

Molly nodded and Tony said it clearly. "We are going too. We're a team and we're safer together."

Gallopade's jaw tightened. "You know it's against my better judgment but after last night, you know the risks. Prepare yourselves and we'll leave in ten minutes."

―――――――

Heija gazed at the bright stars in the dark sky. "First it was the meteor show and now that double moon makes the clouds below look like snow covered mountains. If not for Zor Zanger, this would be an incredible adventure."

"Aye, it is a grand night for flying. Soon we'll have the morning light." Gallopade peered about the darkness for signs of Septars. "I see the red Septar glowing to our right. Is this where we turn, Tony?"

"Veer a tad to the left, sir." Tony directed, looking at his glowing compass. "Good! Rainbow Septar is next."

"I can't wait," Molly chirped. "I love rainbows."

"We might find a pot of gold and be rich!"

"Sure, Tony when apples grow on grapevines!" Molly teased.

Gallopade's head jerked upward, his ears erect. Quietly yet firmly, he commanded. "Be silent, hang on, and dive! We'll hide behind the clouds!" Losing height rapidly, they hid and waited.

The tiny sound Gallopade heard became a clatter as Zor's beast horses with their hooked bat wings flew into the earthlings' sight. Chains rattled around lathered necks and flashes of fire sparked from their metal hooves.

The lead horse slowed and hovered in the air. The long line of steeds hushed when their leader, Black Fire, listened with quivering ears. Smoke curled from his flared nostrils as his eyes raked back and forth over the clouds. His eyes settled where Gallopade and his friends hid.

Razzi and Tony ducked low on the stallion's back. Molly held her mouth trying not to hiccup. Heija feared she might sneeze. Only Gallopade dared to peek at Black Fire through the dark clouds.

After long breathless moments, Black Fire tossed his head and gave a shrill whiny. Clanking his hooves, he darted north toward the red Septar with the black beast herd following. Only a trail of stale smoke remained.

Gallopade finally spoke in a hushed voice, "I feel sure he knew we were here. Then he moved on. Why?"

"How could he see us in this dark?" Heija asked.

"It was just a feeling I had," Gallopade remarked. "Each of you stayed calm and quiet. I'm proud of you!" He eased back into the moonlight, searching the sky for the herd. Soon, he spotted rainbows instead.

Using his quiet voice, the stallion stated. "A good breakfast while watching the sunrise sounds mighty good to me. I'm starved. How does that sound?"

Molly and Tony agreed they were hungry.

"A sunrise through rainbows and good food sounds totally fine to me, even a bit romantic," Heija cooed.

Razzi slouched down behind Tony and mumbled. "Romance my foot! It's a waste of time! I can only hope Double Z ain't hungry this morning."

"The rainbows are magnificent," Gallopade declared. "And look at that. I see a restaurant with an outdoor patio that will be perfect to watch the sunrise."

"And keep an eye open for Zor," Razzi muttered.

They settled beside a long table with a fine view.

Big eyed, Molly peeked around a stack of pancakes, watching a very green woman, eight feet tall, serve food. Her sarong was bright yellow and she had jewelry hanging from her nose to her toes.

With a robust voice, the smiling woman kneeled by Molly. "You enjoy our Septar and rainbows, child? Yes?"

"I love your rainbows, but I miss being home."

"And where is your home? Yes?"

"Back on earth we live on a farm and raise grapes. I miss my Gramps and Meme, but your island is nice. Yes!"

"Yes, child, we are happy to have you. All our food is grown under our life-giving rainbows." The woman turned toward Gallopade. "You will tour our gardens? Yes?"

"Your island is grand, but our business is urgent," Gallopade told her kindly. "We must soon leave. Yes."

"Our city park is next door. A mini tour maybe? Many flowers there for lady. Yes? She will love them!"

"Their flowers do smell delightful." Heija gazed at the stallion with pleading eyes. "May we? Yes?"

"Of course," he said. "A short tour. Yes!"

Heija gave a long sigh. "A spectacular sunrise, good food, grand company, and now lovely flowers make me want to stay here, if not for Esel and the farm."

Razzi watched and listened, but kept surprisingly quiet. The fruit reminded him of Sasha so he ate pancakes. He tried to forget his heartache, so he played games with the children while walking to the park.

Tony pretended to be angry and in gruff tones growled, "Razzi! Why did you do it? How dare you!"

Razzi faked being fearful. "It was Molly!" He squealed. "Molly planned it and dared me! She's evil!"

The boy yelled. "Yeah, Razzi's innocent like a fox! He put these smashed strawberries in my backpack!"

"I never eat strawberries!" Razzi howled. "That's Molly's favorite. Blame her! Cast her in the dungeon!"

"I double dared him," Molly cried out. "But Razzi chickened out. Cluck-cluck-cluck, you're a chicken!"

Acting outraged, Tony exclaimed. "Molly! You schemer! I'll get even! Take her to the dungeon!"

Molly hid behind Razzi. "I wanted some strawberry jam!" She yelled back, giggling still more. "Is that so bad?"

Gallopade and Heija followed, savoring the fun, the sights, and feeling their shoulders touch while walking.

The park's beauty was awesome. A brilliant rainbow loomed overhead. Luscious tropical fruits hung from large green trees and plants. Multitudes of bright colored flowers made sweet perfume. The group followed a sand path and around each curve the scenery became more appealing.

Tony skipped along with a big smile on his face. "Hey, Molly, this place reminds me of our farm. Look!"

"It even has a house and barn like ours," Molly exclaimed. "The grapes are huge." She plucked a grape from vines close to the path and popped it into her mouth. "It's sweet. Gramps would love these."

"I wish Meme and Gramps could see this. They would love it here." Tony noted dreamily.

Molly stopped by a wooden fence to gaze upon the scene. "It really is exactly like our farm. How can that be?"

Gallopade and Heija were gazing another direction so Razzi spoke up. "We know that's not our farm! All this fruit is making me sick. Let's go find Esel."

The children stood by the split-rail fence, still staring toward the farmhouse across a broad field. "Gosh, sis, is that Gramps standing on the front porch?"

Molly squinted. "Tony, I think it is Gramps!"

The old man saw them and surprise filled his face. "Meme!" he called out. "Our kiddoes have returned!" Then he waved to the children. "Where have yah been?"

"Gramps!" Molly said full of emotion. The children began climbing the rails of the fence.

Not wanting to be heard across the field, Razzi warned the children in a low voice. "No, Tony! Wait, Molly! It's gotta be a trick! That can't be Gramps." Razzi needed backup. "Heija, Gallopade, help me stop them!"

They gazed into each other's eyes, not hearing.

"Come kiddos." Gramps called and began walking toward them. "Tell Gramps all about yoreselves."

Tony sat atop the fence helping Molly cross over. He called out. "We'll tell you everything, Gramps. We tried to find a way to save your grape harvest."

"Our crops are fine, kiddos," the man exclaimed as he crossed his yard toward them. "Meme just made a chocolate cake. It'll taste good as we talk."

Both children jumped off the fence, heading toward the man's wide-open arms.

Razzi slid under the fence and ran behind them trying to stop them. "Tony! Molly, this ain't right!" He grabbed the boy's knapsack but Tony kept running.

The quick movements caught Gallopade's attention. He shook his head and said, "What's happening? Where are the children going? Is that Gramps? Heija, wake up!"

The children were halfway across the wide field still running to the lawn and old man. They ignored Razzi.

Gallopade sensed the danger and unfurled his wings, calling out. "Molly! Tony! Razzi! Wait!"

"Why can't they hear you?" Heija asked as her wings opened. "Something's wrong!"

Knowing he could not stop the children, Razzi tried a new strategy. His paws pressed against the ground as he quickly scurried around the children to lead the way.

"You are right! It is Gramps!" The raccoon yelled loud and happily. Bounding ahead of the children, Razzi stopped cheerfully by the old man's side.

Gramps ignored Razzi and waited for the children.

Without caution, the angry raccoon quickly sunk his sharp teeth deep into the old man's leg.

A robust voice thundered in sudden pain. "Ow! You bit me you little fleabag! I'm bleeding! How dare you bite the great Zor Zanger! You ruined my perfect game!"

"I owed you for Sasha!" Razzi cried out in anger as he retreated; however, his escape was not swift enough.

Molly and Tony jerked to a stop when the man bellowed and wildly kicked Razzi like a football. They watched in horror as the animal rolled and tumbled until his head struck a tree and he lay sprawled on the ground.

"You stupid fool!" Gramps roared. "The spiders should have killed you! How did you get away from them? I hope you are finally dead this time!"

Gallopade and Heija landed in the yard, just as dark smoke encircled the image of Gramps. It swirled around and around until it formed a twister, which bumped across the park and soon disappeared.

"Great stormy seas," Gallopade trumpeted. "What just happened? I've never seen anything like that!"

"We thought he was Gramps until he kicked Razzi," Tony affirmed, "but it was Zor and another mean trick!"

Molly ran to Razzi's side and pulled him into her arms. "Razzi, talk to me! Are you okay? He's not moving or answering me. Did Zor really kill him?"

Gallopade trotted to Molly's side. He placed his head near Razzi's chest. "He's still breathing. Maybe he's not hurt too bad. This is all a mystery to me. Why did I not sense trouble? How did Razzi know what to do?"

"Look! His ear is twitching!" Molly said anxiously. "I think he's waking up."

On cue, Razzi's eyes popped wide open. He scrambled to his feet, his fists doubled ready to fight and he shouted. "It's ole Double Z! Run for your lives! Run!"

Molly gently shook Razzi's paw. "Zor has gone away. You saved us, Razzi! We're safe because of you."

"You're safe? Zor's really gone?"

"Yes Razzi," Heija affirmed. "We are grateful for your actions. Gallopade and I were sort of . . . spellbound. I didn't sense danger. How did you know Zor was here?"

The very tense raccoon peered in all directions. "I don't trust that Zor. Did you honestly see him leave?"

"Aye, we saw Zor escape," Gallopade said. "He was wrapped in a whirlwind. How did you know it was Zor?"

The raccoon rubbed his sore head. "I knew that Gramps is back on earth. I waved at you and Heija but you didn't see or hear me, like you were sleepwalking."

"You truly tried to get our attention? Why didn't we respond?" Gallopade asked in amazement.

"Why indeed? This is bizarre!" Heija admitted.

"Zor called it 'his perfect game," Razzi recalled. "Somehow he set us up. But how?"

"We ate the same things this morning," Tony said.

"No, Tony, I didn't eat any fruit, because it reminded me of Sasha. I just ate pancakes."

"I ate a lot of fruit!" Molly gasped her words.

"I did, too!" Heija stated. "Zor must have put something in our fruit to alter our awareness."

Gallopade's built-up frustrations charged out. "Aye, I ate the fruit, too. Zor's so-called games are a disaster! The man is evil! If he hurts one of you . . . I'll . . . ." The stallion caught himself and held his words. "It was a brave thing you did, Razzi. You saved us from that evil creature!"

"Wow! For once, I actually did something right." He grinned then just as quickly frowned. "If Zor comes back, he'll for sure kill me! Can we get out of here?"

"We planned to fly to Esel's place This afternoon; however, we flew all night." Gallopade gazed at Heija. "Do you feel like flying more or do we need to stay here?"

Heija responded quickly. "I've rested enough. Zor messed up our perfect morning. He's always a step ahead of us. The man makes me too angry to rest!"

"Yeah," Razzi snarled angrily. "He's a real rat!"

Molly touched Tony's shoulder. "Do you still have Esel's package that the Wise Ones gave you?"

"Let me look to be sure. Yeah, sis, it is safe inside my knapsack."

After boarding the horses, Tony turned to the raccoon as Heija and Gallopade flew upward. "Hey Razzi, where do you think Zor is right now?"

"Once ole Double Z gets a bandage on his leg, he'll figure a way to get even with me! He's probably working on his next low-down mean trick at this very moment. Since I'm the one who bit him, you know I'm his first target. The only way he would like me is if I was stone-dead."

Thinking about his own words, Razzi pulled his tail around himself and shivered from his head to his toes. "I take back all I said about Zor Zanger being full of hot air. He's a whole lot meaner than everyone said!"

CHAPTER 12

ESEL'S CASTLE

"I see Esel's castle straight ahead! It's all gray." Razzi exclaimed, staring through his telescope."

Excitement gave the exhausted group new hope as they flew. "Wouldn't it be perfect," Heija wished out loud, "if Esel came out to greet us, and he wanted to help us?"

"Aye, that would solve all our problems," Gallopade grunted, while searching the castle and grounds. "It bothers me that no one is around."

"Maybe they saw the beast horses last night," Molly said, "and everyone went inside like in Dome City."

Tony sniffed the air. "I don't smell smoke."

"We didn't smell smoke in the park either," Heija cautioned softly. "And Zor can use a bubble vehicle."

"Yeah, I know all about that." Razzi scowled.

"We've come too far to retreat now," Gallopade declared. "I think it's time to take a closer look."

"This place gives me the jitters." Razzi grumbled.

They glided down and landed quietly in front of the steps that led to the front door. There were only a few bushes, but no flowers around the two-toned gray castle. The horses wings disappeared and they kneeled for their passengers to jump off.

Tony tiptoed quietly up the steps to a massive wooden door. Under a life-sized metal tiger head was the door-knocker. The boy grasped the brass ring and knocked. The tiger's gleaming eyes opened, his mouth flew open showing sharp teeth and he roared.

"He's alive!" Tony yelped as he stumbled backward, nearly knocking Molly over at the bottom of the steps.

The door opened and an elderly woman in a blue uniform was in the doorway. "I heard the tiger's loud roar! I asked Esel to tame him, but he clearly forgot. I am sorry."

Tony's eyes were still on the metal tiger's head.

"Esel returned home last night," the lady continued. "He and the Wise Ones talked. You must be the earthlings. Welcome! Esel is anxious to meet you. Until Esel's other helpers arrive, I am working alone. Please come in."

"Did you hear that? Esel is here!" Molly's jubilant voice rang out and she bolted up the stairs. "Hurry everyone!" She stood by the greeter, smiling brightly.

Tony hoped Esel was not as scary as his tiger.

Molly was quick to follow the lady into the castle, while the others slowly trailed behind, wondering about the many enormous empty rooms along the way.

As if reading their minds, the woman explained. "We were remodeling when Esel was called away. Most of his furniture is upstairs."

After a long walk, they entered a spacious chamber filled with unusual inventions hanging from the high ceiling and off the walls. Comfortable furniture was abundant. The usual lamps, tables, and rugs gave the room a comfort factor. Light filtered through tall stained glass windows high on one wall, splashing color over the interesting room.

"You may freshen yourselves in the bathrooms down the hall." The maid pointed to another doorway. "I will gather a snack and announce your presence to the Master. Make yourselves comfortable." She hurried off.

The earthlings found the bathrooms first. Razzi enjoyed washing his face and paws. Once they assembled back in the large room, Gallopade nervously paced. "Do you think Esel is truly here and he'll help us?"

"I think so," Heija assured him. "We know Bumbles and the Wise Ones love him. When Esel saves the farm, we can go home." She knelt on a royal blue air-cushion. "These big pillows are amazingly comfortable."

The servant returned with a cart full of sandwiches and juices. "The Master cannot leave his experiments at present; however, he'll join you soon. Please eat and enjoy our books, puzzles, and games so you'll not be bored. I'll make arrangements for your lodging and the evening meal." She exited out another door.

Tony watched the woman leave. "That lady keeps reminding me of someone and I just figured it out. She looks like my fourth grade school teacher."

"I remember her," Molly joined in. "You're right. She could be her twin sister if we were on earth."

"Who cares what she looks like?" Razzi grumbled. "I'm just sick of waiting. We came a long way just to wait."

"I know how you feel," Gallopade admitted. "Maybe eating is a good idea. It's been a long day. Growling stomachs in front of Esel could be embarrassing."

Molly served the horses their food in big dishes. "Eat fast," she teased, "before Razzi eats it all!"

"After saving us from Zor, he gets all he wants!"

"Thanks, Tony," Razzi mumbled with a full mouth. "I'm starved! I never ate much after you guys saved me from the spiders. I was too mad and upset to eat."

"Aye. How can Zor have such a cruel heart to leave Razzi with those spiders? Yet, I remember what those wicked witches did to Deborah and me. I guess evil has no heart. If Esel will help us, we're going home!"

Heija nodded in agreement and yawned. "Between the food and these soft air-cushions, I feel sleepy from our long flight. Do you mind waking me when Esel comes?"

"Me, too," Molly whispered with drooping eyelids.

"We flew a long way," Gallopade said. "I'll call you when Esel comes. I'm too anxious to sleep myself."

Razzi brushed the crumbs from his face. "I don't intend to sleep until I talk to Esel no matter how sleepy I get. I just hope he hurries because I'm tired of waiting!"

"I know. How about us playing checkers to pass time," the stallion suggested. "I've not played in years."

"I'll watch," Tony mumbled, rubbing his eyes. "I always lose anyway. It's not my favorite game."

"Okay, you can keep us honest," Gallopade joked. "What color do you want, Razzi, red or black?"

"Red is my lucky color. Wow, how can the girls sleep with Esel so close?" He asked.

Gallopade pushed a checker with his nose. "I guess they feel safe now that we're in Esel's castle."

"I'm glad we got here alive!" Tony admitted with a wide yawn. "I'm still tired after fighting those awful spiders. And that close call in the park today was scary, too."

Gallopade nodded. "Are you going to play, Razzi?"

"I can't decide where to move," the little guy stared at the checkers. "I'm stumped. Tony, where should I move? Tony! Would you believe he's asleep in his chair?"

"I'll be asleep if you don't play soon," the stallion said playfully. "Are you going to move your checker?"

"I'll play, just give me time to think . . . ."

Trying to stay awake, Gallopade forced himself to look around. "It's getting dark! I hope Esel hurries. Okay Razzi, did you play?" He asked. When his eyes returned to his checker partner, the raccoon was softly snoring with his head resting on the checkerboard.

Gallopade fought his own drowsiness. He labored to stand up and stretch his muscles, but his knees buckled. He crumpled to the floor. The room spun. Instant fear clutched his heart as smoke stung his nostrils. He yelled a warning to deaf ears. A gruff voice and haunting laughter filled his senses as he passed out.

"I have them now! Ha! Ha! Ha! They're mine!"

––––––––––––

Strong smoky odors awoke Gallopade. His head jerked and his nose hit the taut confines around him. He was inside a rope cage with a flat wooden base under his body. There was no room to stand or move around. It was dark and he was being carried high in the air.

Iron hooves clanked above Gallopade as two beast horses carried him like a sack of fish, suspended from their strong unique harnesses. They were flying toward the glow of the Kingobe volcano.

"Zor has captured me!" The stallion muttered. "How did that happen? Everyone was sleepy . . . The food! That bloke tricked me again! I'm such a fool! Where's Heija and my buddies? I can't see through this smoke!"

One by one, in the heavy smoke, each of the prisoners awoke with the same frightening reality. Heija searched for Gallopade and her friends. Molly hiccupped. Tony yelled, but his voice was lost in the noise. Razzi pulled his tail over his nose to ward off the foul odor.

––––––––––––

Unknown to the prisoners or the abductors, the Wise Ones in Dome City were watching the unpleasant scene on their big screen. They could see Zor Zanger in his chariot. Behind him were other beast horses in a long line carrying captives in hanging rope cages across the sky.

"I knew this would happen," Birdie cried out. "Zor has captured our earthling friends!"

"It appears to me they are flying toward the Kingobe volcano," Queen Pearl ventured. "How can we help them?"

"We still have the old ray gun," Rose suggested.

"No!" Birdie cried out. "Definitely not! If we kill the beast horses, our earthling friends will also die!"

Conceding, Rose said, "That's true, sis. Although, we must ready the gun if we decide to use it later."

The queen stared at the screen. "Just as I thought, the herd is moving close to the volcano. If shelter exists nearby, it is a perfect hideaway for Zor Zanger. No one dares to go there! Esel was working on volcano energy. Zor has to be the one who stole Esel's ideas! And as we guessed, the heat from the lava is surely the source of Zor's strength. I feel sure Zor has imprisoned Esel, also."

"If that is so, why would Zor take the earthlings to Esel?" Rose asked. "Do you think Zor would threaten or hurt the earthlings to get Esel to tell his secrets?"

Birdie clamped her hand over her mouth. "If our suspicions are true, the earthlings are in appalling danger! Zor Zanger could easily hurt or kill all of them for Esel's secrets. Zor truly is a ruthless coward!"

"It is time for us to go there!" Rose declared.

"No. We must stay put!" the queen firmly replied. "Our powers and equipment are stronger here. If Zor would imprison us, Dome City would be his. We have few choices at this time. Zor is in control. We will send a coded message to Bumbles. Then we must wait and watch."

"Okay . . ." Rose said reluctantly. "Do you suppose there is any chance Esel will get the package we sent him? It could make all the difference."

The queen spoke with tight lips. "That package is only good if Esel is still alive and he receives it. Right now, I imagine Zor has it. If so, Esel and the earthlings are doomed. And we will be next in Zor's direct line of fire."

Birdie squawked with anger. "Zor is an ugly beast!"

"Yes. He is." The queen's words were thoughtful and calm, but the lines in her face crinkled deep and her lips were drawn tightly. After a time she spoke again.

"Zor adores games. Like a cat, he will only kill when he grows weary of playing with his prey. We must hope Esel receives our package in time and is able to use it. At this time, the package is his only chance of survival. However, we must brace ourselves. If Zor Zanger has the package, we may never see our brother or the earthlings ever again."

———

The beast herd soon disappeared from the queen's screen as they plunged into the red cloud layer, descending through the smelly dense clouds. When they broke through the thick vapor into an orange muggy light, they were high above the fiery red volcano.

Razzi stared at the bubbling lava below and cried out. "Zor's really mad at me for biting him. He's going to dump me in the volcano! Help me, somebody. Help me!"

CHAPTER 13

FRIENDLY PERSUASION

Razzi clung tightly to his rope cage as he felt the heat from the bubbling orange volcano below him. Hot vapor made it hard to breath and he nearly fainted thinking he would momentarily be dropped into the scalding lava.

It felt like an eternity before Razzi sensed a slightly cooler breeze touch his nose. He breathed deeply. The beast herd was gliding beside steep cliffs. Steaming rivers of bright molten matter was spilling into glowing creeks that oozed down the steep rocky mountainside.

Further down, the noisy herd still soared frightfully close to sheer stone cliffs. A glow from the volcano spread light through the thick hazy air. Close to the base of the mountain, the air cleared enough to see a bit further.

At that moment, Gallopade could see the lead horse pulling the chariot. It appeared as if he was about to crash into a huge black cliff at breakneck speed.

Gallopade flinched as the horses and their cages were swallowed in an immense shadowy opening.

Zor Zanger shouted. "Guard the entrance!" Several dark forms sprang from nowhere to do as the giant ordered. Gallopade felt their presence and saw the sparks from their hooves more than actually seeing them. The noise echoed against the cavern walls.

The herd quieted and the air cleared deeper into the earth. Dim wall beams lit the way. Gallopade heard Zor shout more orders from his chariot. "Do as I told you." Zor's chariot was whisked to the left and Gallopade was taken by the herd to the right. What was happening? His spine tingled, just thinking of the possibilities.

Next he observed the cave walls widening. His eyes hurt as they entered a brightly lit sizable chamber. The beasts lowered his cage to level ground, bit on clamps, and released the ropes to fall across Gallopade's body.

The beasts following behind repeated the action four more times and left the way they entered. Great iron doors clanked shut locking the captives inside.

Tony was first to work free of his rope net. He helped Razzi. They gave Molly a hand. Together, they freed Heija and Gallopade. The reunion was total joy.

When Molly pulled back from hugging Heija, the girl cried out. "Your harness is gone! Did Zor take it?"

"He must have, while I slept," Heija said with dewy eyes. "Now I realize Gallopade's harness is missing too. What happened after I fell asleep? We were waiting for Esel. Did anyone ever see the Majiventor?"

"No! It was Zor all along," Gallopade groaned. "Zor deceived us twice in one day the same way! I'm furious at myself for not catching on. By the time I heard Zor's laughter, I was passing out."

"I was fooled, too. Did he hurt any of you or steal anything else besides our harnesses?" Heija asked

"Esel's package is missing from my knapsack!" Tony grumbled. "But my other stuff is still here."

"That no-good thief took my cane," Razzi growled.

"Nothing that man does makes any sense. What does he want with us?" Heija asked.

A loudspeaker on the wall made a crackling noise, jerking them to attention. "Please, pass under the blue flashing light," a gentle voice told them. "It is perfectly safe, and I will answer all your questions."

"That's not Zor's voice," Tony whispered.

"I'll bet he's in another disguise," Razzi warned. "No telling what he has in mind this time. Just beware!"

Reluctantly, they passed under the light. Big blue doors swung open showing an impressive room with fine furnishings and fancy chandeliers. Light blue draperies covered the walls and dark blue carpet covered the floor. Good smelling food covered a long dining table.

A tall elderly gentleman with a full salt and pepper beard, a black suit and tall hat stood at the far end of the table. "I am happy you joined me, friends! Abraham is my name. Please make yourselves at home in our cushioned chairs and we will talk about your questions."

Everyone preferred to stand, ready to run.

"Let me see," Abraham pointed to the young girl. "You are Molly." He then called each one by their name. "The great Zor explained each of you to me. It is not often we see a group of visitors like yourselves. Please know you are safe and welcome."

"We didn't come here by choice," Gallopade voiced sharply. "We were put to sleep, taken hostage, and carried here in rope cages without our permission."

"In time you will be happy you came. Zor is sorry your last meal was only sandwiches, so he wanted you to have the best foods possible today. The washrooms are behind the white doors, and then we can eat and talk."

"What do you have in the food this time?" The stallion asked heatedly. "Twice Zor has ruined our meals. As for me, I don't trust his food and I refuse to eat."

The tall man shook his head as he spoke. "I am sorry for your bad experiences. But the food here is fine and I intend to eat with you to prove it."

Razzi crept behind the drapes unseen by Abraham and examined the plain stone walls. Then he hurried with the guys to wash while the girls found their washroom. As they returned, they gathered around the lovely table.

Abraham quietly ate. The food looked good. The earthlings finally ate a few things that Abraham was eating. None of the friends ate much.

With his last bite, Abraham wiped his face with a napkin. "Now we can talk. This is truly a fine place. I can relate to you because I was brought here by force years ago. I fought it at first then decided it was the best thing for me. Zor provided me with all my needs and desires. Let me show you some things behind these drapes."

"How can you show us anything?" Razzi asked. "Those walls are solid stone."

"This is a place full of wonder," said Abraham. He opened one drape wide. Everyone moved close to the window to see a pleasant country side.

Molly spotted a barn and pointed to the upper window. "That barn and the fields are like home, but the house is newer than Gramps and Memes."

"Our dwellings are the finest, with electricity, warm pools, and rich farm lands. Each house will be open to all, soon. There are many modern villages around Old World. Zor is making a whole new underground world."

Tony saw something that took his mind off his fears. "Look! That little yellow flying car is really nifty."

Abraham smiled and bragged proudly. "Yes, Tony, Zor gives each of us a new bubble machine every year. You can pick out your own style and color."

Tony sighed deeply. "I'll admit a speedy car could be a whole lot of fun."

"Yes, and we have many stores," Abraham went on. "Molly will love our library full of exciting books."

Gallopade and Heija were both about to voice their suspicious thoughts when two more curtains opened.

"Look at the fancy desserts," Molly exclaimed. "I always dreamed of ginger bread houses, pies and cakes, but the orphanage wouldn't let us have sweets." The girl pressed her face to the glass. "They look yummy."

"What kind of bribery is this?" Gallopade asked. "What do you want in return for these things you offer?"

"This is not bribery. It is just one of our shops and it will be for everyone who wants the good life."

"Then, where did the Kingobe volcano disappear?" Gallopade asked. "A volcano doesn't just vanish."

Abraham smiled. "The great Zor Zanger controls the volcano to create energy for his underground worlds. Our climate is perfect all year around, and our soil grows everything. Your Gramps and Meme would love this place. They could grow wonderful giant grapes without the worry of storms or starlings to eat their crops."

Heija flinched as she spoke. "Nothing you say makes sense! You know about Gramp's farm and its needs; yet, Zor ordered us to leave this world. Zor tricked Razzi and nearly killed him. Zor drugged us twice. Now he wants us to live in luxury? All you say is totally confusing."

"At first, Zor thought you wished to harm him, but now, he wishes to make up for his bad behavior."

"How does taking us prisoners make up for things?" Heija queried. "How does stealing from us make it better? Where are our harnesses and Razzi's cane? Your words are empty like a dry well."

"Would you have visited us, if we sent you an invitation?" Abraham inquired. "I think not! Zor will return your things, I promise. No robbery took place. Zor is just protecting your possessions. Let us forget the past and enjoy the present. Now, I will show you more windows."

"No more windows or bribes!" Gallopade's patience ended. His voice was filled with command and his front hoof stamped the floor. "Nothing is ever free! Zor needs something from us? Tell us what he wants."

"There is no need for violence, Gallopade," the tall man said, backing away. "The great Zor only desires to share with you. In return he might perhaps ask you to share trivial bits of information." The man shrugged.

"What information?" Gallopade demanded. His voice was still filled with annoyance.

"Since you insist, I'll give you an example. Zor is installing a security system around his property. He must control the entrances and exits and wants a system similar to Dome City." The tall man stated calmly. "Any suggestions you might have would be highly appreciated."

Gallopade's nostrils flared, "We know nothing! Dome City is the Wise Ones' private business! We were only there to find Esel! We believe Esel can help us."

"Esel?" Abraham said. "He is my good friend."

Looking up at him, Molly touched Abraham's hand. "We've been looking for Esel. Is he really your friend?"

"Certainly, child," Abraham answered, sitting down beside her. "Esel and Zor work together making this place a superb place to live. Esel is here helping Zor day and night. Are the sisters missing their brother?"

Molly stared into the man's friendly eyes and she smiled. "Oh yes! The Wise Ones love Esel. They do miss him. They sent him a package for his birthday."

Nudging Molly's back with his nose, Gallopade tried to limit her words. "That's of little importance, Molly. We'll tell Esel ourselves when we see him."

Molly continued to stare straight into Abraham's eyes. She grinned innocently as she stood and talked. "The Wise Ones sent Esel some peanut clusters. They also sent an old watch they found in the attic. It was a gift from Esel's daddy years ago. It's really old and doesn't work, but the Wise One's called it senta-mental. Did I say that right? It never worked but Esel played with it when he was a kid."

"For Pete's sake, Molly, stop your babbling!" Tony scolded, pulling his sister away from Abraham. "Don't pay any attention to her. She's just a kid who makes up stuff."

"I don't either!" Molly snarled. "I tell the truth."

Gallopade breathed a sigh of relief, when Molly stopped talking. "We truly want to speak with Esel. Is he working anywhere around here today?"

Molly interrupted. "Why did you say that, Tony?"

"You were talking too much, sis!" Tony scolded. Still fuming the boy looked squarely into the tall man's eyes. "Molly is just a little girl so . . . ah . . . ah . . . And she was about to tell you about Esel's code book. It's full of secret formulas that only Esel and his sisters can read."

Heija grabbed Tony's shirt with her teeth, and pulled him back away from the man. "Tony, stop looking at that man's eyes. He's compelling you to talk to him."

"What?" Tony shook his head. "What did I say?"

"Abraham is hypnotizing you," Gallopade's angry voice boomed. "It's another scam to seek information."

"I cannot believe your accusations," the old man said, standing up. "This young man and I were only engaging in simple talk. I will find Esel for you."

Molly rubbed her eyes. "What's hypnotized mean?"

"Never mind, child!" Abraham abruptly closed the drapes, his words impatient. "Follow me and I will take you to see my friend, Esel."

Razzi peeked behind the drapery again out of curiosity. He shouted out. "It's all a dirty trick! Abraham lied! Look at this! It's really horrible!"

All the friends hurried to the window. "There's nothing there but hot bubbling lava!" Tony wailed.

"I suspected that all along," Gallopade confided. "It was all just smoke and mirrors!" Angrily the stallion turned to confront the man. "Where did Abraham go?"

"Over here!" Razzi ran to the far side of the room. "He left the door wide open." The others peered over the raccoon's shoulders into the dark.

"He could be hiding anywhere," Heija uttered.

Molly patted Gallopade on the knee and stared up at him. "Does this mean Abraham fibbed and he was really Zor? Did that mean man fool me again?"

Gallopade's anger melted when he saw the girl's trusting eyes. "He deceived all of us, Molly. He wants something, but I can't figure out what. It all revolves around Esel. From what his sisters told us, I believe Esel's a good man and he wouldn't work with Zor. It makes me wonder if Esel is also a prisoner down here."

"For once, something makes sense!" Heija responded. "We know Abraham was fishing for secrets we might know. To take over Dome City he needs the Wise Ones' secrets. Could it be that Esel is down here, too, and won't give Zor the information he wants?"

Gallopade nodded, "That would explain why no one has seen Esel. If he is here, we must find him."

Tony grumbled. "I did everything wrong!"

Molly patted Tony's arm. "Abraham's eyes were so kind, I trusted him. I feel really bad, too."

Gallopade leaned his head close to the children. "Alas, it's not your fault. Zor's a master of trickery. I expect more deceit from him before we get free of him."

Following his lead, Heija tried to help the children feel better. "When we find Esel, he'll answer all our questions, just wait and see."

Molly grabbed Heija's neck and hugged her. "I'm really scared, but I feel better with you and Gallopade here. I love you both so much."

"We love you too, Molly," Heija assured her. "And, don't forget, Esel is very wise. He'll help us."

"Aye, and when we find Esel, he'll know a way out of here," Gallopade added. "And hopefully he can help us keep the farm so we can go home."

Tony looked into his sister's eyes. "I'm sorry I got cross with you, sis. You don't make up stories. I was trying to confuse Abraham, and then he made me say more than you did. Don't feel bad. We'll be okay."

Razzi peered through the open door into the darkness, and mumbled to himself. "I hope things will be okay, but to be truthful, I have some really strong doubts!"

CHAPTER 14

FIRE BELCHING DRAGONS

At first, the dark cavern where Abraham fled was terrifying to the earthlings. After a while, their eyes adjusted and they were amazed how well they could see. Small amber lights here and there lit the way.

The children and Razzi rode Gallopade and Heija expecting Zor Zanger to attack them at any moment. After a long walk, the cave unexpectedly split into three routes.

They selected the cave to their right to explore. After a long walk with little light, they noticed a pinhole of brightness in the distance. It gave the earthlings mixed feelings, but mostly hope for escaping the cave. As the round glow grew larger, the horses' hooves quickened and the radiance was more inviting by the second.

Abruptly, the bright light was cut off as if a door shut. Two enormous glaring eyes filled the open space. Sizzling sounds were heard and smoke filled the air.

"Go back, Heija!" Gallopade quickly shouted loud and clear. "Run for your life!"

The cave lit up when a ball of fire shot out of the beast's mouth, lurching through the cave behind the fleeing earthlings. Screams vibrated through the cavern as Heija ran as fast as her legs would carry her. Gallopade followed on her heels with bright flames biting at his tail and his riders. Even when the fire ceased, the horses rushed on until they returned to the fork in the cavern. They finally paused to catch their breath and regroup.

Still shaking, Tony asked, "Was that a dragon?"

"Without a doubt, it was a genuine dragon," Gallopade confirmed. "His fire nearly cooked us!"

"I thought dragons were only make-believe," Tony exclaimed. "But that thing belched actual fire!"

"Aye, fire spewed out of his mouth like a geyser." Gallopade inspected his legs and swished his tail as he talked. "That was close! I smell scorched!"

"Me, too," Razzi groaned as he sniffed his fur, "and I can tell you one thing for sure. I hate this place!"

"We do, too," Molly spoke for herself and Heija.

When they regained their strength and courage, they picked the center tunnel and moved at a slower pace. Once again, they eased toward a visible pinpoint of light. At the first sound of a dragon's snort, they fled. As they suspected, the dragon spewed fire into the cavern, but they outran the flames quicker the second time.

The third tunnel was their last chance. Seeing another tiny speck of light in the distance, they halted and Gallopade suggested a new strategy. "If Tony and Razzi will wait here, I'll go alone. Without their weight, I can run faster if a dragon fires again."

Razzi and Tony willingly slid to the ground.

"Please be careful, Gallopade," Heija pleaded with apprehension. Her heart pounded as the group watched the stallion move warily toward the light. The opening was square, unlike the previous round openings.

Before the stallion reached the huge entrance, he could see a long way past the opening, into what appeared to be a spacious arena. He estimated it was at least a hundred or more yards long, fifty yards wide and high. It was an enormous cavern.

As he crept closer, he noticed crimson red draperies covering much of the lower walls. He thought about the blue drapes Abraham had opened. Those drapes were used to hide things. Were these the same?

Gallopade inched closer to the huge opening. It had great iron doors swung open toward him. He guessed they held something in or out, but what? A snoring sound caught his attention. Ever so quietly, he peered around the metal corner of the wide entrance toward the noise.

A hefty dragon slept on the ground, with smoke curling from his nostrils. His hind leg was chained close to a metal post, next to a steaming water trough. The stallion saw an old wooden trunk between the dragon and a long row of black drapes, ten feet tall.

The black drapes continued along the left side of the huge room until they met more red drapes in the center of the long room. It all appeared bizarre to the stallion who inched forward into the near acre-sized room, hoping to see a door for escape.

Halfway down the wall on his right side, the red drapes were open, exposing metal bars. That is not good, he thought. As he crept forward, a small stone broke beneath the weight of his hoof. The dragon jerked upright.

To avoid the dragon's fire, Gallopade swiftly retreated back into the cavern. He was still between the opening and his friends when he stopped, waited and watched. Time passed and nothing happened. There was no smoke, no fire, and no glowing eyes? Why?

Gallopade's muscles quivered as he waited in nervous anticipation. After much delay, he edged forward again, very quietly. At the doorway, he peeked around.

The dragon snarled and strained against his chains like an angry watchdog ready to kill an intruder. The beast's tail swung back and forth with smoke coming from his mouth. He flashed a long slithering tongue in and out, not reaching the opening. Enraged, the dragon bellowed and the stallion ran again. Yet, no fire followed.

Gallopade gathered his courage, and slipped to the entrance once again. Seeing no spewing fire, he crept along the wall to his right until he reached the red drapes. At that point, he edged slowly forward to look inside the metal bars. A motionless man in a dirty gray robe was lying on a cot with his eyes closed. The bars were locked.

For a moment, Gallopade wanted to call out, but thought better of it. He backed away, retraced his steps, slid past the dragon, and galloped back to his friends.

Heija had paced anxiously until his return. Upon hearing his story, she whispered. "Surely that poor man in prison is not Esel, the Majiventor! We must find out."

"Aye, we must. So far this dragon has no fire, but he is mean," Gallopade cautioned. "He would kill us if not for that chain. Heija and I should go in first."

"Why not," Razzi said quickly. "We can wait."

"Let us go with you. We'll be quiet." Tony said.

"It could easily be a trap," Gallopade warned them.

"If it is, we still need to be together," Heija replied.

Razzi shivered. He wanted to run, but where? He had no desire be left alone so again he followed.

The group moved forward with Tony on Gallopade and Razzi straggling behind. The dragon bellowed as the stallion led his friends into the arena, moving close along the wall. Molly leaned toward Heija's neck, frightened that the dragon's whiplike tongue might reach her.

Razzi hesitated, afraid to enter the arena. He waited until his friends reached the metal bars before he scooted like a gray streak to catch them. They peered inside.

Before they could awaken the old man, they heard a grinding sound behind them. They spun around toward the entrance they had just walked through. The wide metal doors clanked and locked shut.

A moment later, Abraham slipped through the black draperies and stepped into the arena. His smile was gone. He entered the arena close to the noisy dragon. The beast immediately hushed and cowered at the farthest end of his chain away from the man in black.

Abraham bent down by the post holding the chain, and released a clamp, giving the chain more length. The dragon slunk even further away from the man, and sat in front of the recently closed metal doors.

"That stupid dragon is right in front of the only doors I see, the ones we came through," Razzi's voice was low but panicked. "Do you guys see another way out?"

The bearded man stood up straight, slim as a stove pipe, and walked proudly toward them. Tony realized he looked exactly like Abraham Lincoln's photos.

"So . . . ." The man sneered "You found your beloved Esel. I told you he was here and you could see him. Of course you were stubborn and did it your way."

Backing up, the group sought an avenue of escape.

"Trust me." Abraham spoke with a shrewd smile. "My dragons have all the exits guarded. I very generously let you in. Escaping is a different story. In fact, getting out of here depends strictly on your full cooperation with me and of course our leader, Zor Zanger, himself."

In his hand, Abraham held a brass key with a red strap attached to it. He unlocked the cell door, opened it, and said, "Enjoy your new home!" Hearing the terrible words from inside the cell, the man on the cot struggled to sit up and observe what was happening.

"Go inside, now! Meet your famous Esel. This is what you wanted and what I promised you." Abraham's words were cutting. "You may talk all you want."

"You are locking us inside?" Heija asked.

"That's why I'm holding the keys," Abraham jibed.

Gallopade stood his ground. "I'll gladly do as you ask, but please, I beg of you, let my friends go home. They're no treat. They are helpless bystanders in this."

"Good words for a gentleman, Gallopade; however, only Zor Zanger can help you now. I only do as he bids. Go inside, now!" He ordered. "I'm a busy man! Don't keep me waiting!" The man's face flushed with impatience.

Not trusting Abraham, Heija darted inside the cell's entrance carrying Molly on her back. Gallopade was last to enter the prison cell. The iron bars slammed behind him, and they watched in horror as Abraham turned the brass key and locked them inside.

Tony lashed out in anger. "Abraham, you told us you were our friend! Why're you locking us in here?"

Abraham stood tall. "It's simple. Persuade Esel to share his energy potion with Zor Zanger! If you can do that, my great leader will gladly let you go. Even Gramp's farm might be saved. You'll be rewarded well for your help."

The man turned and walked to where he entered and he slipped between the closed black curtains.

The stunned friends stared at their not so roomy enclosure. High ceiling bulbs gave adequate light. There would be no escaping the metal bars and stone walls. It had taken a lot of work to prepare the large pieces of stone with masonry to make the walls into prison cells.

The floor was dirt. A few old blankets were strewn on two flimsy cots. Razzi peeked through the door in the back wall which led to a windowless grimy bathroom.

The old man sitting on the cot had to lean against the wall to remain upright. His hair was uncombed and stringing over his face and shoulders. The old man's haggard eyes stared at them without feeling or words.

Gallopade swallowed hard and spoke softly. "Sir, are you really Esel, the Majiventor?"

A brief glimmer appeared in the man's blue-gray eyes. He was thin, with a shaggy beard the same color as his thinning gray hair. "And who are y-you?" He uttered.

"Bumbles sent us to find you," Gallopade explained.

"My brother . . . did w-what?" His voice trailed off and his eyes rolled back.

"This poor man needs nourishment," Heija voiced with concern. "Zor must be starving him!"

Tony rummaged through his knapsack and pulled out a chocolate bar for the frail man. The boy opened the wrapper. "Eat this, if you can, sir."

The man weakly clutched the candy with his thin fingers and pulled it to his quivering mouth. His eyes closed as he savored the taste. Slowly, he nibbled.

After a while the frail man was able to speak in a whisper. "Zor quit feeding me. Before that, he fed me very little. Thank you for sharing."

"Here," Tony offered. "Take another candy bar."

"Please keep it for later, child," he replied. "Too much food all at once will sicken me. You are very kind." He pulled his tattered robe close to his neck and gazed at them. "I f-feel a bit stronger now," he acknowledged with a faint smile. "Please, tell me about my brother."

"Yes sir, your brother was healthy the last we saw of him. He sent us here. My name is Gallopade. Because Zor is a trickster, I must be rude and ask you if you are the real Esel. Will you tell us something about your identity that your sisters know, but Zor doesn't know?"

"Why would the Wise Ones tell you anything about me?" The feeble man quizzed back in a low whisper.

"Your kind sisters knew we were looking for you. They helped us prepare for this trip and even gave us a package to deliver to you. Then, of course that devil, Zor Zanger, stole it from us."

The man's forehead wrinkled and he raised up a bit. "My package is in Zor's hands? How did that happen? The package is important and was my last hope to escape."

Gallopade's eyes widened. "You were expecting the package? How did you know? It was a surprise."

Slumping down again, Esel's face drained to an ashen white. Barely audible, he rasped, "I knew Zor was after me before he succeeded in abducting me. I asked my sisters to send me something, before I was taken prisoner. When the Wise Ones could not locate me they must have taken a wild chance hoping you could find me."

"You might say we found you the hard way," Gallopade told him. "We were captured also. However sir, to this point, you have not told us anything that Zor could not tell us. Please show us you are the real Majiventor."

The man feebly reached into his mouth and plucked out a dark wisdom tooth with an imbedded blue diamond on its back side. "Is this what you want to see?"

Heija leaned close whispering. "Thank you sir, we are so pleased to finally meet you."

"What is left of me, you mean," Esel told her as he replaced his tooth. "Tell me everything. I can listen better than talk. How did you find me and why?"

"First off, we are sorry Zor is treating you so badly. And I apologize, sir, for not trusting you," the stallion said.

"Distrust is part of being close to Zor," Esel replied. "You were wise to test for the truth. Your accent tells me you are from Earth."

"Aye, we are." Gallopade relaxed and introduced everyone by name. Each of the prisoners settled into more comfortable positions. The children and Razzi found places to sit on the ground along with the horses. In a small circle the group talked as quietly as possible.

Gallopade started at the beginning with the witches turning Ian and Deborah into wooden rocking horses. He explained how they woke up two hundred years later, and became Gerty and Clyde.

They gave details about Molly and Tony's hardships, how a witch changed Razzi's life forever, and all about Gramp's and Meme's troubles.

Everyone filled in parts of the story about the storm and the makeshift tent. Razzi told how he first saw the little man in the fairytale book. Heija explained about the hope they felt when Bumbles sent them to Dome City. "He suggested we seek your help to save the grape crop. We were in wooden prisons then; yet, we wanted to help."

They told about nearly being eaten in Old World, and how the rocking horses had become Heija and Gallopade with Esel's machine. Then the Wise Ones gave them wings so they set out to find Esel's help.

The old man lifted his hand feebly. "It would be my greatest honor and pleasure to help you, but as you can see, Zor has rendered me helpless. I need my wand, my herbs, my laboratory, and my chemicals to work what appears to be supernatural. Zor covets my knowledge to use for his own selfish powers. He cares nothing about hurting others. Now, he has my package . . . he may win."

"I'm so sorry," Molly whined with a hiccup. "Abraham fibbed to me. He acted like a friend and I believed him, so I told him all about your package."

When Esel heard her words, he gasped and his eyes bulged. "You told Zor all about my package?"

Molly cowered behind Tony. "Abraham hypnotized us," the boy protested. "We intended to keep your secret, but Zor tricked us. My sister only told him about the candy and watch, but I was the really bad one. I told Zor the code book was important. We're very sorry, sir."

Esel eased back. "Do not be afraid of me, children. I am sorry I overreacted. What is done is done. Zor is so focused on what he wants that he will do anything. You saved me with your chocolate and I am very thankful. Let us hope Zor labors hard and long trying to decode my code book. What else did Zor steal?"

Bitterly, Razzi complained. "My gift from the Wise Ones was this bow tie and a fine telescope cane. That ole Double Z stole my cane. It was my favorite gift ever."

Heija hung her head in sadness. "Zor took Gallopade's and my special harnesses."

"Without them," Gallopade whispered, "we cannot fly." For comfort the couple huddled close together.

Razzi spoke up. "Abraham promised he would return our stuff. Does he ever keep any of his promises?"

Esel looked very tired again. "We must hold Abraham to every promise he makes. When he comes back, beg him for everything, especially the code book." The old man curled up on his side then remembered something. He propped his head on his elbow.

"One more thing," he whispered. "I saw Zor place something sparkly inside the chest by the dragon."

"Did you see jewels and tassels?" Heija asked.

"Yes, I think so." Esel's voice was growing weaker.

Gallopade arose and stretched his muscles then stared at the chest behind the sleeping dragon. He spoke quietly. "The trunk is close, but the dragon guards it!"

"Zor hid your harnesses in the safest place possible," Esel told them. "That dragon is so starved, he would eat anything. You folks look like a fine meal to him. Fair warning, beware of that beast."

"Why is the dragon afraid of Zor?" Tony asked.

Esel rubbed his eyes. "A while back, Zor gave the dragons lots of food to entice them into the cave. Once they were all inside, that evil man locked them in. After that, the dragons had no food, except what Zor fed them. The reptiles are intelligent and realized they must protect Zor or starve to death. Zor became their master."

"That lousy man makes me mad!" Tony snarled with tight lips. "He never plays fair. He's mean to kids, old folks, and now dragons. They have feelings too."

Esel yawned. "Zor only feeds the poor creatures tiny amounts of briars and thistles at a time. It is no wonder they are mean. But, that's how the selfish man wants it. He uses everything to his personal advantage."

"Things might look better after we rest," Heija said.

"I must warn you," Esel pointed his skinny finger at the arena. "Zor frees that dragon at night. For some unknown reason, the monster does not blow fire, but his breath can singe you. Sleep away from the bars."

Razzi curled himself by the back wall, under Esel's cot, away from the metal bars. He mumbled to himself. "Without my fur, no one would know me! I wouldn't know myself! I gotta keep away from those dragons!"

Molly had already fallen asleep on the other cot; yet, Tony remained wide-eyed. "I'm too restless to sleep right now so I'll watch for Zor," he told Gallopade.

"Thanks, Tony," Gallopade sounded tired. "I could use some shut-eye. I'll stand guard when you get sleepy."

The stallion turned to Heija and gazed into her sad green eyes. They placed their heads together and he whispered in her ear. "Somehow, Heija, I promise you, we will find our way out of here. We *will* fly again."

CHAPTER 15

STEAMING HOT CHOCOLATE

While his friends slept, the boy sat on the dirt in the back corner; a stone wall on his right and a cot on his left. He wrapped his arms around his bent knees. Tony hoped that keeping watch outside those hideous bars might give him clues which would help them escape.

In the arena, black bats darted around the high ceiling lights. At times the dark streaks zipped around the dragon's head and his steaming water.

A rat family of five scampered single file in front of the cell bars. They moved toward the locked metal doors the earthlings had first entered. Three of the rats were large, one medium, and the fifth was tiny with a stub tail. As they scampered away, Tony pondered their intentions. Did they go out every night looking for food?

Zor must have a kitchen. Even an evil man had to eat. Maybe that tiny rat had lost his tail to a meat cleaver. Ugh! Tony hated that thought. With a shiver, he rubbed the goose bumps on his arms and rolled under the cot on his stomach. Did I hear a door close? He wondered.

Across the arena, near the dragon's post in the corner, Abraham crept through the drapes into the arena wearing a black robe and slippers. He carried sticks in a wire basket, set it on the ground, and peered around.

Seeing no one watching, Abraham snuck quietly along the black curtains. He walked close to the wall. a quarter of the length of the arena and pulled the drapes open wide enough to reveal a glowing chamber.

Abraham entered the light through a sliding glass door, removed his robe revealing his red and white striped shorts. He then laid down on a long cushioned bench.

Tony thought the sight was so funny; he clamped his hand over his mouth to keep from giggling. Abruptly, Abraham stood up, hurried to the open drapes and closed them, leaving the boy to wonder.

When Abraham disappeared behind the black curtains, the dragon snorted and slunk from his corner to sniff the briars. Tony had to crawl quietly toward the bars to watch the beast eat his little sticks.

The beast pulled the briars to his mouth with his tongue and groaned while he chewed the thorns. A sizzling sound could be heard as he drank his hot water and steam rolled from his nose up to the ceiling. The bats zoomed through the gray column.

Tony moved back to his place under the cot lying on his tummy. He imagined what Gramps and Meme would think if he brought a dragon home? He smiled at the thought. My dragon would have a barn full of hay, a cool pond for water, and he would prance across the green grassy fields. The farm would make him a fine home.

Tony's head nodded and thudded against the ground. He sat up with his back to the wall and rubbed his eyes. Don't go to sleep, he scolded himself silently. What if something important happens? I don't want to miss anything. There has to be a way to escape this place.

Tony's eyelids were closing when a click caught his attention. Abraham, in his black robe, withdrew from his bright room. He closed the drapes and walked toward the dragon. The boy was amazed at the man's glowing skin!

Abraham pulled a short wand from his pocket and pointed it toward the dragon's leg. The locked metal band snapped free, releasing the reptile. The trembling brown dragon ran to his usual spot by the locked iron doors.

Why is that monster dragon so afraid of Abraham? Tony asked himself while he watched the glowing man walk to the corner and disappear behind the black curtains. To keep himself awake, the boy idly reached in his knapsack for a chocolate bar. The wrapper crackled through the silence alerting the dragon.

The beast ran toward the sound and stood close to the bars, peering inside, immediately heating the room. Tony stood up and pressed hard against the back stone wall. He waved his hands wildly to scare the critter away. The candy softened between his fingers and as Tony swung his hands, the sweet morsel abruptly spun through the air, falling directly upon the dragon's nose.

Crossing his eyes, the curious beast stared at his nose. His long tongue curled around the candy and pulled it where he could smell it. When the candy disappeared into his mouth the beast made a quick lunge backward, ran in circles, and rolled over in the dirt, kicking his legs.

Standing again, the dragon shook the dirt from his body sending dust in all directions, making Tony sneeze. The reptile darted back to the bars, staring at the boy with pleading eyes. He reminded Tony of a big playful puppy.

Tony threw another piece of candy. The dragon's tongue plucked it from midair and zipped it into his mouth extremely fast. He pranced around, swinging his tail, and he repeat the circling, rolling, and kicking.

Looking down, Tony saw melted candy on his fingers. He smiled and whispered. "From now on, I'm calling you Hot Chocolate. Yeah, I like that name."

The creature returned, pushing his head against the cell bars. His tongue stretched out eagerly toward the boy, and his huge eyes begged for more.

With the reptile's outstretched tongue so close, Tony felt his stomach tighten into a knot. His neck hairs stood on end. He could be eaten any moment; yet, something was different. Strangely, the dragon's breath was not so hot. The boy carefully placed another piece of candy gingerly upon Hot Chocolate's tongue.

With a quick response, the dragon zipped the morsel carefully into his mouth. Once again, he began his dragon dance in the arena. He only stopped when he heard a noise. Like a frightened rabbit, Hot Chocolate immediately turned and ran to his corner by the iron doors.

Tony watched the non-glowing Abraham return in his robe again to the glow room. When the tall man disappeared behind the black curtains, Tony's attention switched to the returning rats. They were carrying morsels of cheese, meat, and bread back to their den. Tony smiled, knowing he had guessed right about Zor's kitchen.

The bats returned to the arena's ceiling. The sleepy boy wondered how the creatures knew night from day in a cave. Each of the bats found their special spot and hung upside down, clinging to the high upper dome. They wrapped themselves with their flexible wings while they slept. Tony also fell fast asleep after the long night's investigation, never seeing Abraham leave the arena.

The dragon's squalling and noisy chains aroused the prisoners from their slumber, except Tony who slept under the cot. The cell was as dreary as the day before. After cleaning up the best they could, the group waited for Abraham and talked quietly among themselves.

"Will Zor give us food today?" Gallopade asked.

Esel yawned. "Zor's cook is a small oriental fellow named, Shoko. He will bring us food, if he can," Esel said. "Zor never allows his cook to carry keys or talk much."

"Could Shoko help us in any way?" Heija asked.

Esel shook his head. "It is doubtful. The tiny fellow is much like the dragons, extremely fearful of Zor."

Molly emptied her shoe. "Shoko won't need to feed Tony for a while, because he won't be hungry. There were three candy bar wrappers tucked in my shoe."

"Quickly child, bury those wrappers!" Esel ordered. "If Zor knows about the knapsack, he will take it away. Tony's food could keep us alive if Zor refuses to feed us."

Molly did so, but could only bury the wrappers two inches down before hitting stone. She smiled at her sleeping brother. "He must be dreaming. He looks happy." Her smile vanished when Abraham returned.

The man walked briskly across the arena greeting his prisoners with a cheerful voice. "Good morning! How are my guests today? You look rested."

No one answered. Heija watched him, pondering how such a cheerful man could be so cold-hearted.

Abraham dangled their cell key in front of their faces as he observed each prisoner. "This place is grim! You see this key in my hand? I'm ready to set you free, if you have my information ready. I presume you persuaded Esel to share his secrets."

"Aye, free is what we want. However, we tried to talk with Esel but he's far too weak." Gallopade explained. "This gentleman needs food and medical care."

Esel was lying across his cot, not moving.

Gallopade went on. "When Esel tries to speak, his memory is hazy. He mumbles about his code book. Maybe with food and his code book in front of him, he could help us. My friends and I are truly hungry, also."

The smile faded from Abraham's face. "Esel's biggest problem is his gigantic stubborn streak."

"Look at him, sir. He's extremely frail," Gallopade stressed. "If Esel can't give us the information you want, how long will Zor keep us here? We're in desperate need to return back to earth to help Gramp's with his farm. Can you help us, Abraham? If you talk with Zor Zanger about our needs, we'll try to help you all we can."

Pulling at his black vest, Abraham's eyes squinted. "If Esel will not share his strength formula, Zor will be very angry. There will be serious penalties. Before you expect pity for Esel, my leader must see Esel's good intentions."

With an effort, Esel rolled over to face Abraham and barely whispered. "Sir, I want to help these good folks. If you will bring food and my code book, it might strengthen both my mind and body. I will honestly try to help you."

"You are bluffing, old man!" Abraham exclaimed. "You know your secrets without a code book. Do not lie to me. You know them by heart. You simply refuse to share with Zor Zanger. You're deliberately being stubborn."

"No," Esel strained to say. "I am old, weary and hungry. I cannot remember as I once could. The code book would help me remember complicated formulas. Without food, I am too weak to think. Please do not punish these fine folks or me for my old age and memory failure."

Heija stepped forward. "This poor man needs food. We've asked you for simple things like food and the code book. You promised Zor would return our harnesses and Razzi's cane, too. Why have you not done that? Do you and Zor have a good excuse for your bad memory?"

Abraham backed up a step. "Returning your property may be impossible right now. Zor Zanger has it."

"But, you promised!" Razzi exclaimed. "What good is that code book to Zor, if he's too dumb to read it?"

"Dumb? You called Zor dumb? How dare you!" Abraham's skin turned crimson. "One more remark from you, Bandit, and Zor will have you boiled in today's stew."

Razzi pulled back so fast, he stumbled and fell. Heija hurried to his defense. "Leave him be! You have lied to us, locked us up, starved us, and now threatened us. Only spineless cowards act that way!"

Abraham yelled in anger. "Shut your mouth, you stupid wench. How dare you call me or Zor names! You'll pay dearly for your insults!"

Gallopade's ears flattened. "Take that back, Abraham! Heija is a fine lady and does not deserve this terrible treatment. She spoke the truth! Zor is the one doing us wrong! You need to apologize to Heija!"

"I'll take nothing back," Abraham yelled, his eyes glaring at Heija. "She'll pay for her words." He pivoted on his heel and marched away at a rapid pace.

Molly looked puzzled. "If he is Zor, why does he look like Abraham Lincoln? He keeps trying to look like a good guy, but he acts meaner than that hungry dragon."

Esel eased up again to a sitting position, stretching his muscles. Looking into each of the earthling's eyes he spoke quietly, but firmly. "Please know that as long as Zor remains in the form of Abraham, he can pretend to be kinder. Zor himself will show no kindness."

"Wow!" Razzi commented. "If Abraham is showing kindness I'm in big trouble. He already wants to boil me in the stew. What would Zor do that was worse than that?"

"You would already be in the stew!" Esel told him.

Razzi shivered and hid behind his tail in the corner.

"We must be very careful about what we say." The Majiventor looked sternly at each of them as he spoke. "Zor is an extremely dangerous man. I hoped he might return our stolen items. Now, to be truthful, it is doubtful. Zor may keep our possessions for spite. He hates for people to say anything bad about his nature."

"This is my fault," Heija confessed. "Abraham made me angry and I lost my temper. I cannot stand bullies, but I must learn to control myself. My temper never helps me or others. I feel so ashamed." She lowered her head.

Gallopade placed his head close to hers. "You only told him what all of us felt. I'm proud of you as always, although; Abraham's threats cause me great concern."

Heija gazed at Gallopade. "You came to my defense against that heartless man and I truly thank you and love you for being so caring and brave. Now it is you I worry about, after you talked back to Abraham."

The stallion hated seeing Heija hurt. "He had no right to speak to you in that manner. You're always gentle, kind, beautiful, and I . . . ." The words came to a sudden halt when his knees turned to jelly and he realized everyone was watching. He loved Heija so much. Why was it impossible for him to tell her out loud? Angry at himself, he quickly changed the subject.

"Look! Tony's awake! Perhaps he saw something last night that will help us get out of here."

CHAPTER 16

ESEL'S SECRET

Tony stretched and opened his eyes to see all his friends waiting for him to awaken.

Molly whispered. "I found your candy wrappers in my shoe this morning, so I guessed you stayed awake a long time. Did you see anything that might help us?"

The drowsy boy crawled upon the cot and grinned. "Last night was sort of exciting," he said quietly and the night's events poured out. Tony enjoyed being the center of attention, hoping something he said would help.

Molly joined Tony on the cot. "Did that dragon really stick his tongue in here? That's yucky! I'm glad I was asleep or I would have screamed with fright."

"He loves candy as sure as I'm sitting here," Tony said. "But it was sort of creepy knowing he could eat me."

Heija shuddered. "I'm thankful this dragon you call Hot Chocolate only wanted the candy."

"If I only had briars to eat, I'd like candy too!" the stallion said, "but what puzzles me, is why Abraham rests in that glowing room? And why does he glow afterwards?"

"I can tell you," Esel said, folding his blanket, "although, it might take some time."

"Time is all we have at the moment." Gallopade moved his head closer to Esel so he could hear well. "Please tell us everything you know."

"As you wish," Esel said leaning against the wall. "Over a year ago, I went to another planet on an important mission. When I returned, a robber had stolen everything from my laboratory and left no clues. All my prepared potions, secret non-coded notes, and my new invention, the image machine was gone.

My notes were about the use of energy from natural sources like volcanoes. It was my hope to benefit millions of people." Esel stopped to catch his breath.

"Now, I realize it was Zor who took my work. My notes guided him in building that glow room! The unique glass on the far side of the glow room changes the volcano's heat into rays of energy. I invented that myself!

Zor has learned the power of my special energy. It not only makes the giant man glow, but the rays strengthen his mind as well as his body. By going to that room often, he wants more power as fast as possible.

"When I saw the volcano's raging fury, I knew it was Zor who robbed me. He poured my secret potion into the sleeping volcano. The potion woke up the Kingobe and it became active again. Since Zor is using that glow room steadily, I wonder how strong he has become."

"If Zor is working with all your things," Gallopade enquired, "what exactly does he need from you?"

Esel ran his fingers through his hair to pull it from his eyes. "A while back, Zor told me he poured all my prepared potion into the volcano. He has none left and no formula to make a new potion. Without it, the volcano will cool soon. If that happens, Zor will lose his strength and he will return back into his miserable weak self again."

"Now I understand why your energy formula is so important to that wicked man." Heija said, peeking around to check the arena.

"Yes, Heija, Zor is heartless. He only thinks of himself. That makes my energy formula more important to us!" Esel said emphatically. "If Zor learns my secrets, I am sorry to say, he will have no use for any of us."

The earthlings all shared a fearful glance, realizing their lives depended on the information they were hearing.

Esel took a deep breath and began talking again. "Zor failed to get my formula when he robbed me, because I had it with me. Soon after the robbery, I visited with my sisters, the Wise Ones. We worked together to create a secret code to safeguard all our written work. At that time, we could see the Kingobe glowing so we invented a potion to cool the volcano. The Wise Ones worked on half of the cooling potion, and I made the other half at my castle. The very day before I was kidnapped, I delivered my half to my sisters in Dome City. It was the last day I was free.

Esel held his head in misery. "I was exhausted when I returned to my castle. I let my guard down and Zor outsmarted me. He used my image machine to appear as my trustworthy maid. While I slept, he stole my wand and brought me here."

"What do you think Zor will do next?" Heija asked.

The old man fixed his wise eyes on her. "Zor will become extremely strong physically," Esel answered. "However, it is not his physical strength that I fear as much as his ability to read our thoughts and memories."

Heija gasped. "He can read our minds?"

"Yes." Esel said bluntly. "He will eventually be able to see our most secret thoughts if he can stare into our eyes. With my image machine, he will not only appear in any form he chooses, but he can make images from our thoughts. His abilities will constantly improve as long as the volcano stays active."

"That's hair-raising!" Gallopade said. "I didn't think anyone could know my thoughts besides my maker!"

Molly sprang to her feet. "Zor must have used your image machine to make Gramps look so real, when we visited Rainbow Septar. I wondered how Zor did it. Razzi bit Zor's leg that day and saved us!"

"Good for you Razzi," Esel patted the raccoon on his head. "Yes, Molly, my image machine can work wonders. I only wish it was working for the good of mankind, and not for Zor's evil uses."

Still happy from Molly and Esel's remarks, Razzi remembered Sasha, before Zor revealed himself. "Where did Zor find Sasha? Did he read my dreams?"

"No, Razzi," Esel answered. "He probably made a good guess. Most males are attracted to pretty females. However, from what everyone is telling me, Zor's powers are growing much faster than I thought. Once he can search my eyes and pull all my secrets from my mind to his, he will not need me."

"Surely, you have some powers left, Esel," Tony said. "Can't you help us escape and somehow stop him?"

"Without my equipment, I am just an old man. My mental strength comes from the knowledge I have learned for many years. That knowledge helps my research and even what appears as supernatural feats. With knowledge, I add specific chemical ingredients and with my wand, great things happen. My wand has electrical impulses that Zor has not yet learned. At this time, I have no idea how long I can keep my secrets from Zor."

"We must see to it, that Zor never looks into your eyes," Gallopade declared. "We must also concentrate on escaping this place and as soon as possible.

"At one time, I thought escape was possible."

"Please, Esel, what were your thoughts."

"Well Gallopade, as I told you," the man stretched out on his cot, "my sisters and I developed a formula to cool the volcano, so Zor would lose his powers. I hoped my sisters would guess Zor kidnapped me and get those capsules to the volcano or me. It was my last real hope. When you told me Zor had my package, my hopes were shattered. I really wanted those capsules! Now, Zor has outsmarted me again by not returning our possessions."

"What are the capsules?" Gallopade questioned. "We thought the code book was what you wanted."

Molly smiled and whispered in Esel's ear. "Does that mean I didn't spill the beans to Zor?"

"You actually said everything perfectly, Molly." Esel gave her an approving wink of his eye. "I didn't tell you before, for fear of putting you in more danger. I hoped the code book would buy us more time."

Hot Chocolate bellowed, alerting the prisoners that trouble was once again arriving.

Abraham looked sleepy as he approached the prison bars. His clothing was rumpled and his hair mussed. He spoke in a quiet, needful manner. "We worked all night trying to learn your energy formula! Zor Zanger is begging you, Esel. What do you want? Power? Freedom? What?"

The tall man's quiet manner was unsettling to the earthlings so they said not a word. Esel remained quiet too, lying on his back, looking at the ceiling.

Abraham shifted from one foot to the other. "Okay Esel you win! I know Zor Zanger promised you he would make you the galaxies' most respected advisor. I can even arrange for your friends to be set free if you can enlighten me." Abraham held out a pen and paper. "Just write your formula here, so we can move on to more prosperous and happy times."

"Fame is not my desire, sir," Esel said quietly. "I would like freedom for my friends and myself. But, Abraham, can you promise me that Zor will help all living creatures, and not just himself, a power-hungry thief?"

"Are you calling the great Zor Zanger a thief?" Redness crept over Abraham's face again.

"I call them as I see them," Esel declared. "Zor robbed the earthling's. They asked you, Abraham, to return their things. You promised that Zor would. He has not. That makes Zor or you a thief!"

Abraham paced back and forth. He no longer appeared sleepy, but brimming with anger. "You're playing this game like a fool, old man. If the great Zor Zanger does not have your formula soon, your precious earthling friends fall into great danger." The man's fist pulled free from his jacket pocket and the large hand heaved several items through the bars onto the ground. "Zor always keeps his promises! But, I swear to you, Zor Zanger is losing his patience. Give your energy formula to me now in a civil way, or prepare to meet the Zor Zanger's wrath!" Abraham turned in anger to leave.

Heija stomped her hoof in the dirt and cried out. "Abraham! You're a bully. We want our harnesses returned! And where is Esel's code book and Razzi's cane? You and your great leader have not kept your word to us."

Abraham left the arena without another word.

Razzi shivered. "I hope Abraham is not having stew today! He was really mad!"

Esel sat up immediately. "Never mind his temper, Razzi!" the Majiventor ordered. "Find every single item he threw between the bars. Find them now!"

"Okay, sir," Molly said, crawling under the cot. "Here's some dirty peanut candy."

"Icky-sticky, candy," Tony groaned. "Here's another peanut cluster."

Razzi grasped an object. "Here's that good-for-nothing old watch. Why didn't Abraham give my cane back instead of this worthless thing? I want my cane back!"

"Quick, Razzi, hand me the watch!" Esel asserted.

"But it's all broken and covered with dirt," Razzi said, dusting it off. "Is it really that sentimental to you?"

"Razzi! Hand it to me!" Esel grabbed the timepiece and placed his back to the bars. "Keep guard for Abraham! Tell me at once if you see him!" Urgency filled his voice.

"What's happening?" Molly asked in a tiny voice. "Is the watch important?"

Barely audible, Esel said. "This old piece of junk may be just what we need. I think the Wise Ones sent it because it does not look valuable. Hopefully Zor has not tampered with it." Dislodging the watch's back panel, the Majiventor shook the case, with his finger pushing on the stem. A metal capsule fell on the cot. He twisted it, and a tiny blue nugget fell out, wrapped in a coded message.

Everyone held their breath, waiting, while Esel studied the code. His shoulders slumped. "We now have two parts of the cooling potion." His voice was weary.

"Why isn't that good news?" Gallopade asked. "I don't understand."

"We need a third part," Esel revealed. "My sisters hoped Gallopade would be wearing his harness when he delivered my package."

"They put something in my harness? Why did they hide the potion in different places?"

"The capsules or nuggets can be explosive if they are placed together for more than a day," Esel said. "This was the only safe way my sisters knew to send them."

"If there are three nuggets," Tony pondered, "one in Gallopade's harness and one in the watch, then where is the third nugget?"

Esel smiled. "Right here, Tony, in my false tooth. You must keep this secret. If Zor finds these nuggets, he will destroy them. They are our only chance to escape this place and Zor! We must not even 'think' about these nuggets, so he cannot see our thoughts. His powers are growing. When he is close to you, make your mind think about the farm or Meme and Gramps. If he learns our secrets now, our lives are not worth a red cent."

Tony gulped. "I know he threatens us, but would he really, honestly harm us?"

Esel lowered his head. "I am greatly sorry, Tony, but the answer is yes, he will. Our lives mean nothing to him. What grieves me even more is that I cannot tell Zor my secret formula to save your lives. If he uses this formula, the whole universe is in danger of destruction. He is evil and has no regard for mankind, much less us."

"There must be a way out of here," Gallopade declared. "What are we overlooking?"

"Too late," Razzi hissed. "The devil just arrived!"

Hot Chocolate squalled and sounds of rattling chains moved toward the prisoners. Molly's eyes nearly popped out when she saw him. A loud hiccup escaped. The menacing giant made Abraham look angelic.

When Zor stood in front of the prisoners, he was so tall his angry eyes peered through the top part of the metal prison bars. His muscles bulged under his black shirt and pants. His knee-high boots were shiny black as was his long cape. Only his eyes and the lining of his billowing cape were bright red-orange. Key chains and Razzi's cane hung from his wide black leather belt.

Gallopade and Heija stood forward in front of the children and Razzi, who gathered close to Esel.

Zor pulled Razzi's cane from his belt and observed their eyes through the bars. "You're a grimy bunch!" His other hand turned the key, clickety-click, opening the lock. He stuck his head inside and snarled. "Heija! I order you and Molly to come out here with me, right now!"

The girl hid her face behind Tony's shoulder.

"Talk to me here," Heija said without blinking. "Leave Molly alone!"

Gallopade stepped in front of Heija, his voice strong. "Leave these girls alone! Take me, Zor.

The giant backed up for an instant and laughed. Then he grabbed the cell bars with his large hands and sparks whizzed through the air. His eyes began to glow like fire and the metal heated to orange around his hands. Smoke floated off the bars.

"You fool! I want Molly and Heija!" Zor roared.

Razzi crept under the cot, covering his eyes.

Gallopade stepped forward into the open doorway. "It's my fault that we're here. It's me you want!"

"Don't tell me what I want!" Zor bellowed, swinging Razzi's cane through the air, striking Gallopade violently across the head. The impact along with an electrical zap knocked the stallion back and to the side of the cell. He hit the stone wall and limply slid to the ground.

Heija went to him and kneeled by his side, her head over his. "Gallopade, my love, speak to me!"

Everyone watched in horror as Gallopade remained motionless with his eyes closed.

The mare screamed with her tears flowing. "You have surely killed him, you monster! What's wrong with you? Gallopade never did anything to you!"

Zor placed his head inside the cell. "You're more spirited than I expected, but have no fear. I can tame you. Do as I ordered! If you do not obey me, you'll look exactly like that worthless stallion." He held the cane up inside the cell ready to strike Heija.

She stood up and glared at him without fear. "If that is your wish, I would rather die than go with you."

Molly bolted from Tony's arms, shrieking loudly. "No! Don't hit Heija!"

Tony reached too late to stop his sister as she fled to Zor's side. "No!" Tony yelled. "No! Come back, Molly!"

Seeing the girl streak past her, Heija shouted, "Molly, don't go out there! Stay in here!"

It was too late. The child was standing by Zor's side. She appeared tiny as a mouse, looking up at the giant. She begged gently. "Please don't hit Heija. I love her."

Heija winced, knowing what she must do. She gazed at Gallopade's limp body, then turned to Esel. "Please, help Gallopade." Another tear slipped down her cheek. Holding her head high, she walked to Molly, touching the girl's cheek with her velvet nose.

Molly grabbed Heija's head and hugged her.

Triumphant laughter filled the arena as the cell door locked. Razzi and Tony wept. Zor picked Molly up and roughly placed her on the mare's back. He took a lock of Heija's mane and led them away.

Tony and Razzi ran to the bars afraid to touch them. They watched the trio cross the arena and disappear behind the crimson drapes in the far corner across from their cell. Clanking metal sounds were heard, and soon Zor reappeared. He looked straight at Esel as he strutted toward the dragon's post. His voice vibrated off the walls.

"Esel, listen well! Now is the time to give me your energy formula. The lives of Molly and Heija are in your hands old man."

Howling with laughter, the giant reached Hot Chocolate who was chained to his post. With Razzi's cane, Zor hit the dragon, with a zap, zap, zap! The dragon gave out agonizing squalls as he leaped backwards, pulling at his chains, trying to escape the zapping cane. After hitting the dragon again and again, Zor spat on the ground, lifted the trunk lid and threw the cane inside. He glared around the arena, smiled proudly and laughed out loud again before taking his leave through the black drapes.

Hot Chocolate shivered and whimpered while licking his wounds.

The cavern quieted again as Esel's weary eyes appraised the damage. Molly and Heija were gone. Where, Esel did not know. Gallopade was bleeding and still unconscious. Would he live or die? Esel wondered. Tears flowed from Tony and Razzi as they stroked the stallions head and neck.

Esel bowed his head in shame and distress. In his thoughts, he beat himself up. All he did was watch. What kind of a Majiventor am I? Nothing but a total failure!

Pulling himself together, Esel stood up and pulled his cot closer to the stallion and the boys. He handed a blanket to Tony to spread over the horse. The old man sat wearily on the cot and pulled the shivering boy and raccoon close to him, wrapping his weary arms around them for comfort.

After they settled a bit, Esel focused on Gallopade. "Okay boys, we need to rub his head and muscles. We must awaken the stallion and get him moving again."

While the boy and raccoon did as Esel instructed, the Majiventor's thoughts traveled to the girls. What can I do when that uncaring arrogant giant returns? And what ghastly plans will he carry out next?

CHAPTER 17

THE DRAGON WILL EAT ME!

Tony and Razzi massaged Gallopade's legs, shoulders and neck, while Esel used a piece of his robe to dab blood from the stallion's head.

"Will Gallopade be all right?" Tony asked intently.

"If I knew that," Esel answered, "I truly would be supernatural." He sighed deeply as he gazed at Gallopade.

Tony's chin quivered when he asked the next question. "Will Zor hurt Molly and Heija like this?"

The Majiventor was hesitant with his answer. "I will do everything I can to keep that from happening, child."

As the stallion lay quietly on the cold dirt, Esel whispered. "I must lie down. Keep up the good work, boys." He stretched out on the cot, shutting his eyes, feeling tired, old, and useless. Defeated thoughts swam in his head. It is time to give up, he said to himself. These good earthlings should not suffer because of me. There is nothing I can do against Zor's strength. If he will let the earthlings go home, I will give that evil man my formula.

Tony eased upon the cot by Esel's side, placing his head on Esel's heart. "It's okay to rest, sir," he whispered, "but please don't give up. We really, really need you."

Esel squeezed the boy's hand. "Bless you, child," he said, wondering how the young boy could grasp an old man's crushed feelings so well. Then Esel recalled Tony's hard times. The child lost his mother in a car crash, his dad left him, and he became the soul protector of his young sister in the orphanage. Yet, Tony remained strong and kind. "I promise, I will not give up," Esel whispered.

"Gallopade blinked! He's waking up!" Razzi squealed as he pulled on Esel's robe.

"W-What happened?" The stallion stammered. "The room is spinning!" Struggling to stand, he leaned against the wall. His eyes widened as he peered around. "Heija and Molly are gone! Did Zor take them?"

With great emotion, Razzi held onto Gallopade's leg and explained in detail about Zor taking the girls away.

"We were sure Zor had killed you!" Tony said, still sitting on the cot holding Esel's hand.

"I'm okay, except for a big headache," Gallopade assured the boy. "What can we do? We can't leave Molly and Heija with Zor. There must be something we can do!"

"If only I knew what," Esel said. "Zor hid his size and strength behind the illusion of Abraham. Now, his powers are stronger than even I expected. Our chances of survival truly grow slimmer every hour his strength increases. He has us in a bad spot."

"I thought witches were the worst, but Zor's just as bad!" Razzi blurted out. "He ruined everything we intended to do. We can't save the farm. He stole Esel's wand. He took Gallopade and Heija's wings so we can't fly away! Zor is totally rotten! He even ruined my cane!"

"What do you mean about your cane?" Esel asked.

"He ruined it! Did you see that thing zap when it hit Gallopade? It's dangerous!"

"No, Razzi, things are not always the way they appear," Esel assured him. "The electric shocks hitting Gallopade came from Zor, not your cane. Before Zor visited us, he soaked in the strength rays to show off his powers."

"But, Esel, sir, I saw lightning zap from my cane," Razzi protested. "I'll *never* touch it again!"

"Honest," Esel said. "I promise, when the time comes and you hold your cane again, it will not hurt you."

Gallopade stared through the bars as Esel and Razzi talked. His heart ached as he searched the arena for some sight of Heija. Then he saw something.

"Esel, come look! The dragon's snoring is sending spurts of air and separating those black drapes." Gallopade sounded excited. "Can you see the wall behind the curtains? There's a key hanging there."

Limping to the bars, Esel peered toward the dragon's feeding area. "Yes, the red cord and key . . ." He uttered. "Zor has taunted me with that key many times."

"If only we could get to it," Gallopade wished aloud. "We could get out of here."

"That's impossible!" Razzi stated bluntly. "Even if we could slip through these bars, the key would be too high, and that hungry dragon would eat us. Hey! Why are you guys staring at me like that?"

"Can you possibly squeeze between the bars?"

"No, Gallopade!" Razzi said quickly with a big gulp. "At least, I don't think so. And if I could, I'd be eaten!"

"Just try to squeeze through the bars," Tony prodded. "We gotta know. You may be our only chance to get out of here. At least try."

Razzi ran to the back wall visibly shaking. "Me and my big mouth!" he groaned. "You know I'm a big coward."

"Zor has the dragon chained right now," Gallopade pointed out. "It's a safe time to try. Just see if you can."

Slowly, the raccoon eased forward. "I want to help but I'm afraid! Even those bars may zap and kill me?"

"No, Razzi," Esel said tenderly. "It is like I told you, the zaps you saw and heard came directly from Zor."

The raccoon barely touched the tip of his paw to the metal bars. His big eyes batted in surprise. "Hey, they didn't kill me! Okay, I'll try, but if you see Zor or that dragon, stop me!" He stuck his head and shoulders through the bars and gingerly twisted sideways.

"He did it!" Tony said behind his hand so only his buddies could hear. A smile filled his young face.

"Wow! It *is* possible. I did it!"

The drowsy dragon lifted his head and snorted loudly. Smoke shot from of his nose.

Without delay, Razzi twisted his way back into the cell much faster than he went out.

Hot Chocolate quieted and was soon asleep again.

"Now that I can get in and out, I'm not so afraid," Razzi said. "I'm going to find Molly and Heija."

"Razzi, if I had arms I'd hug you," Gallopade told the raccoon. "I'm extremely worried about the girls."

"What about the key?" Esel asked. "We cannot help the girls until we unlock this cell."

"I'm not about to be eaten by that dragon," Razzi declared as he squeezed through the bars. While the dragon slept, the raccoon darted across the arena and slid under the crimson curtains. He stopped long enough to listen for the dragon. Still hearing the dragon's snores, Razzi crept along a space between the wall and the drapes until he found another barred cell. To his delight he could see Molly and Heija asleep in the far corner.

Trying to draw their attention, the raccoon found a transparent sheet inside the bars. He shook it and rattled the metal lock to get their attention. The girls never stirred.

Hearing noises, the dragon squalled an alarm.

Razzi peeked under the drapes and ran toward his friends. Still in the arena, he heard a clanking door. Running like a gray streak, he plunged head first between the bars, twisting in the air, then he rolled under a cot. His hand flew over his mouth to keep his breathing quiet.

Zor laid a bundle of thorns in the dragon's wire basket and peered around before he left the arena again.

After Razzi caught his breath, he told his friends about seeing the girls sleeping inside another barred cell.

Gallopade gave a long sigh of relief. "Good! They are still safe," he said. "Now, we must think about how we can free them before Zor loses his temper again."

"*We* can do nothing!" Esel blurted out as he stared at the raccoon. "*Only Razzi can get this job done.*"

"But, how?" Razzi asked. "That dragon will eat me! He's big, strong, and mean. I'm little! What can I do?"

"I'll distract him when Zor lets him loose tonight," Tony said with enthusiasm. "I'll feed him candy bars."

"But, fellows, even if the dragon's not there, I can't reach the key," Razzi argued. "I'm short and it's too high."

"It is possible," Esel declared. "Zor put your cane in the wooden chest and it could help you reach the key."

"No, sir, I can't." Razzi cowered behind the cot. "I saw my cane zap that dragon. I don't want to be fried!"

"The cane is harmless," Esel said kindly. "It is harmless by itself. It has no power on its own. Just like our cell bars, if you touch it or hold it, you will be fine."

"Can't you see," Razzi said trembling. "Either that cane will zap me, the dragon will eat me, or that horrible Zor will come back and kill me! No matter what I do, I die!"

"If I could go for you," said Gallopade, "I would." He started to say more when he heard a new sound.

The stallion's head rose high seeing a small man carrying a tray, coming toward them. "That must be the cook Esel mentioned earlier," he whispered.

Esel nodded and peeked through the prison bars. "Shoko, my friend, you are a pleasant sight."

"Can no talk! Shoko very busy," he said, placing the tray next to the metal bars. His slanted eyes glanced around fearfully. Down his back was a thick braid of black hair that nearly touched the ground.

"Have Molly and Heija been fed?" Gallopade asked.

"Yes, sir, they fed." He stared over his shoulder again. "Can no talk! Must go!" He dashed away.

"Zor is watching," Esel grumbled. "Zor likes to hide behind the curtains so he can stay in control of Shoko."

Razzi handed everyone a piece of dry bread and a cold potato. "Look at this awful stuff! At least it's food . . . . But Zor's a tricky old bird so I hope it's not poisoned."

"Speaking of a tricky old bird, I think it would be good to trick Zor." A rare smile formed on Esel's face. "I will tell him where to find my energy formula."

"But Esel," Gallopade protested. "You said it could never be revealed, not even if our lives were threatened."

"True. I said it and I meant it! However, I want to send Zor on a wild-goose chase. If he searches my castle for the formula, Razzi might have fewer worries."

Gallopade's ears shot forward. "I'm feeling hopeful for a change. When will you tell Zor your secret?"

"My plan is to tell him after the dragon is set loose, although sooner if it becomes necessary."

The irritating sound of rattling chains told the prisoners that evil was in the arena. The giant strutted the full length of the arena trying to impress his observers. Zor entered the red drapes where Razzi had last seen the girls.

"I don't like his manner," Gallopade fretted. "He's far too happy! He must be up to no good."

Keys jingled and metal bars clanked behind the drapes. Zor popped through the corner crimson drapes into the arena again, moved a few long strides toward the dragon's post and stepped behind the drapes directly in front of the prisoner's eyes. They could hear grinding noises and sounds they didn't recognize.

Zor continued to move back and forth, in and out of their sight, smiling, whistling, and laughing out loud. He hid all his activities, knowing he had a captive audience.

"You are right, Gallopade. Zor is far too happy," Esel warned. "Zor is concocting more evil."

Hours passed before the giant was content with his tasks. He paused in the arena to stare directly at Esel. "Yes, old man, this is your last chance! I need your energy formula. Only you can stop this deadly game before it begins. What do you say? Where's my energy formula?"

Esel cleared his throat. "Those dear girls are important to me and yes, I must work with you. Maybe we could strike a bargain? You might actually like my idea."

"Bargain, did you say?" Zor moved closer. "What bargain could you offer, little man?"

With great effort, Esel tried to sit up straight. "I know that you, sir, cannot survive without my energy formula. We still need each other, because time is running out for you as well as for me. This volcano cannot hold its energy much longer before it will cool by itself. Without the volcano's energy, you cannot remain strong.

"Get on with it, old man, I know all that."

"Okay Zor, if you will free my friends now, and let them go back to earth, I will share my energy formula with you. We can work together to build a new prosperous universe with you as our leader."

A slight grin formed on Zor's face and his voice mellowed as he walked toward Esel. "That is what I want to hear. Tell me more."

"First, all my friends must be set free immediately."

Zor unlocked the metal bars, and opened the door, still blocking the exit with his huge body. "As you can see, I've unlocked your cell door, and I promise to let your friends go as soon as I have your energy formula."

"No, I want my friends let go first. When they are set free, I will tell you everything you want."

"We need some trust here, old man. I told you, I'd let them go. We have a bargain, and we have all agreed, so give me your formula."

Esel shook his head. "Trust does not come easy. As you know, I am old and my strength is failing," he said. "My memory is shaky, so the best I can do is tell you where you can find some important hidden notes." Esel hesitated. "Are you positive, you will let my friends go, after I tell you? Will you be honorable?"

"I always keep my promises!" Zor's eyes were fastened on Esel's eyes. The doorway remained blocked.

"Because of your word, I'll tell you what you need to know. Look on the fifth floor of my castle in the blue bed chamber. My notes should be hidden behind the pendulum in the grand father's clock on the east wall."

Zor looked deep into Esel's eyes, and then backed away. He quickly locked the cell door again.

"Why are you locking the bars?" Esel asked. "You said my friends could go free."

"Do you think I'm stupid enough to let your friends run to your sisters for help? I'm not a fool!"

"But you gave your word!" Esel shouted angrily. "My friends need to return to earth. You gave your word!"

"And you gave away your power and fame for their friendship. How far will that get you? You are such a fool, Esel! You now have nothing. I have everything!" Laughing all the way to the dragon, he released the beast and hurried behind the black drapes.

"Zor is a double-dealing rat!" Gallopade showed his teeth in anger as he spoke. "There is no truth in him. But look! In his hurry he left the drapes open and he placed the key on the nail. Are we ready for battle, guys?"

"I am!" Razzi declared. "Zor makes me mad enough to face two dragons! Call Hot Chocolate, Tony. Let's get this show on the road."

"Be careful, Razzi, old pal. Don't take unnecessary chances." Gallopade lowered his head and looked eye to eye with the raccoon. "You are a brave and true friend. I will always be indebted to you."

"Thanks, Gallopade. You're a great friend too." Razzi turned to Tony. "Okay, call your dragon!"

Tony crunched a candy bar wrapper.

Hot Chocolate stretched his neck toward the sound; yet, remained close to his post. After more coaxing from Tony rattling the wrappers, the dragon slunk closer, still looking backwards. Tony tossed the candy high in the air and the dragon ran to it then ate it. He stood quietly with no antics or special joy.

As the dragon ran to the center of the arena to catch another sweet morsel, Razzi pushed through the bars and bolted along the wall toward the old chest. He dared not look back. Hesitating at the open drapes, the raccoon peered at the brass key. It hung even higher than he expected. He ran to the wooden trunk, where he managed to push up the lid and jump in. He eased the lid down and peeked through the keyhole. Tony was still throwing candy to the dragon.

Rummaging around in the darkness of the chest, he felt his cane under some materials. He held his breath and tapped it with his foot. To his relief, nothing zapped. He grabbed his cane and once again, he peeked out to see where the dragon was located. He began to lift the trunk lid when loud noises caught his attention.

Zor burst into the arena with shouts of anger and his eyes blazing. Between the clattering chains and his raging voice, the arena filled with clamor.

Tony, Gallopade, and Esel fell back, pretending to sleep, while the dragon slunk away to a far corner.

Zor hushed and glared around the room, his hands on his hips. He turned and stomped toward the chest, tossing open the lid. His voice ripped through the room like a wind swept forest fire.

"Now you've done it! I see and know everything. Now, I'm really angry!"

CHAPTER 18

DANCE OF RAGE

Cowering on the far side of the arena, the dragon silently watched the hot-tempered giant bluster.

Razzi hid deep in the wooden chest with his heart pounding wildly. He covered his ears as Zor's booming voice circled him. The angry man's reckless kicks slammed the heavy trunk to and fro, jolting the raccoon.

The earsplitting hullabaloo drew the prisoners to the cell bars, where they strained to see. Their faces reflected the puzzlement they felt. Why was Zor not searching Esel's castle? Had Zor seen Razzi get into the trunk? Were all of Razzi's fears coming true?

The wooden chest was the focus of Zor's stare as he repeatedly strutted around it and shouted. "You honestly thought you could trick me and get away with it? I'm here to tell you, you're dead wrong! You're an idiot!"

The agitated man turned away from the open trunk and paced nervously in a wider circle. After ranting and raving, he returned to the wooden box and leaned over it again. "You blundering fool," he snarled as he ran his fingers back and forth over the materials covering Razzi.

Again, Zor stood upright, staring around restlessly. Placing his foot upon the edge of the chest, his voice rumbled through the cavern like a freight train. "I can't believe you attempted this brainless trick. Only a buffoon would dare test me like this!" Zor moved about again, kicking the side of the trunk to show his livid annoyance.

"Zor knows Razzi is in the trunk!" Gallopade uttered. "Our buddy's in grave trouble and we can't help him!"

Esel nodded. "Zor will have no compassion today."

The giant again strutted around the trunk, still shouting. "You pushed me too far this time! Enough of this good fellow stuff for me. I'll make you pay for this!" His skin glowed with fury as he stooped over the chest. Zor flung a blanket out of the trunk onto the dirt, while his right hand searched deeper in the big box.

Silently, Gallopade begged. Watch out, Razzi! Please Zor, go away from that trunk! This must stop!

An abrupt smirk crept over Zor's flushed face. He pulled his arm back, stood straight, and raised the raccoon's telescope cane high in the air. The tyrant's voice echoed off the walls while he swung the little red cane around like an orchestra leader chasing a mad bumble bee. Bright sparks sprayed when the cane struck the trunk. Zor's cape caught air and whirled wildly as Zor lurched one way then another in his stormy dance of rage.

After long moments of theatrical actions and Zor's voice spewing ugly words, the crimson faced man marched to the middle of the arena directly in front of the caged prisoners. He stopped to face them with his eyes glowing like red-hot lava.

"Esel, you are a fool!" Zor shouted. "Don't you know it is useless to send me on a wild-goose chase? You misjudged me, ole man, and I caught you red-handed!"

The prisoners glanced at each other with obvious surprise. The captives abruptly realized Zor's anger was meant for Esel, not Razzi!

Zor placed his hand on his hip. "Esel, you were a fool not to realize your image machine works perfectly for me. With that machine, I'm much wiser than you ever were! Your clever wisdom will never control me again! You and the machine are mine! Soon I'll know all your little tricks and secrets and the world will no longer need you. I'll reign supreme! No one will *even* remember you!"

In unison the prisoners watched the giant at full attention and gradually bunched closer together. They silently hoped the tyrant would not notice Razzi's absence.

The furious man raised the red cane high and continued his arrogant lecture. "Your mental picture of the blue room was perfect, Esel, so I reproduced it on my image machine. The formula notes were not hidden in your clock! Your stupid trick failed, Esel! You'll pay for this!"

Zor clenched his fists. "I outsmarted you for the umpteenth time, Esel. I'm not only great, but I'm growing wiser every day. Your image machine is perfect for all my needs. When I'm through with you and your not-so-wise sisters, the world will think I invented that great machine.

"Soon," he continued, "the universe will be mine and mine alone! No one can stop me now! I'll have respect from all your Majiventor friends, Kings, Queens, and Presidents. Soon, all the rulers will admire my extreme powers and knowledge. And they *will* fear me!"

With his eyes squinted, Zor pointed his finger at Esel. "But you, ole man will be known as the ultimate failure. I'll see to it! Plan to suffer for your betrayal!"

Zor's words gave the prisoners cold chills.

Turning on his heel, Zor strutted toward the red drapes where Razzi had last seen the girls.

Inside the open trunk, Razzi lifted his head from under a moth-eaten blanket and watched Zor leave the arena. The raccoon wasted no time. He jumped from the chest, hitting the dirt floor with his legs running at full speed, clutching a harness in his paws.

The dragon snorted smoke, but never attacked.

The raccoon squeezed inside the cell bars, pulling a harness behind him. He fell to the floor, speaking softly. "The dragon didn't chase me, 'cause he's afraid of Zor! Whose harness did I get? It was dark in that trunk!"

Gallopade placed his head close to Razzi's ear and thanked him quietly. "You made a gallant try my friend; however, this is Heija's harness. Needless to say, my harness and the capsule are still in the chest."

"Doggone it, I'm sorry Gallopade. I was so scared." Razzi slunk under the cot. "I was sure Zor was going to skin me alive the way he was screaming."

"Aye, we feared the same," the stallion told him. A rattle caught Gallopade's attention. "Zor's returning!"

Tony hid Heija's harness under a blanket.

Zor shouted again. "Esel, I still can't believe you tried to trick me. Playing games with me is a lost cause! You know I always hold the winning hand."

Gallopade's spine prickled as he listened to Zor's words. He knew there was dreadful trouble in the making.

The giant pulled open the drapes in the far corner, where Razzi had seen Molly and Heija. The soundproof barrier inside of the prison bars opened enough for Molly's desperate voice to be heard loud and clear.

"Tony! We've gotta help Heija! Zor took her away! I'm afraid for her! And it's lonely and scary here by myself."

"Esel did this to you, Molly!" Zor claimed. "I offered freedom for everyone if Esel would share his energy formula. You could be on your way home if not for that deceiving Majiventor. Instead, he chose to trick me with lies. Try again, Molly. Persuade him to help you."

Molly reached toward her brother through the bars. "Tony, please help me. Think of something! Please Esel, Gallopade, Razzi, think of some way to help us."

Tony reached his hands out toward her. "Stay strong, Molly. You know we'll help you soon. We love you! I'd be beside you this minute if I could."

She cried out. "I love you too, Tony. I miss all of you so bad, and Gramps and Meme too. This is worse than the orphanage, Tony! I really want out of here!"

"I know Molly. I do too." The boy's words were filled with emotion as a tear slipped down his smudged face.

"See, Esel, you made the babies cry. You should be ashamed!" The giant smiled as he toyed with them. He ambled away from Molly, along the far wall until he was directly across the arena from Esel's eyes.

"Now, old man," the giant bellowed. "Watch a real genius at work. I'm the master inventor from this time forward! This will be just the beginning. Zor pulled part of the drapes open to expose a clear glass room.

Gallopade sucked in a deep breath as he saw Heija standing all alone inside the see-through room. She stood proud with her head held high, even though she was totally helpless. Behind her, the menacing red glow of the lava was intense. Fear for his beloved left the stallion woozy and he nearly blacked out. He bit his lip and waited for the evil man's next dreadful words.

Zor yanked more drapes aside, between Molly and Heija's prison cells, revealing another large transparent cubicle. It was filled with all sizes of gray to black wheels. Each wheel had interlocking teeth that fit together with the other wheels.

Tony moaned. "That thingumajig is bad news."

Esel blinked his eyes, inspecting the wheels. "It looks like the inside of a huge timepiece."

Zor boasted. "My clear cubicles are unbreakable. Heija is lovely with the glow around her. Don't you agree?"

The giant entered a side door of the center cubicle and stood inside, appearing small beside the many interlocking wheels. "This is how it works. Watch, Esel!

"This great black wheel lies on its side and is flat like a table. See this large white candle." He held it up. "I'll place the candle on the outer edge of this large table-like wheel. Candles are made to burn so I'll light it!"

Zor was visibly enjoying himself taunting his captive prisoners. "Simple? Huh? I can hear your thoughts. What does this candle have to do with Heija? I love this part!"

Removing a stop-block, Zor set all the wheels in motion. They turned like a clock. Again Zor's cruel voice marched on. "Each wheel turns another, and together they slowly move this big flat wheel around. When the candle makes a complete circle, the flame will make contact with a thick hemp rope.

"Yes, Esel, the rope is fastened to a trap door under your fragile friend's cage. When the rope catches fire, it will burn through, and the floor under Heija will open to the hot lava. Need I say more?"

"No! Let her go!" Gallopade gave an agonizing wail. "Not Heija! Take me! I beg of you, let her go! Take me!"

"Blame Esel, not me! If he will not give me the energy formula, Heija will surely die. Her death will be Esel's fault, not mine!" Zor left the cubicle with the wheels still turning; the candle moving in as low circle of death. Zor locked the cubicle entrance and walked into the arena.

"Esel!" Zor yelled. "This is not a game. You can stop this! How can any secret be worth Heija's life?"

Zor's words were like knives.

"Please, Esel, save Heija! Tell Zor!" Molly begged.

"Now you have the right idea, Molly," Zor grinned with amusement. "Beg little one until Esel saves Heija!"

Zor turned on a speaker for Heija. The system squealed and his loud words boomed through. "Beg for your life, Heija. Molly did! Now is your moment!"

"Oh, Gallopade, it is so good to see you!" Heija's voice cried in earnest. "I was terrified you were badly injured from Zor striking you so hard."

"It's just a bump, Heija. No need to worry about me. It is you and Molly we want safe."

"Zor has not hurt us," she told him. "That is, not yet. Molly is so brave, but she is all by herself now. I'm sorry I couldn't stay with her."

Molly cried out. "I miss you Heija. I miss all of you. I hate being by myself. I wanna go home!"

Tony called out to her. "Be brave, sis. You survived the orphanage, a monster snake, and hungry dinosaurs. You are stronger than you think."

"Aye," Gallopade added. "Remember how you made us fight those spiders to save Razzi. Without you, we might have given up, and we'll not give up this time."

"I remember, Gallopade." Molly told him, rubbing the dampness from her eyes. "W-We're a team!"

"Yes, Gallopade, we are," Heija spoke each word distinctly. "We are the greatest team ever!" She tried to sound upbeat in her tone of voice. "I love each of you dearly, and Gallopade, you'll always be my first and only true love. Flying together was the highlight of my life. I'll always love you." A diamond sparkle slid down her cheek.

Zor held his ears. "Stop it! Lovey-dovey stuff is daft. Beg for your life, wench! You have no time to waste!"

Heija stared at him with malice. How could he sleep at night? She wondered. Taking a deep breath and with purposeful words she spoke again. "Please understand I want to live. Right now, only Zor Zanger can keep me alive. So please, Esel, I beg of you . . . ."

Her words hesitated then flew from her mouth like hornets from a disturbed nest. "No matter what happens to me, never give up your formula to this wicked man. As a ruler, he'll kill all that is good. He is wickedly selfish, vile, and he would say or do anything to get his way. I'd rather die than be under his rule. Please do not . . . ."

Zor turned off Heija's speaker. "Shut-up, you lame-brained strumpet!" He belted out.

Molly stared at Zor. "Please let Heija go. Let all of us go!" Tears flowed down her cheeks as her loudspeaker shut off and her soundproof window shut.

Zor shook his fist at Esel. "That child should be worried about herself! If Heija's time runs out, Molly will be next in line for the crystal cubicle."

Outraged, the male prisoners made an outburst of noise, but Zor paid no attention. He closed Molly's drapes.

Tony crumbled to the floor, hurting for his sister and Heija. "I feel so helpless," he cried out. "I hate this!"

Purposely, Zor left the drapes open in front of the clock room and Heija's see-through cubicle for Esel to see.

His voice boomed again. "Call me, Esel, when you decide to save Heija. In the meantime, enjoy your view of my clock as it counts off the precious moments before Heija dies. When the candle reaches the hemp rope, you will see this is no game! It is real."

The giant strutted toward the wooden chest. He picked up the dirty blanket off the ground and tossed it along with Razzi's cane inside the trunk and closed the lid. Then the evil man marched out of the arena.

After a moment, the dragon slunk quietly toward the open curtains. He sniffed the clear crystal wall where the clock continued to grind, a haunting sound for all the prisoners. His tongue reached toward Heija, swatting the clear glass enclosure, making Heija flinch.

"Call that dragon, Tony!" Razzi commanded with a no-nonsense attitude he had never shown before. "I have to reach our cell key and do it right now."

His sudden energy caused Tony to smile. "Yes! If we can get free, we can set Heija and Molly free. And . . . ."

"No, Tony." Esel shook his head sadly and said. "I am sorry but the keys for their cells are on Zor's belt."

Gallopade raised his head, glaring at the grinding clock. "We must find a way to get Heija out. That rotten wheel is turning way too fast. I cannot stand this!"

The Majiventor was frail, but his voice was firm. "Gallopade, we must do things in order. Razzi must do his job first and immediately fetch our cell key off the wall. Secondly, he must grab your harness from the trunk. If Razzi can accomplish that, we should have the three parts of my cooling potion. The keys will allow us to free ourselves from this cell."

"I'll do my part," Razzi spoke up hastily.

Gallopade searched Esel's face. "What can we do then? I hope you have an effective plan!"

Esel's jaws clamped tightly before he made himself say the next words. "At that time, Gallopade, you must find a way to escape this cavern. You must get around Zor, go outside the cave, and fly directly over the volcano."

Gallopade forehead furrowed. "Why? What are you talking about? How will that help Heija?"

"The three capsules must be dropped into the volcano at the same time. It is the only way to cool the boiling lava in this volcano." Esel replied. "It is the source of Zor's strength. And you, Gallopade, are the only one who can do that. If you can accomplish cooling the volcano, we might save Heija and stop Zor's power all at the same time. Can we count on you?"

"You know I would give my life to save Heija, but that wheel is turning fast. Do we have enough time for all that? If it takes too long, Heija will . . . ." He could not say the words. They were just too horrible.

"Hurry," urged Esel. "Tony, call the dragon with your candy. And Razzi, my friend, prepare to run like the wind."

The boy rattled his candy wrapper and caught the reptile's attention. Soon, a sweet morsel left Tony's hand and whizzed by Hot Chocolate's head. He ran after it.

Before the dragon caught the candy, Razzi was on his way, running toward the old trunk. He immediately found his cane, grabbed it and ran to the key. The red cord holding the key, dangled over a nail. It was still too high to reach. Razzi leaped upward, swinging his cane. He jiggled the key, but could not dislodge it.

Impatiently the raccoon glanced around. The moving candle and Heija's hopeful expression renewed his determination. The dragon was still chasing Tony's candy, so Razzi rushed to the beast's empty wire basket.

The container was heavier than it looked, but the raccoon rolled it to the wall under the key. Razzi managed to turn the basket up-side-down and crawl upon it. It gave him the height he needed and his cane easily moved the cord off the nail. It plopped on the ground.

The success gave Razzi a rush of energy. He grabbed the key, rolled the feeding basket to its original spot and glanced around. His eyes nearly bugged out of his head when he realized Hot Chocolate had slipped up behind him and looked big as a mountain.

Razzi gulped with fear. "H-How did you . . . Oh, yeah, you heard the key. Go away! Go eat candy. I gotta help save Heija!" The raccoon stepped backwards."

The dragon leaned closer with his tail curling back and forth like a cat playing with its prey. His eyes blazed and smoke curled from his nostrils.

Razzi felt the dragon's hot breath, and stepped backward. "Don't look at me that way! I taste awful! Go away you oversized furnace!"

The more Razzi nervously chattered, the more smoke rolled over the monster's sharp teeth. The giant lizard's tongue slithered in and out around the little fellow's head, taunting him.

Razzi's heart pounded fiercely. He was far too small to fight this beast who could flatten him with one foot. He knew running away from this speedy creature was hopeless. He groaned. "Wow! This is bad! I'll cook as that dragon swallows me! Ugh!"

With no way to escape, Razzi took a deep breath and cowered into a small ball, throwing his arms over his head. Nearly fainting from fear, he waited for the dragon's fiery jaws to snap . . . .

Hot Chocolate abruptly squealed, reeled around and ran away, raising dust all the way across the arena.

Shaking like a rag in a windstorm, Razzi peeked at the backside of the dragon. "What happened?" Then he noticed he was still holding his cane up in the air. Hot Chocolate was afraid of it and had run away.

Razzi glanced at his buddies smiling. There had been few smiles since their capture. Elated with his little triumph, the raccoon leaped inside the trunk and soon had Gallopade's harness in his hand. Before he could raise the lid and jump out, he heard rattling chains.

No, not again! Razzi thought. He knew Zor was entering the arena. Peering through a tiny crack in the trunk lid, the raccoon viewed Zor placing thorns in the wire basket. Then the giant stood tall and peered around. The deadly wheels were still turning. He smirked happily and strolled across the arena to enter his glow room. Zor left the drapes wide-open as if showing off.

With the trunk's lid slightly lifted, Razzi's dark eyes watched and waited. When Zor appeared to be sleeping, the raccoon slipped the harness over the trunk's far side away from the glow room. With the cane and key in his paws, the raccoon crawled out by the harness. The lid shut making an unexpected sharp click.

Razzi huddled behind the chest as Zor lifted his head and gazed around. The dragon had returned to munch his thorns, so the giant relaxed again in the energy rays. "Stupid dragon!" Zor grumbled.

From her clear cubicle, Heija watched the dragon back away as Razzi tiptoed back to his friends, holding out the cane. Before the raccoon slipped back into the cell, he smugly handed the cell key and harness to Esel.

Heija watched Esel place the harness on Gallopade. Then Tony fastened the belly band. The stallion looked so handsome in his splendid harness.

Glancing at the deadly candle, Heija shivered. She turned toward her busy friends, hoping the giant would not see them. Please sleep, Zor, just sleep, she thought.

Heija saw Esel pull capsules from his tattered robe pocket, the stallion's harness, and his special tooth. He wrapped the three capsules in a small piece of his robe.

As Esel worked, Gallopade turned toward Heija and their eyes met in a heartbreaking gaze. They spoke a million words in that moment. How had all this happened? He wanted to rescue her! She wanted to be brave for him. They longed to be together again!

Esel tucked the packet inside Gallopade's harness, close to the large control jewel. The elderly man unlocked the cell door, and whispered last minute instructions.

"You must go while Zor sleeps! When you find the exit from the cavern, Gallopade, fly over the volcano. Grab this material I left sticking out and drop this bundle in the hot lava. I can only hope it works!" the old man explained.

Heija's heart pumped wildly as she watched. Go quickly, my love. I will pray for your swift and safe return, she said quietly. I love you even more than life itself.

"I-I hate leaving!" The stallion hesitated as he saw the candle; already a third of the way around Heija's death circle. He had no choice and no time to dally. He must cool the volcano and with great speed!

Gallopade followed Razzi, who held his cane high, warning the dragon. They hurried toward Zor's secret exit from the arena. The stallion's heart was breaking as he halted by the trunk to catch sight of his friends waving and Heija bobbing her lovely head.

The steed nodded in return, his eyes blurring before hurrying on. He pressed the door handle down with his nose to open a large iron door. Razzi held it open as Gallopade whisked through it.

"Thank you, good friend," the stallion told Razzi. "Ease back quietly to help the others. Be careful!"

"I promise, and you, too." Razzi replied seriously.

As the door closed Gallopade knew he must rush to find a way out of the cavern. He trotted past shelves of briars ready to be delivered to the dragon. Beyond those, he passed through a doorway into a lush majestic palace.

Great mercy, look at this! Gallopade gasped. He saw shiny marble floors, walls, and ceilings, with fine furnishings, paintings, fireplaces, elegant rugs and draperies around every room. Giant tables were set with exquisite china. Aqua blue pools with splashing fountains and waterfalls were surrounded with fresh flowers in all colors. Soft music filled the air. Rare treasures were everywhere the stallion observed.

Gallopade quickly viewed each of many rooms, but saw no keys for Heija's crystal room or Molly's prison cell. The exits were also hidden. Time was slipping away!

Beginning to lose hope, he walked into an immense bedroom, with a four poster bed, dresser, chairs, and drapes, all in black and red. This had to be Zor's private bedroom! Even the bedspread was rumpled.

As Gallopade searched the dresser top, he heard the rattling of keys. Zor was quickly approaching!

Swiftly, the golden stallion looked for a closet or place to hide. To his surprise, behind the drapes he found a hidden cavern hallway and he followed it to a metal door. Pushing through the opening, he found himself in the outer cave. He was thankful the door closed softly.

Echoes from his fast-moving hooves reverberated against the walls, forming words in his ears. Heija! Heija! Save Heija! Save Heija!

The dim cave grew larger. His feet barely touched the floor in his great hurry. He traveled a long way before he saw a dim light through the cave's immense opening to the outside world. With mounting excitement, he touched the magic jewel and his wings appeared.

He wanted to shout, whoopee! His better judgment kept him quiet. Flying upward filled him with childlike exhilaration and he knew at that moment he had the power to save Heija. It was a remarkably grand feeling.

Reaching the exit, the floor to his left fell away, revealing a deep hollow tunnel, filled with red glowing eyes. Metal hooves sparked and clanked with a clamor. Wings flapped and rushed toward the intruder.

Gallopade flew from the cavern into the smoky red glow of the volcano. "Blimey! In my hurry, I forgot the beast herd! How can I ever outfly them? Somehow, I must!" He heard them but had no time to look back.

Half way up the mountain, searing pain abruptly jerked Gallopade's leg. Peering back, he saw Zor's lead horse's fiery eyes, anxious to bite again with his bloody metal teeth.

Rapidly, the demon lunged upward and hovered over the golden stallion trying to push him downward.

If Gallopade lost altitude, the whole herd would destroy him. He darted sideways trying to avoid the beast!

Black Fire lunged again, but missed. Taking that moment, Gallopade pumped his wings even harder, flying higher with each push. Reaching the thick cloud layer was his only hope for survival against Black Fire, who had extraordinary speed and power.

The black demon rose higher again and plunged down over the golden stallion. This time, his hooked wings were spread extra taunt. His shiny metal teeth aimed for Gallopade's neck to rip open his jugular.

Knowing a strike on his neck would cause him to bleed to death, Gallopade swooped sideways again, to dodge the black beast's teeth. Saving a wounded neck was good, but a razor sharp wing-hook still caught his shoulder, ripping the hide, and leaving a bloody gash. Pain made the golden stallion's flight upward far more difficult.

Heaving skyward with all his might, he pumped his wings for height, trying desperately to reach the dark clouds. More pain raced up his hind leg from Black Fire's relentless metal teeth. Gallopade gave a strong kick with his hind foot, hitting the black beast squarely in the nose.

Grateful for the dense cloud layer that enveloped him, the golden stallion zigzagged from side to side, trying to lose his opponent. His breathing was labored in the smoke-filled vapor, and his pain was pure misery. All sense of direction was lost in the darkness.

Where was the volcano? He had to find it! Second by second the candle was inching closer to the fragile hemp rope holding Heija's safety. Gallopade's mind as well as his body was filled with agony. He had to find the volcano! Failure now meant his beloved Heija would die! That thought triggered more agony than his bleeding wounds.

CHAPTER 19

TIME IS RUNNING OUT!

Deep in the cave, after soaking up energy rays in his glow room, Zor Zanger's skin gleamed as he strolled toward Heija. With great pride, he admired his deadly invention. "Ah! The candle has nearly gone full circle. My work is perfection!" He bragged loudly.

Zor Zanger glanced at Heija munching on a small pile of dry corn. When the white mare looked at him, she showed him no emotion, just a blank stare.

"No need to worry, Heija. There's still a way out. I'm opening Molly's drapes and soundproof barrier. The speakers are on so you and the girl can convince Esel to share his energy formula. If you do that, I can set you free. That's my promise," Zor strived to sound compassionate with his fingers crossed behind his back.

"Face it, ladies, time is running out! Esel's secrets are not worth your lives! Talk to him! Beg him!"

Heija stood proud and still, except for a slight twitch of her ear. She gazed at Esel, making not a sound.

Esel stared back toward the quiet mare, his face tightly drawn and half covered with straggly hair. He placed his hand on his heart gently patting his chest. The gesture made clear his admiration for Heija. Each understood the necessity of keeping the energy formula from Zor. Their only hope was Gallopade, but where could he be?

Zor paced back and forth. "I can't believe this. Look at the candle, Esel! Heija came all the way here to this world for your help. It's because of you, Esel that she is here. Only you can save her life!" Zor waited eagerly for someone to speak. The total silence drove him crazy.

Molly's voice suddenly rang out. "Please, Mr. Zor Zanger, can't you just blow out the candle? That would not be hard for you to do. I beg you, please save Heija."

"Talk to Esel, not me!" Zor marched toward Esel. "You are known all over the universe for your goodness. Why are you placing Heija in such harm?" Zor turned back to the mare, whose quiet stare stirred his anger more.

"Beg, Heija! Beg for your life! Time is running out!" Zor yelled from across the arena.

Esel could see the candle moving toward the hemp rope and could not hold back his tears. Her bravery was too much for him. "You win, Zor! I cannot let Heija die! I promise I will tell you every ingredient of my energy formula if you will snuff out the candle's fire and save Heija."

"Finally you came to your senses! It's about time! But you are a crafty old soul. How can I believe you? Look at me, Esel!" the giant ordered as he stood close to the cell bars. "I want to search deep into your eyes!"

"Look all you will," Esel told him, "but first, stop that confounded clock. If Heija dies, my secrets also die."

In a flash, Zor reached through the metal bars, and grabbed Esel's neck. The mighty man drew the feeble Majiventor close to the bars and peered deep into the old man's eyes. "Codes are all I see. I demand the formula!"

"I think in codes," Esel managed to mutter in his painful position. "I can translate them for you. J-Just save Heija and *the formula is yours*. Stop that blasted wheel!"

A crooked smile formed on Zor's glowing face and he dropped Esel onto the dirty ground.

"Did everyone hear Esel promise? The formula is mine!" Zor's voice was jubilant. "Majiventors must keep their word! I'll be the greatest ruler of the universe." He banged his hands on his chest as if expecting applause.

"My promise is only good if you keep Heija safe!"

Ignoring Esel's words, Zor continued. "You cannot break a promise!" Abruptly the giant stopped laughing. His eyebrow arched sharply. With searching eyes, he scanned the earthlings again. He demanded. "Where's Gallopade?"

"The rope is starting to smoke!" Esel raised his thin arm pointing to Heija and his weak voice was filled with anguish. "Stop the clock now! There is no time to wait! Stop the clock and I will tell you everything."

Paying no attention to the Majiventor, Zor locked his eyes on Tony. "Where is Gallopade, son?"

Tony moved backwards. "Don't call me son!" He yelled indignantly. "Leave me alone! Help Heija!"

Razzi slunk under a cot away from the giant's searching eyes. The raccoon could see the revolting clock grinding on and tiny swirls of smoke rising from the hemp rope. His eyes blurred with liquid and he trembled.

Growing impatient, the giant grabbed the iron bars with his strong hands. Sparks zinged through the air in all directions. "Tony!" Zor demanded. "Where is Gallopade?"

Tony's lip quivered. "He disappeared!"

The giant's anger grew and he roared, "What kind of trickery is this, Esel? How could Gallopade disappear?"

No excuses came to Esel's muddled mind, only extreme weariness. He pulled himself upon a cot and stared at the smoke rising from the hemp rope. The candle burned brightly. Esel tried to yell out, but his voice refused.

In that untimely quiet moment, the tiniest of squeaks caught Zor's ear. Searching for the sound, he observed the cell door ajar. How had that happened?

Fire filled the giant's eyes as he opened the bars wide and bent through the opening. Zor snatched Esel's arm and jerked the old man through the air like a rag doll.

"How did this happen? And where's that stupid horse? Talk to me you unsightly bag of bones!"

Hearing silence, the giant grabbed the Majiventor's neck and held his face up like a hand mirror. With Zor's free hand, he opened Esel's eyelids wide, staring deep inside the bloodshot orbs, repeating Gallopade's name.

Moments later, Zor's head tilted sideways and his laughter exploded. Once he caught his breath, he shouted for all to hear. "Gallopade intends to cool my volcano? That's hilarious! My beast herd will rip him to pieces. This is the best news I've heard since I captured Esel!

The callous man dropped the Majiventor again like a worthless stinky boot. The old man fell with a kerflop in the dirt. Zor raised his arms in victory and yelled. "Black Fire is the strongest horse alive. Gallopade can't help you! That fool horse is dead, dead, dead!"

Zor laughed, repeating the words over and over."

The Earthlings shivered as the walls echoed, fool, fool, fool, dead, dead, dead. More curls of smoke formed over the candle's flame, making a thin gray column that spiraled all the way to the ceiling.

Hidden in the darkness of the thick clouds, Gallopade listened for bubbling lava. In his escape from the bat-winged beasts, he lost his direction, and now, he was losing valuable time. He was sure the beast horses were waiting for him both above and below the clouds. He knew he was too weak to fight them.

His lungs burned from the bitter smoke in the clouds, and his oozing wounds were sucking his life away. Yet, in his heart and mind one thought kept him moving him onward. Heija needed help! He had no choice but to go above the clouds to find the volcano's orange glow.

———

Still further away in Dome City, a loud alarm had awakened the queen and her sisters. They had tottered from their bedrooms wearing robes and night-caps. Each lady had face cream to match their outfits. Coffee had been poured and they settled in their rocking chairs, near the big screen. When one sister yawned, they all yawned.

Rose adjusted her pink nightcap then whispered. "What set off our alarm at this inconvenient hour, Pearl?"

"That is what I intend to resolve. You will know as I know," the queen replied. "One of our scanners caught something unusual happening near the Kingobe volcano." The queen's night cap was crooked and her eyes drooped.

"I see a horse!" Birdie blinked to improve her sight.

"Black Fire!" The queen exclaimed. "He is dashing about like a humming bird. Why is he so excited?"

"I never saw him move so fast!" Birdie said nearly dropping her coffee.

"He acts like he is looking for something. Now he has jumped back into the cloud layer," the queen stated. "My stars! I see Gallopade, above the clouds now! He is bleeding and appears exhausted. He needs help."

Rose squinted. "Where is he? I cannot see! Will you please make the screen clearer, Pearl?"

Queen Pearl peered closely at Rose. "Take the glasses off the top of your head old girl and use them."

"Thank you Pearl. This is much better," Rose said. "I can see Gallopade, but what is he doing?"

Birdie was wide-eyed. "He is not trying to escape or he would fly in our direction. Esel must be alive! He sent Gallopade to cool the volcano. Those horrible beasts will do anything to stop him!"

"Precisely," Pearl agreed. "Esel found our capsules and gave Gallopade the task of cooling the volcano!"

The queen's expression turned grim. "If we are right, and Esel is alive, we must help Gallopade this very minute. Is the ray gun ready Birdie?"

"It is clean and ready. Shoot at will," she answered.

"We are within the law as this is a true crisis; yet, we must all agree. Do you make this unanimous, Rose?"

"Yes! By all means, shoot now! I see Zor's devil horse again and he has spotted the golden stallion. Black Fire is so strong he may kill Gallopade any minute. Hurry Pearl, aim straight and help our dear one."

"Wait! Should we chance the ray hitting Black Fire?" Birdie asked. "We do not want to strengthen the wrong stallion. It could be a disaster!"

"Sorry, dear. I pushed the button before you spoke. The strength ray is on its way. It is most likely Gallopade's only hope for survival," the queen affirmed.

They watched on the screen intently as Black Fire swiftly closed the distance between the two horses.

"Tell me what is happening," Rose begged. "My glasses fogged up from my steaming coffee."

"Gallopade just glanced backward and saw Black Fire speeding toward him." Birdie told Rose. "Before the beast made contact, our good friend dove downward. The black beast could not stop fast enough, so he spun around and chased Gallopade into the dark clouds."

"I wish I trusted this old ray gun," the queen fretted. "It is ancient and who knows how reliable? It will surprise me if the strength ray reached Gallopade in time. We will keep watch in hopes we see him again. He is so weak."

The Wise Ones stared dismally at the screen, watching several other beast horses flying above the clouds searching for Gallopade.

"Do you suppose we will ever see Esel or the earthlings again?" Rose asked. "This is very unsettling."

———

Gallopade's heart raced when he knew he was close to the volcano. He could feel the heat and hear the hot bubbling lava rolling over the edges of the mountain. Behind him, clanking hooves drew near.

Pushing with the last of his strength, tilting his head downward, he spread his wings and tried to gain speed. Gallopade knew the pain that surged through his body was slowing him. His head felt dizzy and his muscles cramped from the loss of blood. The smoke and gasses made it hard for him to breath. He envisioned Heija waiting for him in her crystal cubicle.

"I must save Heija, even if I die trying!"

———

Deep in the cave below, the rope sizzled and popped as the fire nipped relentlessly at the hemp rope.

Zor glared at Esel's body, sprawled on the ground where he was dropped. The giant shouted angrily. "If I didn't need your stupid formula, old man, I would gladly feed you to my dragon!"

Stooping over, Zor grabbed Esel's hair and dragged him like a bag of trash over the arena's dirt floor, leaving a long flat trail from the old man's limp body.

Heija moaned, wanting to help her friends, but the burning rope also demanded much of her attention.

Tears poured down Molly's cheeks. "Tony! Razzi! Do something! The rope is burning! Heija needs you!"

Her fervent pleas awakened their courage and together they dashed into the arena. What can two little guys do to stop a giant? Razzi wondered. They ran fast and followed Esel's flat trail to the mammoth man.

Razzi held his cane tightly and swung it at Zor's knees, while Tony grabbed the long cape by its hem. The boy dug his heels into the ground trying to stop the giant, leaving long skid marks in the earth while Zor kept walking.

"Give me the keys!" Tony cried out. "Give 'em to me so I can stop those wheels! Please, Zor Zanger!"

Heija's voice pierced the air through the loud speaker. "Listen to me! Please listen."

The commotion abruptly halted. Even Zor tarried in the arena to hear her words.

"Be strong, my friends! Gallopade will return! Believe me; I just know he is not dead. When he returns, tell him I love him with all my heart. Tell him I had hoped to be his wife. And please remember, I love each of you my friends. I'll always love you, no matter where I am. Love will overcome Zor's hate." She bit her lip as the fire on the rope snapped, crackled, and flamed higher.

Frantic, Tony tried to pull himself up Zor's cape. "We'll get you out, Heija!" he yelled. Then he pleaded once more. "We gotta save Heija. There's still time. Give me those keys, Zor! You gotta give me her prison key!"

"Get down, you wicked scoundrels!" Zor sneered. "It's far too late for Heija!" He made a quick turn from Heija's direction toward Molly's cell. The cape billowed and snapped, hurtling Tony away from the slippery cloak.

Molly screamed as her brother tumbled in the air.

The boy hit the ground and rolled like a ball. Jumping up, he shook his head and hurried back to battle.

The giant still held Esel's long gray hair as Razzi continued his feeble attempts to trip the huge man. Molly's pleading face urged Tony to try again. He climbed the giant's cape again trying to reach Zor's head. He wanted to scratch the man's eyes out.

The attempts to stop Zor Zanger only made the giant more agitated. He let go of Esel's hair and twirled around, swatting at the troublemakers like they were mosquitoes. Air gathered under his cape as before, and it billowed like a sail in full wind, once again forcing Tony to the cape's edge. "Get away from me, you blasted trouble makers, before I smash you to mush," Zor warned.

Razzi held to the back side of the giant's boot, trying to get high enough to bite flesh, but failed. He hit Zor's leg with his cane. That didn't work. He tried to climb high enough to reach the keys but all his efforts failed. He jumped to the ground and tried to trip the giant again.

The raccoon jumped nimbly avoiding the huge man's swatting hands and stomping feet. In Razzi's hurry, he forgot about the cape's savage flight as it reeled Tony around at fullspeed. Both the raccoon and the boy collided with a terrific thump. They rolled across the dusty ground like leaves in an autumn wind.

A sharp piercing snap filled the air, ropes whirring, and then hooves scraping and clanking against the glass. A quick squeal from Heija was the last sound they heard.

For a moment, the ghastly sounds paralyzed the earthlings. Even Zor remained quiet momentarily.

"Heija's gone!" Molly moaned before she crumpled to the ground sobbing.

Esel shut his eyes from the misery. Razzi groaned while Tony stared at the empty crystal cage in disbelief. He whispered. "I can't believe it. She's gone."

Spine tingling laughter broke through the silence. "I told you the games were over!" Zor crowed loudly. "Now, it is Molly's turn!" He grabbed Esel's arm and dragged the helpless man toward the girl's cell.

"Not Molly! No! I won't let you!" Tony ran after Zor, trying to stop the immense man the only way the boy knew. He grabbed the billowing cape and began to climb.

Razzi scooted unseen under the cape and grabbed hold of the unsuspecting giant's thigh. With vengeance, he sank his teeth deep into Zor's flesh.

A deep howl ripped through the caverns, as Zor wrenched in pain. He dropped Esel outside Molly's cell, raised his mighty arm high into the air, letting his clenched fist fall hard against the raccoon's head. Razzi's limp body fell clumsily to the ground.

Zor leered fiercely at the quiet little lump of fur then gave him several swift kicks, while snarling. "That's the last time you'll bite me, you sharp-toothed fool! And as for you, Tony, I'm sick of you climbing up my fine cape."

The boy let go and quickly slid down the cape to the ground and ran like a scared rabbit.

Vise-like fingers reached after the youngster, seizing him by the britches. The giant raised the boy high into the air. "Were you going somewhere?" Zor questioned with a crooked sneer.

A blood curdling scream burst forth from Tony's throat. Molly watched, waving her hands and shrieking at the top of her lungs. The exhausted Esel turned away afraid to observe.

———————

Far away, the Wise Ones waited and hoped. Their eyes searched their screen diligently. They saw several beast horses circling over the orange glare. One by one, they slowly disappeared into the clouds, returning to their dark domain. Gallopade was nowhere in sight, and the volcano still glowed as bright as ever.

At length, with tears in her eyes, Queen Pearl spoke, "I am fearful Gallopade is lost. Our brother's plan to cool the volcano is failing." She bowed her head. "This is a sad night; a very sad night indeed."

CHAPTER 20

DRAGONS IN THE LABORATORY

Gliding in the sweltering volcano vapors, Gallopade used his teeth to dislodge the knotted rag holding the cooling capsules. He dropped the bundle and watched it twirl downward into the hot lava below, where snaps and crackles erupted, and then a small green spot appeared.

Gallopade savored the moment when he saw Esel's capsules working. Popping ripples spread outward slowly against the hot lava, making a larger orb of coolness.

The bloody horse had no time to linger as he feared for Heija's safety. Swooping down the side of the mountain, he hurried back to the cavern.

While flying downward, he heard the clanking beast's hooves still searching for him in the thick cloud layer. Hope sprang into his mind. Maybe he could reenter the cave unnoticed if the beast herd was busy elsewhere.

The anxious stallion neared the cavern's entrance with a hopeful heart, knowing the capsules were cooling the volcano and he was returning to his loved ones.

A moment later, Gallopade's hopes turned to anguish. In the darkness ahead of him, sparking hooves showed the silhouette of an immense stallion, guarding the large cave entrance. Gallopade knew it was Black Fire, seeking to finish off the tired and wounded golden warrior.

The daring beast pranced with excitement, lighting the cave with his sparks. He was a fine-looking specimen even if his purpose was wicked. The black steed issued a shrill challenging cry to alert his beast herd.

The weary Gallopade had no time or strength to fight. He needed to return to his loved ones. He longed to pass his malicious opponent quickly so he made a wide circle to gather more speed. He planned to fly through the open high part of the cave's entrance with great haste. That might confuse the black brute's perfect timing.

Black Fire danced with anticipation as he judged the golden steed's arrival accurately and deliberately.

Gallopade spotted the black's hind legs hunched to spring and knew the upper route was certain destruction.

Seeing Gallopade's speedy approach, the black devil placed his devious plan in motion. He lunged upward with immense force, his mouth wide open, aiming his sharp metal teeth toward an exact spot where Gallopade's neck should be in the next second. The jugular was his target. His red eyes burned with pleasure.

Because of recent encounters with Black Fire, the golden stallion anticipated the evil horse's intent. The split second the black steed lifted off the ground, Gallopade made an instant swerve downward, diving low enough to swoop under his enemy's back metal hooves.

The force and speed of Black Fire's acceleration could not be halted. His flight upward was not slowed by grabbing Gallopade's neck; instead the black devil flew directly into the stone ceiling, savagely striking his head. An agonizing squall was heard by all.

Gallopade alighted where the cave narrowed and turned to boldly face Black Fire and his herd.

The wounded demon landed, shaking his bloody head. Blood dripped from his mouth, as he gawked at Gallopade with dull eyes. His twisted wings trembled as he awkwardly turned away. With painful grunts the black horse took to the air and snaked away, retreating with a sick howl. His dutiful beast herd followed him out of sight.

Relishing another victory, Gallopade whirled around and hurried on, hopeful Heija was still safe. He knew flying over the volcano had taken far too long. Questions about her and the other's safety coursed through his thoughts giving him cold chills. What would he find? What if . . . . ?

Reaching the bedroom entrance, the stallion warily entered Zor's red and black bedroom. Peering about, no keys were found so he hurried faster toward the arena where he began hearing loud voices.

The nervous steed pressed swiftly through the last doorway. He remained hidden behind the drapes to scan the arena before charging in. He gulped and froze in place.

The giant was standing at the far end of the arena holding Tony high in the air. Zor was shouting as usual. "Okay dragon, come get your lunch! Tony is small, but he'll taste like a tender young piglet."

Molly clung to her prison bars screaming her heart out. The dirt-covered Esel and Razzi were sprawled dead silent on the cold ground. They were lying not far from Zor's feet. The appalling sight cut into the stallion's heart.

Gallopade's eyes quickly searched for Heija but he could not see inside the crystal room. Was Heija by some miracle still there? He had to enter the arena to see for sure. He listened for the turning wheels, but heard nothing. His legs refused to move. He wanted to help Tony; yet, if Heija was gone, he felt he would surely die!

A loud squall from the dragon pulled Gallopade attention away from his fears. The reptile pranced around his feeding area, watching the giant hold the screaming boy high in the air across the arena.

Anger filled Gallopade with the courage he needed. While Zor was looking at Tony, the horse stepped out, unfurled his wings, and flew rapidly toward the giant.

"Let me down!" Tony cried out helplessly.

Zor swung the boy back and forth. "I'll put you down the dragon throat! Here dragon. Catch him!"

Hoping he was still unseen, Gallopade closed-in to grab Tony's knapsack or pants with his teeth.

From the corner of his eye, Zor saw a streak moving toward him. The giant's mighty arm automatically sprung forward with enormous force. The boy was sent into flight an instant before Gallopade could reach him.

Quickly spinning in the air, Gallopade pushed hard on his wings to catch Tony; however the boy had a vast head start. The child was spinning straight as an arrow toward the excited dragon. Molly's screams gave the golden steed strength to move even faster.

The dragon stood on his hind legs, his tongue eagerly zipping in and out. He anxiously awaited his meal.

Gallopade opened his mouth to clasp Tony's back pack when the excited dragon plucked the boy from the air with his long tongue. The stallion flew in circles overhead with his heart wrenching as he witnessed the terrifying scene. He could hear Molly's cries from across the arena and Zor's laughter and hurtful jeering.

"Even with wings, you are way too slow, Gallopade! You are a total failure! You let Heija die and now Tony!"

Gallopade peered toward Heija's cubicle. No! Where was she? He searched the arena in desperate hope that he might see her. His mind screamed. No, not Heija! The pain of reality made him sick and dizzy.

"She's dead, Gallopade! Dead as dead can be!" Zor yelled without pity. "The volcano is still hot and Heija is toasted. You hear me . . . toasted! You failed her! Now, the only reward you get is watching my dragon eat your pal, Tony!" Zor's laughter was insidious.

The hurtful words stabbed the stallion like dozens of knives. His eyes stung as he slowed to a hover just out of reach of the dragon. Only anger and the children's wails kept Gallopade from collapsing in a heap of sorrow.

The dragon twirled the boy around in circles just below Gallopade's reach. Then the reptile rolled his tongue up and down with Tony in the middle of the roll. Swinging his tail to and fro, the dragon became more excited as Tony yelped. Several times, the big guy held the boy out in front of his crossed eyes, as if surveying his grand meal.

Gallopade watched the dragon playing with Tony like a little toy. Soon the toy would be a meal! There must be something the stallion could do, but what? Each time Gallopade moved closer, the dragon pulled Tony away.

Zor's relentless voice shouted across the arena. "Eat him you stupid fool dragon! Stop messing around and eat him or I'll flog you to death, you no-good useless stove!" He pulled his whip out and snapped it in the air.

The dragon turned his back to the noisy Zor Zanger.

The giant jumped up and down, yelled and cracked his whip again. The threats poured out even louder.

The beast stopped playing and cocked his head sideways, listening and watching Zor. The dragon's eyes stared at Tony, and back at his noisy whip-cracking master; back and forth, back and forth while the giant ranted. Abruptly, the dragon blinked his eyes and stomped his front foot in anger. He arose on his hind legs and unwound his long tongue toward the flying stallion.

Gallopade cautiously moved closer afraid to believe what was happening. Could a dragon jest? Would he snap the boy back when the stallion came close?

Tony smiled as he positioned himself on the end of the dragon's tongue to climb on Gallopade's back. The boy grabbed a handful of dark mane and scrambled atop his flying steed. He hugged Gallopade's neck and then wiped tears and perspiration from his face with his sleeve.

"Jeepers, I'm glad to see you Gallopade. Zor told us you were dead!" Tony babbled. "Hot Chocolate likes me! I thought he did, but I didn't know for sure until now. It was a little scary!" Tony pulled a partly melted candy bar from his knapsack and tossed it to the wide-eyed dragon.

"Thanks, Hot Chocolate. I'm glad you're my pal."

The giant watched in awe, and then grew angrier than ever. He cracked his whip. "Why did you let that kid go, you stupid fireless idiot? I'll never feed you again!"

Snorting smoke to the ceiling, the dragon bellowed a fierce battle cry and charged toward Zor Zanger.

"No, you fool, stop!" The giant snapped his whip. "I'm your master! I'm the great Zor Zanger. Get back!"

The huge beast forged ahead even when the leather thong lashed him. The dragon eyes burned and he flinched while wrapping his long tongue around the whip's handle. He tore the flogger from Zor's grip. Hot Chocolate swung his tongue like an arm and cracked the whip toward Zor.

"Stop the beast! Help me, someone!" Zor howled as he ran for cover. "The fool creature has gone mad!"

Molly smiled the moment Tony was rescued and now seeing Zor run was actually funny. Each time Zor's pace slowed the dragon snapped the lash again.

The dragon chased the huge man the full length of the arena and back again. The giant ran in large circles and small circles trying to escape. When the screaming giant reached a place he could escape into an empty cell or an exit door, Hot Chocolate zapped the whip at the man, changing his direction. Zor screeched like a scared child. He ran and ran until he could not catch his breath.

Exhausted, the giant finally fell in the dirt. "Don't hurt me! I can't handle pain!" He begged.

At that point, the dragon dropped the whip and wrapped his tongue around the man, rolling him up like a tight burrito. Clamping his mouth down, Hot Chocolate left only Zor's head and legs showing. Obviously happy with himself; the dragon pranced about like a proud warrior still holding his captured enemy tightly.

Tony patted the stallion's neck and said, "I think it's safe for us to fly down and see about Razzi and Esel."

Gallopade was thankful for the guidance. His mind was numb. He felt sick and drained of all hope and drive. His heart was overcome with a painful longing for Heija.

When they landed on the ground close to Razzi and Esel, the boy slid down close to the raccoon. "He's not moving and awful cold. I'm afraid for him."

Esel sat up and stretched his painful body. "I did not want Zor to know I was alive," he murmured. Slowly he arose and hobbling toward the boy and quiet raccoon. He stiffly kneeled to feel Razzi's pulse.

Behind them Molly's voice whispered. "Zor Zanger kicked Razzi awfully hard. I'm afraid Zor killed him."

"Ouch!" Razzi barked. "Stop pushing on my head, Esel! I'm too sore to be dead! Where's ole Double Z?"

Tony picked the raccoon up in his arms and carried him to Molly. "Razzi's okay, sis. Nothing seems broken."

Molly reached through the bars to rub Razzi's back and talk. "The dragon likes Tony, but Zor might get eaten!"

"That would be a great day!" Razzi mumbled.

Seeing Razzi in kind hands, Esel turned to the stallion. "These boys put up a valiant fight. Your wounds tell me you fought, too. We are grateful for your safe return. Heija was also very brave. She never gave in to Zor." Esel's voice faltered. "I cannot talk about her now. I must stay focused! We need Zor's keys to set Molly free."

Tony joined Esel. "I want to help, but how?" the boy said. "Zor's keys are on his belt in the dragon's mouth."

"That chore will be tricky," Esel replied. "Zor and the dragon could still be quite dangerous. "Can you entice the dragon to our empty prison cell? If we work it right, we could grab the keys and lock Zor in the cell all at once."

"If Zor gets loose," Razzi warned, "he'll be meaner than ever. He's had time to rest!"

"But we gotta get Molly out of that cage," Tony insisted. "If that's the only way, Esel, I'll call the dragon."

Esel shook his tired head. "We will try," he said limping toward their empty cell with the boy.

When the boy pulled out a bar of candy, the dragon rushed so eagerly toward Tony, the boy had to step backward into the open cell to avoid being trampled.

"If you let me down, I'll be good," Zor avowed.

Seeing the clear danger, Esel yelled. "Wait, Tony! Come back! This will never work! We will try another way."

Tony tried to run out of the cell, but Hot Chocolate was in the way. The boy shivered when he saw the excited reptile drop Zor, swipe the candy bar, and turn away to roll playfully in the dirt.

Zor jumped to his feet, brushed himself off in the doorway then crept toward Tony, who was backing away.

The boy trembled in the corner with no place to go.

Molly screamed as she watched the scene unfold.

"You made my favorite dragon into a fool pet!" Zor grunted. "Since he won't eat you, I'll crush your bones myself. You can't get away from me this time, kid!"

Tony's eyes widened, knowing he was trapped. Having no options left, he fell to the floor and shrieked.

The shrill scream made Zor cover his ears.

The lights flickered and the earth shook. Tony peeked around his fingers in time to see the fearful dragon slink away. Across the arena the glow through the clear cubicles was blinking with orange and blue-green flashes.

"No!" Zor cried out. "It's happening like Esel said. My volcano is cooling!" Zor's rage erupted and his large hand reached out for Tony. "I'll break your scrawny neck!"

In midair, Zor's hand jerked and withdrew into his shirt-sleeve. His cape crept up around his face. A miserable moan escaped as Zor wiggled out from under his heavy cape and he quickly jumped out of his boots to keep from being trapped. The giant was shrinking!

Tony watched the startling sight as the man's skin turned green, his clothes fell to the ground, and he grew smaller by the second. The boy saw his chance and seized Zor's keys then ran like a scared rabbit into the arena.

Esel locked the cell door before Zor could escape. The naked man hid behind his cape, grumbling lividly.

"What happened, Esel?" Tony asked. "Did my scream cause the earth to shake and Zor to get tiny?"

"No, Tony," Esel replied. "Happily, Zor ran out of energy. I knew he was using the glow room often; however, I did not realize he needed extra energy just to maintain his powers. The strength he used while fighting us and running from the dragon took all his energy away so he reverted to his old self. Now that the volcano is cooling, he will remain small. Hopefully, his giant days are over! I am ever so thankful he never learned my energy formula!"

Raising the keys, the Majiventor jangled them above his head. "Look, Molly, Zor is in prison and you will soon be free."

The little green man's thick gray eyebrows pinched over his deep set angry eyes. He shook his tiny fist from behind his cape and yelled. "You just think you won! You wait. I'll show you! I'm still the great Zor Zanger!"

"He's little but still mean," commented Tony as he took a carrot from his knapsack and tossed it to the dragon. They trailed behind Esel as he hobbled to Molly.

Gallopade limped behind, his body aching, but it was the pain in his heart that rendered him helpless.

Molly bolted from the bars and ran into Tony's arms. She then hugged Razzi and Esel. Lastly, the big eyed girl went to Gallopade and hugged his drooping head.

"Zor said you were dead, but H-Heija told us you would come back." Molly poured out her heart. "Heija said she loved you and hoped to be your wife. Flying with you was her favorite times. She also said she would always love us no matter where she was. Heija was like a mom to me. I love her and miss her like you do, Gallopade."

Their tears cascaded like a summer storm as the children, Razzi and Esel huddled close around Gallopade comforting each other, forgetting the world around them.

A piercing clatter interrupted the quiet as the group shared their extreme grief. They peered around with smudged faces to see dishes and food on the ground in front of the seldom seen cook. His voice wailed.

"Look! Zor escaping! Get him fast!" Shoko yelled as he pointed to Zor's locked cell. "See, he goes!"

The children and Razzi dried their tears on the run. Esel and Gallopade shuffled in the same direction.

"See! Zor's feet! Hole in wall!" Shoko told them. "See! Zor's clothes on ground. He naked!"

Esel paled. "Shoko is right! The devil has escaped through a secret passageway. With my image machine, he could become dangerous again! We must stop him!"

"Come. See!" Shoko pulled Esel toward the double iron doors, already unlocked by the pintsized cook. "I show you best way. Shoko not so dumb like Zor say."

"Where are you taking us?" Tony asked.

"To lab on lower floor. Zor will get there fast with short-cut. We must hurry. I turn on lights."

With a gasp, Tony said, "It's a hidden passageway!"

"Thanks, Shoko!" Esel said, "Show us the way!"

The cook shivered. "Mean dragons nearly cooked me before! Very scary! I show you partway."

Gallopade's grief turned to anger. "I'll lead and find Zor if it kills me! He must be stopped!" The stallion trotted down the pathway ahead of everyone.

Shoko shouted after him. "Watch out for dragon! He burn your tail! I follow Molly."

Even Hot Chocolate tagged along. The good-sized corridor with its steep path led to a generous room where other tunnels linked together. On the far side of the space, light seeped from under a large metal locked door.

Pointing his finger, Shoko whispered. "Door leads to lab. A chain inside locks it."

Tony and Esel pulled on the wide rail handle, but the iron door refused to open. As they tugged, a rebellious roar rumbled through one of the adjoining tunnels.

"Bad dragon!" Shoko warned. "He kill us! Run!"

Gallopade's anger worsened. "Everyone pull at once!" he directed and they did. The door refused to open.

Smoke swiftly filled the room before they could retreat. Everyone huddled down behind Gallopade, except Hot Chocolate, who gave a shrill squall of his own and met the oncoming dragon. While charging, his back feet dug into the soil and pelted the group with dirt.

The dragons tangled, making circles, their tails barely missing the frightened viewers. Sparks and fire shot upward and the bellows and roars were deafening.

Poor Hot Chocolate, Tony thought. I hope he lives.

A moment later, the noise turned to gurgles, toots and puffing sounds. As the smoke and dust settled, the two dragons stood side by side, their necks entwined. They were gazing deep into each other's eyes.

"What you know?" Shoko rejoiced. "They are lovers! Zor kept them apart. Unhappy mates much meaner."

Tony's giggled and whispered, "That cute dragon must be Hot Chocolate's long lost Marshmallow."

"Heija would like that name." Molly uttered sadly.

"Aye, Molly." Gallopade's eyes glistened over. He could hardly speak. "Heija would truly love that name." He abruptly changed the subject. "I know Zor is up to no good! That greedy coward has ruined my life. I want to make sure he can't hurt others. We must stop him!"

After more futile attempts to open the locked door, Hot Chocolate moved in close to the door. He rolled his tongue around the handle. Marshmallow copied him. They pulled until a loud snap was heard. The chains inside the door broke and the door opened to another hallway.

Tony tossed candy to the helpful dragons.

"Lab door straight ahead," Shoko's fears had vanished. He showed them the way.

Gallopade pushed inside, immediately spying Zor staring back at him. The tiny scowling man held a glass beaker of steaming purple liquid in his green hand.

A lab with cluttered shelves of bottles, liquids, and powders were on Zor's right side. Behind him was a draped area. To his left were comfortable sofas, tables, and chairs for his private use. "You followed me!" He hissed in a raspy voice. "How dare you!"

"Stop threatening us, Zor!" Esel spoke with authority none of the earthlings had heard before. "I want my belongings! Where is my wand?"

Zor appeared haggard with his wrinkled face, gray hair, bloodshot eyes, and crinkled clothes. With no warning, Zor cast the glass on the floor in front of his pursuers. The beaker broke. As the liquid sizzled, Zor fled.

"Catch that murderer!" Razzi cried out and charged forward, but found he was running on air.

Esel held the scruff of Razzi's neck and decreed. "Go back to the hallway immediately!" He pushed Razzi toward the door. "These fumes are deadly! I must find my wand." Holding his nose, Esel rushed to the shelves.

The group obeyed the Majiventor. Gallopade shifted from one hoof to the other wanting to catch the little evil man who caused everyone so much grief. Razzi paced in circles, while Molly, Tony, and Shoko stood quietly and waited for word from Esel. The dragons rubbed noses and cooed, catching up on lost moments.

After what felt like an eternity, Esel found his wand. He quickly tossed two powders over the spill and waved his newly found wand. The poison disappeared. He raised his hands with glee. "Look at my delightful wand! I am once again a real Majiventor! It is safe. Come back in now."

Another twist of his wand and the drapes behind Esel also vanished, revealing a soft pink lighted stage.

Gallopade jerked to attention and made a sudden dash into the pinkish light. "Great mercy, how can this be? It's Heija! She's not moving or aware we are here! Is she still alive?"

CHAPTER 21

ZOR'S CRUEL GAME!

With wide eyes, Gallopade pleaded, "Please tell me, Esel, is Heija alive? I can't tell if she's breathing!"

While the stallion waited, Esel bent over the mare, placing his ear near her heart. The children, Razzi, Shoko, and the dragons stood quiet as statues watching the Majiventor place a mirror under Heija's nose. Finally, the elderly man stood up, his face still ashen and stern.

"Heija's heart is barely beating."

"She's alive!" Gallopade gasped. "Thank heavens!"

Esel's face remained grim. "Zor gave her a drug to cause this deep sleep and I have no idea what potion he used. She needs an antidote right away to stay alive."

Perplexed, the stallion probed. "Antidote?"

Esel studied the vast collection of bottled liquids and powders on the wall of shelves before replying. "Zor used one or more of these countless chemicals you see before you to keep Heija sedated. The word 'antidote' is a remedy to awaken her. It is hard for me to see well in this dim light. The electrical power is weak since the volcano is cooling. I need more illumination."

Tony jumped up. "I'll light the candles, sir."

"Yes, Tony," Esel approved. "I remember you telling me about your grandfather teaching you to always be careful with fire. He is a good man. Carry on safely."

"Gladly, sir. But first, can you tell me how we saw Heija fall into that horrible hot lava and now she is here?"

"That is a fine question, Tony. I can tell you what I think happened as I work and you light the candles. We know Zor's favorite passion is playing cruel games. I believe he used my image machine to make his most malicious game ever. He projected Heija's image from this stage to the crystal cubicle upstairs."

The Majiventor pointed to the stage. "See the glass panels still behind Heija on three sides and panes of glass leaning against the wall? If all those pieces were placed together on the stage, it would make a perfect cube. Zor created an illusion so real, I imagine even Heija believed she was in the arena and about to die."

Esel carried his first mixed antidote to Heija and placed it under her nose to smell. After no respond from the mare, he limped back to the work area. "The illusion was so real, we all believed Zor. Heija was truly brave. When the rope burned through, Zor must have added some sound effects to make her death appear real to us."

Working constantly, Esel said, "Now I know what Zor meant when he was captured and swore revenge. The green devil sneaked out through his secret passage and hurried here to poison Heija. Had it not been for Shoko and everyone's quick actions, Zor would have succeeded."

Esel tried a second mixture. Heija lay still as stone. The old man reasoned as he worked on another possible antidote. "Zor ran down here, found his old clothes then removed the front part of the glass cube to reach Heija."

Pointing to the floor, Esel asked. "Remember the purple liquid Zor dropped? He planned to give it to Heija! When we ruined his plan, he hoped to kill all of us!"

"Zor's a mean horrible rat!" Tony asserted.

Taking a deep breath, Esel went on. "We arrived just in time! It grieves me to think Zor may still win his sinister game. Unless I find a potion soon to awaken Heija, *she will surely die!*"

Esel's words etched into Gallopade's mind like hot lava. "Please sir, keep trying. Please keep Heija alive!"

"You know I will do all in my power to save her," the Majiventor promised. "I grew to love her dearly myself."

After hearing Esel say Heija might die, Razzi felt his fur stand on end with burning rage. "I'm going to find ole Double Z and make him tell us what potion he used!"

"I go," Shoko offered. "I show you secret doors and tunnels. We stronger than him now."

"I'm going, too!" Tony declared. "And you, Molly?"

"I'll stay here with Heija, but be extra careful!"

"We will, sis." As Tony followed Razzi and Shoko out of sight, the dragons followed the boy.

Molly sat on the stage gently speaking and stroking the mare's soft mane. "Can you hear me, Heija? You told me to be strong and I'm doing my best. Now, I want you to be strong and come back to us. I love you, Heija. We need you. Please open your eyes." Tears rolled down the little girl's cheeks as she talked lovingly to the mare.

Gallopade listened to Molly and watched as Esel assembled new potions, trying to revive Heija. Each time the remedy failed, the stallion grew more concerned.

Minutes dragged into hours. The candles burned lower until some sputtered out. Esel continued his work.

The search party eventually returned depressed and empty-handed. They immediately saw Esel's somber face and Heija still lying on the stage. The sad sight told the story. Razzi and his helpers slumped with disappointment.

Tony shrugged and whispered. "I'm sorry, Gallopade. We hoped Heija was okay by now."

"She will be, soon." The stallion assured him.

"Zor escaped to the outside world," Razzi bemoaned. "We couldn't find any tracks or scent so we think he flew away in his bubble vehicle."

"You did your best," Gallopade replied. "You might as well rest until we awaken Heija."

Molly crept from Heija's side to the couch beside Tony and Shoko. Her little head nodded from lack of sleep.

Razzi asked Gallopade to join him in the outer hall where the raccoon shared his feelings. "This is all wrong! Heija and you came here to help us! You're both good folks, but you're the ones suffering. It makes me so mad to think that tiny no-good green feller escaped safely. That selfish rat is probably laughing right now. I'd bet my fur he's planning more trickery as we speak. It's not fair!"

"I know how you feel, Razzi. I appreciate you sharing your feelings. My dad used to tell me life is not always fair. He told me to remain honest and work hard, and it will work out okay. With that in mind, our group can know we honestly did our best and for good reasons. We even gained valued friendships along the way."

Gallopade lowered his head closer to Razzi. "Zor, on the other hand, with his self-seeking ways did not win, no matter what. His heart is cold and his bad deeds will haunt him the rest of his life. He is a lonesome, gloomy person; growing old without good friends or any kind of love."

"I can't feel sorry for him!" Razzi let slip. "But you're right. Zor's too mean to have friends!" The raccoon's anger fizzled into fatigue. He shrugged and slunk back to the couch where he curled his aching body between Tony and Shoko. "I'm glad I have friends," the raccoon muttered.

Gallopade limped stiffly back to Heija's side.

The weary Majiventor trudged from the workbench to the stage time after time. Three large candles remained on the sturdy table helping Esel find his ingredients. The only other light was the pink glow over Heija's quiet body.

Gray mice gathered in rows to watch. The dragons sat in the corner, silently observing. Even the bats lined up across the ceiling to witness the event in the eerie light.

Gallopade stayed close to Heija, swaying from one side to the other on his throbbing legs. He watched every movement the Majiventor made. Each time Esel lowered Heija's head gently down to the stage floor and her limp body showed no signs of movement, Gallopade's body felt heavier and his spirit grew more troubled.

Exhausted and bewildered, Esel limped to the stallion. The old man's shoulders drooped and his frail body wavered as he whispered. "I am at a loss . . . There are no more antidotes in my mind. I am extremely regretful." His words were hardly audible. "I must rest. I am at my wit's end." Then he repeated the words he had said before. "I am sorry to say this, but prepare yourself. If Heija does not awaken soon, she *will surely die.*"

All of Gallopade's pent-up anguish surfaced. "No!" he moaned. "Please Esel, you must remember more! We cannot stop now!" The stallion's heart was breaking as Esel slumped into an overstuffed chair near the others.

"I am sorry, my friend," Esel whispered. "My memory is totally blank. I have no choice. I must rest."

Shaking his thick dark mane, Gallopade moved closer to Heija's side. *She will surely die* echoed like clashes of lightning in his mind. A severe pain filled his chest and swelled inside of him to the screaming point.

He placed his head by hers. "Come back, Heija. Please come back," he pleaded. "When I first saw you, I loved you. I dreamed of marrying you when your name was Deborah. Your beauty and goodness filled my heart."

His words rushed out. "I wanted to tell you how I longed to marry you. Yet, I told myself it was not fair to you. I had no riches like your father and I could not support you in a manner you deserved. Back during the thunderstorm when we were human, you told me you loved me! That opened my eyes and I wanted to share my feelings with you. That's when those malicious witches broke down my cabin door and changed our lives."

Gallopade looked to the ceiling, took a deep breath and began again. "When we woke up in wooden prisons, it seemed impossible to talk about marriage. Yet, I loved you. It was your company that kept me sane. You helped me endure. We talked for hours, dreaming of freedom and how we wanted to help our friends." Again he halted to lick his dry lips and inhale.

"After the miracles in Dome City, we were set free. It was a great time! We ran together in the park like young folks in love. Even more incredible, we were given wings and we flew! Except for Zor Zanger, our life together was like a grand fairy tale. I wanted to tell you my feelings time after time. I nearly told you on the upper terrace after rescuing Razzi. For some unknown reason, telling you my feelings out loud terrified me. I was a total fool!"

Gallopade shuttered as he remembered. "Then Zor captured us and again our freedom was stolen away. Your courage the whole time astounded me. Seeing you in that glass cubicle next to that horrid clock tore me to pieces. I was powerless to help you. My journey to cool the volcano took far too long. I knew I was losing precious time. When I returned and you were gone . . . I died inside."

"Now, my bonny lass," the stallion said softly. "You are alive here in front of me. I can touch your face. It's like a miracle! Still, I need you to come back to me in spirit. Please Heija, hear me! You must live! I cannot lose you now! I need your forgiveness and love. I truly love you."

He stopped to see if she was moving. Her body was still lifeless. "I'll tell you how much I love you now and forever if you will let me. Please, Heija, come back to me!"

He nuzzled her golden mane, but Heija remained dead silent. Not a muscle moved. Gallopade's body, mind, and spirit was exhausted and his hope was waning. Heija was not responding to the potions or his pleading. His pleas grew more despairing.

Gallopade raised his head and wailed a long agonizing moan. His eyes filled with forlorn tears as he placed his head close to hers. "Heija, my darling, please come back! I can't lose you now! I love you too much!" His heart-wrenching tears slid down his cheeks and splashed upon her forehead. "I love you with all my heart. Please hear me, Heija," he begged in sincere rasping whispers.

"Please, Heija, wake up!" As he pleaded, he felt a tiny quiver. Gallopade's head jerked upward. "Wake up, bonnie lass!" He called urgently. "Wake up!"

Heija's eyelids trembled then blinked. Ever so softly, she spoke. "Did I hear you calling me, Gallopade?"

He placed his head close to hers. "Yes, dearest. It's me. I called you. Don't go to sleep! Stay awake, Heija!"

"I will. I had a perfect dream. I saw our past and heard your voice calling me. Why were you calling me?"

His head gently touched hers. "It was no dream," he whispered. "I talked about our past and I told you I love you, my darling. I've always loved you. I loved Deborah, Gerty, and of course I love you, Heija. I love you with all my heart. And I'll be forever thankful for you."

"I've waited so long to hear you declare your love for me," she whispered. "I knew you loved me; yet, I wanted to hear it from you. I can never hear it enough."

"I'll tell you until I grow too old to talk then I'll still love you! You're my first and only love, my dear Heija! I always have and always will love you. You keep my heart beating." He pulled back, reared upward with glee, and called out to surprise their sleeping friends.

"Get up sleepyheads! Hallelujah! Heija's awake! I told her I love her and she woke up!"

Heija arose to her feet, stretched, shook herself, and stepped off the stage next to Gallopade. As they rubbed their heads together, everyone hurried to them and snuggled close with hugs, giggles and happy tears.

Razzi clapped his paws and cheered. The mice danced about the tables and shelves, the dragons wagged their tails, and the bats zigzagged around the ceiling. It was a happy party for all, especially Gallopade and Heija.

After the excitement quieted, Esel explained his opinion. "In my exhausted state, I forgot the most obvious remedy of all, called the Lover's Tear. Zor used it, knowing Gallopade was locked in a prison cell upstairs. As long as the lovers were separated, his plan worked perfectly. Now you are together and Heija is fine. Zor lost this game!"

"Hurray!" Everyone yelled and cheered.

Heija nodded happily. "Thank you for finding me. From the time Zor took me away from Molly, I was placed here, although I felt like I was there in the arena. I could see and hear you, just like I was there. After the rope burned, a blue mist surrounded me. After that, I have no memory until Gallopade's wonderful words awakened me."

"The mist released in your cage was started when the rope broke," Esel guessed, still adding the facts together. "Zor had no need for your illusion after that."

"What happened after I fell asleep?" Heija asked. "I saw the boys trying to stop Zor. It was a terrible fight. How did you win over his strength and cold-blooded ways?"

"It's too much to tell all at once," Tony said. "Razzi got knocked out! Zor threw me over the arena to the dragon! He caught me then let me go. He caught Zor, and then Zor got away and tried to kill me. The volcano started to cool and suddenly he shrunk and turned green!"

"I wish you could have seen all that, Heija," Esel told her. "They were all brave. Gallopade even had to fight Black Fire and his herd outside the cave."

"Aye, Zor's beast herd saw me leave the cave," the stallion said. "Black Fire was truly faster and meaner than a barrel of snakes wanting to kill me. I lost my way trying to dodge him. By the time I reached the volcano, I was weak. I think seeing the capsules begin to cool the hot lava made me feel better.

"Black Fire waited on me in the entrance, but he wasn't as smart as he thought. He guessed wrong and hit his head on the cave ceiling mighty hard. His herd followed him when he flew away. That felt good, then I saw Heija's cubicle empty . . . I never hurt so badly in all my life."

"And even through all that, Gallopade still helped save me." Tony told Heija. "Hot Chocolate helped, too."

Everyone laughed about how funny Zor looked, running from the dragon. The group talked and answered Heija's questions, while Shoko left, prepared food, and came back with a meal. Even the dragons ate well. The contented friends talked until one by one they fell asleep. Hot Chocolate and Marshmallow kept watch for Zor.

———————

Upon awaking, Gallopade beamed as he observed Heija sleeping close to him. He realized Esel was gone. After quietly arising, the golden horse met Shoko in the hallway. The friendly cook showed the stallion a quick way to the front entrance where Esel was working.

"This is a grand morning, gents," Esel greeted his friends. "As Shoko knows, I woke up early and most of my work is complete. Having my wand back is a great gift. I made a flying vehicle with my image machine for Shoko so he can return to his wife. If she will agree, they are invited to work for me in my castle. I need a good cook and someone to look after the place especially when I travel."

"Shoko happy," the cook said as he hurried off.

Esel smiled blissfully while explaining more. "All my property is now transferred back to my castle. I have left nothing here that Zor can use against folks. I put my image machine in a locked area where Zor cannot find it."

"Because Hot Chocolate saved our lives," said Esel, "I have prepared a special food room for him and the other dragons. I will drop off new food from time to time and they will never go hungry again. I have left them a special push button flare cannon that will send colors in the sky above the clouds if they ever need us. Now that I know these good-hearted dragons, I will visit them often."

"That is incredible!" Gallopade affirmed. "I'm happy for them. By the way, what will happen to Zor's beast herd and why are they not here?"

"I fixed that problem first thing this morning," Esel stated "Zor had transformed cave bats into horses. Being bats again made them happy. Of course Black Fire's head and wings were painful. I treated him so he will be okay."

The stallion sighed with relief. "Who would have guessed they were cave bats? Black Fire was vicious!"

"He was cruel because Zor made him that way!"

"That makes sense! Zor loves making bad things happen. If only he worked that hard for peace." Gallopade glanced around. "Is that extra bubble vehicle for you, sir?"

The man's answer was quick. "Yes. I plan to visit my sisters and study your problems back on earth. That is my first priority. I hope by the time you reach Dome City, I will have all your problems solved, Gallopade."

"Aye, that is music to my ears!"

Just as Gallopade spoke, Shoko guided the other earthlings from the cave, with the dragons following. When everyone was informed about Esel's activities and his plans, Esel asked them, "Would you prefer a flying vehicle or your wings to take you back to Dome City?"

"Wings!" Everyone said at once.

Shoko had retrieved Heija's harness from the prison cell, and she was anxious to try her wings again.

Esel boarded his flying bubble. "Just as I thought. By the time you folks reach Dome City and refresh yourselves, I plan to solve your farm problems back on earth. I just hope we are not too late."

Hugs were shared before Shoko and Esel glided out of sight, going upward into the cloud layer.

"Shall we go also?" Heija asked.

The stallion pranced with enthusiasm. "I'm ready!"

The children waved to the dragons as the horses rose gracefully in the air. Tony tossed candy to them. "I'll miss you! Take care," the boy called out and waved until the clouds blocked his view.

When they popped out above the dark smelly clouds into the fresh sunlight, cheers filled the air.

"We won!" Gallopade yelled happily. "We found Esel and we are flying again! Heija is alive and we are free!"

The mare flipped her tail in the breeze. "And Gallopade loves me!" Heija added contentedly.

"I don't want to be a wet blanket," Razzi murmured, "but, what if we're too late to save the farm?"

"We should know by tonight, ole buddy," Gallopade replied. "So, until then, can we celebrate? I want to sing, laugh, look at flowers, eat lunch on Rainbow Septar, and enjoy our love and freedom every second of today."

Heija clicked her front hooves together and cried out. "It's a great day to be alive and to be free!"

"It is also a great day for me to love you, Heija!" Gallopade said proudly and without shyness. They talked, laughed, and sang all the way back to Dome City. The delightful day and their enchanted flight passed all too quickly. At sunset, Jay-T, the overseer, opened a panel for the tattered group to enter the transparent dome.

"You look ghastly!" Jay-T said honestly. "More wounds than the first time I saw you! Did you fight a war?"

"We not only fought a war, we won the war!" Heija respond proudly. "Surely you have talked with Esel."

"He was too busy to talk. He went straight to the lab with his sisters," the flying turtle answered.

"Well, we faced Zor and our mighty team reduced him to a little green man," Gallopade boasted with joy. "We thank you and the Wise Ones for all the gifts you gave us. Each of those gifts helped us survive."

"That is grand news, indeed. I am astounded and elated you are all alive," Jay-T affirmed. "Miracles do still happen! Come. The Renovation Center awaits your arrival."

Special treatment was once again given to each member of the group, according to Miss Mabra's instructions, including a medical room to heal their wounds. When the refreshment was completed, Jay-T escorted them to the Wise One's gracious home.

Gallopade turned to Heija. "Why am I so nervous? It's not like we are facing Zor! It's the children I worry about. If we're too late, they'll be terribly let down."

"It does seem like forever since we left earth," Heija admitted. "I feel anxious myself."

CHAPTER 22

GOOD NEWS AND BAD NEWS

"We are overjoyed to have you with us in our home again," Queen Pearl said as everyone gathered in their meeting room. "Esel updated us on your horrendous struggles with Zor Zanger and how you saved his life. We are thankful you survived and grateful for the courage each of you displayed during extremely harsh conditions."

The queen stood by her purple rocker while talking. "Our brother, Esel, is still working in the laboratory, trying to find answers to help save your farm home on earth. Rose, Birdie, and I, helped Esel all day, gathering data. He is sorting all the facts right now. We hope he will soon have good news for everyone."

"Thank you, ladies," Gallopade said. "We're truly anxious to hear Esel's news and hope we're not too late. Jay-T told us it was your strength ray that helped me deliver the cooling capsules into the volcano. I was in bad shape and wondered what happened when my pain dulled. Esel and all of us would have died if not for your help."

Pearl smiled as she spoke. "Thank you, Gallopade; however, we are the ones indebted to you. The five of you risked your lives to save Esel. If Zor had our energy formula today, he would be ruling us now in a dreadfully cruel way. None of us would have our precious freedom!"

"Pearl is right!" Rose agreed. "Instead of grief, we have much to celebrate tonight. Jay-T is opening the dome to display fireworks! Our city has arranged a grand party in your honor, and everyone is waiting in our backyard."

"Double wow-wow! A real party!" Razzi yelped. "I'm ready, thanks to these wise ladies. They gave me a new red tie and a new cane. Mine were beat up. Let's go!" He grabbed Molly's hand and twirled the giggling child around.

"Follow us!" Pearl waved her purple cane. "It is time." The group trailed the ladies. Fond memories poured back as everyone remembered Gallopade and Heija learning to fly. It was such a grand unforgettable day.

A great crowd cheered when the earthlings appeared. The lawn was filled with colorful tents and all kinds of amusements. Fireworks exploded, trumpets blared and drums rolled. The excitement was happy and loud.

The night was filled with good food, entertainment, and music. A play was presented showing the perils that the earthlings encountered in the cave with Zor Zanger.

The town citizens did everything they could to show the earthlings their love and gratitude. There was a circus with acrobats, gymnasts, and jugglers. For the young ones, there were whimsical games, even a dunking pool for Razzi. The dark sky was either filled with fireworks or crisscrossing colored light beams.

Gallopade and Heija walked together, soaking in the sights and sounds. They watched the children and Razzi enjoying the food and games. Other children joined them, trying to know the earthlings better.

"This is different than the cave," Heija said. "There are so many sights and sounds all at once; it is making me a bit woozy. Do you think these folks would be upset with us if we flew to a quieter place for a short time?"

"I feel overwhelmed myself." Gallopade noted. "We could use some quiet time together. You are all I need."

They spread their wings and glided away from the noisy crowd. She raised her head happily and replied. "And you are all I need. It's like a wonderful dream come true."

"If this is a dream, Heija, it's the best one ever."

After a while of quiet talking and flying, they felt calmer. They rejoined the crowd and enjoyed talking with many of the curious locals.

While circulated among the crowd, they over-heard various comments. One man asked, "Why is Bumbles not here?" Another woman asked Jay-T, "Where are our leaders? They should be celebrating."

Heija also had concerns. "This waiting is making me a bit nervous, too. Even the Wise Ones appear anxious."

Gallopade nodded. "They are waiting for Esel and maybe Bumbles, too. I'd like to thank him," he grinned as he spoke, "even if he did drop us in a swamp to be eaten!"

She responded with a kiss on his nose. "Besides that, Bumbles put us in a place where we can live again, laugh, and fly. I want to thank him, too. I hope Esel is not delaying because he has bad news."

With a quick change, Heija's somber words burst into giggles. "It's Jay-T. He's singing harmony with two other turtles. Listen to his fine voice and rhythm."

Gallopade enjoyed listening to the trio, loving their tempo. He felt so joyful, he began dancing his father's jig. It took a while for all four hooves to cooperate.

Heija tried to join him and tripped over her hooves. Laughing at herself, she tried again. The steps were not as easy as she thought. It was so pleasant having fun again.

As the turtles warbled a long high note, a cold spray of water drenched them and their instruments. Everyone hushed and peered uneasily toward the water fountain, where a small familiar form splashed and spluttered.

His voice was extra loud and grouchy. "No. I say! Leave me alone! Let go of my arm! I am fine! Thank you anyway, but go away! I just made a small miscalculation!"

With his wet robe, crumpled hat, and squishy shoes, the Majiventor trudged slowly toward his horrified sisters. "Do not say a word, ladies!" He grumbled. "I know, I am two hours late, but it could not be helped."

Seeing the earthlings, Bumbles quickly grinned from ear to ear. He made a wide turn around his sisters, and hurried directly to Gallopade and Heija.

"I've heard great things about you!" He greeted them. "When I first met you under that tent, I knew right off you were special folks and now you have proved it!"

Bumbles looked at them closely. "Look how you have changed. You are no longer Clyde and Gerty, but Gallopade and Heija. You look perfectly wonderful."

"Yes!" Heija replied. "Thanks to you, sir, we also have wings!" She pranced around showing the dripping little man her new wings and body. Feeling overjoyed, Gallopade pranced and showed off also.

"I highly approve of your renovation." With his words Bumbles beamed. "This is much better than those stiff wooden things you were wearing. How do you feel?"

Before they could answer, they heard the queen's stern call. "Theodore!" She tapped her watch. "It is time!"

The old Majiventor tipped his wet hat. "Excuse me, friends. My sisters must keep their schedule." He ambled toward the Wise Ones, his shoes sloshing with each step. The sisters collected all the earthlings together and directed them to follow Bumbles to the side of a large stage in front of all the assembled Dome City inhabitants.

The three Wise Ones stood center stage. In her pink gown, Rose introduced each earthling, and then guided them to stand near the queen in her purple gown. Next to the queen, stood Birdie, wearing a swishy green gown and holding a fancy box. As each earthling was introduced, Pearl lifted a golden medallion on a golden chain from the box and placed the gift over each of the hero's heads.

Bumbles, still dripping, sat nearby grinning widely as the earthlings received their golden gifts. When the last one was given to Gallopade, the Majiventor held his droopy hat and sloshed near his sisters and the loudspeaker.

"Hello, Dome City!" He waited for the cheering to ease off. "Our earthling friends have received golden medallions today, given only on rare occasions for true courageous behavior. Our five visitors from earth have shown great bravery to rescue my fine brother, Esel, from the evil giant, Zor Zanger."

The crowd clapped and shouted. It continued on and on, embarrassing the earthlings, except for Razzi of course, who loved every minute of the ovation.

Bumbles continued. "Our earthling friends and Esel outsmarted Zor Zanger and cooled the volcano. Zor's evil intentions were blocked by our brave visitors. We hope Zor stays hidden and never returns. We rejoice in peace!"

The audience shouted approval, knowing Zor Zanger was not an immediate treat. After the applause, Bumbles raised his hands. "We are forever grateful to these heroic earthlings. Before I end this program, I want to explain a few things about these exclusive gold medallions."

Molly held her medallion and smiled at Bumbles, melting his heart. He winked at her and resumed.

"These medals give our earthling friends lifetime rights to our world to visit or live here permanently. They are always welcome to call us for help or friendship. These medallions make them one of us, forever." The applause was deafening. After it settled a bit, Bumbles concluded.

"Now continue your party and enjoy the night. Thank you for your kind and cheerful attention."

The audience gradually returned to the festivities. As things quieted, Bumbles took his friends to the fountain to speak in private. "These medallions are precious so please take good care of them. Crooks love gold so you may want to keep them secret especially back on earth."

Bumbles leaned against a stone wall to talk. "These gifts have special powers. If you need us, click your teeth gently on the gold piece five times, then press your medallion against your heart. You will be found by us in a short time. We are forever in your debt."

As the earthlings thanked Bumbles, he turned and excused himself. "I must dry off, but I will return quickly."

"I wish Meme and Gramps could see all this," Molly said brightly. "Can you imagine what they will say when we fly over the farm together? It will be such fun."

Esel, dressed in a fine white linen robe with gold trim, arrived just in time to hear Molly's words. His jaw muscles tightened into a grimace.

"Esel is back!" Gallopade acknowledged. "Did you find some answers? Are we too late to save the farm?" The stallion asked quickly. "You look disappointed."

The Majiventor made an effort to smile. "I have good news about the farm. I am sure we can save Meme and Gramp's grape harvest without any problems."

Squeals of happiness sprang from Molly, Tony and Razzi. Esel still was not as happy as Gallopade expected. It made the stallion feel a bit uneasy.

Esel continued. "Let me tell you what I have worked out. The positions of the stars were perfect when my brother, Bumbles, sent you here. You won't believe this, but you are in a delayed time warp, which means you will return to the farm three hours before you left."

After the earthlings reacted to the bizarre news, Esel began again. "The storm will be in progress when you return and the mountain road will be blocked. At that time, we can direct the main storm's power to the pass, so it will clear the rocks from the blocked road. Your grandparents can return the next day. How does that sound?"

"Incredible!" Heija said in total amazement. The others shook their heads in agreement.

"After that," Esel said, "we know the birds are still gathering in the valley. A harmless scented potion added to the rain clouds is my solution. Humans cannot smell it; yet, the birds will hate it and fly away. That same potion will also help the grapes grow larger and taste wonderful."

Esel smiled and spoke proudly. "Your worry about too much rain can also be solved. I have arranged for a slight breeze to move the clouds away just at the right time. The grapes will be ready for picking the next day. Once they are harvested, your grandparents will sell them and the profit can pay off their bank loan."

"Great mercy," Gallopade remarked. "No one will know that Majiventors helped us. Our trip can be secret!"

"Yes, and another good thing has happened on its own." Esel said. "The news of your farm problems spread through your grandparent's hometown. That goodness is not of our making. It is an act of pure kindness. You will know more about this after you return home."

Tony jumped with joy. "We have a home, Molly! We can stay there forever!" He and Molly twirled about with delight and Razzi jumped up and down like a Yo-Yo.

Tony hugged Esel. "Thank you, sir! We're really thankful to you for helping us keep our home."

Esel was extra solemn as the children and Razzi ran to the stage to thank the Wise Ones and Bumbles.

"Heija, is Esel okay?" Gallopade whispered. "He seems distracted to be so full of good news."

"I noticed that, too." she answered softly. "Something is wrong. He was much happier this morning. Maybe he is tired. Should we question him?"

When Esel moved closer to Gallopade and Heija, his face was long, pale, and quite grim.

"We are worried about you, sir," the stallion voiced. "Are you not feeling well or is something wrong?"

Heija leaned close to listen.

Esel's face crunched into a frown. He appeared older and his words were hesitant. "We, . . . w-well, we went through a lot back in the cave together and you saved my life many times over." He stopped and cleared his throat. "It breaks my heart to be the bearer of bad news for you." He stopped, unable to say more. His eyes filmed over with liquid and he had to sit down.

From the stage, Queen Pearl called Esel. She pointed to the large clock on the wall. "Time is quickly running out. If the farm is to be saved, we must catch this opening in the star cycle. The earthlings must leave soon!"

"Yes Pearl, I will not be long," Esel told her.

"Do hurry!" The queen turned and walked away.

Esel's face turned gray as he spoke. "I failed to tell you this news earlier, because I wanted you to enjoy the time with your friends and the ceremony our city so kindly prepared for you. Now I must tell you quickly. Please know this is very hard on me to have to tell you."

"Just tell us, Esel." Gallopade said. "We know you would not intentionally hurt us. What is this bad news?"

Taking a deep breath, Esel began. "We have laws that we must follow here in Dome City. It is our duty to abide by them. The law says very clearly that our creations or renovations must remain here in our world. The children and Razzi may return to their home on earth along with their rocking horses, Clyde and Gerty. However, according to the law, the two of you must remain here. I am truly sorry. I understand how hurtful this will be for all of you."

At that same moment, Queen Pearl was trying to tell the children and Razzi about the law. A hush fell over the crowd as the word spread in little murmurs. Even the music stopped as if silenced and hurt over the sad news.

"No!" Molly cried out. "I don't believe you! Why are you doing this? They are our best friends. This is not right! No. I won't let this happen! We just got back together!"

"Please know, child, we do not wish to hurt you." Birdie tried to hug her, but Molly pushed her away.

Rose tried to sooth the children. "There are many reasons why the law protects our new creations. If they get sick, we can help them. It is for their best interests, I assure you. They will have a good life here. If Gallopade and Heija return to your farm, humans there would not understand the things they can do. In our world, they are accepted, safe and loved. The law must be obeyed."

Molly's lower lip protruded as she spoke. "What is best for them is to come home with us. We love them!"

"We are truly sorry," the queen explained. "In Dome City, we sisters make the rules for what is best for our inhabitants. We cannot show ourselves to be above the law, or change the law on impulse. We must be law abiding citizens! Please try to grasp our position."

"Understand my foot! This is rotten to the core!" Razzi blurted out. "Rotten! I say, rotten!"

"Razzi is right! We helped save you from Zor!" Tony barked. "Now, you treat us this way! It's really rotten!"

Molly hiccupped as tears slid down her cheeks. "We just got Heija back. We thought she had died! She's like a momma to me and I can't lose her again. Please don't rip us apart. We're a team! I don't care about your silly rules. I want them to come home with us!"

"Time is running out children," Esel said with his eyes blurring. "None of my strategies will work unless you go back at this time. If you want to save your farm, you must leave now. Our galaxy time-tunnel for traveling will soon disappear. It will not reopen for a month. The grape crop will be ruined by then."

Tony took Molly's hand. "Come on, sis. If Gramps and Meme don't keep their farm, their hearts will be broken, and it's the orphanage for us. After all we've been through; we can't let our grandparents down now. Gallopade and Heija know that. I'm sick about it, but the law is the law. We'll leave for now then return real soon."

Gallopade nodded with his muscles flinching. "You must go. I'm truly sorry. We came here to save the farm. Now that the Majiventors and the Wise Ones have granted our wish, we must abide by their rules. Maybe someday they can change the law. And when you come back, we'll fly everywhere." He tried hard to smile.

Molly's chin trembled. "I don't want to go. I love you too much, but I don't have a choice this time."

While the teary-eyed children told everyone goodbye, Esel moved close to his brother, Bumbles. "Theodore, the earthlings and I became really close down in that miserable cave. They were my comfort and my helpers. I grew to love each of them. Could you grant me the privilege of sending them safely home? I would be tremendously honored to do so."

"I know you are close to the earthlings and have their best interests at heart, my brother," Bumbles replied, "however being the eldest, I still have high authority. I sent these earthlings to Dome City, and it is my duty, desire and intention to return them safely to their home. I gave them my word. I must be the one to send them back."

"I will stand aside if you insist brother." Esel's face was pale as he turned to hug the children. "I have grown quite fond of each of you. I will miss you. Thank you for everything. Remember Dome City with good thoughts and please return soon," he said.

The raccoon surprised Esel and jumped into his arms to give him a furry hug. "I know you would change the law if you could," Razzi whispered.

"That is true. I hope everything will work out well at the farm and you will be happy," Esel murmured.

"We'll come back soon," Tony promised with a glum face. "We have to come back soon!"

The children turned to Heija and Gallopade.

Molly clung to Heija's neck. "I can't say goodbye," she sobbed. "I just can't."

"I love you, little one," Heija said, trying not to cry. "We'll have many good times together in the future. Always keep your golden charm safe so you can return soon." Her voice cracked with emotion.

Tony hugged Gallopade's head. "Leaving you really hurts," he managed to say. "Riding a wooden horse or even a real horse won't be the same after flying with you."

Gallopade's throat tightened. "I know. It will hurt but we have no choice my devoted friend. You carry our hearts with you. We wish you a safe trip home and I know your grandparents will be thrilled. I'm glad we could help."

Razzi hugged Heija's front leg and his eyes glistened. "I will even miss you, Heija. The only good thing about all this is the fact that you are real now, not just spirits inside wooden horses. I'm happy about that, but I'll honestly miss you. Thanks for everything."

"I will honestly miss you, too, Razzi." Heija sighed then said, "I sincerely mean it. And please watch out for the children and their needs like you always did so well."

"I promise," he told her before being pulled away.

Bumbles hurried the children and Razzi to the center of the stage. "Stand close now, children. You will soon be safely home. We wish you well."

Tony brushed tears from his face and picked up Razzi. Molly held onto Tony's arm.

Quickly, Queen Pearl rechecked her telescope and pushed buttons and dials in a small room beside the platform. "The stars are still in line. You have time if you say your words now!"

Molly quickly called out to Heija and Gallopade. "Stay strong. We'll always love you, no matter where we are." She brushed the tears from her cheeks and waved.

The Wise Ones, Esel, and all of Dome City, along with Gallopade and Heija watched as Bumbles proceeded to swing his wand, in his usual awkward fashion. He sung out his words strongly. This time, things happened on the first try. Blue smoke swirled around the earthlings and tinkling music could be heard. Poof! They disappeared.

Esel shook his head. "I can only hope my dear brother did it right and those precious children will have a safe trip home. Otherwise, who knows where they might end up, maybe Mars or Jupiter!"

CHAPTER 23

SMALL MISCALCULATION

A rooster's high-pitched crowing awakened Molly. She blinked her eyes then slowly gazed around her blanket tent still strewn over the rocking horses and herself. Tony and Razzi were sprawled amidst pillows and blankets. Her fairytale book was still open on the floor.

"We're home!" Delight filled her whisper in an instant of surprise. Everything appeared exactly as it was when she went to sleep during the lightning storm.

The young girl crawled from the makeshift tent in yesterday's clothes. She yawned and uncovered the wooden horses' heads. Gently Molly touched Gerty's painted nose and stroked Clyde's brown mane. Her smile faded and she shivered from the emptiness she felt.

Turning, Molly hurriedly opened the window curtains and looked outside. She knew by the sunshine the storm had passed. The sunny brilliance splashed over the valley and she saw no damage. Everything looked new.

She was thankful the storm was gone, but her heart felt sad. Molly shuffled back to the tent with doubts. She whispered. "Was Heija and Gallopade just a dream?"

"No, Molly, they were real." Tony answered. He joined her outside the tent, rubbed his eyes and yawned. "Heija and Gallopade got their wings in Dome City and we flew to Esel's castle. It was real, sis," he told her clearly.

Molly gave her brother a hug. "Thank you, Tony! I was scared part of the time, but I wanted it to be real, not just a dream."

"I know. Zor Zanger nearly killed us in that cave. He was creepy. But it was great when we flew together again."

"Flying was so much fun! It really happened!" She touched Gerty's wooden head. "These rocking horses will never be the same. I miss Heija and Gallopade so much. How can we ever have fun without them?"

"I don't know. We had to come back so Esel's plan would work. Things were happy one minute and sad the next. Everything was perfect until the Wise Ones told us Heija and Gallopade had to stay there." His eyes stung, just thinking about it.

"Doggone it anyway!" Tony turned toward the window to hide his tears and snarled. "Why did they make that crazy law anyway? I missed Gallopade and Heija before we even left Dome City."

"Me, too. I felt sick inside." The young girl said while watching the raccoon stretch. Before his eyes opened, curiosity filled Molly. "Razzi, can you still talk?"

"I could always talk! Can you still hear me?"

"Jeepers Razzi, I can!" Tony exclaimed.

"Me, too!" Molly squealed and kneeled to hug him.

"Wow, don't choke me!" He grunted. "I used to talk to Clyde and Gerty all the time, but you couldn't hear me. Now the wooden horses don't talk. That makes me extra glad you can hear me. At least this way, I won't be so alone; however, I'll miss Gallopade. Okay . . . I confess I'll miss Heija too. And I never thought I'd ever say that!"

"We'll all miss them," Tony grumped sullenly.

Molly nodded in agreement as she petted the raccoon's back. "At least for now, we've got each other. Hearing you talk, Razzi, is great. It's like a miracle!"

Razzi pulled his tail around him. "Now that I think about it, if everyone can hear me, I'm in big trouble! Real raccoons can't talk! If folks hear me, they'll think I'm odd. The next thing you know, a circus will lock me in a cage like a freak. I'll be taken far away from here all by myself."

"No! We won't let anyone do that!" Molly's voice was protective. "We'll keep it secret and not tell a soul!"

"I agree! Mum is the word," Tony declared. "If we told folks about our adventures, no one would believe us anyway. We can bury our gold medallions in the barn some place safe and make a secret pact between us to keep our mouths shut about all that has happened."

"What about Meme and Gramps?" Razzi asked. "They might accidentally hear us talking sometime."

"They love us," Molly insisted. "They wouldn't put you in a circus! I think they might even believe our story."

"Me, too," Tony agreed thoughtfully. "But let's not take that chance for now. We can tell them later if we feel it is right. Until then, I think keeping our secret is best for all of us, including Meme and Gramps. They have enough worries without us making more. Are we a team on this?"

Molly and Razzi nodded their heads in agreement. With that settled, they sat in a circle on the floor, shaking hands to paws to confirm their secret bond. They placed their medallions in a cardboard shoe box and hid it under the boy's bed, until they could hide it in the barn. Next they ate some bread and jelly for breakfast and talked about their enchanted flight with Gallopade and Heija.

Afterward, they were clearing away their blankets and pillows from the front room when they heard a horn beeping outside. They bounded outside.

"Molly! Tony!" Meme called out. "We have worried about you all night. You look good enough to squeeze!" She grinned and gave the children big bear hugs.

"How did you get through the pass?" Tony asked."

Gramps smoothed his mussed hair. "Yah know, Tony, it was the strangest thing. In all my years, I ain't seen nothing like it. Thet road was packed with rocks and mud last night. I saw it with my own eyes. Then early this morn, all those rocks and even the mud was gone. It's a miracle! Thet road is so clean yah could eat off it.

"Now, Gramps! None of my family will ever eat off an old road!" Meme asserted. "I think the high winds and water just washed all that jammed up mess down the mountainside. It did look good and clean."

"Yep, thet's what I just said," Gramps declared. "Now, let's get busy!"

Molly and Tony looked at each other and grinned. It was difficult not blurting out what they knew and all the experiences they had during the night.

Tony pulled a sack of groceries from the truck and handed a lighter one to Molly. "We're just surprised and happy you're home. It was a long night. We missed you."

"We missed you too," Meme told him, reaching for more sacks to take into the house. "I'm glad to tell you, your Aunt Sharlene is coming home soon. Her heart is fine. It was just indigestion. Isn't that wonderful news?

"Yep!" Molly mimicked Gramps, trying to act happy as possible. She hoped no one noticed her sadness for her missing friends, Heija and Gallopade.

"There's more good news," Meme added. "Your uncle Joseph told a friend we needed help harvesting our crop. This morning, cars and trucks gathered by the hospital as we checked on Sharlene. Joseph told us that all those folks volunteered to follow him out here to help us with the grape harvest. They're probably on their way."

"I checked the fields as we came in and even after all thet bad wind and rain, those grapes are perfect. Look Meme!" Gramps yelled, grinning ear to ear. "The trucks and cars are coming down the road behind Joseph and Sharlene. It's a great day already! We're truly blessed!"

"It's a beautiful sight." Meme was jubilant.

"Well we can't just stand here jack-jawing. Time is a-wasting." Gramps called with glee. "While Meme and the kiddos take in the groceries, I'll show the pickers our baskets. We're about to pick the best crop ever! I hope we can get it done before those devil birds arrive again."

Everyone worked hard the next week including Molly and Tony. Razzi wanted to help, but figured if he did, folks might wonder. Many of the visiting helpers ate and slept on the farm until the harvest was picked and every single basket was delivered to the raisin factory. That was a great day for Gramps, Meme, and all who helped.

Several weeks later, Gramps noticed Tony push Clyde away and kick his foot against the floor. "What's wrong, Tony? Don't you like riding Clyde anymore?"

Tony's face flushed. "Clyde's okay. It's just me, sir. I feel a little too old to ride a wooden horse. I didn't intend to hurt you. I'm sorry. I'll go to the pond and fish a while."

"Sure, thet might be good." Gramps said gently.

The boy ran outside and across the field all the way to the pond. His thoughts were on Gallopade and Heija. Big tears flooded his eyes. How could a wooden horse be okay after flying on his magnificent steed? Tony kicked at the sod and threw rocks while he had a good cry.

Molly grew quieter each day. She smiled less and cried herself to sleep each night. She would hug Meme and cry on her shoulder, but Molly would not share her sorrow with her grandmother.

One evening, Meme spoke to Gramps. "Something is wrong with our children. I just don't know what. I'm worried sick about them. They grow sadder each day, but won't tell me why. Maybe they need more friends."

Gramps had seen the signs as well. He just shook his head, trying to understand.

Early one morning after breakfast, Gramps talked with Uncle Joseph. "I think the children have outgrown Clyde and Gerty. They act bored nowadays. I guess wooden horses are jest not exciting enough anymore."

A grin appeared on Joseph's face. "Say, old man, I didn't tell yah my problems. Would you believe we might be able to help each other."

"Yah don't say," Gramps answered, throwing feed out to the hens. "Tell me what's on yore mind."

That evening after supper, Gramps asked the children to sit with him on the porch swing. Meme was in her rocking chair. The crickets chirped and the evening birds whizzed through the sky. The sun was sliding over the mountains and the clouds shimmered with golden edges.

Gramps appeared serious for a change. His usual smile was missing as he talked. "The two of yah have had long faces a lot lately. Can we do something to help?"

"No, Sir," Tony replied, "We're okay."

"What about you, Molly?" Meme inquired.

The girl bit her lip. "It's nothing, I'm okay." Molly responded as bravely as she could with a forced smile.

"Is it something that Meme and I are doing wrong?" Gramps gently asked.

"Jeepers no, we love you and we love it here. We just miss . . . uh . . . some old friends," Tony declared.

Gramps stroked his beard. "Well, I've been thinking. We need to do something to work off all these bad feelings. Yore grandma and me think new chores might be the answer. With more exercise you might sleep better."

Tony and Molly shared a nervous glance.

Gramps continued. "I think we should begin tonight. You can walk out to the barn and put some clean straw in the stalls. That should give you a good workout."

"You want us to work after dark in the barn?" Tony asked, his high voice quivering. Seeing Gramps serious face, the boy shrugged. "Uh . . . okay, if you say so."

Molly stared at Gramps with her mouth open. She could not believe her ears. Evening time was always Gramps and Meme's family time.

"You'll catch bugs in your mouth if it hangs open much longer," Gramps said without a smile. "I've noticed you and Tony don't ride your rocking horses anymore. I guess you have outgrown 'em?"

The girl shrugged. "I guess. Gerty's nice, but it's hard to love a wooden horse. Maybe I'm growing up."

"That's the way things are sometimes," Gramps remarked thoughtfully. "We all grow up, things change, and we're never the same again."

Joseph and me can carry Clyde and Gerty back to the attic tomorrow. Go now and see about your chores. Fill those stalls with fresh clean hay. And about those leather harnesses, I like to look at them now and then. Jest carry them to the barn with you and hang 'em on a nail."

The children obeyed reluctantly and went inside the house to the wooden horses. They unbuckled the harnesses off Clyde and Gerty then returned to the porch. They hugged their grandparents and began their stroll toward the barn with Razzi tagging along.

Out of hearing distance from their grandparents, Razzi whispered. "Wow! I listened to all that. What's wrong with Gramps? Did you do something bad to tick him off?"

Tony shook his head. "Not intentionally! I just miss Gallopade and Heija and I've not been myself. How can we enjoy wooden horses after soaring around the sky on flying horses? I'm sorry about making Gramps and Meme worry. I gotta try harder to be happy around them."

"Me, too, but . . ." Molly hesitated, "if Gramps gets mean, I'm going back to Bumbles' World! I miss Gallopade and Heija so much. It hurts worse every day!"

"Yeah," Tony declared. "Maybe we should go back to Bumble's World! We had a great time when Zor wasn't after us." He thought for a moment. "But the way I see it, if we leave Meme and Gramps, they'll be lonesome and miserable like we are now. That isn't right."

"So what'll you do?" Razzi asked.

Molly looked at the cows across the field and shrugged. "It puts us in a bad place. I guess we could . . ."

Tony grabbed Molly's mouth just before they entered the barn. "Shush, Molly! I heard a strange noise!"

"Sure, Tony," Razzi goaded. "I seem to remember that Gramp's has cattle! Just grab a broom and chase them out while we start putting straw in the stalls."

"No!" Molly whispered. "I just saw all our cows on the far side of the field."

Clink-clatter-clank sounded from inside the barn.

"That was one of Gramps metal buckets being knocked over," Tony whispered.

Razzi bolted back to the field. "I'm getting out of here," he told them. "It might be a mountain lion or a wolf. They can rip a fellow like me to shreds. Let's get Gramps."

"Razzi's right! Gramps will know what to do."

"No, Molly. Gramps might get ticked off if it's only a squirrel or opossum." The boy picked up a pitchfork by the barn door and crept quietly inside. Molly tiptoed behind him in the dim light. Razzi watched. They looked behind the tool chest and in the first stall, expecting a wild animal to jump at them any moment.

Turning their eyes upward, toward the loft, they scanned the second floor of hay. There were no signs of activity up there. Then another rustling sound stirred from two stalls away. Razzi ran behind the tool chest.

Before the children had time to move backwards, a large head poked around the stall and stared at them. Then another head peered over the next stall wall.

At first in the darkness, the children let out squeals and backed up. Quickly, Tony lit the lantern and hung it on a high nail. In the light both children gasped.

Hearing their gasps, Razzi peeked around the chest. "Double wow-wow!" He barked. "It's a miracle!"

Molly was crying happy tears as she hugged Heija and Tony held Gallopade head with giggles of joy. Razzi jumped around like popcorn on a hot skillet, making joyful yips. The jovial noises overflowed across the field.

Hearing laughter and happy noises from their porch, Meme exclaimed. "My word, Gramps, those kids sound happier than I've heard them since the storm. Where did you find those horses? Did Joseph help you?"

"It was his idea! Two fine horses, too fancy to plow, showed up in his barn, back around harvest time. When Joseph found 'em, they were not branded. My brother advertised the horses, but no one could identify 'em. Joseph was busy on his farm with the harvest and I was busy here so we never talked much the last several weeks.

"My brother decided it was best to sell 'em. When I told him about our kiddos being sad, he wanted to give the horses to Molly and Tony. 'No' was my answer. I told him my wife and I had discussed buying a real horse. With that in mind, Meme, I hoped you wouldn't mind us buying both the horses. Joseph gave us a real bargain!" Gramps said.

"I'm totally thrilled," Meme replied.

"So while I read with the children this evening, Joseph and a friend slipped the horses into our barn. The strange thing is that the real horses are the same colors as our rocking horses. Can you believe thet?

"Really? That's odd. Well, that's a grand surprise for our children, Gramps. I'm so pleased the farm is all ours once more. And if those horses make our children happy again, I'm overjoyed! Tomorrow, I want to see the newest part of our family."

"Looky there, Meme. The children are running this way." He stood up smiling. "I see big smiles on yore faces for a change! You must enjoy the new chores!"

"If those fine horses are our chores," Tony exclaimed, "then we love our work!"

"Yes," Gramps affirmed, "we bought 'em for our special kiddos. But yah must take good care of 'em and love 'em. I can tell they are really fine animals."

"We'll love them more than you can imagine, sir," Tony declared sincerely. "Thank you both very much!"

Molly hugged Meme. "I've never felt so happy," she chirped. "This is really home now that all my loved ones are together. This was the best present anyone ever gave us. I love you both more than I can ever tell you."

"I love you too," Tony called back over his shoulder, as they dashed back to the barn.

"That's what I wanted to hear," Meme murmured with happy tears dripping down her cheeks. "I do wonder what Molly meant by *all her friends were together*."

"Who knows how youngsters think? They're good kids," Gramps told her, taking her hand as they stood up. "The kiddos and animals need time to get to know each other. They'll most likely be up most of the night, if I guess right. Since it's been a long day for us, and morning comes early, let's turn in. They walked inside still holding hands.

The lantern glowed in the barn and tension was in the air as the children fit the leather straps on the horses. Being so short, both children had problems getting the harnesses in the proper position to fasten. The jewels sparkled in the lantern's glow.

Razzi leaned against the wall. "You're slower than cold molasses. Can't you guys hurry faster?"

"Stop complaining," Molly groaned. "In Dome City, it was easier. They did it for us."

"Sure," Razzi told her. "Everything in Dome City was easier and extra special. The Wise Ones and Jay-T were always surprising us. I miss that concrete pool with its glow fish and my robot helpers. We sure had fun!"

"Once Zor was gone, it was a perfect place until we had to leave without Heija and Gallopade," Molly's voice quivered. "That was awful! By the way, Razzi, you could help me if you want us to hurry faster."

"No thank you." Razzi backed away. "If I helped and something failed to work, like their wings not being there, I'd catch all the blame."

"Don't even think that way, Razzi!" Heija pleaded with big eyes. "We just have to fly again!"

"You will. I was just . . . never mind." Razzi wrung his hands. "I have to admit, I honestly love flying now."

"I knew that!" Heija said playfully. "It just dawned on me . . . the children can hear our voices here on earth. I hope that means we can still fly!"

"I think Bumbles made it happen," Razzi told them. "I never thought I'd say it, but he's a good-hearted chap."

"I hope he visits us again," Tony added. "By the way, that reminds me. We have our medallions hidden. Where is yours, Gallopade?"

The stallion's ear flinched. "Check the large pocket in my harness. I hope I still have it."

Tony grinned as he pulled the chain and medallion from Gallopade's harness. "It's been with us the whole time! I'll keep it with ours in the shoe box."

"Add Heija's also," Molly said. "I just found it. And, look, I have her harness fastened. We're ready to fly!"

"Hurry, Tony, I can't wait." Gallopade's eagerness showed. "If Bumbles remembered the medallions, I'm sure he made it possible for us to fly here on earth. We just have to fly; it's part of us now."

"Wait a jiffy until I hide your medallions with ours." When Tony returned, he grabbed the lantern. "Let's hurry out back so no one will see us."

Everyone followed the light. "You try your wings first, Gallopade," Heija suggested.

Tony hung the lantern on a hook behind the barn.

Gallopade excitedly moved from hoof to hoof. "Together would be better," he countered.

She nodded and the horses touched their noses to their harness jewels. Poof! Beautiful feathered wings appeared as lovely as they were in the other world.

"Double wow-wow!" Razzi cried, leaping about.

The children jumped up and down, too. Gallopade pranced from hoof to hoof, making fancy little kicks. "My father would be proud of me. Not only can I fly, I can still dance his favorite jig."

"Only now, it's doubly well done, because you use four legs!" Heija said gleefully. "Your dad couldn't do that!"

"He was never a horse," Gallopade teased back.

"Yet, I know he's proud of you," Heija said seriously. "I remember falling in love with you as you did your dad's favorite jig."

"I'm thrilled you did. I loved you, too." Gallopade stopped dancing to touch his head to hers. "That early love has blossomed into a forever love."

"Hey! No more mushy stuff! Let's fly!" Razzi yipped.

"Razzi has a great idea!" Tony said. "Let's fly!"

Heija and Gallopade gave each other a loving glance and chuckled as they knelt and let the children and Razzi climb atop their backs. Once everyone was well seated, the horses pranced around the backside of the barn in a large circle as the anticipation grew.

Everyone ready, Gallopade asked.

"Go," Tony commanded. "Up, up and away!"

A bright yellow moon lit the valley below. The long rows of autumn colored grapevines were soon beneath the winged horses as they carried the children and raccoon high in the sky. Everyone breathed in the crisp air and gazed at the many twinkling stars over them. This was a special ride for each member of the group. They flew toward the mountains away from the farm house.

"I've never felt so free in all my whole life!" Gallopade told Heija.

"Nor I," she purred. "This is truly wonderful."

"We must thank Bumbles for all this," Gallopade said. "It had to be Bumbles that made this happen. His mistake happened on purpose. The law had to be kept by the Wise Ones and Esel, but who could blame a lovable Majiventor named Bumbles for a small miscalculation?"

"You are exactly right! No one was able to do it, but Bumbles," Heija replied. "Thank you Bumbles!"

"Thank you for our wings, our freedom, and our wonderful family," Gallopade added. "And thanks for this fantastic *enchanted flight*."

"Thank you!" Tony and Razzi both yelled.

Molly called out. "We love you Bumbles wherever you happen to be."

———————

"Of course, Bumbles and his nephew, Bobby watched the earthling's *enchanted flight* with all the sights and sounds on their three-dimensional story screen.

Stretching back in his floating chair, his face covered with cookie crumbs, Bobby said. "You were right, Unc. I'll remember Gallopade and Heija's story a long, long time. I imagine their story isn't over yet. Will you tell me more about their adventures another time?"

Bumbles waved his wand. The screen dimmed and the wall was just a plain wall again. Placing the wand over his ear, a smile crept over his tired face.

"Yes, Bobby, that would be fun. Heija and Gallopade had many more great adventures, with Molly, Tony, and that rascal, Razzi." Bumbles placed his hand over his mouth and yawned. "Right now, it is late. The next holiday you visit me, I will be happy to tell and show you another fine story. There are many."

The end, until next time.

ENCHANTED FLIGHT BOOK 2

Kiko's Treasure
Author: Donijo Ash

During the holidays, Bobby wanted to hear another Majiventor's story with Gallopade, Heija, Tony, Molly, and of course the rascal, Razzi. In book two, a new cast member draws the earthlings once again into the perils of Old World. There are amusing moments, ventures to new places, and more formidable situations.

As we look in, Gallopade's serious expression melts into a smile. "Why are we worrying? Bumbles can fix this problem; all we have to do is contact him."

"No, no, no! Forget that! If you trust that over-the-hill Majiventor; we'll end up lost on some strange planet in outer space."

"But, Razzi, he got us home last time," Molly reminded him. "I trust him."

After a long talk, they decided to send a message to Bumbles with their unique medallions. They restlessly waited, until a terrible racket above the barn caught their attention. Hurrying outside, Tony sucked in his breath and exclaimed. "It's Jay-T from Bumbles' World, and his vest is caught on our barn's weather vane. He can't get loose!"

Gallopade spread his wings, flew upward, grabbed Jay-T's vest, and pulled the winged messenger off the high metal bar. They landed safely beside their friends.

"I make foolish mistakes when I am rushed! Why does everything happen at once? What is wrong here?" Jay-T barked point blank without so much as a hello or thank you.

"It's Heija . . . she needs Bumble's help," Gallopade answered.

"My stars . . . this is more bad news! There are no Majiventors available at present to help you. This is Bumble's region, but I must inform you, our fine friend is missing. It is just dreadful!" He shuttered in fear as he spoke. "Zor Zanger is back!"

"Ole Double Z is back?" the raccoon repeated, trying to fake a bravado he did not feel.

"Yes, Razzi, and he is stronger than ever. Yesterday, Zor made a frightening appearance over Dome City, riding an ugly giant buzzard. He laughed then shouted to everyone in the city that he had captured our dear friend and leader, Theodore Bumbles. The Wise Ones and I are worried sick over this.

"With the help of a new invention, the Wise Ones sent me here to see about you folks. If Heija will return to Dome City, I feel sure the wise ladies can help her."

After a group discussion, Razzi reluctantly agreed to journey back to Bumbles' World with his friends. "Our team must stick together," he said daringly, although his instincts were begging him to stay home. Moments later, only footprints remained visible by the barn in the earth's soft soil.

The earthlings were once again pampered upon their return to Bumbles' World. While they ate a fine meal, Razzi began detecting a new problem. He accidentally dropped a small crumb on the floor. As he bent over to find it, a tiny ball of light zipped around under the table. He heard a female's sharp voice.

"You are a messy, messy bad boy!"

"Who said that?" Razzi asked. Then he peered around with wide eyes, seeing nothing. He quickly realized his friends and the Wise Ones were staring at him with questioning eyes. He smiled shyly and returned to his food to avoid the extra attention.

The tormenting invisible voice kept whispering close to Razzi's ears, ridiculing him and calling him a bandit.

"Who are you? Show yourself or go away!" Razzi whispered under the table. "I guess you're scared to show yourself for fear I'll punch you!"

The mocking continued through the evening until Razzi could take no more. If he saw the light again, he planned to catch it; and he tried. He made a wild leap upward, but instead of catching the light, he hit the wise Queen's drinking glass. Bright green liquid covered her face and purple hair.

"I was trying to catch that bright . . . you know . . . zipping ball . . . Oh never mind. No one believes me. I'm really sorry." Razzi hid his face in humiliation.

In a firm voice, Queen Pearl called out. "Kiiiikkkkoooo!" At the same time, she swung her wand and the spilled liquid was gone. Her face and purple hair were spotless again.

"Kiiiikkkkoooo?" Razzi repeated fearfully to himself, thinking the queen was saying weird angry words because of him.

Instead, the queen quietly explained to Razzi about the ball of light. "Kiko is the name of the voice you heard. She spells her name, K-i-k-o. I venture to say she *is* our *little* problem. Her father, Joseph Tee, was a scientist and his work was testing various genetic materials inside eggs. One day an earthquake hit and most of his work was broken or ruined. He salvaged what he could and placed the remaining eggs in incubators. One day, a little baby amothamal was hatched. Joseph named the baby, Kiko. She happily bonded with Joseph, and called him father.

"Everything went well for a while until the war. Joseph decided to send Kiko away to a remote planet. She was raised with distant family relatives and spoiled a bit. Joseph missed her and prepared many things for her return. He wanted a good life for his sweet Kiko. By most standards, Joseph was quite rich; but, sadly, he was killed in the bombings.

"When Kiko came of age, her adopted family gave her an envelope from her father containing a map with instructions to her inheritance. It could lead to valuable gold or jewelry, or it may even be stolen by now. No one knows. The bombs may have destroyed whatever Joseph wanted Kiko to have. Yet, she has high hopes it will still be waiting for her. Of course, if Zor Zanger has the map Bumbles was carrying, Zor will want all the treasure for his selfish and evil purposes."

"A blur of light flashed in front of the raccoon's face. "The treasure is mine! I just have to find it. Only I can read the map. Say, Bandit, do you still want to punch me?" She materialized. "You should know I'm way faster than you."

With his eyes bulging, Razzi responded. "You are tiny as a sparrow!"

Queen Pearl spoke softly "I rather hoped you two would be friends."

"It is most unlikely," Kiko said curtly. "I don't like this bandit, and I'll soon be leaving this place."

"Razzi is a raccoon, not a bandit," Pearl said kindly. "He is a courageous and kind fellow."

Razzi couldn't believe the kind words being said about him.

With curiosity, the other earthlings had gathered to listen to the conversation. Gallopade asked the queen a question. "I'm worried about Bumbles. Is there some reason he didn't take Kiko with him when he left for Old World?"

"Yes, of course!" Kiko quickly answered, sounding annoyed. Then seeing Gallopade, her voice softened and she nearly smiled. "Bumbles told me Old World was filled with destruction and terrible dangers. He said once upon a time the planet was a wonderful place to live, just as my father hoped it would stay. But after the devastating war, a polluted cloud layer encircled the entire land surface."

Kiko took a breath and resumed. "Bumbles, the Majiventor said he wanted to scout the area for existing landmarks on my map; and then upon his return, we would travel together. He told me it would take him less than a week, but as you know, he left two weeks ago and has not returned."

Heija shivered. "All this brings back dreadful memories."

"What about Bumbles' brother, Esel?" Tony asked. "Kiko could use another Majiventor's help."

"Esel is across the universe, in the middle of a serious outbreak of sickness and death. He cannot return to us until he finds an antidote for those countless ill." Queen Pearl told them. "And we sisters have no choice, except to stay here and care for Dome City.

Gallopade and Heija glanced at each other, knowing they must help. "This is the way we see it," he declared. "Bumbles' life is in grave danger. There's no time to spare. We want to find him as quickly as possible."

"We must hurry!" Tony rapidly approved.

Molly grabbed her purse.

Razzi's hair bristled. "Oh no, here we go again!" He groaned while wringing his hands.

About the author

My name is Donna Jo Solomito Ash and southern Indiana is where I grew up. My husband, John, and I met after my high school graduation, married the next year, and had two wonderful children. We soon moved to California to find work. Later we followed John's work in Aerospace to other states. From youth, I loved art and it was a constant in our lives. Oil painting kept me busy until the toxins in the oils made me ill.

During that low period in my artwork, my sister, Rita Riggs, told me with my whimsical side and my active imagination, I should be writing. "I have no training and nothing to say!" I quickly chided her. Unknowingly, I was very wrong. A day later, I observed a toy rocking horse and felt its need for freedom. My imagination took wings; thus, my writing began. In two weeks I had five hundred handwritten pages, a beginning, middle and an end. I soon learned telling a story and writing it for an audience were two entirely different things. Rewrites became common for years. I also began creating other novels and published a few magazine articles. It was fun.

Dyslexia has troubled me all my life. Just reading was a constant problem, especially as I grew up. I offer this information to help others with Dyslexia. Although it never goes away, you can overcome it; and with work, accomplish things you never imagined. My book is personal proof of that.

My husband and I now enjoy living in southern Alabama, liking the short winters and abundant sunshine. I write, paint some, enjoy God's wonderful gifts of nature, and our family. We are thankful for God's love every day.

Edwards Brothers Malloy
Thorofare, NJ USA
May 15, 2013